ALONG
THE
BROKEN
BAY

FLORA J. SOLOMON

LAKE UNION

PUBLISHING

Published by Lake Union Publishing, Seattle
www.apub.com

Amazon, the Amazon logo, and Publishing are trademarks of Amazon.com, Inc., or its affiliates.

ISBN-13: 9781542093637 (hardcover)
ISBN-10: 1542093635 (hardcover)

ISBN-13: 9781542043236 (paperback)
ISBN-10: 1542043239 (paperback)

Cover design by Shasti O'Leary Soudant

Printed in the United States of America

First edition

ALSO BY FLORA J. SOLOMON

A Pledge of Silence

ALONG
THE
BROKEN
BAY

To my rising stars: Rebecca, Maria, Michael, Lee, and Finn

Some terminology used in the novel is meant to reflect the time and is not in any way a representation of the author's opinions.

Chapter 1

THE PEARL OF THE ORIENT

*I view the formidable defensive arsenal on Corregidor Island,
the Gibraltar of the East, and my chest swells with pride for
my country, the United States of America.*

—Ray Thorpe, Corregidor, December 1941–May 1942

Manila, Philippines, December 1941

A tinny squawk from a loudspeaker woke Gina. *"You inside! Lights out!"*
She reached for her husband but found his side of the bed empty. Ray,
an army reservist called to active duty two weeks ago, was stationed
on Corregidor, a small island off the tip of the Bataan Peninsula. She
pulled his pillow closer and nestled it under her cheek to breathe in the
scent of him.

The squawk blasted again. *"You inside! Lights out!"* She opened one
eye. The clock read 3:10 a.m. After sliding out of bed, she tiptoed in the
pitch dark to the window and peeked from behind a blackout shade,
seeing the dim glow of an army truck's shielded headlights. The blackout drills were an unneeded disruption—a nuisance, in her opinion,
and taken full advantage of by the criminal element in the city. Light
from across the street flicked off.

She tucked the shade around the window, then fumbled until she found the flashlight on the night table. With her hand covering all but a sliver of the beam, she walked down the hall to check on Cheryl. The five-year-old was curled on her side. A lock of hair draped across her cheek, and her baby doll lay on the floor where it had fallen. Gina smoothed Cheryl's hair off her face, covered her with the Winnie the Pooh blanket, and picked up the doll and placed it at the foot of the bed. Nothing seemed amiss, and no sound came from the maid's room off the kitchen.

The house was too quiet with Ray gone; every squeak of the floorboards was magnified as she returned to their bed. She sat on the edge and lit a cigarette with a flick of a lighter, shielding the flame with the palm of her hand. Ray hoped to come home soon to attend the Junior League Christmas dance, and she'd had a dress made for the occasion—red, his favorite color, and slinky, his favorite style on her. She grinned, a half-hearted attempt to summon good humor. Gina wished he were there to share the cigarette. For twelve years she had slept with Ray by her side, and tonight her body ached for him.

Gina slept until Isabella appeared with a breakfast tray she set on the table before removing the blackout shades on the windows. The room filled with light. Isabella, at age twenty-four, was a friendly, capable girl who had worked for the Thorpes since she was a teen. Gina yawned and stretched her arms over her head. "I'd like to sit on the lanai this morning, Isabella."

While Gina closed her eyes for another ten minutes, Isabella wiped the morning dew off the outdoor furniture with a towel she kept tucked in the waistband of her uniform and then retrieved the colorful chair cushions from the storage room. Finally she placed the breakfast tray, newspaper, and mail on the table. "Is there anything else, Miss Gina?"

Gina reluctantly pushed the cover back. "Yes. I'll be going to town this morning. Have Miguel check the car for gas . . . and oh, Isabella, I'm expecting a delivery for the Junior League. Please sign the chit for me."

As chairwoman of the Junior League's fund-raising committee, a job that on some days kept her busy from morning until night, Gina relied heavily on Isabella's help and believed for certain the household couldn't function without her.

After slipping on a cotton robe and satin slippers, Gina stepped onto the lanai that overlooked her yard and the neighborhood of red-roofed houses similar to hers, all oriented to take advantage of the views and the breezes off Manila Bay. Filipino gardeners were raking under the white oleander tree that shaded the yard and trimming the pink and purple bougainvillea bushes that defined the lot line between her and Vivian's houses. Gina detected the scents of jasmine and gardenia, which reminded her of her father, a master gardener who lived in Seattle, Washington. She picked up the morning *Tribune*, then scanned the news:

> US secretary of state Cordell Hull expressed a pessimistic view of US-Japan relations. Months of discussions have not reached a stage where actual negotiations toward a peaceful settlement can take place.

She put the paper aside. Tensions were rising between the United States and Japan, causing concern among the expat population. Weeks ago Ray had urged Gina to take Cheryl to Seattle and stay with her father until the threat of war with Japan was ended, but Gina had stubbornly refused. General Douglas MacArthur was preaching a reassuring message: with a newly bolstered army, recent shipments of heavy artillery, and airplanes equipped with the newest technology, Manila was the safest place in the Orient. Gina had confidence in the general.

As she sorted through the mail, Gina saw a letter from her dad, and she smiled. Oftentimes, thoughts of him preceded the delivery of his letters, an uncanny occurrence. When she opened it, a picture fluttered out and landed close to her foot. She picked it up and saw it was of her tall, lanky father standing next to a child-size snowman. On the back he had written,

To Cheryl from Grandpa Milo,
My friend Mr. Snowman says hello.
Love sent your way.

Gina opened the triple-folded letter to see her dad's familiar handwriting, a bit shakier now.

December 1, 1941

My Dear Angelina,
Yes, we had snow here in Seattle, almost unheard of this early in the winter. It's a soft, wet snow, and as I am writing this letter, Mr. Snowman is quickly melting into a puddle.

I recently read unsettling news. The military has been evacuating wives from the Far East islands. That tells me one thing, my daughter: you are in dangerous territory. I worry for you and your family and encourage you to come to Seattle, where it is safer. Your company would be most welcome.

Give my regards to Ray and my love to Cheryl.
Love you,
Dad

Her dad had never been one to mince words. She knew he was lonesome. Gina's mother had died before Cheryl was born, a sadness she had never completely reconciled. However, now, as close as both she and her dad desired to be, they were at an impasse where to reside—he not willing to leave his friends and garden projects in Seattle, and she and Ray not inclined to give up Manila's rewards.

The door to the lanai opened, and Cheryl, dressed in a blue school uniform, skipped to Gina for a goodbye kiss. Gina and Ray had wanted a houseful of children, rowdy boys and girlie girls, but the miracle had never happened. In her thirties now, she felt time was running out to give Ray a son. She handed Cheryl the picture.

"A snowman? What's snow?" Cheryl questioned.

"It's sort of like frozen rain. When there's a lot of it, you can clump it together and make snowmen."

"He looks cold."

"Yes, snowmen are cold. They like it that way."

Cheryl studied the picture. It had been over a year since she'd seen her grandpa, but they had a bond that he kept strong through letters and pictures. "I miss Grandpa Milo. When can we go see him?"

"Maybe this summer when school's out. I miss him too. We'll talk about it when Dad comes home."

Cheryl clapped her hands.

Luisa, Cheryl's young amah, called, "Time to go, Cheryl."

Cheryl waved the picture of Mr. Snowman. "Can I take this for show-and-tell?"

"Of course. Be good, my love." Gina kissed her daughter goodbye.

⌇

At her dressing table Gina brushed her dark hair until it shone, then arranged it into a twist at the back of her neck. She applied light makeup to brighten her cheeks, eyes, and lips. From the many colorful linen and silk dresses, skirts, and blouses hanging in her closet, kept tidy by the laundress, she selected a favorite rose-colored dress that complemented her coloring. She slipped on jute wedge-heeled shoes that were comfortable to wear and then accessorized her outfit with matching enamel-and-brass earrings and necklace, a variety of gold bracelets, and a vintage square-cut opal ring.

Inspecting her image in the full-length mirror, she posed with her hip jutted out and a bigger-than-life smile like when she was onstage. She sometimes missed it, the excitement traveling around the world with the Follies Musical Revue Inc., basking in the applause and accolades lauding her sultry voice and smooth dance moves. Loving the lifestyle, she'd thought she would be a chanteuse forever, but then, while she was in Manila, Ray had appeared in the audience of the Alcazar Club, where she was working—he handsomely blond, blue eyed, and the life of any party. Their casual dates had quickly moved to a romance. Never believing she could love anything more than traveling, singing, and dancing, she'd been blindsided when she'd fancied the stability of marriage and a family with this remarkable man.

Gina mused for a while. She wanted Ray home . . . they'd hardly been apart since the summer they'd met, when he'd delighted in showing her the hot spots in town. A native of California and a UCLA grad, Ray had spent his boyhood summers in Manila visiting his grandparents, his grandfather a cofounder of Wittig and Thorpe Civil Engineering, a company that had ridden the wave of the Americanization of the Philippines in the early twentieth century. Ray had taken over the company and had carried his grandfather's stellar reputation forward.

Gina put her hand-beaded party shoes into a tote, and before leaving, she gave Isabella dinner instructions for her to pass on to the cook.

⁓

The area underneath the house served for storage, laundry, and a car park. Gina's maroon LaSalle roadster gleamed, but Miguel, the houseboy, continued to polish it. He babied the car like it was his own. "Her all gassed up. You want the top down?"

Gina glanced at the clear sky. "Yes, that would be nice."

Miguel lowered the top. "Be careful on Dewey Boulevard. Big accident! A tree is over the road. You drive around it."

Gina slid into the driver's seat. "Dewey's wide enough to land an airplane. Someone drinking too many palm toddies?"

"Maybe. Many weddings at the hotels last night, soldiers and their ladies. Big doings in the mansion by the bridge. Many Bentleys and Mercedes. Pretty cars."

It was a short drive to the city center. From the top of the Jones Bridge, she had a view of the busy port area filled with foreign freighters, tankers, and island steamers that stevedores loaded with everything essential for the smaller islands dependent on regularly scheduled deliveries. Crowding the waterway and lining every inch of the riverbank were bancas, outrigger canoes, a popular source of transportation around the Philippine archipelago of seven thousand islands. Cascos, flat-bottomed dinghies, housed gypsy families who supplied Manila's shops with woven bags, sandals, pottery, and colorful beads that Gina bought to give to friends or wear for fun.

Progressing over the bridge, she passed by the art deco architecture of the theater district before arriving in the business quarter, where forty years of American investment had brought modernization to the flourishing area. She slowed to carefully steer through masses of autos; two-wheeled, pony-drawn taxis called calesas; families on bicycles; jaywalking pedestrians; and even dogs, every vehicle, person, and animal claiming their right-of-way. White-gloved traffic directors stationed at intersections did little to lessen the chaos. She scooted into a parking spot.

The commercial district bustled with men going about their business in the banks, office buildings, and posh restaurants; women lingering in front of shop windows; and masses of soldiers and sailors seeking a good time. A bevy of young Filipino girls ambled toward her, giggling at their conversations and wearing traditional dresses with huge puffed sleeves made from finely split pineapple fibers, the trains of their long skirts tucked into their waistbands. Gina relished the colorful vivacity of this area.

She entered her destination, Chan's Tailor Shop, a storefront that sat behind the more significant buildings. Chan kept the wealthy women of Manila dressed in copies of the latest Parisian fashions, and Gina owned several of his creations. The tinkle of a bell announced her arrival. Mei, the tailor's wife, wearing a peacock-blue silk dress, came through a curtain from the back room. "Good morning, Missy Gina," she chirped. "I get dress, you try. Here, please." She held the curtain for Gina to pass by.

Chan sat hunched over a clattering sewing machine while two of his four sons worked at large tables with bolts of colorful shantung silks and paper patterns. As with everywhere in this city, the radio was playing, and an announcer droned on about the American-Japanese negotiations. Gina tuned it out.

In the dressing room, Mei helped her slip into the red silk dress, zipping up the back and smoothing the neckline and sleeves. "It very pretty on you."

Gina turned to face the mirror and admired the dress, which draped perfectly over her generous bust, small waist, and rounded hips. She loved the jewel-tone color and snug fit. Ray would be pleased.

"For the Christmas dance?"

"Yes. Ray's coming home, if the army will let him. It's not a sure thing." However, Gina was counting the days until they would dance the night away at the festivities—and later she would dance just for him. The image of the intimacy made her vision go dreamy.

Chan came into the room, and Gina stepped into the hand-beaded shoes she'd be wearing with the red dress. He checked the fit around her bust and hips, the lay of the neckline and cap sleeves, and then marked the correct hem length with tailor's chalk. He took a step back.

"Beautiful. You be the prettiest lady in the room. Good advertisement for me."

Gina struck a pose, flirting a bit and standing with attitude. "Good ad that I am, do I get a discount?"

Mei chuckled.

"Yes. Free delivery. You my favorite customer."

Gina smirked—she and every other woman in the Junior League, all like herself, with money to spend and time on their hands. "My Junior League friends got your number, Chan. You're a flatterer."

"Yes, me a flatterer. It comes cheap. You enjoy new dress. My son deliver to you this afternoon. Merry Christmas."

For all the lighthearted banter, there was always a sadness about Chan. Mei had confided to Gina one day when Chan was especially sad that in 1937, soldiers of the Imperial Japanese Army had entered his Chinese village near Peiping and wantonly raped and murdered the men, women, and children quietly living there, including many members of Chan's large extended family. Chan, Mei had said, had no love for the Japanese and greatly feared an invasion.

~~

Christmas was a favorite holiday in this country, and the Junior League dance was the highlight of the season for Gina and her sorority sisters. She walked to Heacock's mezzanine, where she was lunching with three. Carols played over the department store's speakers, and lights twinkled on Christmas trees, raising her sense of well-being. Her sisters were waiting, sipping the first Christmas martinis of the day, candy canes hanging from the rims of the stemmed glasses. "Flyovers," heavyset Stella said as Gina took her place at the table.

"What about flyovers?" Gina asked, thinking that war talk intruded on every milieu these days.

Blonde and bespectacled Vivian, Gina's next-door neighbor and best friend, drawled in her confident, debutante Atlanta, Georgia, way, "It's tonight. Another practice drill. A big to-do over nothing . . . a war on our nerves, that's all it is. The Japanese wouldn't be foolish enough to attack us, and we don't want a war with them."

Gina said in jest, "At least not until after the Christmas dance. I've got a new dress I'm dying to wear."

Edith missed the humor and snapped, "Don't be so shallow, Gina. I would die to get to the United States, but my mother is living with me, and she's too sick to travel. Ed and I sent our kids to my sister in Chicago. It's one worry off my mind, but I feel so damned guilty."

Vivian placed her hand on Edith's. "Honey, don't fret so. Your kids will be okay. I'm sorry to hear about your mama."

"Thanks. She's been slowing down for a while."

"Well, don't worry. If Japanese planes show up in our skies, it'll be over in a blink. We'll bomb those Nipponese islands straight off the map." Vivian lit a cigarette and blew out a long stream of smoke. "That'll be the end of it, and they know it."

Slightly embarrassed, Gina said, "You'll be all right here, Edith. Manila's the safest place in the Orient."

Stella scoffed. "That's MacArthur's story. A big bluster in my opinion to fool the Japs into believing it. We're nowhere near ready for war. And there's no telling what the Japs will do or when they'll do it. They're crazy as crackers." She grabbed a handful of mixed nuts from the bowl on the table. "Anyhoo, I'm staying in Manila. I don't want to leave my horse, Tomboy, or my husband . . . in that order."

Gina and Viv exchanged an amused glance. Gina cackled. "Stella, you're terrible."

"Yeah. Paul's a good guy. He built us a bomb shelter. He lined the floor and walls with bamboo so it doesn't seem so much like a cave. The roof is reinforced, and there are a couple vents. He was a fireman in New York, so he knows all about those things. It's big enough for a crowd. Feel free to duck in."

"For bombs and bridge?"

"Or 'Kumbaya.'"

Edith flicked a tear away. "My worst fear is we'll end up in an internment camp. Mom would never survive that."

Stella's demeanor softened. "It wouldn't be so bad for a few weeks. I'd be there to help you keep her comfortable. Does she play bridge?"

Gina said, "If things turn ugly, I'm taking Cheryl to our cottage near Pilar on the Bataan Peninsula. You and your mama are welcome to come and stay with us. The invitation is open to all of you."

Lunch with her friends lasted through two martinis and a rum-fortified coffee, followed by window-shopping along trendy Escolta Street. The four tipsy women laughed away the hour while they assessed the dresses, shoes, and hats in the storefront windows and pointed out to one another the diamond earrings, bracelets, and brooches they expected to find under their Christmas trees. After wandering into Chinatown, they purchased baubles and doodads to fill Christmas stockings for their many children.

Gina loved being with her friends whiling away the time, and she basked in the city's vibrancy and savored its diversity—a perfect blend of the colorful old and the pristine new. It was a privileged lifestyle the Pearl of the Orient offered her, and she trusted that General MacArthur would never let the Japanese anywhere near it.

⌒

At home, she found Cheryl on the terrace with Luisa. The amah, from a large Filipino family and just out of her teens, never seemed to tire of Cheryl's constant bilingual chatter.

"Mama." Cheryl waved a paper. "I need to take a snack for the Christmas party. It says so right here." She handed the important paper to Gina. "Can the cook make those coconut maca . . . maca . . ."

"Macaroons." Gina kissed her child's chubby cheek and sat on a chair next to her. "She will if you ask her politely. What did you learn in school today?"

"I drawed triangles and squares. Do you want to see?" She took a fat pencil and wide-lined paper from her school bag and demonstrated her new skill.

The child resembled Ray, with the same wide-set eyes, short nose, and square jaw, but her dark coloring came from Gina, with hair almost black, eyes deep brown, and skin that tanned dark enough to seem almost native. She looked tiny sitting at the round rattan table, her face in studied concentration and her feet not quite touching the floor.

She drew more triangles, this time in a chain. "Harry says there's going to be a war. I told him there wasn't either, and he stuck out his tongue at me." She stopped drawing. "He's a very rude boy, Mama."

Cheryl had a sassy way of talking that reminded Gina of her mother. Stifling a smile, she mirrored her daughter's knitted eyebrows and pursed lips.

Cheryl asked, "What's a war?"

Gina's knitted brows turned into a frown. She and Ray had never discussed the rumors of war with Cheryl around. "It's when men fight, honey."

"Is Daddy going to fight?"

"No. Daddy builds roads and bridges. He won't fight." At least, Gina hoped and prayed not.

"Will Harry's daddy fight?"

Harry's dad was Major Davy McGowan, an important figure at Fort Santiago, an ancient thick-walled fort down by the Pasig River that was now home to the US Army Thirty-First Infantry. Gina and Davy's wife, Sissy, worked on school projects together. She liked Sissy's easygoing nature and Harry's polite manner. The families hobnobbed at the ubiquitous cocktail parties and cookouts held among their clique. "He's a soldier, so he might have to, but we hope not."

"If he does, will he get killed?"

Startled by the question, Gina rapidly blinked. "What makes you ask that?"

"Harry started to cry, and his mama had to come to school to get him. He said if his daddy went to war, he might get killed. What's it mean to get killed?"

Gina didn't want to have this conversation with her five-year-old. The child should be dancing around in her new dress, excited about the upcoming party. She carefully chose her words. "It means getting hurt very badly. When we say bedtime prayers, we'll ask Jesus to keep Harry's daddy safe."

That answer satisfied Cheryl. When she finished her snack, Gina hugged her tighter than usual. Cheryl wiggled away and ran off to find the cook to ask politely if she'd bake macaroons for her school party.

A war with Japan, only speculation, nonetheless was touching Cheryl in ways Gina hadn't realized. She pondered the ugliness of the unending news, ubiquitous gossip, and wild speculation swirling around her child like a hurricane—it would be good to get away from the tension this summer. She read through her dad's letter again, and unexpectedly, feelings of love and loneliness brought her to tears. How very much she missed seeing his handsome face, hearing the sound of his voice, and savoring his loving embrace folding around her.

Chapter 2
WAKING UP TO WAR

I watch the Japanese bombing Manila just three miles across the North Channel. In impotent fury, I can only pray that Gina and Cheryl escape the carnage.

—Ray Thorpe, Corregidor, December 1941–May 1942

Gina felt Isabella tap her on her shoulder, and she heard in her half sleep, "Wake up, Miss Gina. Mr. Ray is on the telephone."

The clock read 7:00 a.m. Ray never called this early in the morning. Maybe he was excited to tell her he'd gotten leave, and he'd be home in time for the Christmas dance. He'd know she'd be pleased. She slipped on a cotton robe and hurried to the phone.

Ray's voice was barely audible over a background of commotion. He asked, "Do you have the radio on?"

She didn't like the tone of his voice, and it was a strange question to ask this early in the morning. She answered hesitantly. "No . . . what's going on, Ray?"

"Nothing good. The Japanese bombed Pearl Harbor early this morning. It was a surprise attack, about three hundred Jap warplanes, they're guessing. At least four of our ships were sunk, and four others were damaged, maybe more. They don't have a final count yet. The harbor's on fire." Ray's voice broke. "They're estimating a thousand men are dead."

Gina could only gasp. "A thousand?" Tears came to her eyes. "So then . . . we're at war?" Just saying it sent a chill up her back. She heard a deep sigh.

"I'm afraid so."

It couldn't be. General MacArthur had assured them that Japan would never dare attack the American bases in the Pacific. She motioned to Isabella to bring her a glass of water. "Are they coming here?"

"We don't know." The phone crackled and buzzed. "This line is bad. Can you hear me?"

She held the phone tighter against her ear. "Not very well."

He spoke louder. "We don't know what the Japs are doing. They could be on their way to the Philippines or not. Can you get to Stella's bomb shelter?"

Gina felt her knees go weak, and she quickly sat down in the chair by the phone. The answer came out a croak: "Yes." She cleared her throat. "Stella said there's room. Do you think we'll need to?"

"Maybe. If you hear sirens, get to the shelter. In the meantime, prepare for the worst. Get money from the bank. Stock up on groceries and medicines. Have Miguel service the cars. Get to the cottage in Pilar if you need to get out of Manila. Miguel will tell you when it's safe to drive. Take Route 7. Are you there? I can't tell with this crackling."

"Yes, I'm here. Are you all right, Ray? Are you safe? Can you come home?"

"No, I can't come home—no one can leave—and yes, I'm safe. I'm working in the Malinta Tunnel. It's a huge complex the military uses for storage. It's bombproof. They're converting some of the side tunnels into offices in case MacArthur has to flee Luzon. Men are lined up to use the phone, sugar. I need to hang up. Give Cheryl a kiss for me."

"I'll do that, and a hug too. We love you. Be careful. Are you sure you're not in danger . . . ?" The line went dead. After she hung up the phone, her fingers lingered on the receiver as her mind raced through all Ray had said.

Standing nearby, Isabella clutched at her necklace, an amulet that she believed protected her from any peril. Luisa, who had arrived to walk Cheryl to school, was teary eyed. Gina poured a cup of coffee and lit a cigarette.

Isabella said, her voice tense, "It's bad, isn't it, Miss Gina?"

Gina deeply inhaled and then said in a way she hoped sounded calm to her maids, "It's not good. The Japanese bombed Pearl Harbor earlier this morning. It's best we prepare in case they come here. Luisa, Cheryl will stay home from school today. Let her sleep. When she wakes up, I want you to keep her busy. If she asks questions, bring her to me. Dry your eyes, please. I don't want you scaring her.

"Isabella, have Miguel take you to the grocery store. Buy as many canned foods as you can. When you get back, I want you to pack for us. We might go to the cottage. Tell Miguel to service Ray's car—gas, oil, and tires. I have some errands to run. Don't be afraid. I'm just being cautious. General MacArthur promised he wouldn't let the Japanese anywhere near Manila."

Gina thought she sounded confident while talking to her maids, but her stomach felt tied in a knot. She warmed up her coffee and turned on the radio, hearing about the multiple air strikes on Pearl Harbor, the ships sunk and others on fire, the innumerable casualties, and the overflowing hospitals. She struggled to retain an impassive front.

The announcer's voice rose. "Just in! Japanese attack planes have been spotted approaching the Philippines. Stay tuned. News is arriving as I speak."

The coffee cup dropped from Gina's hand and smashed on the counter. She saw Isabella stiffen and heard Luisa gasp. Gina steeled herself and addressed her maids. "The best we can do is stick with our plan. If the Japanese come here, we'll be ready. Let's get busy."

~

Gina drove into the city center in heavy traffic. Her mind churned. Would enemy planes come from the north or south? She should have asked Ray. If from the south he could be in their path, and the thought made her shiver, regardless of his reassurance that he was safe in the tunnels. Had he said how much money to draw out of the bank? She didn't remember. She wished he were here to take care of these details so she could be home when Cheryl awoke. Her child would be frightened. Gina stepped harder on the gas pedal.

The business area was swamped, and Gina had to park the car blocks away from the bank. She joined the end of a slow-moving line that started at the bank's door and snaked around the block. The woman ahead of her was crying, and the man behind her cursed the line's crawl. As the sun rose higher and hotter, a kid arrived selling water he dipped from a bucket at a centavo a cup. What she would give for just a swallow—but thinking better of it, she waved the boy away.

Inside the cavernous bank, the impatient crowd jockeyed shoulder to shoulder for space, and Gina pushed her way to one of the many service windows. She placed her passbook on the counter. "I'd like to withdraw all but ten pesos."

The harried-looking clerk opened Gina's passbook. "Two hundred pesos a week is the limit, Mrs. Thorpe. It's a new ruling this morning." She mechanically recorded the transaction, counted out the bills, and passed them through the window.

Gina leaned in and whispered, "We're good customers. Let me talk to the manager."

"Take the money and get out of the way," a red-faced woman behind Gina hissed, using her generous body to shove Gina aside.

Someone else growled, "Move along, lady."

Gina thrust the two hundred pesos into her purse; how would her family survive on the meager amount? She fought her way to the outside, where people were jabbering about strange lights they'd seen in the east and objects in the sky they swore were Japanese paratroopers. She walked a block to the Chinese drugstore, where she picked up vitamins and aspirin and was elbowed by a man who grabbed for the last bottles.

Her arm ached where she'd been jabbed, and a blister had formed on her heel. Gina limped to the car only to find a truck had double-parked beside her. Blocked in, she sat on her bumper and watched the merchants tape their windows and stack sandbags in front of their establishments. Feeling in a surreal world, she wondered how this could be.

A man in a red hat shouted, "The Japs are at Clark," causing a panic in the street. Clark Air Field was fifty miles north of Manila. Gina paced and stewed, learning through talk on the street of countless casualties happening at Clark and that the newly arrived B-15 bombers and P-40 fighters, Manila's main source of air defense, had been parked in rows on the ground and were being demolished by heavy Japanese bombing and strafing.

My God, my God. General MacArthur promised this wouldn't happen.

By the time Gina arrived home, Isabella was in a frenzy. "You go, Miss Gina. You take Miss Cheryl and go to the cottage. If Japs come here, it be very bad for you." Her hand gripped her amulet.

"Hush," Gina snapped. "You'll scare Cheryl." She looked at her maid's terrified face and softened her voice. "We're okay. If anything happens, it's not going to be this minute. We have time to think of what to do. Shush now, please."

Cheryl, still in her pajamas and her little face tearstained, ran to Gina. "Are the bad guys coming, Mama?"

"Bad guys?" Gina knelt down and dried Cheryl's tears. "Where did you hear that?"

"At school. Harry says the bad guys are coming to get us."

Gina led Cheryl to the rocking chair, wondering what else Harry had told her. She pulled Cheryl onto her lap and wrapped her in a protective embrace. They rocked quietly for a moment while Gina gathered her thoughts. "Some Japanese people want to live in Manila, honey. You may see their airplanes in the sky. They're not bad guys, and they're not coming to get us." Gina paused, wondering how to prepare her daughter for danger without scaring her. "General MacArthur will tell the Japanese to take their planes and go home. They'll be gone soon; you'll see." Gina hoped it was true. "For now, we'll stay snug in our house. Maybe later we'll go to the cottage."

Cheryl was crying, and she rubbed her eyes. "I want Daddy here."

Gina felt like crying, too, but she pushed down her feelings and forced her voice not to waver. "So do I, but General MacArthur needs him to stay on Corregidor. Would you like to send him a message?"

Cheryl nodded, her dark eyes large and teary.

"It will be our secret communication channel to Daddy."

"What's a secret communication channel?"

"It's like a telephone. Link pinkies with me." She showed Cheryl how to entwine their little fingers. "Now close your eyes and talk to Daddy."

Cheryl frowned. "I don't know what to say."

"Then I'll go first." Gina closed her eyes. She knew Ray's leanings, and she wished to tell him to stay inside the tunnels where he was working and not to take risky chances. Instead she said, "Ray, sweetheart. Cheryl and I are together, and we're sending our love and kisses. We miss you. Be safe. Come home soon." Her voice cracked. "Your turn, honey."

Cheryl scrunched her eyes closed. "Daddy, I miss you. I love you. Isabella and Luisa are crying, and my tummy hurts. I'm scared. I want you to come home." She opened her eyes. "Do you think he heard me?"

"I know he did. You can talk to him anytime you're afraid and tell him you love him. Do you want me to rub your back?"

Gina felt Cheryl relax and her breathing slow as she rubbed her back. They rocked for a while longer, Gina savoring the heaviness of her child's body against hers while contemplating all she must do to keep her safe.

General MacArthur wasn't able to protect the islands from Japanese aggression. For six days their bombers crisscrossed the sky attacking US military bases scattered throughout the Philippines, leaving behind wide paths of destruction.

Goose bumps formed on Gina's arms when she heard a buzz and felt a vibration. From her window she saw formations of Japanese fighters approaching the bay.

Air raid sirens wailed in the city, the howl turning Gina's blood cold. She hurried Cheryl and her maids to Stella's backyard, where a dozen neighbors were gathering. Gina got in line behind Vivian and her two daughters, Maggie sixteen and Leah six. "You doing okay, Viv?"

"We're hanging in there. Leah won't let go of my skirt, and Maggie has pulled into herself. And you?"

"I'm jittery all the time, and Cheryl's weepy. She wants her dad."

Stella hurried the edgy crowd down the six steps into the shelter, while her two little boys ran in frantic circles, aiming imaginary guns at the sky. "Pow!" they hollered. "Bam! Bam!"

Stella's five-year-old daughter, Ruthie, passed out flashlights.

"Mama," Cheryl whispered and pointed. "Ruthie looks like a boy."

Indeed, Ruthie's red hair was shorn, and she wore a boy's shorts and shirt. The child strutted through the crowd apparently proud of her new look.

Stella explained in a whisper, "I figure Ruthie will be safer . . . you know . . . as a boy." Her voice quavered. "Anyway, it's just for a little while."

Gina and Vivian exchanged a quick glance.

Two bare bulbs dimly lit the interior of the low-ceilinged, bamboo-lined shelter, and storage benches edged the perimeter. Gina and Cheryl sat on the bench next to Vivian and her daughters, both girls wide eyed.

When the drone from outside swelled, Stella closed the door. "With this many people in here, it's going to get hot. We have water and an air supply. Please, stay calm. Say a prayer. We'll get through this."

Ruthie squeezed in next to Cheryl. "My daddy built this shelter, and he let me help. You want to play go fish?" She took a deck of cards from her pocket.

"Okay," Cheryl said, wiggling off Gina's lap. "I like your shirt."

Ruthie's toothless grin revealed her delight. "It was my brother's. He outgrew it. You want to play, too, Leah?"

Gina watched the girls sitting on the floor playing go fish and wished she could be so easily distracted, but her ear was tuned to the growl from outside, which had increased to a roar. And then, *boom*! The shelter shook, and the lights went out. Another *boom*! In the inky black, the little girls screamed. Flashlights flicked on, and Cheryl jumped onto Gina's lap.

"It's okay," Gina said, not sure it was. She wrapped her daughter in a protective hug and covered her ear with the palm of her hand. Cheryl popped her thumb into her mouth, closed her eyes, and snuggled in tight.

The beams from multiple flashlights illuminated frightened faces—some in wide-eyed panic, some sniffing and crying, and others with lips moving in prayer. In time the air became hot and rank from close quarters and nervous breathing. Sweat ran down Cheryl's cheeks and dripped off her chin.

Maggie said, "She needs water, or she's going to dehydrate, Miss Gina. I'll get her some."

A squadron of warplanes directly overhead roared a cacophony of discord that made the ground under Gina's feet pulsate. Feeling panicky again, she tightened her grip on Cheryl, who squirmed in the restraint. When the bombs dropped on the harbor, one after another and another, the floor in the shelter buckled, and dirt filtered through the ceiling. Gina ducked her head and clamped her jaw shut to keep from yelping.

"Holy shit," someone yelled. "It's going to cave in on us."

"Let me out," another shouted. "I'm not dying in this dirty tomb."

Gina sensed a scuffle and heard muttered epithets. She cringed back against the bamboo-lined wall, Cheryl clamped so tight to her chest they could have been one.

"I want Daddy!" Cheryl whimpered.

So did Gina, and her thoughts slipped away to her last sight of Ray, he dressed in jeans and hefting a duffel, as clear as if he were standing beside her. "You look like a kid, not an old married man with a five-year-old," she'd teased.

"Hold that vision, babe. I'll be back before you turn around twice." He'd run his hands through her hair like he was petting a kitten.

After what seemed a lifetime, the booms and roars faded to a diminishing buzz, and when the all-clear sirens blew, Stella opened wide the shelter's door. Carrying Cheryl, Gina emerged to murky light and a sticky-sweet smell. Toward the harbor, columns of black smoke spiraled upward.

Vivian murmured, "Lordy, I never . . ."

Cheryl whimpered, "Will the bad guys come back?"

This time, Gina didn't correct Cheryl's supposition. "Probably. We'll be safe in Miss Stella's shelter."

"I don't want to go back there."

Still feeling the buckling ground and the rain of dirt, hearing howls of fear and prayers of despair, Gina didn't want to go back there either.

~~~

The Japanese returned the next day to continue their bombing raids on Manila Bay's harbors, destroying docks, warehouses, storage sheds, and anything that floated. Gina, Vivian, Isabella, and the girls, traumatized yet again, trudged home from the shelter. Her voice husky from the smoky air, Gina said to Vivian, "You want to come in for a while?"

"Thanks, I was hoping you'd ask."

It was a shaky group that entered Gina's living room, the mood subdued, everyone processing one more distressing experience. The little girls leaned on their mothers, and Maggie sat by herself in a corner, watching out the window. Isabella brought in glasses of Filipino lemonade called calamansi and a plate of peanut butter cookies. Her eyes were large and dark.

"Thank you, Isabella. Help yourself to a glass of wine if you like."

Knowing her friend well enough to communicate in signals, Gina gave Vivian a nod.

Vivian said, "Maggie, please take the girls to the playroom and keep them busy for a while. You can take the cookies with you."

Maggie's pretty face turned sullen. "Why do I always have to watch them?"

The girls retreated, and Vivian's gaze followed Maggie. "She sasses back about everything. It's wearing, and I sure don't need it right now."

"She's sixteen, half grown up and half still a kid . . . one scared and not wanting to show it." Gina handed Vivian a vodka and tonic, noticing both their hands were shaking. "And she's worried about her dad. Where's Theo now?"

"He's at Clark Air Field. The hospital up there called for additional surgeons. I'm proud he volunteered, but holy cow, Gina, I need him here. The girls need him here." She patted her chest and coughed. "This smoky air kicks up my asthma. I can hardly breathe. How about Ray? Is he still on Corregidor?"

"As far as I know. He's living in a bombproof cave. The Malinta Tunnel, he called it. MacArthur has offices there, so Ray might be safer than we are." She swirled her drink, and ice tinkled against the glass. "I've decided to take Cheryl and Isabella to our cottage. There are beautiful beaches close by. It will be safer there away from the military bases and the harbor. Why don't you come with me?"

"Are you sure? Do you think it's safe to be on the road?"

"I don't know, but it can't be any worse than sitting in Stella's shelter or waiting for a stray bomb to come through my roof. I'm barely holding it together for Cheryl's sake, and she's jumpy as a bedbug. It's a three-hour trip. It's a chance I'm ready to take."

Vivian took a long time to answer. "I'm tempted. I'm really tempted, but I want to be here when Theo returns from Clark. How long do you think we'd be gone?"

"A couple weeks, maybe. Until MacArthur clears the skies."

Vivian glanced out the window at the smoke-filled horizon, and then her gaze went to the playroom. She raked her hands through her hair. "Our girls have to come first. Theo will understand. When are you leaving?"

"First thing in the morning . . . God willing."

Chapter 3
LEAVING MANILA

I'm billeted in a complex of underground tunnels. Exploring a series of passages, I discovered a fully stocked one-thousand-bed hospital, and I cringe at the implication.

—Ray Thorpe, Corregidor, December 1941–May 1942

The morning started in chaos, with Miguel not able to pack all the necessities for living at the cottage into the trunk of Ray's Cadillac and teary-eyed Isabella wringing her hands and pleading, "Miss Gina, no make me go. My mother old—she needs me close by."

"Isabella, you have sisters who can care for your mother. It's only for a short time, just until General MacArthur stops these bombings. We'll be back before you know it. I need you at the cottage. I can't do this alone. Come with me, please?"

Isabella nodded a damp-cheeked yes.

"You're a dear," Gina said. She went to her bedroom closet to access the wall safe where she kept her jewelry. Ray had always been generous with his gifts, and each piece brought a memory of celebrations and intimate pleasures. She slipped on her diamond-and-sapphire wedding ring and selected a diamond necklace and earrings, her last birthday present from Ray, and a few other pieces she enjoyed wearing. She wrapped the jewelry in a satin case and put it in her purse with the money she had withdrawn from the bank. Left secure in the safe was a treasure trove of her most costly gold, diamond, and gemstone pieces.

Gina packed a few clothes—she wouldn't need many at the cottage—and added some for Ray just in case. On a whim she added a polo shirt of Ray's that Cheryl had worn for a nightgown after he'd left, the short sleeves hanging nearly to her wrists and the hem to her ankles.

There was little room in the car for six people, each carrying their own treasures. Gina drove, and Vivian rode shotgun with boxes of food and sundries crammed under both elbows and on the car floor. Isabella, still sniffing; two big-eyed little girls; and Maggie, hugging her dad's black medical bag, sat in the back with totes piled on their laps and under their feet.

"Three hours to the cottage door," Gina announced to her passengers, trying to keep her attitude positive, but the reflection of her house growing smaller in the rearview mirror brought on a shiver. She forced her sight forward, glad Vivian was beside her for support.

They joined a long line of trucks and cars heading out of the city, the vehicles packed with families, their household belongings tied to their transports' tops and running boards or stuffed in back windows. As they approached the bridge over the Pasig River, traffic slowed to a crawl. A trolley car lay on its side, telephone wires hung to the ground, and the poles leaned cockeyed. Glass from broken windows covered the street for blocks, and gangs of young boys were looting the unprotected shops.

Ahead, Gina saw the destruction worsened, and she drove around chunks of debris in the road. The walls of Intramuros, the walled city that had survived since the sixteenth century, had cratered, and the roof of the Santa Catalina School lay in rubble. Thick smoke billowed from the twin towers of the ancient Santo Domingo Church, and ferries left in the bay listed and smoldered.

"I figured the docks would be damaged, but I didn't expect this." Gina's voice was thick with emotion.

Vivian agreed, her voice hoarse. She sat with her arms hugging her body.

Isabella mumbled in her native Tagalog under her breath.

"I don't know what I'm supposed to feel," Maggie said. "Anger? Hate? Rage? I have friends at school who are Japanese. I like them. And what about Professor Yokota, who lives down the street? He's always been nice to us."

As had the workers in the Japanese spa Gina frequented. Conflicted herself, she didn't know what to say to Maggie. Vivian was quiet, too, and the question remained unanswered but not forgotten as they drove in silence through blocks of rubble.

Beyond the city center, bumper-to-bumper traffic included oxcarts and hundreds of walkers—mothers, fathers, aunts, old grandpas and grandmas, and black-haired children, even the youngest carrying bundles on their heads, in their arms, or strapped to their backs and chests. It seemed the whole country was trudging to somewhere else, their bodies stooped, their faces sad.

Gina inched the car through miles of rice paddies where workers in conical straw hats and knee-length pants worked to salvage their crops and repair strafed fields. Huge-horned water buffalo called carabao dragged plows through the muck or soaked their massive bodies in mudholes to cool off, passively tolerating white herons that perched on their broad backs.

Gina maneuvered around an American troop truck that lay on its side twisted and smoldering, and then she circumnavigated several potholes as big as bathtubs. "Lordy, Viv. Why are the Nips bombing the farmers' fields?"

"Beats me. Maybe they plan on starving us."

"Don't say that! MacArthur will clear them out in a jiffy." It was a chant Gina let roll on a loop in her thoughts.

Leah said from the back seat, "Mama, I need to use the bathroom."

Cheryl added, "It's hot back here. I'm thirsty."

Gina stopped at a nipa-roofed roadside store that was nestled in a stand of acacia and flame trees. The girls hopped out of the car and made a beeline for the outhouse.

Inside the store, colorful *parols*, star-shaped Christmas lanterns, hung from the ceiling, and festive Christmas music played on a radio, the ambience in contrast to the anxiety emanating from the milling crowd. Gina whispered to Vivian, "Did you pack Christmas gifts?"

Vivian nodded. "A few. Just in case. But we'll be home before Christmas, don't you think?"

"I did until we drove through Manila."

Vivian purchased bottles of sarsaparilla for everyone and the last bag of pretzels in the store from a one-toothed crone manning the cashbox. The old woman took her money. "You no go to Clark Air Field?"

"No. To a cottage," Vivian said.

The woman's eyes shone overly bright. "That good. Ladies go to Clark to find missing husbands. But nothing there. It flat. Boom! Boom! Boom! The whole ground shake. Scare my ponies near to death."

As she stood next to her mother, Leah's face turned ashen. "My daddy's at Clark."

The old woman glanced at Leah but ignored her fear. "My son found a hand on the road. Right off some soldier's arm. He buried it, and I put a flower on it. An awful thing, it—"

Aghast, Gina and Vivian quickly herded the girls out of the store and into the car.

The traffic had thinned, making driving easier. Isabella fingered the amulet, her eyes closed and her lips moving in a silent incantation. The little girls squabbled, and Vivian minded the sky as they drove by miles of sugarcane fields. A glint caught her attention, and she adjusted her glasses on her nose to better focus. "Japanese planes! Get off the road, Gina! Right now!"

Gina made a hard right, and the car barreled through the head-high stalks of sugarcane, bouncing those inside around before it stalled. She clutched the steering wheel like it was the only thing between her and death, while Vivian searched for her glasses, which had been flung from her face. The little girls cried for their mothers, and Isabella chanted louder.

Her voice shaky, Gina called, "Is anybody hurt?"

Maggie said, "I bumped my head. I'm okay."

Hearing the planes roar overhead, they all hunkered down and prayed Japanese bullets would fail to find them.

It took a while and the help of a farmer and his carabao to pull the car out of the field. The three-hour trip stretched to eight. Gina turned off the main road that rimmed the perimeter of the peninsula onto a steep, serpentine mile-long climb that led to the cottage. The tin-roofed structure, one of many tucked into the hills, almost disappeared in the surrounding vegetation—a mixture of hardwoods, ficus, bamboo, and towering poinsettias with vibrant-red plate-size blooms. Vines from strangler figs had overgrown the porch.

Gina kicked through the vines and unlocked the front door, and everyone went inside except Isabella, who wouldn't get out of the car. She sat with her eyes closed, her lips moving as she rolled her amulet in the palm of her hand. Gina went back to the car and nudged her shoulder. "Isabella—"

The maid's eyes popped open. Her pupils were huge and her voice strangely breathy. "We not stay here, Miss Gina. I feel evil spirits around us. The toddy cats restless. The birds no fly. The howler monkeys quiet. They *know*."

Gina didn't need this anguish right now. "You talk nonsense. There are no evil spirits. The airplanes are scaring the animals. That's all."

"Ooohh! Nooo!" Isabella's breathiness turned to a moan, and her big eyes glazed over. "My *lola* told me evil spirits hide in the trees. They come out when danger nearby. Tonight I hear them whispering. They planning. They snatch the weak. Please do not stay here, Miss Gina." She covered her face with her hands.

Gina had heard these beliefs before. Hundreds, maybe thousands of superstitions permeated all strata of the Filipino society. "Your grandmother told you a made-up story. I tell you there are no evil spirits."

Isabella put her hands down. "My *lola* old. She knows strong magic. She knows what you not know."

Gina coaxed the reluctant maid out of the car, the frightened woman crying and babbling, "Lots of night animals in jungle—toddy cats, tarsiers in the trees—they restless. Deer and wild pigs, running. Crocodiles hiding . . . no go near the river's edge."

Gina had no thought of going anywhere. "Viv," she said while leading Isabella into the cottage, "get Isabella a cool washcloth for her forehead, please. Maggie, would you be a dear and make Isabella a cup of tea?"

With Isabella quieted, Gina passed out room assignments. "You take the guest room, Viv. The girls and Isabella will sleep in the loft." She opened a door, showing off a bathroom with running water, a shower, and a flush toilet, luxuries in a rural cottage.

The individuals dispersed to settle in—Cheryl excitedly showing Leah her stash of games and books, Maggie helping Isabella cook and serve a meal of rice and canned tomatoes, and Vivian retiring to write a letter to Theo. Gina moved her things into the main bedroom, feeling relieved to be off the road and hidden away in the remote countryside. She should have come sooner and saved days of stress. She cracked open a window to freshen the air. The moon shone as large and bright as she'd ever seen it, and she took a long minute to enjoy it, wondering if Ray was thinking of her and enjoying it too. "I miss you. I love you," she whispered.

In the morning Gina answered a knock on the door. A young man handed her a basket of freshly picked vegetables. "My mom says hello. She told me to ask if I could paint your roof."

His mom was Mrs. Flores, who looked after the cottage when it was empty. Gina noted Arturo stood a foot taller than when she'd last seen him. "My roof? Is there something wrong with it?"

"It shiny. The Japs see it from the sky. I paint it green. We not want Japs to see we are here. Mom said to tell you we turn lights out at night too."

It hadn't occurred to Gina that retreating to her cottage could put the local people in danger. "Of course. We'll be cautious. Please paint the roof for me." Gina handed him money for the green paint. "Tell your mom thank you for the vegetables and that I'll stop by to visit soon."

━━

Days lazily came and went. Gina and Vivian lay on a large, flat, sun-heated rock beside a waterfall that created a crystal-clear pool. Water lotus grew thick at the pool's edge, and Gina plucked a fist-size purple flower off its tall, willowy stem and tucked it behind her ear, thinking the fragrance more exotic than any perfume she had in her collection.

Her gaze went beyond the girls playing in the waterfall to the far side of the pool, where the tops of the bamboo formed lacy patterns against the cloudless sky. She lay back on her towel, feeling secure enough to let her vision go out of focus.

"Mommy, are you sleeping?" Gina felt a pat, pat on her face.

She half opened her eyes to see Cheryl, whose arm was bandaged from her fingertips to her elbow. Gina bounded up, every fear of the last weeks rushing back to her. Leah appeared with her head wrapped mummylike in gauze. Both little girls were giggling.

"Maggie did it." Cheryl pointed to Maggie, who sat with a medical book on her lap and a roll of gauze in her hand.

Maggie grinned and gave Gina a little wave. "Just practicing."

Gina heaved a sigh of relief. "Anyone else getting hungry?"

Three women and two bandaged little girls walked back to the cottage, on the way meeting the laundress, who was carrying a bag of dirty clothing and linens that Isabella had gathered up. The old lady's rheumy eyes widened when she saw the girls. "Okay? Okay?" she jabbered.

Gina assured her, "Yes. Okay. Just play."

The old woman shook her head and smiled. "Nice girls. No want them hurting."

The families had been at the cottage for almost three weeks. The Japanese continued to bomb the islands, and General MacArthur seemed to have no way to stop them. Gina said, "Maybe this is going to drag on longer than we thought."

She hadn't heard from Ray since the one phone call, and that seemed so long ago. She had no idea what was happening on Corregidor or if Ray was safe inside its massive system of tunnels. She craved information, and what little she heard on the radio was always bad . . . the Japanese ruled the air and sea.

Vivian received a letter from Theo stating he was back in Manila and working at the hospital, a madhouse, in his words. He was glad she was with Gina and safe in a small village away from devastation. He hoped to see her soon but didn't know when.

In the evening Gina turned on the radio, and when the announcer mentioned General MacArthur, Vivian and Maggie stepped closer to listen.

"In a defensive measure today, the US Far East forces destroyed interisland steamers and hundreds of smaller vessels in Manila Bay and the Pasig River, paralyzing domestic shipping, including mail and newspaper deliveries.

"Explosions are being reported in northern Luzon, the result of US Far East forces blowing up railroad bridges. Communications equipment are also being rendered inoperable. This is Michael Camp at KZRH, broadcasting from Manila. Stay tuned for updates."

"Destroying interisland steamers," Gina mumbled. "This is worse than I thought. We're being isolated, Viv. My lord, what's MacArthur up to?" Cheryl leaned against her, and Gina lifted her into her arms.

"Sounds like he's preparing for a Japanese invasion." Vivian reached for a cigarette, and then Maggie lit one too.

"You don't smoke," Vivian said.

"I do now," the teen answered.

Leah wrapped her arms around Vivian's waist. "Is Ruthie going to be all right?" she asked about her friend who'd had her red hair shorn.

Gina and Vivian shared a worried glance.

Viv said, "We'll pray for Ruthie and her family, honey. They have their shelter, and General MacArthur is working hard to keep them safe." She snubbed out the cigarette, turned off the radio, and took her daughter's hand. "Anybody up for a game of go fish?"

~

Gina had no interest in celebrating Christmas. However, on Christmas Eve Arturo brought over a small pine tree he had dug up and planted in a bucket. Isabella found craft supplies in the cupboard and showed the girls how to make paper chains and *parols*. Maggie baked ginger cookies, and Vivian opened a bottle of brandy.

Gina found her guitar in the back of the closet, and after a few minutes of tuning and strumming, she had the group singing "Jingle Bells," the music lifting everyone's spirits.

Cheryl cheerily said to Leah, "My daddy's coming home. Mama got a new red dress, and they're going to a dance."

Gina stopped strumming the guitar, and the room became quiet. She'd taken for granted that Cheryl knew plans had changed, and there was to be no dance, no red dress, and no Daddy for Christmas.

Leah said snottily, "He's not coming home. There's a war. Daddies have to stay at work."

Cheryl's face crumpled. "My daddy is too coming home. You're an old poopy head, Leah." She ran to Gina and buried her teary face in her lap.

Gina carried her sobbing child to the bedroom, feeling like a horrible mother. How could she have neglected to inform Cheryl of this most basic information? "Honey, I'm sorry. I should have told you. General MacArthur needs Daddy to stay on Corregidor. He has very important work to do." She rubbed Cheryl's back and dried her tears while trying to control her own. "I have something special for you. You want to see what it is?"

Cheryl sniffed and nodded.

Gina retrieved Ray's shirt from a drawer, the scent of Old Spice still lingering.

Cheryl held it against her cheek. "It smells like Daddy."

"You can sleep with it if you'd like to."

Cheryl scurried onto the bed and laid her head on the pillow with Ray's shirt against her cheek and her thumb in her mouth.

Gina gently pulled the thumb out, and Cheryl grunted, "Umm!" and popped it back in.

"All right, baby. You win." Blinking back tears, she kissed her daughter on her forehead and left her alone with her thumb and her daddy's shirt, thinking it a poor substitute for his loving arms.

⌒

34

After both little girls were asleep, Vivian shooed Maggie away too. "You know the rules. Santa won't come until all kids are asleep, and this Santa is getting very tired."

"All right," Maggie grumbled behind a grin.

Gina and Vivian retrieved the Christmas gifts and wrapping paper from a closet where they were hidden. Gina held up a Shirley Temple doll with its golden curls, polka-dot dress, and Mary Jane shoes. "I hope this perks Cheryl up. She's always on the edge of tears, even when she's laughing."

"Leah too. Kids feel these things more than we think. My dad was away for months during the Great War. I was about six. I remember crying myself to sleep. I'd be more worried if Leah wasn't touchy." She opened a box and showed Gina a pair of boots.

"For Maggie?" Gina asked of the rhinestone-and-mesh ankle boots.

Vivian shrugged. "What can I say? She has a taste for the exotic. She gets it from Theo's mother. What did you get Ray this year?"

"A watch with a calendar. He hinted about it for weeks. I left it in the safe with my jewelry. Do you think it will be there when we get back?"

Vivian nudged her glasses up. "Who knows? It's beginning to look like *if* we get back. We'll stick together, right? You and me. We'll help each other through this?"

"All the way."

Together they finished wrapping the few packages: a child's tea set for Leah, a few games and books for the girls, and extra money and a pocketbook for Isabella. Seeing wrapped presents under the small decorated tree brought a feeling of warmth to Gina. "Merry Christmas," she said to Vivian.

"As merry as it can be."

That night an acrid smell seeped into the cottage, and Gina checked outside for evidence of a fire. A strange light glowed on the horizon, and dogs in the nearby village howled. "Manila looks like it's on fire. Do you think the Japs bombed it off the map?"

Vivian joined her on the porch. "Pray not."

Gina prayed not, too, and wondered if her house that overlooked the bay was being consumed along with irreplaceable letters, albums of priceless photographs, and artifacts that nudged memories of her and Ray foraging for treasures in backstreet galleries and bookshops, a pastime they enjoyed together. She rubbed the back of her neck with both of her hands, massaging the tops of her tight shoulders. Would the bad dream never stop? She cursed General MacArthur's incompetence.

Gina went to bed with worry on her mind and entered a dream state, seeing her eighteen-year-old self working at the Follies—hard muscled from hours of dancing, voluptuous from a generous diet, jeweled, oiled, and fringed—while she whirled like a dervish, struggling to keep up with the frantic plucking of zithers and mad beating of percussion on a stinking stage, in the blazing spotlight, and under the watchful gaze of her nemesis, a fiery-eyed sheikh.

She heard howling first, and dread caused her to pant as her head twisted and turned on the pillow. A horde of big-booted Japanese soldiers swarmed the stage. She smelled their sour, hissing breaths and felt their rough hands rooting like mad dogs' snouts under her jeweled brassiere and fringed hip skirt until it ripped and fell away. Pushed to the floor, she landed on a mesh ankle boot, and she heard Maggie scream. The terror of it woke her in a sweaty panic, and she bolted upright, heaving to breathe.

She was safe in her cottage, but her heart wouldn't stop pounding. Turning the kerosene lamp on its lowest setting, she carried it to the loft, her shadow following her up the stairs. The girls were safely asleep. *It was just a bad dream.* But the terror of it lingered.

Downstairs she poured two fingers of bourbon into a glass, extinguished the light, and stepped out to the porch. The glow on the horizon had grown brighter and now reached higher in the sky. *Something is going on.* Still sweaty, she shivered while hugging herself and sipping the bourbon. *Ray, I'm frightened. I need you.*

In the morning she found Vivian pacing in the kitchen, her body held tight as a coiled spring and one hand massaging the back of her neck. "What's going on, Viv?"

Vivian's voice trembled. "It's on the radio. The Japanese troops landed north and south of Manila. They say fifty thousand soldiers with tanks and artillery are advancing toward the city."

Gina's insides turned icy. Japanese troops were just three hours away. She sank into a chair.

Vivian's hand shook as she lit a cigarette. "What do you think we should do?"

"Stay put. We're hidden here. MacArthur will clear the Japs out soon enough."

"Maybe not. Seems his troops threw down the weapons and ran away."

"Viv, that isn't funny."

"No, but it's true."

Chapter 4

TRAPPED ON BATAAN

*Bataan is surrendered to the Japanese. What next, I wonder?
Corregidor, I'm certain, but I resist accepting the unthinkable
eventuality.*

—Ray Thorpe, Corregidor, December 1941–May 1942

To save the population from further ravages of war, General MacArthur
declared Manila an open city, thus announcing he had abandoned all
defensive efforts. Behind his evacuating troops, warehouses were burned
and ammunition dumps ignited. The city lit up with the fireworks.

That strange glow, Gina remembered.

Over one hundred thousand soldiers and civilians poured into the
Bataan Peninsula, a small jut of land thirty miles long and fifteen miles
across its widest point. A single road snaked down the east perimeter through several small towns, including Pilar, near Gina's cottage,
and then halfway up the west edge. The craggy peaks of the Zambales
Mountains covered most of the interior. Corregidor Island, where Ray
was stationed, lay off the southern tip.

Soon the grinds, grates, and whines of convoys moving the vast
populations along the road reverberated to Gina's cottage a mile above.

Vivian and Gina stayed close to the radio to follow every scrap of news. "Just in," the announcer shouted—

Then nothing.

Vivian rotated the dial, turned the radio off and on, unplugged it, and plugged it in again. She slapped the top with the flat of her hand, and still, there was no response. Irritated at the loss, she snapped, "Nothing! It's dead. Shit." She looked around to see if the girls were within hearing distance.

The afternoon dragged on with no information. Gina paced, and Vivian smoked. The families played a half-hearted game of Parcheesi, but nothing held their interest. Late in the day, Gina said, "Viv, let's drive down to the main road. Maybe somebody can tell us something."

"Let me come too," Maggie said. "I'm going crazy here."

On the way out, the three women each grabbed a canteen of water and a pack of cigarettes. Gina parked the car at the main road to watch the American-Filipino army passing by in an eerie, dark parade—mile after mile of tanks, buses, trucks, jeeps, and every conceivable make of car commandeered from civilians. Filipino families rode in rickety oxcarts or walked with their worldly possessions tied to their bodies. The air reeked of acrid fumes, and the setting sun was clouded by roiling dust, causing Gina's eyes to water and Maggie to sneeze. Some soldiers waved and whistled, and a few pulled over to chat with the three pretty women sitting in a Cadillac offering cigarettes and drinks of water.

Gina handed the canteen to a soldier. "Our radio's out. What's going on?" His blue eyes and blond hair reminded her of Ray, and a sudden longing arose. The insignia on his uniform identified him as a medic.

He took a long gulp of water. "Stars and Stripes are down; the Rising Sun's flying over Manila. Goddamn. MacArthur pulled us out. Said he wanted to save the city. A little too late, in my opinion."

"Only the city?" Gina asked, wondering what was happening to Ray on Corregidor, just a stone's throw across the North Channel.

"Yes, ma'am. Far as I know."

Vivian offered him a cigarette. "Where were you stationed, medic?" She had to shout to be heard.

"All around, but mostly Philippine General."

"Do you know my husband? Dr. Theo Parker?"

"Yeah. He went to Clark when they asked for volunteers."

"Do you know where he is now?"

The medic shrugged. "He could be here. Or he could be in Manila with patients too sick to be moved. In which case . . ." He took a long drag on his cigarette. "Not to be the bearer of bad news, ma'am, but if he's in Manila, he's probably been taken prisoner by now."

Gina saw Vivian's smile disappear and the corners of her mouth twitch, and she wished to comfort her, but words had to be shouted.

Maggie folded her arms. "But he'll be all right?"

Her question went unanswered.

Three other soldiers joined them, and Gina offered the canteen and cigarettes. "Any of you boys been to Corregidor?"

"Where?"

"No."

"Never heard of it," the last one said while smiling at Maggie.

Never heard of it. Gina's jaw clenched. How could he not? It was the island protecting their precious Manila Bay. Somebody must know something. Had it been bombed? Were soldiers still stationed there? Where was her husband?

A jeep screeched to a stop, and the soldiers scuttled away.

Vivian bit her lip. "Don't look now, but a big honcho's coming this way. He's got a driver, and look how he walks."

The gray-haired general, dressed in wrinkled khaki and chomping on a smoldering pipe, approached and hollered over the rumble of a passing tank. "What are you women doing here?"

Vivian answered, "We're watching for our husbands, sir."

His voice boomed. "Holy mother of hell. Does this look like a picnic area? Jesus! Where you staying?"

Dust churned from the road, stinging Gina's eyes. She pointed. "About a mile that way. I have a cottage. We thought we'd be safer here than in Manila."

The general scowled, every line in his weary face sagging. He continued to holler. "No place on this godforsaken island is safe. Nip fighters will be strafing this area before you know it, and the artillery forces are right behind the planes. Get yourselves hidden and stay put, the higher up the better." Jamming his pipe between his teeth, he held his hand out. "I'm taking this car. Give me the keys."

Gina, stunned at this turn of events, stuttered, "Y-you can't."

"Yes, I can," he growled. "My injured men need a ride. Give me your keys."

There was no disobeying that order, and Gina held out the keys, but her fingers wouldn't loosen on them.

Vivian nudged her and hissed, "Give him the keys, Gina."

She forced open her hand, and the general grabbed the keys and tossed them to an aide. As he strode back to his jeep, he shouted over his shoulder, "Don't wait! Not another hour! Get yourselves hidden!" With that, he sped away with Ray's car right behind him.

"Shit! You damn bastard!" Gina screeched as she watched Ray's car disappear. In anger, she flipped the general's back a double bird.

Vivian slapped her hands down. "You want us thrown in the brig?"

"Right now I don't give a damn shit. I feel like I've been mugged. How . . . ?" She gulped air. "How are we supposed to"—she mimicked the general—"get ourselves hidden?"

With no other option, Gina stewing, Vivian angry, and Maggie bewildered, they hiked back to the cottage.

After a time, Gina said, "I think the cottage is hidden well enough by the foliage. It can't be seen from the road or the sky. Everything we need is here, and who knows what we'd find higher up. I think it's best we stay."

Vivian's voice rose to a higher pitch. "Are you kidding? You left out one little detail. Didn't you hear the word *strafing*? Bullets go right through foliage. The general put the devil in me, Gina. I'm not staying anywhere the Japs are within spitting distance. I'm taking my girls and going higher up the mountain, even if we have to walk."

Gina objected. "How will Ray and Theo find us?"

"My hope, darlin', is alive."

⌇

Arturo was pacing on the porch when the women returned from the main road. "Señoras, my cousin just came from Manila. He say the Japanese army moving fast. Bad for Americans. Mama say you go to Señor Ramos's ranch, or you be trapped here."

Vivian jumped on the information. "Whose ranch? Where?"

"Señor Ramos. He owns a big ranch in the mountains. You go. I show you the way."

"We can't. The car is gone, and the road's blocked by the army." Vivian grabbed onto Arturo's arm. "Can you take us tonight in your cart on the back trails—"

"Viv, no . . . in a cart, on a narrow trail, in the dark. You could fall off a cliff."

"I'll take that chance. By hell, high water, or oxcart, I'm leaving."

"I sorry, Señora. The back trail too steep for my cart."

Vivian's eyes widened. "Oh my God, we're trapped on this peninsula."

"We'll be okay, Mom," Maggie said, but her voice sounded tiny.

⌇

Without a radio news was hard to get, but Arturo kept Gina and Vivian informed of what he knew. Battles raged on the north end of the peninsula, the stronger Japanese army pushing the American and Filipino troops farther south. Field hospitals swelled and then overflowed with wounded and sick soldiers, and graveyards were quickly filling with the dead. With the ports blocked and one hundred thousand soldiers and migrant civilians needing food, hunger and disease were as much of a threat as the Japanese soldiers. Rice fields soon lay barren, and vegetation was stripped of anything edible; animals of all sizes became scarce as both armies and civilians slaughtered them for food. Water supplies dried up or became polluted, and malaria, typhus, and beriberi took hold.

At the cottage, the families endured. Mrs. Flores shared her supply of tea and jerky and showed Vivian where to find persimmon-like fruit and sour rattan berries.

Looking skeptical, Vivian asked, "What should I do with them?"

"Cook them into your broths. They give a good flavor."

Arturo supplied the families with rabbits, pigeons, and once a hunk of wild pig that kept them fed for a week.

Maggie searched the forest for edible weeds and fruits. Tickled at her find one day, she trotted home. "I found a patch of native corn. There's a lot there. Enough to share it with Mrs. Flores."

⌁

Isabella did her best to make the mismatched and scrounged food edible and kept their drinking water potable. The little girls did their share by helping with the cleanup.

It was Gina's job to shop at the local markets, calling for treks along hilly mountain trails to whatever market was open that day. She savored her time away from the tensions always present in the cottage brought on by fear of what lay ahead, barely edible food, and too much togetherness. She had learned to pay attention to the sounds and sights around her, as she had been followed one day and had her parcels stolen by a shrunken soldier. She'd handed them over without a whimper but cursed his skinny bones when he was out of earshot. Now she carried a stout stick and was always ready to use it.

Today's market was a meager affair, with only a few stalls set up and many locals purchasing the stringy meats and underripe vegetables. The little money she had was disappearing too quickly, and Gina shopped frugally, buying a rabbit that was killed, skinned, and gutted while she waited; a bag of okra; and a jug of carabao milk, wondering how she was going to carry it. Stepping back from a stall, she bumped into a man wearing a tattered army uniform. "Sorry," she muttered.

"My pleasure," he answered.

Gina stopped short. She recognized the voice. "Theo?" She squinted in disbelief. A belt cinched up his khaki shorts, and his shirt fell off his shoulders, but it was blond-haired, green-eyed Theo. Never had anybody looked so good to her.

Theo flashed an open-mouth grin. "My lord, Gina, you're so dark I thought you were a local. Is Vivian with you?"

Gina felt tickled to give him good news. "She's at my cottage, and so are Maggie and Leah. They're fine. We're all fine." She saw worry drain from his face. "Where did you come from?"

"I'm at the Ninety-First Field Hospital about ten minutes from here by jeep. Been there a couple weeks. I knew you had a cottage around here someplace. I've been looking . . . I was hoping . . ." His eyes twinkled, and he laughed for the first time in a long while, Gina suspected. He asked, "Have you heard from Ray?"

"No. Last I knew he was on Corregidor."

Something flickered in Theo's eyes that made her feel weak kneed. Her purchases suddenly too heavy, she dropped them on the ground. "What do you know about Corregidor?"

"Nothing, really. It's heavily fortified. MacArthur and his wife and son are there holed up in those tunnels. Ray's probably eating better than we are."

"Do you really think so?"

He shrugged and offered her a cigarette. They both lit up. "Can you take me to Vivian?"

Leah spotted them first, and she let out a shriek: "Daddy's here! Mama! Mama! Come quick! Daddy's here!" Vivian and Maggie emerged from the cottage and ran to Theo's open arms. The three enclosed him in a circle of love, kisses, and happy tears.

Cheryl ran to the jeep, clapping her hands, her eyes wild with anticipation. "Where's my daddy?" Her head snapped left and right.

Gina knelt down to Cheryl's height and took her hand. "Honey—"

Cheryl jerked her hand away and balled it into a fist, her face contorted with anger. "Where's my daddy?" she shouted while stepping away. "Why didn't you bring him too?" Wailing, she turned and ran into the cottage with Gina right behind her, but there was no consoling the little girl, who wanted her daddy more than anything in the world.

She lay with Cheryl until her cries turned to whimpers and then sleep, not knowing what else to do but hold her close.

Theo's visits to the cottage were determined by his workload. Days would go by with no sign of him, and then he'd arrive weary, smelling faintly of ether, and his boots so mucky he'd leave them outside. Often he'd sleep so soundly that Vivian would poke him to see if he responded.

When awake and fed, he told how makeshift medical units were moved around as needed and set up in minutes, with tents affording cover and generators supplying power for the lights strung over the surgical tables. Patients arrived by bus, jeep, or mule, and doctors performed surgeries around the clock.

"Take me back with you," Maggie said. "I hate just sitting and waiting. I can work. I'll do anything."

Theo growled his displeasure. "It's not like our clinic in Manila. It's no place for a young woman."

"You have nurses," Maggie argued. "How am I any different?"

Theo looked at his daughter as though he were contemplating that question.

Gina agreed with Maggie. "I'll volunteer too. I've got two strong hands and time to spare. I need to feel useful."

"We all feel that way," Vivian added.

"You don't know what you're getting into," Theo argued, "It's not what you think. It's not what you can even imagine."

The three women stared him down until he acquiesced.

⌇

Theo was right: they had no idea what they were getting into, and when they returned to the cottage after a shift, not one word was said about the drippy gray ugliness they'd witnessed or the sour smells of the miserable place or dying men lying on the ground for lack of a cot, the surgeries without anesthesia, the screams, the shrieks, the severed limbs, the buckets of blood, the vomit, the shit, the gore—

⌇

Word that a convoy of fresh Japanese troops had landed at Lingayen Gulf north of Manila Bay came through the bamboo telegraph, a loosely constructed communications network of priests, shopkeepers, itinerant workers, guerrillas, and gossips that permeated the islands. Within days, the stronger, well-armed enemy blasted their way through the American and Filipino defenses, and Bataan was surrendered to the Japanese. All American and Filipino forces, including medical personnel and patients in the field hospitals, were taken prisoners of war.

The news felt like a punch to Gina's gut, and she couldn't keep a meal down. Maggie retreated into her medical book, the girls squabbled over a game of go fish, Isabella clung to her amulet and mumbled prayers, and Vivian, her body hunched and arms crossed, paced the room's perimeters.

"What now?" Vivian asked. "The Japs will have free run of the islands."

Gina didn't know. "We stay hidden and sit it out."

"But Theo . . ."

The look on Viv's face made Gina wonder if her friend, this once-sheltered debutante, would break under the weight of the happenings.

Chapter 5

THE DEATH MARCH

Our leaders abandon seventy thousand American and Filipino soldiers to Japanese cruelties. I don't believe. But then, I believe. And then I despair.

—*Ray Thorpe, Corregidor, December 1941–May 1942*

April 9, 1942, US Army major general Edward P. King surrendered Bataan to General Masaharu Homma. Under pressure to rid the peninsula of the American-Filipino army, Homma ordered the seventy thousand soldiers to be marched sixty-five miles to prison camps in northern Luzon. The news sent Gina to her bedroom to privately deal with her sorrow. She heard a soft knock on the door.

"It's me," Vivian whispered.

"Don't let the girls in," Gina instructed and swiped her hand across her teary eyes.

Vivian opened the door a few inches, slid through, and closed it. She turned toward Gina, her back against the door as if she needed support. "Mrs. Flores just left. She said our soldiers are marching along the main road. The Jap guards aren't giving them food or water. Theo—"

Vivian's body began to slide down the door, and Gina helped her into a chair and rubbed her back. "We'll take food to the men. Rice balls and coconut. There are canteens in the cupboard we can fill and hand to them as they walk by."

⌁

The morning sun had just begun to peek through the dense hinterland growth, and the dew-heavy air shimmered silver, forecasting a blistering-hot day. Bees buzzed around flowering hibiscus, and birds chirped; however, their love calls were eclipsed by the raspy caws of circling crows. Carrying canteens and as much food as they could spare, Vivian and Gina started their downward trek. Near the main road, the quality of the air changed, and Gina breathed through her mouth to block an acrid stench.

The main road was rutted by heavy footfalls and tire tracks, and at intervals were splotches of black goo covered with flies that swarmed when they walked by. Gina bent and picked up a gold wedding ring half obscured in a rut. The inscription on the inside of the band read, *Love forever. M & L. 1939.* She showed it to Vivian. "Someone must be heartbroken about losing this." Nearby, she uncovered a picture that had been stomped by a hobnailed boot. The writing on the back gave names to the faces: Martin and Lynette, he looking smart in his uniform and she young and pretty in a frilly wedding dress. Scavenging along the edge of the road, she found a trove of rings, fountain pens, watches, and rosaries. "Why would the men be dropping these?"

Vivian muttered, "To keep them out of the Jap pockets is my guess." She stirred through the orphaned objects as if she were searching for something of her own, before wrapping them in a banana leaf and hiding them behind a rock.

They filled the canteens with water from an artesian well. Nearby a bamboo bridge crossed a ravine thick with weeds and grasses. Gina pointed out a stream that ran along the bottom. "Ray says the fishing is good here. He brought Cheryl with him sometimes."

Stepping a few feet off the road, Vivian picked up a white under-shirt attached to the end of a disabled American rifle. She held it up. "Looks like a flag of surrender. The poor guy. God help him." She threw the makeshift flag down.

Gina found a single boot, a crutch, and then a bloodied hand snagged on a bush. She flinched back, and a wave of acid welled up from her stomach. What had gone on here?

A wizened Filipino woman came out of the brush and left a sack of bananas by the well. Gina recognized the rheumy-eyed laundress who did washing for the cottage. "Ma'am," Gina said, signaling her, needing to tell her what she'd seen, but her voice failed.

The woman's eyes widened when she saw Gina. "No stay here," she said in a crackly voice. She flipped her hands in a shooing motion. "Bad here. Dangerous for you." She turned and scurried away.

"Wait," Gina called, but it came out as a croak. She considered Vivian, who was scrounging in the weeds picking up rings and watches and intently inspecting each one. They could be of no help here. She sipped from the canteen still in her hand. "We should go back, Viv. We can leave the food and water. It's dangerous for us. It's worse than I thought."

"All the more reason to stay," Vivian snapped. "I need to see Theo with my own eyes. You go back if you want, but first show me where I can hide."

Gina deliberated the worst of scenarios for Vivian: seeing Theo at the mercy of a cruel enemy, or not seeing him at all. There was no good choice. Whatever the outcome, her best friend couldn't be left alone. She pointed out the dry place where she used to sit while Ray and Cheryl caught perch in the stream, the bamboo now grown thick around it. "We can hide here."

Hundreds of birds flocked out of the trees, their flapping wings stirring the air like an approaching storm. Monkeys stopped hooting, and tarsiers silenced their high-pitched squeals.

"The men are coming," Vivian whispered.

Sunlight dimmed under the flocked birds, and finding it hard to take a full breath, Gina felt as if in a surreal world. A rattle in the distance turned into the squeaks and pings of bicycles. The women scrambled into their lair.

Vivian slightly parted the camouflaging vegetation to view the Japanese soldiers, whose rifles were strapped to their backs. Fat bundles were tied behind the seats of their bicycles. Following the bikes were the captured American and Filipino soldiers. They marched five across in long columns, a procession of the weariest, most pitiful-looking men Gina had ever seen—their faces gray from caked-on dirt and days-old stubble, their hair greasy, and their bodies bone skinny under what was left of their tattered, filthy uniforms. Some hobbled on crutches, while others leaned on friends. An almost imperceptible murmur of moans, epithets, and prayers accompanied them along with that sour stench. Tears flooded Gina's eyes and left a trail down her face.

Vivian, holding back a moan, leaned forward to see. "Is Theo with them?"

Gina was certain a familiar face in this horde of downcast eyes would be impossible to identify, and a known gait in this mass of shuffling feet would be distorted. Vivian would learn nothing of Theo's fate here.

Peeking through the foliage, the women studied the guards, who stopped to smoke, drink from the well, and compare the American watches that lined their arms from wrist to elbow. Their thirst and nicotine craving sated, they returned to prodding the prisoners with sticks and switches past the well, denying them the water their dehydrated bodies craved. When one man stumbled, a guard stabbed him in the buttocks.

Vivian gasped and stood in the blind, poised to run to the stabbed soldier, but Gina pulled her down and clasped a hand over Vivian's mouth. Vivian pushed the hand away and swiped at blinding tears.

All morning and into the afternoon, trapped in their jungle jail, Gina and Vivian gaped in horror at the urine and shit stains on the soldiers' trousers and the blood and sweat that drenched their shirts. Gina cringed and covered her ears to block out the pitiful cries of the injured and gritted her teeth when a guard barking, "Speedo, speedo," tripped a soldier tottering on crutches.

A half-crazed prisoner broke ranks and wobbled toward the well, his tongue lolling and his resolve obvious. "Halt," a guard bellowed, and when the prisoner didn't stop, the guard raised his sword and severed the prisoner's head with one practiced chop. Blood spurted like a fountain as the prisoner's body crumpled, and his head rolled in the opposite direction.

In a surge of rebellion, other prisoners roared, trampled the guards, and swarmed the well for a gulp of the life-giving water that flowed so freshly and freely. During the fray, some brave or demented prisoners hurled themselves into the ravine, and a contingent of guards opened fire. Allied blood turned the water in the stream crimson. Gina pulled her legs up to a fetal curl as the scenario unfolded, her eyes squeezed tight and her hands over her ears to block out what she couldn't possibly process.

~

The parade of marchers ended as it had started, with the rattle of bicycles. When the clatter and clank faded, Gina and Vivian crawled out of their hiding place. Bodies lay in a heap by the well, and others were sprawled on the road, some beaten so severely that pulp replaced their faces. As they searched, hoping to find some men alive, circling crows swooped down, screeching and pecking in a mad head-to-head competition for a piece of the booty. Screaming obscenities, Gina threw fist-size rocks at the black-feathered birds that caused them to contemptuously flutter a few feet away, but they soon returned to their feasting.

Panting at the exertion, Gina picked up a stick and sat beside a lone soldier who lay sprawled in the dirt. A blond kid, like Ray, she noted. A blue eye peeked out from a half-closed eyelid, and when she reached over and closed it, she saw a Saint Christopher medal hidden under his khaki shirt. *Overlooked*, she figured. *Lucky guy.* She guessed her humor was as dark as the world around her. His class ring read, *St. Michaels HS, 1941*, and ink scrawled on the back of his hand read, *Carolyn*.

Gina furiously whacked the stick on the ground to deter approaching crows as she screamed, "Git! You dirty buggers." Sighing, she bowed her head and pinched the bridge of her nose to stem tears. The kid was nineteen years old, if that. She straightened his bloody shirt over the bayonet wound on his chest. There were a mother and father somewhere worried about him and a pretty girlfriend named Carolyn. She went through his pockets and found a wallet that held his identification, Gerald Kent, and a plastic sleeve of family pictures that she flipped through, the tightness in her chest moving up to her throat. She put the wallet and ring into her pocket, believing his parents would want what was left of him.

She heard a growl, and every nerve in Gina's body prickled. She looked up to see Vivian confronted by a rangy dog, snarling, his teeth bared and muzzle wet with blood. A stout stick lay near Vivian's feet, and when she took a tiny step toward it, the dog lowered his head and growled again, deep and guttural.

Gina fumbled to pick up a rock, and when she saw the dog crouch to spring, she heaved it, missing but distracting her target. In one smooth move Vivian swooped up the stick and slammed it across the creature's muzzle. He yelped and slunk away, but others skulked close by, and Vivian, clinging to her stick and a rock, retreated.

Beyond Vivian, a cadre of Filipinos emerged from the hills, some with wheelbarrows and shovels and others carrying crosses. As they came closer, Gina waved one over, wanting Gerald to be buried before the scavenger birds and wild dogs tore apart his young body.

Gina helped the Filipino load Gerald's body into the wheelbarrow, noting the dead weight of it, and as they worked, she told the local man about the soldiers who had escaped into the ravine. "There may be some bodies in there too."

"You find, I bury." The Filipino held up four fingers. "Four days they come, and each day more die. They march with no food, no water, and when weak and fall down, they stabbed. I watch for my son marching. I told they come tomorrow and the next day and the next one after." He bowed his head in grief. "You find, I bury," he muttered again. "Dead men left on ground bring sickness to my village." He carted Gerald Kent away.

Gina watched him leave, her grief pulling her down into a dark place the depth of which she'd never before known. Certainly, there would be retribution for an atrocity of this magnitude. Somehow, sometime, somewhere, someone would pay, and she itched to be there to help it happen.

___

She joined Vivian, who was looking into the ravine that was thick with vegetation and stank of decay. Two bodies lay facedown at the bottom with shallow water flowing around them, the backs of their shirts stained crimson. "It's getting dark," Gina said, hoping Vivian would suggest returning to the cottage. Instead, Vivian plunged through the waist-high foliage.

"Someone might need help," she said. "Come on."

They tramped along the water's muddy edge, searching for footprints or a piece of a uniform of those who'd tried to escape snagged on a broken branch. "They came out here." Vivian pointed to where the reeds and grasses had been crushed. The women followed the trail that zigzagged deep into the wasteland so dense it seemed to close in behind them.

"We're going to get lost." Gina pushed back panic.

"We're not lost. I used to hunt with my dad. I think we're on a deer run. If I'm right, it will lead us back to the stream. Let's go a little farther."

As Vivian predicted, the trail led back to the stream, where thousands of fiddler crabs and beetles scurried underfoot, and Gina's wet shoes made sucking sounds in the black sludge. There were no further signs of the escaped prisoners.

"Maybe they're hiding," Vivian theorized.

"Or a local helped them escape," Gina added, hoping it was true.

The trail dipped into a hollow. The stream narrowed to a trickle, and clumps of sawgrass and sedges thickened, their sharp blades catching Gina's pant legs. She wanted out of this dark ravine, far away from its swarming insects, sounds of dripping water, and foul smells.

Vivian stopped abruptly. "Don't go any farther!" She choked and coughed. Weaving on her feet, she grabbed hold of a nearby tree and fell on her knees in the muck and retched.

Gina pushed ahead to where masses of prisoners lay in scattered heaps in the scummy quagmire, their bodies covered with swarms of black flies. Wild pigs lifted their heads as she approached but then went back to their gory feasting on the human entrails strewn haphazardly around. Gina's hand flew to cover her nose and mouth, and it was then she saw the men were tethered together, their faces, necks, and hands bound in barbed wire. Gina froze. Her knees went soft and gave out from under her.

Vivian half dragged and half carried Gina away from the hollow, where the evil was so thick it sucked out the air. Collapsing against each other, Gina gave way to sobs that boiled up from the depths of her soul while Vivian stood dead eyed and nearly comatose. Gina held Vivian's cold hand as they trudged along the upward path that led to the comfort of home and family.

Whiffing smoke, Gina lifted her head and sniffed. The locals burning bodies? Roving Japs torching the nearby village? The girls! Mrs. Flores! Arturo! "Can you smell it, Viv? Smoke? Let's hurry." She pushed to move her legs faster along the uphill trek, but each hung on her body as heavy as a fence post. More smoke thickened the air. "Got to hurry," she mumbled under what little breath she had in her.

Gina saw flickers of fire before the women came into the clearing and witnessed the whole of their fire-consumed cottage.

"Oh my God!" Vivian screamed, clawing her way up the last hill. Gina's core turned ice cold, and she screeched, "Cheryl! Maggie! Leah! Isabella! Oh no. My God. No!"

Chapter 6

ESCAPING BATAAN

I watch the tunnel's entrance for a tank or a flamethrower.
Instead, a man appears—short, mustached, and bespectacled.
A sword strapped to his belt drags on the ground. How danger-
ous can he be? I soon learn.

—Ray Thorpe, Corregidor, December 1941–May 1942

Gina kicked at the front door of the cottage until it gave way, but the resulting roiling wave of heat and smoke drove her backward. "Cheryl, Maggie, Leah!" she shrieked. "Isabella! Where are you?" Vivian crashed through the back window with the same searing outcome.

"No!" Gina screamed, preferring to die herself than lose her daughter. Turning, she saw two Japanese soldiers approaching with grins on their faces and bayonets aimed at her heart. Beyond fear and with tears streaming, she bellowed, "My little girl!" She pointed to the billowing smoke. "She's six years old!"

The soldiers didn't respond.

Gina made a cradle with her arms. "My baby," she cried and pointed again to the smoke curling out the doors and windows.

Concern washed over one soldier's face. As he jabbered with his companion, a jeep nosed out of the jungle and raced full speed toward them. One soldier shot at the vehicle and jumped into the underbrush, while the other stood big eyed and frozen. Gina cowered and covered her eyes so as not to witness the impact.

She heard a sickening thud and Theo yelling, "Get in."

Frantic, Gina shouted, "The girls."

"Taken care of. Hurry! Get in!"

Gina and Vivian hopped into the jeep. "How? Where?" Gina questioned, but she was thrown back by Theo's tromping on the gas pedal. With Arturo pointing the way, Theo sped to the waterfall, where Isabella and the girls were hiding behind a stand of bamboo. They scrambled in, Cheryl and Leah on the seats with their mothers and Maggie and Isabella scrunched on the floor.

Gina had no control over the tears of relief that flowed down her face.

"Hang on tight," Theo yelled, and Gina clung to her daughter. Off again, the passengers were bounced and jerked, but Theo didn't slow down until they were far enough along the bumpy and twisted trails to be out of immediate danger. When the jeep stopped, Arturo passed around a canteen of water, and everyone got out to stretch their legs.

Vivian, shaken and pale, placed her hand on Theo's arm. "The march . . . the cruelty . . . the soldiers . . . I thought . . . oh my God, Theo, I thought you—"

Theo explained. "I was sent to Corregidor to pick up pentothal. It was supposed to be a one-day trip. I couldn't get back and had to hire a boat. I got here this morning and found Arturo. He told me that Japs were all over the area and that Isabella had taken the girls to hide behind the waterfall."

"Isabella," Vivian said. "How can I ever thank you?"

"Make that 'we,'" Gina added, reaching over to give Isabella a hug, remembering how she had coerced her maid to come to the cottage.

"You're the best, Isabella. I'm in your debt. Thank you." She tried to smile, but not even a grin would form on her still-trembling lips. She turned to ask Theo, "When you were on Corregidor, did you see Ray?"

"No. I didn't get past the dock. The place is being bombed to dust. Except for the guys managing the batteries on the island's perimeter, most everyone else is holed up in the Malinta Tunnel. When the Japanese invade, and it's inevitable, the soldiers will be taken prisoners of war. I'm sorry, Gina."

Gina's heart sank. There was no good alternative.

Theo addressed the others. "We need to leave. Everyone back in the jeep."

Gina settled Cheryl on her lap. "We fooled them, didn't we, Mama? We hid, and the bad guys couldn't find us."

Gina's eyes searched her daughter's, and she wondered how Cheryl would process today's events. Did she even realize the danger she'd been in? "You were very brave." She kissed Cheryl's forehead, tasting salty sweat. "We have a long way to go. Close your eyes and rest." She tightened her hug to encircle Cheryl in a zone of love and safety.

"Where are you taking us?" Vivian asked.

"To the Ramos Ranch. Señor Ramos will find a place where you can wait out the war." He turned to Arturo. "How do you find your way around up here?"

Arturo shrugged. "It's a map in my head."

The long ride gave Gina time to ponder, and the events of the day played like a horror movie through the recesses of her rattled mind. Occasionally, her body uncontrollably twitched, and more than once a moan escaped from her throat. Time slowly passed. Cheryl slept on her chest. Vivian crooned a lullaby to Leah, Maggie and Isabella sat twisted like pretzels on the jeep's floor, and Arturo in the front seat chain-smoked.

High in the hills of Bataan's mountainous interior and fronting miles of grassland, they came upon a sign on a stone arch that read, **Ramos Ranch. Est. 1910.** A cowboy astride a horse met the jeep at a scrolled wrought iron gate. He wore a handgun on his hip and had a rifle slung across his saddle. A large hat obscured most of his face. "What can I do for you folks," he growled. The horse shook its shaggy head and whinnied.

Theo answered, "Good day, sir. We're here to see Señor Ramos about renting a cabin."

The cowboy leaned down and peered into the jeep, where the families huddled—dirty and traumatized, the little girls clinging to their mothers. Arturo's hand shook as he lit another cigarette.

The cowboy opened the gate, and they followed him along a meandering road to a low-roofed house, where he tipped his hat and trotted away. Theo knocked on the front door, and when a maid answered, he disappeared inside.

Maggie said, "We're homeless, aren't we? I've never even thought about being homeless." After being quiet for a minute, she mumbled, "Well, this ought to be an adventure."

Theo returned and slid behind the wheel of the jeep. "You'll be staying here tonight. Señor Ramos has a cabin near a barrio called Tinian. It comes with a houseboy. He'll take you there tomorrow on horseback. I paid three months in advance for the cabin and ordered food and supplies." He started the jeep and followed the meandering road past barns and corrals to a whitewashed outbuilding. Inside were several bunk beds, and on the end of each were a pillow and blanket.

To Gina, the surroundings hardly registered. She took Cheryl to the outhouse and helped her wash her hands and face in water from the hand pump. Cheryl asked, "Are we going back to the cottage?"

"I'm afraid not. It was on fire, honey. You didn't see it?"

"No. Isabella made us hide in a cave behind the waterfall. I didn't want to go in there."

"I'm glad you were brave. Isabella did the right thing. Come—let's go back."

On returning, she saw Theo and Vivian standing close, he handing her money and she crying. He waved Gina over, and when she approached them, Vivian said, "Theo's leaving in the morning."

Gina gasped. "You can't."

"We need more provisions than what's available here, warm clothing and medical supplies especially. I'll never find my way on the back roads into the city. I'd like Isabella to go with me."

"But, but . . . ," Gina stammered, wondering who would unpack and organize for her. "Did you ask her? Does she want to go?"

Theo called, "Isabella, come here a minute, please." He explained the situation.

Isabella's eyes lit up. "I go. I help Dr. Theo."

"I don't c-cook," was all Gina could think to say.

"I live with my mama. She old. She needs me."

Gina's mouth fell open. "You're not coming back?"

⌒⌒

Vivian poured them all a generous whiskey from a bottle that Theo had brought with him. Gina slugged hers down and held her glass out for a refill, hoping the burning liquid would anesthetize her brain and erase every insane memory of the last eighteen hours.

The sun was setting, and the stars were peeking through a blue-black sky. Sitting on the edge of her cot, Cheryl said, "I don't want to stay here."

Gina said, "It's just for one night, honey."

"I want to go home."

How could she tell her child she didn't have a home? Gina struggled to steady her voice. "The important thing is we are all together. Being together is our home wherever we are."

"Daddy's not here. We're not all together." Cheryl began to cry.

Gina reached out for Cheryl, but her daughter pulled away.

Gina lay on her bunk and pulled the pillow over her head to block out the light, the noise, and her thoughts of running a bayonet through the whole goddamn Japanese population. Her hand on her heart, she felt a seed of hate beginning to swell like a malignant cancer.

Theo, Isabella, and Arturo left before dawn. Gina stood watching in the early-morning dark with her eyes bugged open and her mind in a muddle. How could she cope when she couldn't even think?

⌐

The single-file caravan—two families, four cowboys, and an oxcart full of food and supplies—ambled along a dusty trail through Señor Ramos's vast pasturelands, where countless numbers of gray, hump-backed cattle grazed.

Gina hunkered in Sugar's saddle, her eyes on the ground, her back rounded, and her shoulders taut. She needed to be alone, and she allowed Sugar to lag behind the others while she wept and pondered whether life with all its pain, with all its anguish, with all its hate and cruelty, was worth living. When a squadron of Japanese planes flew over, making Sugar skittish, Gina patted her horse's neck and soothed her with calming words: "It's all right. You'll be all right." Sugar quieted, and soon Gina's body relaxed into the animal's plodding rhythm. She lifted her gaze to the beauty and grand scale of the high-reaching Zambales Mountains, now backed by a golden sky.

Ray had often suggested they vacation high in the mountains. "You should experience it," he had said. "It's rustic and wild . . . . a different way of life. Whenever I'm in the mountains, I realize how little a man needs to survive. It's life renewing."

"No, thanks," she had said, declining every suggestion of a mountain vacation. "The cottage is rustic enough for me." Now she wished Ray were by her side, seeing what she was seeing and saying, "Didn't I tell you it was grand?"

Vivian fell back to be with her. Worry lines had appeared on her forehead and dark patches under her eyes this morning. She turned her head slowly as if her neck were stiff.

"You ride like a pro, Viv. I haven't figured out how to turn Sugar around yet. Are the girls okay sharing a saddle with the cowboys?"

"The cowboys have them giggling, and that's a good thing. By the time we get to wherever we're going, they'll have a repertoire of trail songs."

"Oh, lovely. Not bawdy?"

"I hope."

Soon they entered a forested area where light dappled the ground, rainbow parrots and yellow-breasted sunbirds flitted from tree to tree, and families of long-tailed macaques, perched on high branches, threw seedpods at the caravan. The trail continued up and switched back around and then switched back again. High up now, Gina took in the long view of the mountain's majesty and its forested endlessness. She realized its immense capacity for refuge and doubted that Ray would ever find her up here. She pushed the thought away.

Ahead ran a stream that cut a blue ribbon through acres of golden grass, and beyond that were farmers' fields and rice terraces that stepped down the mountainside. The trail led to a barrio of a dozen nipa huts nestled in the jungle trees, a church, and a general store with a porch and several rocking chairs.

"The barrio of Tinian," a cowboy announced as they rode through. "Mrs. Bueno at the general store will keep you supplied with the basics." He waved at a wispy-haired old woman sitting in a rocking chair smoking a pipe. A dog beside her barked, and she quieted him with the touch of her hand. The cowboy pointed to a ribbon of clay that meandered through the farmers' fields below. "The village of Katana is about a two-hour walk down that road. You'll find government offices, schools, churches, and a larger market there."

Beyond Tinian, the caravan turned onto a narrow path that wound back into the jungle, and a baritone voice of a cowboy melodically boomed, "Beee it evvver so hummmmble, there's no-o place like . . ."

Gina couldn't see much of anything through the tangle of vines and thick stands of bamboo, but from up ahead, she heard Vivian moan, "Ooooh my . . ."

Chapter 7

SETTLING IN

I douse the American flag with gasoline and toss on a match.
In sobering silence, I watch it burn.

—Ray Thorpe, Corregidor, December 1941–May 1942

As she turned on a bend in the path, Gina saw the reason for Vivian's groan. Before her were two thatched-roof nipa huts constructed from bamboo stalks bound together with thongs of rattan, giving them the appearance of giant wicker baskets. One looked occupied, with two camp chairs out front and blue-and-white-striped towels and three shirts hanging on a clothesline.

"Lordy," Gina murmured. "Those huts have to be infested with every critter in the jungle." She dismounted and joined Vivian. "Tell me we're in another bad dream."

"Could be worse. It comes with a houseboy. Let's see what's inside."

They each grabbed a little girl's hand and walked hesitantly on the narrow plank that led to a landing four feet up. Maggie followed in three long strides.

When Gina opened the door, a bird fluttered out of one of the two uncovered windows. Gina startled, and Cheryl tugged at her pant leg. "I don't want to go in there."

Inside, woven half walls separated the space into three rooms. A rattan couch and chair with cushions, a coffee table, and a dining table and four chairs furnished the largest room. Along the back wall were waist-high cabinets with open shelves underneath that held wooden plates, bowls, clay pots, and a kerosene lamp. A shallow rectangular structure filled with sand and flat rocks was built into the countertop. "Any idea what this is?" Gina asked.

"It might be a stove," Maggie guessed, pointing below. "Here's wood and matches. I don't see a sink anywhere."

The smaller rooms each held two double beds with kapok mattresses, on one of which Leah jumped and lay spread eagle. "It's soft," she announced. "Can I have this one?"

Cheryl jumped on the other. "This one's mine."

The cowboys brought boxes and bags from the oxcart and stacked them against a wall. When they had emptied the cart, one man repaired the broken blinds on the windows, and another fixed the door so it would close all the way. After tending to their horses and carabao, they left with a thank-you from everyone and a bottle of brandy from Vivian.

The girls were whining that they were hungry, and Gina evaluated the impossible kitchen. "Where do we start?" She realized how much she was going to miss Isabella.

"Here." Vivian put a bottle of brandy, three Cokes, a bag of peanuts, and a bunch of bananas on the table.

"Not much of a dinner, Viv."

"We'll survive. I'm too tired to look for the can opener."

"We're missing a chair," Leah said.

Maggie stacked up boxes of canned goods to chair height. "For you, Leah. I anoint you queen of the can."

Cheryl giggled, and Gina smirked.

There were sounds of footsteps on the plank, and a scrawny little man wearing khaki shorts and a buttoned-up cotton shirt came in the door. He was barefoot, and his left foot twisted inward, causing him to limp. His face was brown and lined, though he didn't look old. He carried a large bamboo tube and a bundle of wood. He dropped the bundle and pointed to the thatched roof. "New. Keep you dry." He smiled broadly.

"Well, that's a plus," Vivian said. "And who are you?"

He shook his shaggy head, seemingly not understanding. He pointed to the bamboo floor. "Smooth. Nice." He showed more white teeth.

Gina didn't think this stranger a threat, but she was still wary. "What is it you want?"

"I Popo. Señor Ramos say I help."

With what? Popo didn't seem robust enough to be of any help. More exhausted than she remembered ever being and repulsed by this hut that housed birds and who knew what else, Gina suppressed her doubt and said with a stiff smile, "Thank you. We need help. Do you know someone who can cook?"

"You cook. I show you." He filled a round-bottomed pot with water from the bamboo tube, placed it on the circle of stones in the sandbox stove, pushed several sticks of wood underneath it, and lit them with a shiny Zippo lighter. "Easy. I bring you water and wood every day."

"He needs to wash his hands, Mama," Cheryl said.

Gina frowned and said, "Shhh," but saw Popo's fingernails were black. She made a hand-washing motion.

"Ah." He poured water onto his hands and let it drain through the floorboards.

"How about that," Vivian deadpanned. "No sink to scrub. Isn't this our lucky day?"

Popo bobbed his head. "You lucky. Nice here. Children hungry. You make rice; I bring you chicken."

"You lucky," Gina muttered after Popo left. The girls were fussing, and she hoped it didn't take him too long. She rummaged through the pile of goods on the floor and found the rice and two cans of peas, and then she pawed through a woven bag. "Any idea where I'd find a can opener?"

"Mommy," Cheryl whispered. "I got to go poopy."

"Of course you do," Gina snapped and was immediately sorry for her sharp retort. She took Cheryl's hand and in a softer voice said, "Come on. Let's see what we can find."

Outside, Gina took in the view for the first time. Trees, brush, and tangled vines formed a solid wall of green vegetation around the entire perimeter of the cleared area. Banana, coconut, and wild orange trees filled the space between the huts, affording a semblance of privacy and sweetening the air. Along the back was a garden fenced with chicken wire. She heard but didn't see running water. She didn't see any activity at the other hut.

"Mommy," Cheryl pleaded.

"Oh, I'm sorry." Gina spotted a roof of what she guessed was an outhouse tucked behind a clump of bamboo. Approaching it, she checked for wild animals or snakes. A rat skittered out when she opened the door, and both she and Cheryl yelped and jumped back.

"Don't make me go in there," Cheryl cried as she clung to her mother's arm.

Gina inwardly groaned. *Brother, what else?* She tried to make light of it. "Well! That was a surprise, wasn't it?"

She held her breath as she warily opened the door wider to check for anything that flew, slithered, or hopped. As she coaxed Cheryl to do what needed to be done, she fought off a cloud of black flies and blacker sadness.

Back inside, she found Maggie trying to light the wood under the cooking pot and Vivian working to lower woven shades over the windows to keep the birds out. "They've built nests in here." She pointed to several. "Did you find an outhouse?"

"Yes. Up front behind the bamboo. Take paper and a stick." She found a roll of toilet paper in a bag and placed it by the door. "Use this sparingly." Seeing long faces, Gina asked the little girls, "You want to help me make beds?"

They made up the beds with blankets and pillows. Gina pondered how many people and critters had slept on those beds. She tented them with mosquito nets, and Cheryl and Leah crawled inside and played a hand-clapping game to the words of a newly learned trail song. Gina was glad they could entertain each other.

Popo returned with another bamboo tube filled with fresh water, and their dinner—the feathered corpse of a chicken, its head lolling to one side.

Gina's face went white, and she felt a giggle welling up inside her that she tried to hold in, but when a guffaw escaped Vivian, their eyes met, and hysterical laughter erupted from both, followed by Gina's sob of despair and gush of tears. She felt everyone's gaze. Taking a deep breath, she composed her face and dried her eyes on the hem of her blouse. "Sorry. Just a little overtired."

Popo stood openmouthed, his face a mask of disbelief.

Maggie accepted the chicken with a cordial thank-you. She tossed it onto the counter and began plucking its feathers. "I'm not afraid to work with my hands. I did enough of it working in the clinic with Dad. I learned that not everyone had maids and cooks. I'm going to think of this time up here as an adventure."

Gina took notice of the young wisp of a girl's take-charge attitude. A positive attribute? A cover?

Popo showed Maggie how to clean the chicken; cut it into pieces; season it with the garlic, oregano, and cumin he'd brought with him;

and fry it in lard. He added salt, pepper, and chopped cashews to the boiled rice, and the two chastened women had to admit that everything tasted delicious.

Before leaving, he filled a kerosene lamp with fuel and showed the women how to adjust the wick and light it. He said with that beautiful smile, "I be back tomorrow. I help you," and this time Gina believed him.

Later, while Gina was giving Cheryl a sponge bath and getting her ready for bed, the child said, "My head hurts."

Gina felt Cheryl's forehead; it didn't feel warm, but it was hard to tell in the humid heat. "Anyplace else hurt? Your throat? Your tummy?"

"No, just my head."

"You might be overtired. I'll see if we have medicine for your head." She supervised Cheryl's toothbrushing, another ordeal in a hut without a sink, and then searched through the boxes for a first aid kit and medicines, worrying that a headache was the beginning of a serious illness. Mosquitoes carried many tropical diseases, including malaria and dengue fever, both long term and debilitating. She returned to Cheryl with half an aspirin and a glass of water, wondering about the nearness of a doctor—or whether there was one.

Cheryl rubbed her bloodshot eyes. "I want to say good night to Daddy. He doesn't know where I am." A tear rolled down her cheek.

Sadness descended on Gina again. "Oh, honey, so do I. It might be a while, so we have to be patient. Link pinkies with me. Let's send him a message."

Cheryl squeezed her eyes shut and wrinkled her nose as she concentrated on her message. She opened her eyes. "I told Daddy I loved him, and I'm going to be patient. What's *patient*?"

Gina sighed. "It means we have to wait and see what happens. Go to sleep now." Gina kissed her good night.

As tired as she was, Gina lay awake a long time, processing all that had happened so fast and listening to the sawing sound of cicadas, the mournful hoots of owls, and the horrific screeches of those hunted and caught. She worried about Theo, Arturo, and Isabella, who were traveling a dangerous road. Cheryl, who lay beside her, cried out in her sleep, and Gina rubbed her back until she quieted. Gina needed to be soothed too. She wanted Ray beside her. Was he alive? Was he suffering?

⌐∕

It rained during the night, making everything outside drip, but inside the hut it was dry, as Popo had promised it would be. "Yoo-hoo," someone called, and an older woman walked through the door. Built square as a box, she wore a faded blouse and cotton slacks that were cinched up by a length of rope. On her feet were leather boots. "My dears, you must have Popo build you some decent steps. Hi. My name is Edna. I'm your neighbor."

Standing closest to the door, Vivian welcomed Edna. "I'm Vivian. This is my friend Gina. The dark-haired child is her daughter, Cheryl, and the two blondes are my daughters, Maggie and Leah."

Edna pushed a package into Vivian's hand. "Mountain trout. Best you eat it today. My brother, Marcus, and I were fishing yesterday. We missed your move-in. Have you learned how to use what passes for a stove yet? Keep an eye on it. If the clay lining breaks away, the coals fall on the wood below, and you'll have a fire. It happens a lot. Marcus and I do most of our cooking on a grill he built outside. You're welcome to use it."

"Thank you." Vivian motioned toward the table. "Would you like to sit down?"

Edna took a chair at the table. "I'm tickled to have someone living here. It's been rather lonesome. Marcus and I are originally from Ohio. Where are you from?"

"Seattle," Gina said, "but I've moved around some."

"Atlanta," Vivian said.

"No husbands?"

"Not here."

"That's too bad. Marcus could use the help. The jungle would eat this place up in a week if he didn't keep chopping it back. But I'm glad you're here, with husbands or not, and the children are a bonus and a blessing. I can show you around if you like."

The families and Edna inched down the plank to the ground. She pointed to the banana, coconut, and wild orange trees. "A boy from the village cuts down the fruit for us. I don't suppose you have a bolo."

Gina took her last step to the ground. "No. Do I need one?"

"Yes, to open the coconuts and to cut back the vegetation. Personally, I feel safer with a bolo by my door—not that there has been any trouble, but you can never tell, out here like we are."

Open coconuts? Gina couldn't imagine.

Vegetables grew in the fenced garden, and Edna pointed them out. "This was here when we arrived. We cleaned it up and added a few raspberry bushes for tea." She reached down and pulled a handful of weeds and tossed them aside. "The women from Tinian come by a couple times a week to sell fruits and vegetables, and Mrs. Bueno's store has the basics—you can buy a bolo there. Anything out of the ordinary, you must place a special order. I'll introduce you. She's quite a character."

Gina and Vivian exchanged an amused glance.

Not far from the garden stood an old chicken coop. "We had chickens, but they disappeared right after we got them. The culprit turned out to be an iguana. Marcus found him living in a hollow tree down by the stream. He smoked him out and shot him. That fella was six feet long if he was an inch. We ate well for a while."

"Did the meat taste like chicken?" Gina asked, tongue in cheek.

Vivian frowned. "Do iguanas attack people? Are they a danger to the kids?"

"Not usually, but watch the little ones. There are snakes and wild pigs. Coconut rats live in the fruit trees."

Cheryl practically climbed up Gina's leg, and Gina clutched her, trying to hide her own disgust.

Edna's brow furrowed. "Don't be afraid, honey. The critters run away when they see you coming."

Cheryl wrapped her arms around Gina's neck.

Edna started down a cleared path. "Follow me. The stream's this way."

The path to the stream wandered through a forest of giant dipterocarp trees, whose smooth, straight trunks supported knotted and curled strangler vines that wound from the dark, ever-wet jungle floor to the sunlight above, forming a tangled canopy. Orchids and bromeliads peeked through the canopy, adding unexpected splashes of purple and orange. Tiny finches, warblers, and flycatchers with feathers every color of the rainbow flitted from tree to tree, along with buzzing bees, large monarch butterflies, and swarms of moths.

Something screamed loudly enough to make Gina jump, and the jungle came alive with a cacophony of squawks, howls, and whistles. Who would have thought a jungle was such a noisy place?

Cheryl clung tighter to Gina's neck.

They came to the rocky edge of a fast-moving stream. Edna pointed to a bamboo platform that held two water barrels. "That's our shower. It rains often enough to keep the barrels full. I like to sit over there and meditate." She pointed to a place where water pooled and then rippled over flat table-size rocks. "It keeps me sane." She showed them the spot where it was best to do laundry and another of smooth rocks where they could catch freshwater shrimp. "The trick is to snatch them quickly from behind."

The women took off their shoes and sat on the rocks and let the water flow over their feet while Cheryl and Leah waded nearby in search of shiny stones. The scowl on Vivian's face mirrored Gina's thoughts. For years neither one of them had lived without servants. Even at the cottage Gina had hired local women to do the cooking, cleaning, and laundry, and she had always had Isabella or an amah to care for Cheryl. Edna's matter-of-fact acceptance of this primitive life made her curious about the woman's background. "I'm wondering, Edna . . . this place couldn't be any stranger to me than if it was on the moon; how is it you . . . um . . . get by so well here?"

Edna picked up a stone out of the water, studied it, and put it in her pocket. "Once you're settled, it's not so bad. Before I came to the Philippines, my husband and I worked at a missionary school in rural China. Life was rough there too. I learned to make do with what was on hand." She found another stone and added it to her pocket. "Missionary Headquarters ordered us to leave when the Japanese invaded in 1937. They suggested we come to the Philippines because it was 'safer.' So much for their advice. My husband died, and by then Marcus had moved from Ohio to Manila, so I came here. He's principal of the Santa Catalina School, and he hired me to teach biology and botany." Sadness crossed Edna's face, and she sighed. "We kept the school open as long as possible. I pray for those poor, sweet girls. God be with them." When she rose to leave, she inspected her feet and ankles. "Always check for leeches. They flick off easy enough if you find them right away. It's harder after they burrow in."

Appalled, Gina struggled to stand, her little-used muscles rebelling against the horseback travel and heavy work. Calling the girls back, she and Vivian checked their feet and ankles for leeches.

Edna handed Cheryl and Leah each a stone from her pocket and pointed out flecks in them. "Gold. You'll find lots in this stream."

~

Edna coached the families through their first weeks of mind-numbing bewilderment and near catatonia from lack of sleep. There were days of burns and cuts, slivers, more bug bites than Gina thought a body could endure, and fear when Cheryl's ear ached and she ran a fever.

Banana leaves that Edna kept stacked in the outhouse replaced toilet paper, and reusable rags that required washing substituted for sanitary napkins. Grime under her fingernails was impossible to remove, and her hair turned to a bush without the lotions she used to tame it. They each purchased one set of clothes from Mrs. Bueno's store.

"These are boy's shorts," Cheryl protested.

"Mine are too big," Leah complained.

However, the deprivations became insignificant after they heard the news that traveled the bamboo telegraph. Corregidor had fallen into Japanese hands after weeks of massive bombing, and those soldiers who had survived the carnage had been taken prisoner.

Despondency crushed Gina, and ugly scenarios blocked rational thought—life without Ray wasn't an option. Cheryl needed a father, and Gina desperately wanted another chance to give him a son. Alone by the rippling stream, the words of poet Astor Laslo ran in an endless loop:

the agony of losing you
is only eclipsed
by the fear of never finding you

Across the stream, three miniature deer—a buck, a doe, and a fawn—lifted their heads and twitched their ears, as if listening to Gina's whispered plea: "My dearest, give me a sign that you are still with me on this earth."

She sat still as a stone, listening, watching, and waiting for a whisper in the breeze, a point of light reflecting on the water, a birdcall perhaps, or a wave of positive assurance. Her heart almost stopped beating when the buck walked into the forest, leaving his doe and fawn alone by the water's edge. Gina cried out her sorrow and fear of her future.

Life in the nipa-hut camp settled into a humdrum existence of endless, hot, dirty, backbreaking work that Gina had to make palatable or perish. While doing chores, she escaped her reality by dreaming she was in a more familiar world, singing in Italian and French the songs she'd performed while touring Europe with the Follies, and the diversion nourished her soul. She knew by the fit of her clothes that she had lost weight, but her muscles were firm, her joints flexible, and she could finish most long, hard jobs without needing to rest.

Chapter 8
LIVING IN THE SKY

I am an alien in my own world, where no one anymore speaks my language.

—Ray Thorpe, Corregidor, December 1941–May 1942

Gina had adjusted to living by the rise and fall of the sun. There were no shadows now, so it must be noon. She found the crisp morning air refreshing, the cool mountain water invigorating, and the garden-fresh fruits and vegetables vitalizing. She had learned to fish and catch shrimp and cook them over an open fire. She could crack open a coconut and peel a pineapple with a bolo, as well as clear a path with it, each learned task bringing with it a sense of accomplishment at her self-sufficiency. Though she missed her maids, cooks, houseboys, and amahs—oh, how she missed them—she had an appreciation for the long hours of hard work they had done for such a pittance in pay.

Edna had set up a school class for Cheryl and Leah and taught reading, writing, and math using Marcus's books for the basics and hands-on learning for practical applications. With the individual attention, Gina thought both girls were advancing beyond their grade levels.

Popo meandered up the path, carrying a hollow bamboo tube filled with a day's fresh water and a jute bag of logs he had chopped into usable lengths for the stove. He was stronger and more helpful than she had first thought. He'd built the stairs soon after they'd arrived and tilled the soil to extend the garden. Though Tagalog was his native tongue, he knew some English, having gone through grade school as the mountain people did, and could communicate with her on an elementary level. Today there was something on Gina's mind, and she wanted to talk to him.

When they entered the hut, a gecko scuttled in, a sign of good luck according to Popo, and she had gotten used to them scurrying around. As usual, he was smiling. He bobbed his head in greeting and then filled the water jugs and the woodbin. A cockroach skittered out from under a log, and he stomped it dead with his bare foot.

Gina grimaced. There were some things she would never get used to, like the cockroaches that hid in every crevice, the insects that she had to shake daily out of their bedding, and the coconut rats that jumped through the trees during the day and slunk about inside the hut at night. Popo said they were good eating, but even the thought was revolting to her. Ants had been a problem until Popo had showed her how to soak the ground around the hut's supports with oil. She crossed her arms and leaned back against the counter. "Popo . . . how hard is it to keep chickens?"

At first his face went blank, but then he laughed. "Easy, easy." He used his hands to help talk. "Little house. Fence . . . wire to keep out iguanas and wild pigs. You feed . . . ahh . . . scraps from you eat. That is all. You get eggs."

Iguanas and wild pigs. Did she want to invite them into the yard? Seemed like there was always a downside. In half English and half pantomime, she said, "How many chickens would I need to feed seven people?"

He bobbed his head and held up six fingers. "You need six chickens. I help you build a coop. I look for good layers."

In the yard, Gina showed him the small structure in lousy repair that had housed chickens. He shook his head. "No good. I do better." He grabbed a section of wire fence and gave it a hard tug. The posts gave way, and the wire and wood flew in all directions. "Eyee!" he hollered, and his hands flew to his face. Blood oozed between his fingers.

"Popo!" Gina gasped, her body tensing with distress. "My God! Did it hit your eye? Let me see."

Blood dripped off his chin when he peeled his hand away. His eye was intact, but a gash extended from the top of his ear to the corner of his mouth. He fumbled in his pocket for a bandana, which he folded into quarters and held over the cut. "I go home now."

"No, I wouldn't hear of it." She took his arm and pulled him forward. "Come with me. We'll fix you up." By *we* she meant Maggie, who had shown herself to be a competent nurse. Inside the hut she called for the teen, who examined the wound and cleaned it with a mild boric acid solution.

"Some splinters need to come out, Popo. I'm sorry. I'll be very careful, but it's going to hurt a little."

Popo's eyes grew wide, and he moved to leave, but Maggie grabbed his hand and began chanting a riff. "One, two, three and we be done. Miss Gina, would you please bring Popo a cup of water? Okay, Popo? Quick pick and we be done? You no get infection, and I be happy." She nodded, and Popo mimicked the movement.

By the time Gina brought water, Maggie was murmuring to Popo while picking at the wood fragments with tweezers. "Open your fist. Make your hand floppy like a fish. Think floppy hand, fishy hand. Close your eyes and think of cool water washing over your fishy hand. The cool water is climbing up your arm. It's at your elbow now, and your arm feels like a floppy fish. I don't know what color the floppy fish is, Popo. What color should we make your fish?"

"Fish no color." His voice sounded dreamy.

Gina stood off to the side, mesmerized.

"Done." Maggie held up two wood fragments for Popo to see.

"Done?" he repeated, still in a daze.

Maggie dusted the wound with sulfa powder and covered it with a dressing. "It will be a little sore. You feeling all right?"

He took a deep breath. "Sí."

She handed him six aspirin and the glass of water. "Two now, two tonight, and two in the morning. Come back and see me in two days." She held up two fingers, and Popo nodded. After he left, she said to Gina, "I wish Dad would return with meds. He's been a long time in Manila, and I'm down to my last bottle of aspirin."

"He should be back soon," Gina said. "It's hard to move around when you have to stay hidden." She picked up the bloody rags, which would be washed and reused. She saw a little of herself in Maggie, curious and independent, having left home at barely seventeen to travel with the Follies. "You had Popo in a trance. Where did you learn that?"

"At the clinic, I guess. I worked a lot with the kids. It was one way I learned to distract them. Sometimes it works. Sometimes it doesn't. Popo's pretty suggestible."

"My dear, you're an angel."

Maggie scoffed. "Tell that to my mother."

"She only wants the best for you."

"I know. I just need more space."

With increasing numbers of people moving to the mountains, the produce available from the local women had decreased, but the garden had filled out and was taking up the slack, and the chickens they'd purchased were laying plenty of eggs. Additionally, Edna and Maggie scoured the jungle for tubers, greens, berries, and mushrooms used for food or medicines. This was a sore point for Vivian, who privately called Edna a witch doctor after she'd almost killed Leah, Vivian felt, by dosing her with sugar melted in a teaspoon of turpentine to rid her little body of intestinal parasites. The child had been up all night crazy with pain, though Vivian had to admit that Leah had passed the offending worms in the morning, and the malady appeared cured. Nevertheless, she'd told Maggie that her father wouldn't approve.

"Yes, he would," Maggie had retorted. "Edna taught biology and botany at the high school in Manila. She lived off the land when she was in China. Where could I find a better teacher?" In defiance of her mother, Maggie continued to work with Edna and catalog the appearance, location, and usefulness as food or medicine of each new plant she found.

Theo returned, guided by a cowboy from Señor Ramos's ranch, each man riding one horse and leading another loaded with bundles. After the welcome homecoming, Theo told the latest news. "You would hardly recognize Manila. The streets are filled with Nips, and guards are on every corner checking residence IDs. Propaganda is everywhere: Asia for the Asians. The locals are scurrying around, keeping their heads down. Some Americans are still in hiding, but most have been interned on the University of Santo Tomas campus. It won't take long for that to turn into an overcrowded stink hole."

Gina winced, imagining Stella and her three children and Edith and her frail mother interned in a Japanese-run camp for the long haul, not the few weeks they'd so glibly fantasized. Despite the hard life in the mountains and the nipa hut's meager comforts, she was glad to be free.

Theo passed around a pack of cigarettes and offered lights. Gina deeply inhaled, enjoying the familiar buzz; they had been out for a while. He said, "Thanks for letting me take Isabella."

Gina didn't remember it that way. But she was physically stronger now, more self-sufficient, and confident she could survive this uncomfortable interlude in her life. She was able to say, "I'm glad she was helpful to you, and I wish her well."

Theo nodded. "Very helpful. I had to stay hidden, and she was my intermediary. Dr. Lopez at Remedios Hospital donated medical supplies and drugs. Father Morgan from Malate Church sent clothing and blankets. You remember him, don't you, Vivian?"

"Of course. He runs a charity mission through the church, and you wrote him a generous check every Christmas. Not in my wildest dreams did I ever think we'd be on the receiving end."

Later, Theo took Gina aside. He looked pale and tired, like the trip had taken its toll. He spoke in his gentle way. "I suppose you heard. The men on Corregidor were captured. They were taken to Bilibid Prison. I saw them coming into the city."

Gina's eyes searched his for more information. "Did you see Ray with them? I heard hundreds were killed during the last bombings."

"I wasn't that close, but there were thousands, Gina . . . Ray could have been one."

Gina called to mind the bloodied, beaten men on the march. Expecting the worst, she steadied herself. "Tell me more, Theo. I need to know the truth."

"The truth is the men are dehydrated, hungry, and dirty. The Japanese are petty; they push the prisoners around and steal anything that glitters. But these men haven't been abused like what you saw on the march. I'm so sorry you had to witness that. I know it has left its mark on you. It has on all of us."

Yes, a mark and that kernel of hate she felt growing. "What happens to the men now?"

"Bilibid is just a temporary holding facility. Most men stay a few days or weeks before being trucked out to other prison camps."

"Trucked? They're not being marched?"

"No."

"Trucked," she repeated, somehow finding that small piece of information comforting.

Theo kept the horse he arrived on; and several times a week he and Maggie, who rode behind him, roamed the mountainside, visiting the barrios in the area, chatting with the local people, learning their dialect, and attending to their medical needs. Often they returned carrying bags of rice or beans and today vegetables that Gina cleaned, cut up, and roasted on the grill for their evening meal, along with mountain trout Marcus and Edna had caught and cleaned that afternoon.

With Cheryl and Leah playing go fish with a new deck of cards Theo had brought back, Vivian lit candles and set up for bridge, a common evening's entertainment.

"You're quiet tonight," Vivian said to Theo, whose mind seemed to be wandering.

He put down his cards. "Sorry. I was thinking about Señor Ramos. I heard he and his foreman were picked up by the Kempeitai yesterday."

A pall came over the room. The Kempeitai were the military police of the Japanese army, a punitive branch of a harsh force trained in espionage and counterintelligence and known for their unique torture techniques to ferret out local resistance. Gina folded her cards. "His ranch is halfway up the mountain. How did they find him?"

"A sympathizer or a bounty hunter. Or maybe the Japanese just want his cattle. At any rate, we have to be extra cautious."

That night, Gina, in a recurring dream, heard the rattle of Japanese bicycles and the directive of the captors: "Speedo, speedo." She slunk behind the throng, carrying a gunny sack, collecting body parts of American soldiers with the intent of returning them to their families. As always, she awoke gasping for breath.

❧

Days later, two men on horseback came to the edge of the clearing. Gina stepped inside the hut, where they couldn't see her. Both men were

Filipino, but they weren't like the local farmers she had seen at the store in Tinian. These men wore expensive boots and hats and carried guns in holsters attached to their belts. They sat on their horses and gazed at the huts as if they were looking for something.

Cheryl and Leah skipped toward the door, and Gina waved them back and put her finger to her lips. "Shhh." She took inventory of the others' whereabouts—Vivian cutting up vegetables in the kitchen, Edna and Maggie at the stream catching freshwater shrimp.

Marcus walked across the clearing to the Filipinos. He was square built like his sister but tall, with big hands and big feet. When not clearing brush around the perimeter of the camp, he'd be in the jungle hunting or at the stream fishing, often bringing home meat or fish for the evening's meal. A quiet man, he liked to read, which was a problem with so few books available. Edna had told Gina he was fluent in several languages.

From the door of the hut, Gina, unable to hear the conversation, tried to catch the gist of it by studying the men's body language. Marcus stood rigid with his feet apart and arms crossed, not offering his handshake in greeting. The Filipinos stayed in the saddle. One gestured toward the cabin, and she pulled back into the shadow and shushed the girls again. She hoped Edna and Maggie stayed out of sight at the stream. They needed rules for when strangers showed to hide and stay safe, a topic for this evening's conversation.

After a time the Filipinos turned their horses around and left.

Vivian came up behind Gina. "What was that all about?"

"Beats me. Let's go find out."

Marcus took off his hat and wiped the sweat off his brow with a kerchief he'd pulled from his pocket. "They said they were looking for a place to live, but my gut tells me they're scouting for Americans. Seems we have a price on our heads now. I spoke to them in Spanish and told them we were from Argentina. I'm not sure I fooled them. We may have to move farther up the mountain."

Vivian's face clouded. "It will be colder . . . more primitive. People don't live there for a reason. We'd never survive."

Marcus gazed at the mostly uninhabited peaks in the distance. "My guess is that's the Japs' plan."

Chapter 9

GUERRILLA BEGINNINGS

I'm fenced in by barbed wire, trapped under a blazing sun, and given little water. I watch the sky for American planes. None come. It can't be. My country wouldn't surrender me to a cruel enemy.

—Ray Thorpe, Corregidor, December 1941–May 1942?

Gina, returning from Mrs. Bueno's store with her arms full of packages, saw Vivian hurrying toward her. Viv's voice was urgent. "I'm glad you're back. A nurse showed up with a wounded soldier tied on the back of a mule. His clothes are covered with dried blood. The strange thing is Cheryl ran up to him like she knew him. I grabbed her back. I thought you'd better know."

Gina frowned. She didn't want Cheryl running up to any stranger. She'd have a talk with her. "Where's the soldier now?"

"With Edna and Marcus. Theo examined him. The guy's out of his head with malaria and who knows what else. His pants are full of holes like"—Vivian swallowed—"oh God, Gina . . . like he'd been stabbed multiple times with a bayonet."

Vivian's eyes filled with tears, and Gina blanched.

"The nurse—her name is Clara—wants to leave him here with Theo."

"Did you learn his name?"

"Davy something."

No. Please don't let it be . . . But they were on an island. "Not Davy McGowan."

"Yes, so you know him?"

Gina's voice quavered. "Yes! Cheryl and his son, Harry, are in the same class at school. He's a major in the army. You met him once, Viv, at a birthday party I threw for Ray. Tall, good-looking guy. Brush cut. A scar under his right eye. I must go see him."

Gina thought she was prepared, but it sickened her to see Davy's once-robust body shrunken, jaundiced, and covered with oozing wounds. A patch protected one eye, and when he opened his mouth, she glimpsed broken teeth. She forced her widest smile, and to cover her shock, she reverted to the trash talk she'd learned while traveling with the Follies. "Holy cow! You look like a piece of shit, Davy. Tell me how you're really doing."

His laugh brought on a paroxysm of coughs.

Gina's hand flew to her mouth. "Sorry. I didn't mean—"

"A breath of fresh air," he wheezed. "Everybody's been pussyfooting around me. It's good to see you, Gina. I'm top notch. Clara here rescued me, didn't you, honey?" He waggled his finger toward a sturdy woman standing nearby, counting supplies and vials of medicines.

"I sure did. I thought he was a dead deer in the weeds and almost walked by, but then he moaned. I stuck him with morphine and packed him on the back of my mule. Finding this camp with a doctor was serendipity or divine intervention, depending on your beliefs. Personally, I think someone up there is looking out for him."

Davy tried to sit up but fell back and began to shiver.

Though Gina covered him with blankets, his tremors became more violent. He tried to speak, but Gina only recognized the word *Cheryl.*

"What about Cheryl, Davy? Is there something I need to know?" He didn't respond, and Gina waved Clara over. "I think he's in pain. Isn't there something . . . ," she started to ask, but Clara was already by the bedside with her syringe of morphine.

"This will put him to sleep." She administered the drug. "I'm going to change his dressings while he's out. I have to debride some wounds. It's not pretty. You may want to step outside for a smoke."

"I'll stay and help."

"I'd rather you not. You look pale, and I don't have time to watch you faint. Go get some fresh air."

Gina was glad to get away from the smell and gore. However, the sun beating on the porch made it hotter than Hades. She was breathing hard and felt light headed. She diverted her attention by looking around, seeing Clara's mule tethered to a tree and Edna in the garden picking green beans for tonight's meal. Maggie had scratched a grid into the dirt and was teaching the younger girls how to play hopscotch. Gina tried to concentrate on Cheryl tossing a stone onto a grid and hopping in a pattern around it, but overhead a flock of screeching crows caught her eye, and she watched them circle over something they'd spotted on the ground.

In a blink Gina's memory flashed back to Bataan, where the crows had been circling and cawing, the flies buzzing, and the stench of death so rank she had breathed through her mouth. As clear as real life, Gerald Kent's dead body lay at her feet with one blue eye half-open. Gina bent down over the body to close the eye; his skin was cold and rubbery to her touch.

Clara stepped onto the porch.

Gina jumped up, and Gerald Kent's body disappeared as quickly as it had appeared. Confused as to what had just happened, she patted her chest and took a deep breath. "Just a little light headed. Seeing Davy was more of a shock than I thought. Is he going to recover?"

"He'll live. He may not walk. Don't tell him, not yet. Just surviving's enough until he's stronger."

Clara didn't know Davy's determination, and Gina couldn't imagine him bound to a wheelchair. She asked, "Where did you find him?"

"By the side of the road between here and Katana. I've been traveling these mountain trails for a few months. My husband and I ran a clinic over by Angeles. He and one of our nurses were killed by the Japs while I was out back in the privy. When they left, I grabbed all the drugs and dressings I could carry on the back of that mule. I'll stay in these mountains until my supplies run out. There are hundreds of soldiers like Davy around."

⌒

Gina visited Davy often, at first bringing books from Marcus's meager library to read to him. As Davy grew stronger, he wanted to talk, and she listened to his stories about the men in his unit, some of whom had been killed or were missing. He sometimes cried and then apologized for being weak. When he spoke of Sissy and Harry, his voice was fervent. "If the Japs find out they are my family, it won't go well for them. I have to get them out of there."

Not an easy task. Gina knew of only three prisoners who had escaped from Santo Tomas, and they had been caught, tortured, and killed, the whole camp a witness.

As soon as his wounds were healed, determined to walk, Davy began to exercise his legs, instructing Gina how to add resistance. Soon he was crawling and, in time, hobbling on two canes Marcus had made for him.

One day he hobbled outside by himself and sat in Edna's chair, a great accomplishment. Gina joined him. Together they watched three squirrels play tag in the trees. After a time, she reached over, took his hand, and asked the question of which she'd been curious. "Were you one of the men marching, Davy? I was there. I saw some of it." She clenched her jaw to keep from elaborating. This wasn't her story. She felt his hand squeezing hers.

"No. I wouldn't surrender. I hid in the hills. There was a handful of us. We helped the prisoners escape by hiding them in hollow trees or obscure caves. A Jap patrol caught up with me later and did this." He waved his hand over his body. "They left me for dead. But miracle of miracles, Clara came along."

Standing nearby, Clara nodded. "And you don't need me anymore, Davy. It's time I moved on."

"To where?" Gina liked Clara as a friend and didn't want her to leave. Over the weeks while caring for Davy, Clara had told Gina how she'd come to the Philippines from Idaho, a young nurse looking for an adventure. She'd fallen in love with a Filipino doctor, married him, and stayed.

Clara said, "Davy used most of my supplies, and I need an income. A job opened up at the Red Cross in Cabanatuan City. I'm going to apply for it."

"But . . . ," Gina sputtered.

"Yes. I'm an American. The nurse in our clinic who was killed was Lithuanian, and she had Red Cross credentials. Her name was Clara Jacob. I assumed her identity and adopted her mule."

The first thing Gina noticed when she woke the next morning was that Clara's mule was gone. She found Davy on Edna's porch, leaning heavily on his canes. "She's a woman of her word. She's right . . . I don't need a nurse, but I'm going to miss her."

Gina was too. She envied Clara's practical skills and her swashbuckling grit. "If there's anything I can do to help—"

"There is! I'm going to have Marcus build me a lean-to. You can be my cook."

Gina grimaced. Being a cook wasn't what she had in mind. She'd been mulling over the bigger picture: revenging the atrocities, the needs of the masses, giving of herself as Clara did. However, believing her prowess woefully inadequate, where to start? "You might prefer to eat your words other than my cooking, Davy."

Word spread about a doctor in the area, and other wounded and displaced soldiers began arriving to see Theo. Most received treatment and moved on, but some cleared pockets in the jungle, built lean-tos, and stayed. The population of the camp grew.

Vivian and Maggie worked as nurses for those who needed medical care, while Edna attended the expanded garden and chicken coop. Marcus cajoled local farmers to donate rice, meat, and supplies. Popo became a jack-of-all-trades, the girls helped wherever they were needed, and Gina learned how to cook for a crowd.

⌒

Japanese planes crisscrossed Luzon and dropped thousands of leaflets that fluttered down like giant snowflakes onto those below, stating that all Americans must surrender to the Japanese military within four months or face execution when later captured.

"Not a good choice here." Gina held out the leaflet. "We have until September to be imprisoned or executed."

Vivian gave the leaflet a glance. "They left out the option *to disappear*. Theo thinks we're too visible, and he wants to go higher. Something's up between him and Davy."

The stray soldiers who had now become permanent residents numbered eight. They bummed cigarettes from one another and traded harrowing stories of how they had outwitted their captors. They discussed best methods of retaliation—for the sadistic torture, the starvation, the vicious brutality, and their dead buddies. They damned the Japanese and their smirking faces that they hungered to smash into oblivion—slowly, one at a time—make the buggers watch their comrades squirm like they'd done to the soldiers.

Gina and Vivian complained to Theo and Davy about the foulness that had crept into the only place they had to live, but both men agreed the soldiers needed to vent their anger and sorrow and suggested the women keep the kids out of hearing distance.

"It's not that easy," Vivian snapped at Theo. "You know Maggie wants to work with you. She's obsessed."

"Then she'll have to toughen up," Theo retorted, and Gina wondered when he had become so callous.

＝

At the stream, Gina used a bar of lye soap and a fist-size rock to pummel a stain out of Cheryl's shirt, a technique Edna had shown her. She jumped when a young man suddenly approached in her side vision, big beaked and Ichabod awkward. He wore khaki pants and a soldier's shirt, and a hand grenade hung from his belt. *Another stray soldier—a friend or a foe?* She stood, her fingers tightening around the rock.

"I'm sorry." His voice was high pitched and nasal. "I didn't mean to frighten you. Can you take me to your leader?"

His request was so ludicrous she laughed out loud, but her fingers remained tight on the rock. "Leader?"

"Someone in charge of this guerrilla camp. I'd like to help with the resistance. I have some information that will be useful."

Guerrilla camp? Resistance? Gina had suspected something was going on. Lately when the men gathered around the campfire, they often spoke in furtive whispers. She hedged. "What are you talking about? Who are you?"

He snapped to attention. "First Lieutenant Robert Louis Stevenson, ma'am. Philippine Military Academy, ROTC. I wish to become involved with the guerrilla army."

Wish to become involved? Gina laughed at the strange fellow, who looked young enough to be her son. Davy could decide what to do with him. She gestured. "Follow me."

~~~

Later she learned that the information Stevenson brought was indeed valuable to those inclined to make mischief. The Japanese were stockpiling ammunition just a day's walk away, and Stevenson had a map to the site and knowledge of the number of guards and their schedules.

The next morning, Davy, Marcus, Theo, Stevenson, two other soldiers strong enough to walk, and five of Popo's Filipino neighbors to whom Davy had assigned military rank gathered at the camp. With them they had a carabao and cart, six rifles, a box of ammunition, a dozen hand grenades, three homemade bombs, five pitchforks, several bolos, and two days' worth of food and water. Not an army equipped to raid a Japanese ammo depot, Gina knew.

All day and night, the women waited and watched for the raiders to return.

"They've got the element of surprise," Gina said.

"The Filipinos know the lay of the land," Vivian offered.

"I don't think Marcus could shoot another human no matter his skin color," Edna added.

The raiders returned the next day with a cartful of Japanese guns, ammunition, TNT, and dynamite and wild stories of triumph. That night, with the men still full of bravado, the talk around the campfire turned from the boastful hypothetical to concrete planning.

~~~

After a series of successful forays harassing the Japanese, Davy singled Gina out. "Walk with me." He led her to the firepit, where the last embers were glowing. They sat on a low bench, and Davy placed a log on the embers. A mosquito buzzed around her, and she swatted it away.

"Anopheles." Davy slapped at another. "The females are the deadly ones. They carry malaria. Are you taking your quinine?"

"When I can get it. Japs blocked supplies." She knew Davy had something else on his mind besides mosquitoes and medicines. "What's up?"

He lit a cigarette for each of them. "I want to bring you up to date with our plans."

"Our plans? I don't remember being privy to any plans."

"Me, Marcus, Theo, Stevenson—"

"Stevenson? He's in on your plans and not those of us directly impacted? He's just a kid."

"Maybe so. But it turns out he knows a lot about blowing up bridges. He and a couple of his ROTC friends have been harassing the Japs, and they want to be part of a larger group. The raid on the ammo depot was just the beginning—we have more arms and explosives now and support from the locals. There are Filipino soldiers out there itching for retribution. Popo found a place, farther up and better hidden, where we can set up a compound."

Even in the dim light of the embers, Gina saw fervor on Davy's face, and it scared her. A compound of men crazed with hate was no place for women and children. "Have you told Edna and Vivian about your grand plan? I'm sure they'd be interested." She hoped he heard her sarcasm.

"Not yet. We'll work it out with them."

"Then why are you telling me?"

"We have other plans for you. But then, maybe you're not interested." He got up to leave.

"Maybe I'm not. I don't know your *plans* for me, so why don't you tell me."

He sat down. "We're all stuck on this island, Gina, and there's no leaving. None of us knows what we're doing. We're making up plans and rules as we go. I don't have to tell you what we're up against; you've seen what the Japs do!" He took a long drag on his cigarette. "Just stop giving me flak."

Her voice softened. "I'm sorry. I'm listening."

"We're forming a guerrilla unit. For this to work, we need a contact in Manila who can solicit money and send it to us. We think it could be you."

"Uh-uh," she uttered in surprise. It was the last thing she had expected to hear. "Why me? You don't like my cooking?"

He grunted. "No. It's because you can be a pushy broad, and that's what it's going to take."

That made Gina laugh. She had never thought of herself as a broad of any kind. "So you dump me in Manila and then what?"

"Marcus has ties to the resistance organizations. They'll help you change your identity. You could pass for Spanish or Italian."

"Italian. My grandparents were from Italy. I speak a little of the language."

"There you go. We'll give you a list of contacts. You'll explain what we're doing and ask them for help."

"That easy?"

"No, but that's the bones. You'll have to find a place to live. The Nips are in your house."

Gina had half expected that news, but it galled her to hear it, and she wondered if the Japanese had cracked open her safe, a gold mine for them. Powerless, she swallowed down this one more torment. "Give me some time. I have Cheryl to think about. She's my priority."

"Don't take too long. Keep in mind Manila's under Jap rule, and you'll be rubbing shoulders with the enemy. With all you've seen, do you think you can do it? Be sure of your decision."

⟋⟍

Gina stayed by the fire after Davy had left and contemplated his request. She could do it. She had the chutzpah and knowledge to support this fledgling band of guerrillas, and soliciting money for a cause was in her blood . . . letters, phone calls, knocking on doors, and telling the story of a mission and a need. However, the thought of living in a Japanese-held city, with loathing inside of her churning like a hurricane, was terrifying. Hiding her emotions wasn't in her nature. *You can be a pushy broad.*

And then there was Cheryl.

"It's a harebrained idea," Vivian said when Gina told her. "Manila? Taking Cheryl? How can you even think of it? You'll be like Daniel in the lion's den. If you're caught, you'll go to prison, or worse, and then what will happen to your darlin' child?"

"But Viv, we can't survive up here without help, and I know I can get it. And maybe I can find out what happened to Ray."

"Then go if you must, but leave Cheryl with Theo and me. She's like one of our family now anyway."

Gina stewed, knowing she could be a valuable asset to this camp but not wanting it to be at the cost of her daughter's well-being. While in the garden with Edna, she raised her concerns.

Edna shook dirt off a turnip and placed it in a pile for that night's dinner. "Cheryl will adjust either way. But she's a child, and she has no filter. The danger is she'd say something that would give away your true identity."

"But how can I leave her? She's already missing her father."

"We're as close as any family here. She'll be loved and looked after. If it doesn't work out, you can come back."

Davy returned from a foray that hadn't gone well, and he added pressure. "I need your answer," he growled, but then he disappeared behind the closed door of his hut.

Before sunrise, awake and still fretting, Gina saw Davy sitting alone by the firepit. She joined him. "Have you been here all night?"

He shrugged. "It wouldn't be the first time."

She knew that to be true. The sortie to cut Japanese communication lines had gone sour, and Davy had lost two men. Loss always took its toll, leaving him brooding and despondent.

"Our scouts saw Jap patrols headed this way," he said. "We'll have to move higher up the mountain. Have you decided what you're doing?"

"You know I'm tempted to say yes, but I'm concerned about leaving Cheryl."

Davy poked at the fire. "I understand. No parent wants to be separated from their child. But between Vivian, Maggie, and Edna, Cheryl will be loved and nurtured. I'd leave Harry with any one of them in a heartbeat." He threw the poker down. "In the new camp, there will be an area set aside for families. It will be homier, and there will be a schoolroom. The children will be shielded from the worst of what goes on here."

Gina had heard of the new plans, but she still wavered. "How long do you think I'd be gone?"

"It's anyone's guess. If it doesn't work out for either you or Cheryl, I'll get you back here. I promise."

Gina felt an urge to be more useful than working as a cook for a small band of guerrillas. She trusted Davy and knew Cheryl would be all right with Vivian and Theo, though she expected their parting to be a hard one. "You promise to get me back here if it doesn't work out," she reiterated.

"On my honor."

"All right. I'll work for you in Manila. When will I be leaving?"

"In a few days. Marcus will set you up."

The sky was beginning to lighten, and Gina had breakfast to cook. She poked at the fire and added a log, feeling both excited and fearful about the future she had agreed to. "You know I'll do my best, Davy. I hope I don't let you down."

While Marcus worked out the details of the trip, Gina began her preparations to leave. Foremost on her mind was telling Cheryl that she would be staying with Vivian. She waited until they were alone at the stream, a place where Gina found it easy to talk to her daughter. Today they were searching for stones flecked with gold. Upon seeing one, Gina pointed it out to Cheryl, who picked it up and put it in her pocket.

"I've been thinking, sweetheart, about going back to Manila."

Cheryl clapped her hands. "Yay! Are Miss Vivian and Leah coming too?"

Gina sighed. She was off to a bad start. "No. I'm going by myself. I have important work to do for Major Davy. You're going to stay here with Miss Vivian, Leah, and Maggie."

Cheryl's face scrunched into a frown. "I can help you do work for Major Davy."

"It's grown-up work, honey. I'll be very busy, and Manila wouldn't be the same for you. Your friends are gone, and the school is closed. I won't be living in our house. You'll be happier here with Leah and Maggie."

"When will you be back?"

"I'm not sure. But I promise just as soon as I can be."

Cheryl kicked at the water. "No! Daddy's gone. You can't go too. He won't know where to find me if you go away."

Gina wasn't prepared for that argument. She didn't know where Ray was or if they'd ever be together again. She took Cheryl's hands in hers. "That's not so. Daddy will always know where to find you."

"But how can I talk to him if we can't link pinkies?"

Gina felt her child's pain as if it were her own. She kissed the palm of each little hand and said softly, "You can talk to Daddy anytime you want to just by whispering your love to him. He'll hear you. Sweetheart, you're going to stay here with Miss Vivian. I'll be back as soon as I can. I love you. Daddy loves you. I promise we'll all be back together, but I don't know when. Now, let's go back to the cabin, and you can help me pack."

Gina carried Cheryl back to the camp, the child sobbing on her shoulder. At the cabin Cheryl struggled out of her mother's arms. "I'm afraid to be all alone by myself," she bawled. "I'm just a little girl." She ran inside, and through the window Gina saw Vivian swoop her into her arms. Gina's heart almost broke in two. She walked out to the garden and tugged hard at the weeds, her tears salting the soil. *This damn war. This damn, damn war!*

Chapter 10

MARCUS

I march past silent crowds through the streets of Manila to Bilibid Prison, stripped of all personal belongings, including my identity and my pride. My cold curiosity helps detach my mind from the jitters of my reality.

—Ray Thorpe, Bilibid Prison, May 1942–October 1942

With Gina having made her decision about going to Manila, Davy charged ahead with his plan. He gave her cash and a list of names and addresses of people in Manila to contact. "Keep this hidden," he said. "Better yet, memorize it and then burn it."

She looked over the list, recognizing a few names, mostly Filipino higher-society men and women whom Davy, Theo, and Marcus knew and trusted. "How much should I tell them?"

"Only as much as you need to. That we're a guerrilla unit harassing the Japanese. We need money for food and guns. Don't reveal our position or our size. That will change anyway. I'm looking for a runner who will be your contact to me."

"How will I know him?"

"Good question." He squinted at the horizon. "How about he will ask if you like strawberries, and you reply, 'I prefer mangoes.'"

"You're joking. I didn't know you were an Agatha Christie fan, Davy."

"Get used to the cloak-and-dagger."

She felt a tingle of anticipation. "Can I add my own friends to the list?"

"If you trust them, yes, but be careful, Gina. Don't reveal too much to anyone. We're new at this, and none of us know where it's going to lead. Our fate is in your hands."

The smirk left Gina's face, the weight of the responsibility becoming real. "I'll be careful. I'll work hard for you. I promise."

That night Gina formed a pocket in her brassiere by picking out the stitches between the lining and the fabric. She studied the contact names to commit them to memory before inserting the list in the pocket and sewing it shut.

~

The trip would be a hard one, along back trails to avoid Japanese patrols. Marcus would travel with her part of the way, with Negritos guiding them through the rain forest to the bay. She'd continue alone by boat into Manila, where a man with a cart would take her to Malate Church.

When she heard the plan, Vivian muttered, "Are you crazy? The Negritos are headhunters."

"Don't, Viv. I've struggled enough with this. The guides Marcus hired are not headhunters. They're just mountain people. Family oriented, Marcus says. They know the trails better than anyone. I trust Marcus's judgment." She sniffed. "I'm the one going home, so why am I the one who can't stop weeping?"

"Guilt maybe? You inherit a ton when that first baby is born. Cheryl will be fine, Gina. I love the child as much as I love my own. Besides, with her here, I know you'll be sending us food and supplies—and maybe a goody or two—on a regular basis."

Vivian was probably right, though Gina wouldn't admit to being so self-serving.

Vivian reached into her pocket. "I have something for you and Cheryl." She handed Gina two gold chains; dangling on each was half a heart-shaped locket. "My mother had these made when I was a child and she was ill and in the hospital for a long time. She gave me one and kept the other. The hearts snap together as one. I want you to take them for you and Cheryl. Tell her whenever she is lonesome to touch the locket, and you will be thinking of her. It helped me through a sad time."

Gina was warmed by Vivian's offer of such a precious object. "Oh no. I can't accept what is so cherished to you."

"Yes, you can. And I want you to. And I pray I'll never need them again myself."

"Viv, you're closer to me than the sister I never had. I love you. What happened to your mom?"

"She's hitting sixty. She and my dad are looking forward to a retirement on a beach somewhere."

Not wanting a teary morning send-off, Gina decided to say her good-byes that night at the party Vivian organized. It was a big group that gathered around the firepit: Vivian, Theo, the girls, Marcus and Edna, Davy, Popo, several displaced soldiers, Robert Louis Stevenson, and a gaggle of ROTC kids. "I'm going to miss you all," she said to the somber gathering. "I promise to work hard to make your lives easier."

"Hear, hear," a soldier called out. He tapped a rhythm on a bongo drum and chanted a limerick:

We're sending a girl to Manila
Who's pure and sweet as vanilla.
What the Japs don't know
Is the girl's a pro
Who works for the underground guerrilla.

With that, a bottle got passed around, and the party livened up with dancing and drinking to the strums of a guitar, the scratch of a fiddle, and the bongo drumbeat to keep the rhythm moving. The gaiety continued until the fire died.

*

After the party, Gina carried Cheryl, who was already half-asleep, to her bed. The child had been weepy and clingy for the last few days, increasing Gina's guilt and causing her to constantly rethink her decision. After helping her into her pajamas, Gina said, "I have something special for you." She showed Cheryl the two half-heart-shaped lockets and how they clipped together as one.

Cheryl's eyes widened as she inspected the gold pendants, clipping them together and taking them apart. "It's like a puzzle. Can I keep it?"

"Yes, you can keep one, and whenever you get lonesome for me, you can touch this heart and know that I love you and will be thinking of you. I'll do the same." Gina fastened one chain around Cheryl's neck and the other on herself. "Know I love you more than anyone else in the whole world. And nothing will ever change that." She lifted her sleepy daughter onto the bed and then climbed in beside her and cuddled with her, Cheryl clinging to the locket and Gina breathing the scent of her daughter until the child was fast asleep.

*

That night sleep never came, and Gina, her hand often going to the locket, gave up the prospect. Alone on the porch, she thought about all she was leaving. She'd made friends and carved out a life here, however hard and humble. The night air smelled fresh and earthy, and the full moon hung so low she felt she could reach out and touch it. Tree limbs and swooping bats showed as silhouettes against the moon's glow, an ever-changing black-and-white scene. Why had she never noticed the beauty?

≈

At dawn, Gina met Marcus in the yard. As instructed, she had packed only a few clothes and personal items and a small amount of food. Marcus wore a pack on his back and a bolo attached to his belt. He handed Gina a package. "This is from Edna. She said it's for the trip."

Inside Gina found a pack of Lucky Strike cigarettes, a thermos of water, and two candy bars. "American cigarettes! Where'd she find them?" Gina sniffed the pack.

"She's been hoarding."

"I have to thank her!"

"She'll understand. Let's go. We're meeting the guides on the other side of Katana."

They strode along the path, and as they walked, the sky lightened. Beyond the town Marcus pointed out a lone tree in the distance. "We're meeting the guides there. Don't be alarmed when you see them."

"Why would I be?"

"They're a little different. Good people, though. Nomadic. Their ancestors came to this country over thirty thousand years ago."

Gina glanced at Marcus. He seemed to know something about everything.

Waiting for the guides to show, Gina opened her bag and retrieved mangoes and hard-boiled eggs. She gave the mangoes to Marcus to peel while she shelled the eggs. She opened Edna's thermos of water and took a long swig. "Wow!" She coughed and choked. "Your sister's full of surprises!" She handed the drink to Marcus, who took a swallow and sneezed it out his nose.

"Edna's vodka." He wiped his nose and laughed. "I should have suspected."

Giggling, they ate the eggs and mangoes, smoked, and passed the thermos back and forth as the blazing sun rose higher in the sky.

"Maybe we've been stood up," Gina said.

"Maybe. Or they're hiding in the trees watching us. It wouldn't be unusual."

A dozen diminutive, dark-skinned, woolly-haired men, carrying bows and arrows, came into the clearing. Despite Marcus's warning, their appearance gave Gina the willies. Knives of varying lengths were tucked into their G-strings, the only clothing that covered their taut, muscled bodies. As they neared, Gina saw ritual scars on their backs and arms, and teeth that had been filed to points.

One stepped forward, shook Marcus's hand, and then turned to her. Marcus said, "Shake his hand, Gina. He learned the greeting from an American soldier."

Oh, Lordy! She needed another swig from Edna's thermos. She reached out to him, and the little man almost pumped her arm off.

While the leader and Marcus negotiated, Gina sat on the ground, and the Negritos squatted in a circle around her. When she dug into her pack of belongings, they scooted in closer to watch. The little men smelled feral, and Gina recoiled. She handed a small bag of dried fruit to one man and motioned for him to pass it around. Marcus beckoned for her to come.

"We'll have four guides. There are two trails. One is longer but an easier walk. The other is steeper but shorter. Do you have a preference?"

"The shorter one, of course."

The guides helped each other balance the supply bags on top of their heads. Relieved to be on the way, Gina trotted behind their long strides. The trail climbed so steeply in places that she clung to tree roots to pull herself up, and when it turned downhill, she slid on the seat of her pants, and grit scraped her elbows and forearms. They stopped to ford streams or briefly for drinks of water and meals of fruit, dried meat, or an egg, at which time the guides rearranged the bundles on their heads.

Endless time went by, and the sameness of the green gorges and peaks, the chirps of the birds, and the howls of the monkeys became background to Gina's senses. Winged insects disturbed by their passage rose in clouds around her head as she pushed her way through openings so narrow she had to wiggle through sideways. With one hand she swatted at the insects that crawled down the neck of her blouse, and with the other she protected her face from flicked branches. The soil, black and wet underfoot, seeped through the holes in the bottom of her shoes, while scraps of songs played and replayed in her head and kept her mind off the pain in her back and legs.

The guides stopped the trek, and Gina took her eyes off the ground. She was standing on a ledge that overlooked the forest canopy, a rolling swell of green, brown, and gold that stretched to the horizon. After conversing with the guides, Marcus approached her. "How are you holding up?" he inquired.

She wasn't going to admit that she was tired, hungry, thirsty, and dirtier than she had ever been. She hoped she didn't smell bad too. "I'm doing fine. Do these guys ever stop?"

"They're going to cook us a meal down there." He pointed down the hundred-foot cliff to a clearing where a small waterfall trickled off the rock face into a stream—an idyllic setting in which to rest. But Gina groaned as she imagined the long, circuitous trail to get from here to there. It would take hours to walk.

"We're taking a shortcut," Marcus continued as if reading her mind. He pointed to the guides a short distance away, who were busy tying vines together into what might be a harness.

Gina checked to see if Marcus was grinning—making a joke, maybe—so she could slap at his arm and call him a tease. But his face was chalky. He said, "I'm not good with heights. It's like a force is drawing me over the edge. Does it affect you that way?"

"No, I'm okay with it." She noticed the worry in his eyes. "I'm sorry. You should have said something. We could have taken the easier route."

He shook his head. "I'll tough it out. My mother always told me to face my fears." He glanced at the cliff. "Somehow I don't think she meant *that*."

A guide was being lowered down the rock face, taking little steps and hops, as if it were easy, fun even, Gina thought. At the bottom he stepped out of his harness, and the guides at the top pulled it up. After lowering down the packs, a guide beckoned to Gina.

The little man passed the vines behind her back, around her waist, and between her legs and tied the resulting three loops in a tight figure-eight knot, and then he fastened the lowering rope vine to it. Trussed and tied, she stood with her feet planted on the edge of the cliff and leaned back into the harness. It cut into her groin, and she wiggled to readjust it, but no amount of wiggling helped.

"Be careful, Gina!" Marcus barked, and then he addressed the guides. "Be careful with her . . . if anything happens, I'll—"

The harness gave a bit, and a cry of surprise escaped from her throat. She saw Marcus turn away and walk into the woods, his hands covering his face.

Recovering, she called, "I'm okay. Marcus. I'm okay!"

She took her first baby steps backward as the guides worked the riggings and lowered her down. The ride down the cliff was thrilling, and when her feet touched the ground, she laughed in delight. As she stepped out of the harness, she saw Marcus standing as far back from the edge as he could, his arms folded and his body rocking. *Lordy,* she thought. *What is this doing to him?*

Marcus landed a few minutes later, his eyes overly bright and his body soaked in sweat. When he tried to stand, his knees knocked together, and he fell back. "Give me a minute for my head to stop spinning." He added, "This is embarrassing."

"It shouldn't be. Can I get you something? A drink of water?"

He nodded and blew out a breath through puffed cheeks.

Rummaging through the packs for water, she found Edna's thermos. "Thank you, Edna!" she exclaimed. She took a swig herself before handing it to Marcus. They clapped and shouted bravo when the last guide rappelled down the cliff. When all were on safe ground, the four guides disappeared into the jungle.

Marcus watched them leave. "Two guides are scouting the trail ahead for Jap patrols, and two are hunting for dinner." He grinned. "Sorry. I forgot to ask your preference . . . herb-crusted roast beef with caramelized onions, potatoes, and carrots, or pancetta salmon kabobs with parsley vinaigrette? You choose; I don't have much of an appetite."

Gina chuckled at Marcus's offering. Glad for the break, she took off her shoes and waded into the stream, splashing water on her face and running wet hands through her hair. "Come on in. It will cool you off," she called to Marcus, whose face was still ashen. She flicked some water his way. He took his boots off, sat on a rock, and dangled his feet in the water.

He observed her curiously before he spoke. "What's your background, Gina?"

"Why do you ask?"

"Because you're different. I don't know any other woman who would do what you just did, and I've heard you singing in French. I find you intriguing."

Gina shrugged. "Hardly intriguing. I traveled through Europe with a musical revue company. They did some light opera, and I learned some French, German, and a little Hungarian. I knew Italian from my grandmother. We were booked at the Alcazar Club in Manila. It's where I met Ray. You know the rest." She splashed water his way again. "How about you, Marcus? What brought you to Manila?"

"A job. I was a high school principal in Ohio. Married almost fifteen years . . . my wife died of cancer. Her name was Shelly." His jaw clenched.

Gina felt a desire to hug him. "I'm sorry," she said.

"Thank you. It was a sad time in my life. My church in Ohio supported the Santa Catalina School in Manila. The principal had just retired, and my pastor asked if I'd be interested in the job. I came to love that school and the people. Leaving it was a lot harder than leaving Ohio." He reached for the vodka and took another swig. "Thank you, Edna!" He gazed around. "Those buggers ought to be back."

The hunter guides returned and held up two dead monkeys.

"Uh-oh," she whispered to Marcus. "I may get sick for real."

He snickered. "I'll hold your head."

The guides cooked their meal over a fire started by rubbing bamboo sticks together. The dinner, a concoction of monkey meat, rice, bamboo shoots, and a pinch of an unfamiliar spice that gave the dish a distinctive flavor, was served on a large banana leaf. Gina sat in a circle with the others and ate with her hands from the common leaf, so hungry and spent she didn't give a thought to health or hygiene. Marcus held a conversation in a mixture of Tagalog, English, and pantomime with a young man whose grin revealed filed teeth. He moved his arms like rocking a baby and held up three fingers. "Three something," Marcus said to Gina, and she nodded and smiled.

Sipping some kind of alcoholic brew, Gina and Marcus watched the guides pitch lean-tos for the night. Gina asked, "When will we get to the bay?"

"Tomorrow evening. You'll be on your own then. You up to it?"

"Kind of late to ask that, isn't it?"

"Hmmm. Yeah." He reached deep in his pocket for an envelope. "I'll give you this now in case things are hectic later. I know Davy gave you money to live on while you're getting established. Here's a little more." He extended an envelope.

She placed her hand on her chest. "Thank you so much, my dear friend, but I can't accept it. You need it for yourself."

"Not really. I have more. All I need. Take it, Gina. None of us knows what you're getting into. I'm not so sure you should even go. It's a lot to put on your shoulders."

Now that she was away from the familiar surroundings of the Tinian compound, the task charged to her was taking on an ominous scope, making Gina second-guess her ability to carry it out. "I feel the weight. But I think I'm up to it."

He pressed the envelope toward her. "Take it. Eventually Cheryl's going to need shoes, and she won't find any up here."

That argument made it easier, and Gina accepted the offer. "Thank you. I'll pay you back, one way or another."

Marcus rolled his eyes. "Geez, just take it. It's a gift."

In the morning the trip down the mountain resumed. It was dark by the time the Negritos led them into a village where nipa huts lined the water's edge and fishing boats bobbed on windswept waves. A man at the end of one dock waved them over.

"That's Moody," Marcus said. "He'll be taking you across Manila Bay tonight."

So this was happening. Marcus, her protector, her last contact with the friends she trusted, was leaving her on the shore of this vast bay in the hands of a stranger named Moody.

Marcus noted the rising winds and thickening clouds. "You may get wet."

Chapter 11

MOODY

Q. What's a Japanese girl's favorite holiday? Erection Day. Q. Why are there never any Japanese bingo players? They disappear when they hear B-29. Q. Why wasn't Jesus born in Japan? He couldn't find three wise men or a virgin. I laugh. I cry.

—Ray Thorpe, Bilibid Prison, May 1942–October 1942

Gina sat huddled in a small motor launch on the water's edge, holding a giant banana leaf over her head, inadequate protection from the monsoon rain that was pouring down in sheets. She was traveling across the bay to a shack just outside Manila, where she would stay until a farmer picked her up and drove her into the city. Cold, she wrapped a blanket around her body. "How long will this last?" she yelled to Moody over the howl of the wind.

He tapped his ear and shrugged his shoulders, indicating he hadn't heard her. It was a moot question anyway, Gina knew. The storms during the rainy season could last two days or an hour, a factor Marcus, with all his planning, had been unable to figure into her trip. When the wind let up and the rain lessened to a drizzle, Moody pushed the boat away from the shore with a pole. It rocked in the choppy current as he tried to tease the engine to life, repeatedly pulling the cord, but it sputtered and died. After he primed it with alcohol and adjusted the choke, the motor caught hold. Moody flashed Gina a smile. Reassured by his smile and on their way again, she relaxed a bit.

There wasn't much to see in the dark night on the black water, except a few points of lights on the coastline, and there was nothing to hear except the muffled putt-putt of the small motor. Woozy with fatigue from the long hike down the mountain, Gina lay on the boat's wooden seat and went into a half sleep. The fishy smell, the rock of the boat, and the drone of the outboard motor all took her back to her childhood, when she'd fished with her father on Puget Sound and learned the difference between a perch and a rockfish and how to bait a hook. On those excursions he'd told stories of his childhood and his parents, vaudevillians who had immigrated from a small village in Italy. Gina adored her feisty grandmother, who had taught her how to move gracefully and project her voice from the stage.

When they neared the shore, clouds rolled over again, and the wind picked up, rocking the boat and swirling the water. "Hang on," Moody hollered, and he set the throttle at full speed. The craft skipped across the water, each slap of the waves on the hull jolting Gina so hard she clenched her teeth to keep from biting her tongue. A bolt of lightning hit close by, and the hairs on her arm stood to attention, just as a cloud opened and the world turned gray with the downpour. The boat slowed and stopped. Moody hauled her onto a wobbly dock barely visible in the driving rain and pointed to a small tin-roofed building. "Go in there," he shouted as he fought the wind to tie down his boat.

Gina hurried along the dock and across a muddy street to the building. The sign over the door read THE SHIP SHACK. She banged on the door until a grizzled old man answered. A brown-and-black dog stood alert beside him. After stepping into the dimly lit interior, Gina gazed around the store stocked with fishing gear, hats, tools, knives, and several shelves of books. A clock on the wall read 2:35 a.m. Both the man and dog eyed the bedraggled woman with curiosity.

Gina addressed the old man. "Moody said to come in here."

He cupped his hand to his ear and shouted, "Speak up, girl."

Gina felt her body jump.

"Moody said to come in here," she shouted back.

"Fool!" the old man sputtered in his too-loud voice. "Shouldn't be on the water. Didn't expect no one in this storm." He disappeared into a back room and returned with a towel that he handed to Gina.

"Are we close to Manila?" Gina patted her face and arms dry.

The old man grunted, and she wondered if that was a yes or a no. He lit a lamp with hands that were gnarled with arthritis, all the while mumbling something Gina could not decipher. He nodded toward her. "Come with me."

The dog followed along as the old man led them across the uneven floor to the back of the store and up a narrow staircase. The low-ceilinged room at the top reeked of oil, and a blackout shade shielded a small window. Boxes and barrels, fishing rods, nets, and tools cast eerie shadows in the dim lamplight. A cot against the wall was covered with bedding that looked well slept in.

Gina felt tears forming from hunger and cold, or maybe fear, and she felt the stab of guilt she had been grappling with all day at leaving Cheryl behind. She quieted herself by chanting in her mind, *All this will be worth it—you'll see.* Not a hollow promise, she hoped.

The old man rummaged in some boxes for blankets and dry clothing for her to change into. "You are very kind," she loudly said, but he gave no indication he'd heard her.

His voice boomed, startling her again. "There's a privy out back." He and his dog descended the stairs.

Alone, she put on the dress the old man had given her, detecting a moldy smell. The motion of the boat and the odor of the fuel had left her woozy, and she wanted a comfortable bed with clean sheets and soft pillows. There was no comfort in this room, with its plank floor and rain hammering on the tin roof.

Her nerves were jangled from the long day's travel. Sitting on the bed, her hand went to the locket, and she wanted more than anything in the world to be with her daughter right now, singing the lullabies her mother had sung to her.

⌁

A door downstairs banged shut. Moody's voice filtered up the stairs. "Son of a bitch. It's a screecher out there. Hey, Bandito, how you doin', ole buddy? Yeah, you like that, don't you? Here, take this. Good dog."

Gina envisioned Moody scratching the dog behind his ear. She heard stomping on the stairs.

Moody, still dripping with rain, stepped into the room, followed by Bandito, who was carrying a newspaper in his mouth. She studied the man, who was shorter than she was and slightly bowlegged. His hair was as black as any Filipino's, but his eyes were hazel and his skin a golden brown. Was Moody his real name?

From a bag he removed bottles of beer and a bowl of rice and vegetables and placed them on the table, then took the newspaper from Bandito and tossed it aside. "Good boy," he said, pouring beer into a bowl for the dog. He opened another beer for Gina and handed it to her. "You comfortable enough? Need anything? Dry clothes, blankets?"

Gina thought a hug from her daughter would be nice. She said, "Thanks. Your dad took good care of me. I don't think he heard me say thank you."

"Don't worry about it. He knows. Go ahead and eat; you look hungry."

"Thank you. I am."

He leaned back in the chair and ran his hand through his hair. "Man, I could use a towel." He reached over and grabbed Gina's. "Tonight, don't leave the building unless you need to use the privy. Have my dad check the alley before you go out. We're close to Manila, and the Japs wander up this way."

Gina drank the beer, it going down easily, and Moody opened another, which she accepted. No doubt she'd have to use that privy in the alley with Japs roaming around—not a pleasant thought. She drank the second beer more slowly and ate the rice and vegetables, which settled her queasy stomach. "What time are we leaving?"

"Early. My mom will wake you up. She wanted me to give you this." He reached into his shirt pocket for a packet of powder. "Stir it in a cup of water. It will help you relax."

"Oh. I won't need it—I'm so tired I could sleep standing up. Tell your mom thank you, though."

He pushed the packet closer. "It's not for tonight. It's for the trip. We rigged up a cart, and you'll be hidden in it. Mom says it's not fit for a dog. It's not that bad. I rode in it once just to see. But take the powder if you panic in enclosed spaces."

Gina choked at the description of her vehicle and covered it up as a cough. She wiped her chin. "How long's the trip?"

"Two hours or longer if we get hung up at the checkpoints. There are three. Any movement or sound could give you away; then we'd both be guests of the Japs in Fort Santiago."

The trip sounded odious. She glanced at the packet of powder. No. She needed to be in full control of her body and mind on the dangerous trip with this strange man. She left the packet on the table.

Bandito woofed, and his legs twitched in his sleep.

"Rabbits," Moody said. "He lives to chase them. Anything else? Any questions?"

Gina's mind was fuzzy with fatigue, and the beer had pushed her over the edge. "I can't think of any right now."

"Okay. Sleep good." He slapped his leg, and Bandito's head popped up. "Come on, boy." The dog stretched and yawned and followed Moody down the stairs.

Gina picked up the newspaper that Moody had left and read the headline news. José P. Laurel had been elected president of the Republic of the Philippines, and a pact of alliance had been signed between the new republic and the Japanese government. Former adviser to General MacArthur Señor Salvador Estevez had been released from prison after declaring loyalty to the Japanese and had been appointed an adviser to the newly formed legislature. The print blurred before Gina's tired eyes.

She lay down on the odd-smelling bed, still dressed in the garment Moody's father had given to her, and the next thing she knew, someone was coming up the stairs. With her head still buried in the pillow, she opened one eye to see a wizened Filipina carrying a basket. The woman smiled and put the basket of fruit and biscuits on the table. "For you, miss."

Gina sat up and rubbed the grit from her eyes, thinking the night had disappeared too quickly. The woman pointed to a pitcher of water and a basin.

Gina guessed the woman was Moody's mother. "Thank you, madre. You're very kind."

The woman nodded. "I wish you well."

Still half-asleep, Gina poured water into the basin, filled her palms, and held them to her face, enjoying the moment, a normal one. Her hand went to the locket and her thoughts to Cheryl, still snug asleep, she assumed, and when she awoke, Vivian would provide a good breakfast and Edna a school lesson. Gina already missed her best friends.

She had slept in the dress she would wear today, a dreary smock, but who would care? From the basket she selected a banana and a biscuit, a satisfying breakfast. Peeking from behind the blackout curtain, she saw Moody and a lanky man in the yard preparing a slat-sided horse-drawn cart for the trip. She picked up her bag full of wet clothes to join them. "Morning," she said.

"Morning to you," Moody said. "This here's Deke. This is his cart, and he'll be driving."

Gina nodded to Deke and then inspected the bed of the cart, where a tarp and bunches of bananas partially camouflaged a small coffinlike structure. She crossed her arms, glad for the first time that Cheryl wasn't with her.

Moody gestured at the small bunker. "The sides are lined with bagged charcoal. Deke will put a mattress down. You'll be safe in there. We'll be stopped at three checkpoints. The guards will search for contraband by stabbing through the bananas. It will scare you, but you can't move or make a sound until I give you an all-clear."

"Okay," Gina said, certain she could endure anything for two short hours, but after Deke completed the hideout and Gina climbed onto the moldy-smelling mattress mottled with stains of unsavory colors, her heart began to pound. A tight squeeze—there was barely any headroom.

Moody handed her a canteen of water. "You're sure you'll be all right?"

Resolute, she nodded. "I can do it."

"Then here we go."

Moody and Deke piled bags of charcoal and bunches of bananas over the top and sides of the bunker until the space became even more tomblike. Gina's heart raced so fast her breathing couldn't keep up with it, and she felt she could die in this crypt—and no one would be the wiser until it was too late.

With the first strides of the horse, the cart jerked. "It's going to be bumpy for a while," Moody called back to her. "Close your eyes and concentrate on your breathing. Long, slow breaths. It will slow your heart rate. You're going to be fine."

Gina latched on to his words, finding the sound of his voice comforting. She followed his instructions, and her anxiety lessened. Moody seemed to know what she was experiencing, and she wondered how many people he had smuggled into Manila—a dozen, a half dozen? Was she the first one? Did he have a backup plan, if something should go wrong? She wished she had asked him more questions last night.

The cart bumped along the rural road and then turned onto a smoother highway. Gina relaxed a bit. Her thoughts drifted to the people working in the underground, awed by how far their reach extended—from a hotbed in Manila, according to Marcus, to ranchers like Señor Ramos to the guerrillas forming in the mountains to fishermen, boatmen, and farmers scattered all through the country. The realization of its magnitude and her anticipated part in it brought on a poignant connection to the Filipino people she'd not felt before.

The cart's speed dropped to a crawl, and Moody called, "Checkpoint. Be still. Be quiet."

She put her hand on her heart, hoping to slow its beat.

The cart inched forward and stopped. She heard Japanese voices demanding licenses and identifications. Gina, sensitive to every sound, detected footsteps circling and then the thump of a bayonet jabbing through the slats into the bananas. A yelp tried to escape, but Gina gritted her teeth and stifled it. Charcoal dust rained down, and she swallowed the need to cough. When the cart moved forward, she began to cry, and there was no place for the tears to go but from the corners of her eyes into her ears.

"All clear," Moody called. "Only two more to go."

Only. The temperature in the cart rose to unbearable; the air stayed thick with charcoal dust.

"Checkpoint," Moody called twice more, and each time Gina experienced the harsh voices, jackbooted steps, and jabs of the bayonets. Her heart thumped so hard again she had to steel herself to keep from jumping out of her skin.

After what seemed an eternity, she heard the city's church bells chime nine o'clock. Her hopes soared—Saint Sebastian's or Santo

Domingo's? Gina wanted out of this cave, and she bit her tongue to keep from shouting Moody's name. The cart took a sharp turn to the right and stopped.

Moody called, "Hold on, Gina. We're coming." A moment later she glimpsed a sliver of light and Moody's face emerging from behind the bananas. He opened the tomb, and a soft pink hand tugged at Gina's. Rising, she squinted against the bright light of day and found she was in the courtyard of Malate Church, standing beside a priest dressed in white vestments now streaked with soot. The priest nodded toward a doorway. "Quick, come with me."

While Moody and Rocco transferred bananas to a garage where the priests stored food for Manila's most impoverished populations, Father Brady James Morgan led Gina inside the crumbling seventeenth-century church, where she felt the cool peacefulness of it for a moment before her world went black.

Chapter 12

FATHER MORGAN

Without stopping to think, I aid a soldier who has fallen, and I suffer a beating for it. The insult to my sense of decency is worse than the guard's cruel blows.

—Ray Thorpe, Bilibid Prison, May 1942–October 1942

Gina heard her name and struggled to pull out of the darkness. She was nauseated, and her left arm felt restricted. An unfamiliar voice said, "Take a couple deep breaths, Gina."

How did he know her name? She opened her eyes and saw she was lying on a bed in a stark room. A priest in his vestments and a doctor in a white coat stood beside her. An IV dripped into her arm. "Where am I?" she asked. She tried to sit up, but the nausea redoubled to a gag, and she lay back. Cold, she felt clammy too. When she saw she was covered with coal dust, the events of the last hours came to her. She asked more urgently, "Where am I?"

The priest said, "You're in the nuns' quarters at the Malate Church. You're dehydrated, and you passed out. Dr. Lopez started an IV. You should feel better soon. Lie here and rest for a while. When you're ready,

Miss Lyda, my secretary, will bring you clean clothes and show you where you can shower."

Dr. Hernandez Lopez took Gina's pulse and flashed a light in her eyes. She wondered whether he knew how she'd gotten into this weakened state. He didn't ask. "As soon as your stomach settles, I want you to drink half and half water and juice. No coffee, tea, or alcohol for the rest of the day. Do you have any questions?"

She couldn't think of one and shook her head.

"All right, sleep for now. You're safe here."

The two men left the room. "Wait," Gina croaked, but they were out of earshot. How long had she been here? Where was Moody? How much did they know?

She slept the rest of the day, sensing someone coming in periodically to check her IV but not waking her. When she sat up, Miss Lyda, a gangly woman with her hair pulled back in a bun, provided her with underwear, a skirt, a blouse, and slip-on shoes. "They're from our charity closet, but they're clean. Dr. Lopez said I can remove the IV. I left a towel, soap, comb, and such in the shower for you, two doors down on the right."

Gina grimaced as the needle was removed from her arm and a bandage put in its place. "A shower? Do you think I really need one?" She held up her coal-blackened arms.

Miss Lyda smiled. "Keep the bandage on for a few minutes, and then shower. When you're ready, Father Morgan would like you to join him for dinner."

Gina scrubbed the coal dust out of her hair and off her body with multiple applications of shampoo and soap. The warm water rushing over her felt wonderful, and she basked in it as long as she dared, letting her mind wander. The trip was harder than she had anticipated, and as much as she missed Cheryl, she was glad she had not exposed her to it.

Dr. Lopez . . . where had she heard that name before? While toweling dry, she remembered—his name was on the list of contacts Davy had given her.

⌁

"You look much more comfortable," Miss Lyda said. "Is there anything else you need?"

"Maybe another change of clothes? The few I brought are soaked and dirty."

"Of course. I'll let you choose from what we have. Come with me now; Father Morgan is waiting." She led Gina through a thick-walled stone passageway, past ornate pilasters and octagonal openings on the way to Father Morgan's office, soon passing through a vestibule where an elaborately carved glass case enshrined a small statue of a woman. The miniature stood erect, ornately dressed in beaded purple-and-white vestments with her hands outstretched, as if offering comfort. A gold medallion-shaped crown framed her ivory face and graceful features. Gina stopped to admire her.

"She's beautiful, isn't she," Father Morgan said as he approached from a side room. "She's Nuestra Señora de Los Remedios, Our Lady of Remedies. She was brought to this church in 1624 from Spain. Our young mothers recovering from childbirth, or those with a sick child, pray to her for a fast recovery. Our Lady has been known to perform many miracles. Sadly, we're going to be locking her away." He turned to his secretary. "Thank you, Miss Lyda. I'll take Gina from here."

Gina walked with Father Morgan down another long hallway.

"Nothing anymore is sacred," he said. "The Jap soldiers come into this church and sleep on our pews and defecate on our floors, and that's the least of what we deal with on a daily basis."

"Oh, Father. How do you handle it?"

"By rising above it and focusing my energy where it matters. To survive in Manila, you must learn to do that too."

"I couldn't possibly. I've seen too much . . . our men marching north. The Japanese are a cruel race. I have fear and loathing for them deep inside of me."

"My dear, I, too, have seen what the Japanese do. The Filipino soldiers come to our hospital half-alive and full of hate. We heal their bodies and, hopefully, their souls so they can return to their families and be useful. Given time and with help, I expect your soul will heal too."

Gina didn't want her soul to heal. Her hate for the Japanese was deserved, appropriate, and righteously savored, and she doubted she could live up to Father Morgan's standard. Irritated by his benign acceptance of Japanese cruelties, she said, "I doubt that, Father." She felt his sidelong glance.

In his office, an arched window overlooked a tropical garden anchored by a stately statue of Queen Isabella, a once-beloved Spanish monarch from the mid-1800s. The furniture was dark and heavy, and a side table was set with dishes, glasses, and cutlery. He motioned to Gina to sit on the leather couch and took a side chair himself. "I was getting worried for you this morning. So many bad things happen on the road nowadays." He pressed his fingers against a tic in his left cheek. The twitching muscle relaxed, leaving his square-jawed face serene. "Davy McGowan's a parishioner here. He sent word that you were coming. How is he?"

"Better. He was stabbed multiple times before he escaped the Japs. It was touch and go for a while."

A frown creased Father Morgan's forehead.

"How much do you know, Father?"

"I know that you're working with him, and you need a place to stay until you're issued a residence pass. That alone tells me more than you realize, but fill me in."

Gina told him a brief history of her moves from Manila to her cottage to the mountain hut, Davy's arrival, and the beginnings of the guerrilla unit. Father Morgan listened, in turn frowning and nodding until Miss Lyda arrived with a food cart.

At the side table he gave the blessing before serving the hearty vegetable-beef soup from a tureen. Gina broke apart a baking powder biscuit and poured herself a glass of carabao milk. "How did you avoid the internment camp, Father?"

"I'm Irish. All six of us priests are. Our American brothers and sisters are interned in Santo Tomas. May I ask . . . where is your husband?"

"He was working on Corregidor. I heard the men from there were sent to Bilibid." All Gina's fears and desires tumbled out. "I don't know if he's with them. Can I find out? If he's there, can I see him? Or send a package of clothing and food?" she pleaded. "Or at least a letter?"

"My dear. Hundreds of prisoners are processed through Bilibid every week, and almost all are transferred to other prison camps. The Japanese don't release the prisoners' names. We have no way of knowing who passed through. Promise you won't do anything that will bring attention to yourself or your husband. It would be dangerous to you and those around you."

"I promise. I won't. I know the Japs' cruelty, and I hate them for it."

"Be very careful. Hate strips the vitality out of one's life. It consumes energy that can be channeled elsewhere—like volunteering at Remedios Hospital. We've just recently opened. The ladies from the Catholic Women's League keep the hospital operational, and we are always short of help."

Gina listened with interest. The money Davy and Marcus had given her wouldn't last long. "Can you hire me? I'll be needing a job."

"No, unfortunately I can't. Our funds are limited. We've begged and borrowed every piece of equipment, and most of our staff, even our doctors, are volunteers. Don't rule out volunteering. It's an opportunity to meet people and integrate yourself into the new society."

He folded his napkin and placed it on the table, signaling the end of the meal. "As soon as Miss Lyda has you ready, I'll take you to Señor and Señora Estevez's hacienda. The decision to accept you into their home wasn't made lightly. It's a precarious position for them, and you must strictly follow their house rules. I can't stress that enough."

Miss Lyda led Gina to a small room and showed her a neatly folded nun's habit. "You'll wear this outside. There's a bit of art to putting it on."

Gina suppressed a smile; a nun she had never been. She stepped out of her skirt and blouse and into a cotton slip. Miss Lyda helped her into an underskirt, a black serge tunic pleated at the neck, an apron called a scapular, and a belt that held it all together. She slipped black shoes onto Gina's feet, hung a silver cross around her neck, attached a rosary to the belt, and slid a silver ring onto her left hand. "Now the pièce de résistance." She stuffed Gina's hair under a white cap and secured it with a bandeau and a starched linen wimple that covered her cheeks and neck. Over that she arranged a black veil. "The skirt's a tad long. Be careful not to catch the toe of your shoe on it. One last thing." She handed Gina rimless glasses. "No prescription in these."

After having worn cotton slacks and shorts for months, Gina felt weighed down by the layers of material, and the wimple felt scratchy on her neck. She took a few cautious steps in the unfamiliar shoes, hoping she wouldn't trip on the overly long skirt.

Father Morgan's calesa was waiting in the courtyard. He nodded his approval at her appearance and handed her a fake residence pass with a picture of a nun who resembled Gina somewhat. "You're Sister Margaret Mary. If we're questioned, let me do the talking. I'll say we're on our way to a funeral. With all the disease in the city, there's enough of them around lately."

Clutching a bag of her sodden clothes and another with clothing Miss Lyda had given her, Gina ducked her head and climbed under the buggy's canopy. "Do you think we'll be stopped?"

"We're never sure. If the Japanese are anything, they're unpredictable."

The driver maneuvered the buggy through Manila's streets crammed with people walking, riding bicycles, or in horse-drawn vehicles. Only a handful of cars was seen, and neither a bus nor a trolley was evident. Japanese flags flew boldly atop buildings, hung limply from street posts, and even fluttered from bicycle handles. Japanese soldiers wearing white pith helmets and carrying rifles patrolled the streets, demanding ID checks and expecting civilians to bow and make way.

Gina swallowed dryly. Manila's magic was gone, replaced by an undercurrent of fear potent enough to be sensed by an observer. Believing herself vulnerable even with a fake ID and wearing the habit, she sat back in the seat where she couldn't be seen. After a time, the buggy drove through an iron gate and down a long driveway, stopping in front of a hacienda-type house that Gina hoped was her safe haven.

Chapter 13

FRANCA

I'm one of nine thousand men imprisoned in this camp. Disease is rampant. Cruelty is unrestrained and violent. I'm losing weight rapidly, and I'm having long stretches of hopelessness.

—*Ray Thorpe, Cabanatuan prison camp, October 1942–January 1944*

A Filipino maid opened the massive front door of the hacienda. "Father Morgan, Sister. Please come in."

Sweltering under the heavy nun's garments, Gina gladly stepped inside, where thick walls insulated the interior from the day's ruthless heat. She had forgotten what splendor was—this foyer was larger than the whole of her nipa hut. An elaborate gold-and-crystal chandelier hung from a high-beamed ceiling. On a round table underneath the fixture, an urn as tall as Cheryl held big-headed sunflowers, colorful zinnias, and natural grasses. A curved staircase of polished mahogany ascended to the right.

The maid said to Father Morgan, "Señora Estevez was called away. She asked that I take our guest to her room and make her comfortable."

Father Morgan put Gina's bags of clothing, one still wet from the trip, on the floor. "I'll be leaving then. Give my regards to Señora Estevez." He turned to Gina. "We'll be in touch. Don't forget what I said about volunteering."

"I won't, and thank you, Father."

The maid picked up Gina's bags. "I am Millie. We will be going up the stairs." She pointed to the right.

On the way, Gina glanced through arched doorways to see marble fireplaces, thick-legged tables, and couches upholstered in heavy damask. Holding the long habit's skirt, she followed Millie up the staircase, hoping she wouldn't trip. In a wide hallway, life-size paintings of dark-eyed men in full military regalia and women with enigmatic smiles and wearing elaborate dresses stared down at those approaching. Gleaming swords and guns, from palm-size pistols to long rifles, were displayed on the walls or in glass cabinets.

"Your room is here, madam." The heavy door glided open to a chamber swathed in gold velvets and royal-blue damasks. A four-poster bed dominated the space, with an ornately carved wardrobe against the opposite wall. Millie led her past a windowed alcove that held a table and two cushioned chairs to the bathroom. Gina peeked in and almost fainted with delight at seeing a big bathtub and fluffy towels.

Millie placed Gina's bag of belongings on a luggage stand. "Are you hungry? May I bring you something to eat?"

"No, thank you. I had a meal with Father Morgan. When will Señora Estevez return?"

"In a couple hours. She asks that you not leave this room, madam." Millie pointed out a call button by the bed. "If you need anything, you can buzz me here. Is there anything else I can do for you now?"

There was nothing Gina wanted more than to soak in that big bathtub. "No, thank you. What should I do with these?" She gestured at the nun's garments.

"Leave them outside the door, and I will send them back to Father Morgan. If you have anything you would like laundered, put it outside the door too."

⌇

Gina peeked in the wardrobe, finding a cotton robe and slippers. A few books were on a shelf, and the Manila *Tribune* was on the nightstand. The headline caught her eye: "US Forces Surrender the Malinta Tunnel." She stepped to the window to better see the accompanying picture, a horde of American soldiers exiting the tunnel with their hands held high and under heavy Japanese guard. She studied each face, hoping to see Ray's, seeking assurance that he had survived the bombing of Corregidor, but none were familiar. She tossed the paper aside.

The bathroom was a dream come true, with thick bars of soap, bottles of shampoo and lotions, a drawerful of grooming accoutrements, and even a bottle of clear nail polish. *Señora Estevez must be an angel.*

She stripped off the cumbersome nun's garments and immediately felt pounds lighter, and then she drew a bath, adding a handful of lavender bath salts, swirling it into the water and sniffing the lovely scent. When she stepped in, sat down, and lay back, "Ahhh" escaped from the back of her throat. She closed her eyes to enjoy a moment of peace and pleasure. However, *Estevez* came to mind. Where had she heard that name before? She mulled it over. From the Junior League—there were so many women—or a school friend of Cheryl's, or a client of Ray's, perhaps?

She breathed deeply to clear her mind, hoping to induce a few moments of peaceful feelings, but Vivian's face crossed her inner vision. She'd be shaking out the girls' bedding now, getting rid of whatever bugs had crawled or flown into them. Did she hear Cheryl crying? Her hand went to the locket. Was Maggie consoling her child? Gina squeezed her eyes closed. She wondered if Marcus had gotten back to the camp yet.

There was no clearing her mind, with its too many worries and much wondering, and there was no enjoying the sensations of a scented bath knowing the deprivations of those closest to her. She defaulted to the once-mundane tasks: shaving her legs and underarms, a job more difficult than she expected; clipping her nails and filing them smooth; and brushing her teeth with mint-flavored toothpaste. Pulling the coverlet back on the bed, she ran her hand over clean, crisp sheets, then selected *Gone with the Wind* off the bookshelf and sank back into soft pillows, reading the first pages before feeling lonesome for her loved ones and the guilt of unwarranted indulgence. It was then the flood of tears came.

$\backsim$

Gina woke up when Millie came into the room carrying a tray with coffee and juice and placed them on the side table. Disoriented, Gina sat up and pulled the sheet to her chest. She realized she was in a comfortable bed in a beautiful room. Sunshine streamed through the window. "It's morning? I slept through the night?"

"Yes, ma'am. Señora Estevez thought it best. Breakfast is on the sideboard in the morning room. She will meet you there when you're ready. Is there anything else I can get you now?"

It had been a long time since she'd been asked that question, and Gina smiled. "No, thank you, Millie. I'll come downstairs."

Gina's thoughts went to Cheryl and how much she would have loved sleeping in this big bed. She would be waking up soon and eating breakfast, possibly today a bowl of berries, before her school session with Edna.

Real coffee! It gave her a boost. She sipped the coffee and prepared for the day, brushing her hair, which was softer this morning, and slipping on a dress too small in the bust and too big in the hips. She sighed, remembering her closetful of tailored dresses of not so long ago.

As she left the room, last night's lost memory came to mind. *Estevez.* She had read his name, Señor Salvador Estevez, in the newspaper while at Moody's fishing shack. He had been arrested and later released from Fort Santiago for something. Her hands were cold, and she realized she felt shaky inside too.

~

In the morning room, Gina found a woman with velvety skin sitting in a winged chair reading the newspaper. Dark hair curled around a friendly, open face, a short nose, and hazelnut eyes. The woman put the paper down and held out her hand. "Welcome to my home, Mrs. Thorpe. I'm Señora Estevez. Help yourself to breakfast on the buffet, and come sit with me." She moved to a table that was set for two with colorful stoneware and pewter.

Gina selected one egg, two slices of bacon, and a cup of sliced mangoes and bananas. Millie brought her a cup of coffee.

Once they were settled, the señora asked, "Are you comfortable in your room?"

"Yes. It's a beautiful room. This is a gorgeous house."

"Thank you. The land has been in my husband's family for over two hundred years. It was once a pineapple plantation. Before the Japanese came, I was having the house modernized—plumbing, heating, and such." She gestured to a door that led outside. "You're welcome to use the garden. You'll find it pleasant out there. I must ask you not to go off of our property until you're issued your residence pass, for your sake and ours. People caught without a pass are arrested. As you can imagine, that would be a bad situation."

Gina was anxious to get started on her mission. "How long does it take, Señora?"

"Please call me Franca, and I'll call you Gina. How long it takes depends. A few days or a month. A letter from my husband to Colonel Ito of the Kempeitai may speed it up. It's never a sure thing."

Curious, Gina asked the question she had been pondering. "It's very generous of you, and I appreciate it, but why are you and Señor Estevez willing to help me? You don't even know me."

"Oh, we do, better than you think. Your husband, Ray, is well respected in the business world. We know you as a prolific fund-raiser for the Junior League. Where is Ray now?"

"I don't know. He was on Corregidor. I've had no word of him."

"Unfortunately, that's not unusual. And your little girl, Cheryl?"

Gina smiled at hearing her daughter's name. "I left her in the mountains with friends."

"That's rough, but leaving her there is for the best. Manila's not the city it used to be. I'm sure you've noticed the sentries on the streets already. Let me tell you where we stand. I'm sure you're wondering. Señor Estevez and I know that you're here to raise money for Major Davy McGowan. When Davy contacted Father Morgan saying he needed help getting you set up in the city, Father Morgan came to us. It was a hard decision. Señor Estevez spent two months in Fort Santiago, you see. It was in all the papers, so you probably already know. He wasn't seen as cooperating with the new administration. Men are found floating facedown in the Pasig River for doing less. He's in their good graces now, but we're being watched. You will be, too, until you change your identity and can disappear into the city. You have a cover story, don't you?"

"Yes, I do."

Gina had gone over her story until she sometimes believed she was Signora Angelina Aleo, born in Milan, Italy, and raised in Vancouver, Canada, by her mother's sister. She had come to the Philippines with her Canadian husband. He had worked in the gold mines in northern Luzon. There had been a mining accident. It was presumed he had been killed, though his body had never been recovered. It had happened years ago, just before the mine had closed.

"I worked with Marcus to select names and dates that couldn't be traced. He suggested I grew up in Canada to account for my good English."

"Yes, you need to keep practicing the details. If you're ever questioned by the Kempeitai, they'll pick up discrepancies in a heartbeat. I've been asked to help you get started. As long as you're staying here, I'll quiz you on your story until it's second nature." Franca's gaze wandered to outside the window, where wide-leaved plants and red hibiscus surrounded a waterfall and grotto that held a statue of the Blessed Virgin. "Secrets. Always lies and secrets. It's not the way it was." She flipped her hand in resignation.

Gina spent her days in sequestration under Franca's tutelage, preparing for a new life in the occupied city.

"You must learn to bow," Franca said. "The Japanese man is arrogant. You must be silent and compliant to him and always bow. If you don't, he'll slap your face. Accept the slap. Don't put up a fuss. If you show any resistance, he'll beat you. You'll see it often happen on the street. Pretend you don't notice." She demonstrated the bow, and Gina reluctantly copied it—a stiff tilt forward from the waist with hands clasped together. "Keep your head down. Don't look a Japanese man in the eye. If one yells *tomeru*, that means 'halt.' Believe him and do it. Don't ever run away—he'll shoot you in the back."

Gina felt her face pale. She had heard about the beatings but not the shootings.

Over lunch or while walking in the garden, Franca quizzed Gina about her invented life as Signora Angelina Aleo, often tripping her up on the details and stressing the importance of keeping them straight.

So thorough was her tutelage that Gina wondered whether Franca had mentored others through this passage of change. An artist forged Gina new identity papers, and Señor Estevez bribed a clerk at city hall to obliterate all records of Angelina Maria Capelli Thorpe from public files.

"You need to meet with Colonel Ito, the head of the Kempeitai, for your residence pass. Señor Estevez will call his office to set up an appointment."

"Is there any way I can get out of it?"

"No. He'll ask you a few questions. You'll take an oath and sign a paper. It only takes a few minutes."

A few minutes face to face with a Japanese officer of the Kempeitai, answering questions she was bound to stumble over, giving herself away as well as those helping her. It sent a chill up Gina's spine. Señor and Señora Estevez had no idea what they were asking of her.

～

Gina found a spot in the garden where she could bask in the sun to keep her skin dark so as not to stand out in a crowd, though it was a moot point, she thought, since she was inches taller than most Filipinas.

Millie came into the garden. "Miss Gina, a man at the door is asking to see you. He says his name is Miguel."

Miguel? Her former houseboy? What could he possibly want? Gina straightened her clothes and hurried to the porch, where Miguel stood with his hands in his pockets. When he saw her, he whispered, "I told to ask if you like strawberries."

"Oh! I see." Caught off guard, Gina had to think. "I prefer mangoes." She stepped back and smiled. She knew Miguel to be steady and faithful, and he would be a good contact between her and the camp, but it was a dangerous job, and he had young children. "Please come in."

She signaled Millie, who was passing by. "Please bring us some tea and a snack of some kind. We'll be in the morning room."

Miguel followed Gina to a small table by a window that overlooked the garden. They sat opposite each other. "It's good to see you, Miguel. Where are you working now?"

"With my father. He has an orchard of fruit trees. He is glad to have me with him. He is older now. Has aches and pains."

"And your wife and children?"

"She do fine. We have four kids now. New baby girl three months old."

"Congratulations! That's wonderful news. That balances your family, two and two. And you're a runner for Davy?"

He leaned in close and spoke in a whisper. "Major Davy, I call Stargazer."

Gina strained to hear. "You can speak up. Stargazer what . . ."

He spoke a fraction louder. "He ask that I be your runner. I say you, I be honored. You call me when you need me. I go up the mountain fast by horseback or slower with cart. It depends."

Gina's brow furrowed. "Are you sure? With the kids? It's dangerous for you."

"Everything dangerous nowadays." His hand went to an amulet hanging on a leather thong around his neck. "I know the trails Japs not know. They get lost easy. I know caves where to hide. I good shooter with a gun."

The excitement in Miguel's eyes surprised her. He had never seemed the kind of man to live on the edge.

Millie came into the morning room carrying a tray with glasses of iced tea and slices of banana bread. Gina offered Miguel a piece. "Major Davy moves around. How do you find him?"

Miguel waited for Millie to leave the room. "I go to a checkpoint. I have a code. They point the way." He reached into his pocket. "I bring you a letter." He handed it to Gina.

Gina put the precious letter aside. "Thank you. How will I contact you?"

"I give you telephone number. Ask for Flash, like Flash Gordon." He grinned, and Gina did, too, at her laid-back houseboy's alter ego. He reached into another pocket. "When I check your house, I found this on Mr. Ray's nightstand. He gone. I think you want it." He handed her Ray's onyx ring.

"Oh, Miguel. Ray must have left it out. Everything happened in such a rush. How can I thank you?"

"Thank-you not needed. I wish I could have found more for you. Japs are living in your house now."

"That's what I heard. I'd still like to see it."

"No. That not a good idea."

Gina had Millie wrap up a loaf of banana bread for Miguel to take with him. She walked him out. "I'll be moving soon. I'll call you with my new address. Miguel, have you seen Isabella?"

"Yes, ma'am. She lives with her mother and works in a market stall. She sells *anting-anting*." A crocodile-tooth bracelet dangled from Miguel's wrist as he waved goodbye.

A perfect fit for Isabella, working in a market stall selling amulets to protect against evil forces and charms to bring good luck and good health. She called after Miguel, "Tell Isabella I'm glad she's happy, and I wish her well."

～

Gina returned to the morning room and slid Ray's ring onto her thumb. The last time she'd seen it, they had been dancing the rumba at the Jai Alai Club, and she'd teased him about the wiggle of his hips. Though he claimed to have no rhythm, Ray was an adequate dancer and open to practicing intricate steps and nuanced moves that sometimes led to tangles, trips, and peals of laughter. And then there were the nights he'd push the lanai furniture back and put on a record, and they'd dance under the light of the moon, and if Cheryl joined them, they'd circle their private ballroom as a threesome. She wondered if they would ever dance as a threesome again. Slipping off the ring, she read the inscription on the inside of the band. *Forever.* How long was their forever? Had it already slipped away? She sniffed and put aside the ring and her disturbing thoughts. She opened the letter and saw Cheryl's childish scrawl.

> *Dear Mama,*
> *We moved and I cried becuz I was afrad you culd not find*
> *me. Miss Vivian said that you always no where I am. Are*
> *you done in Manila? Can you come and get me?*
> *I love you.*
> *Cheryl*
> *PS Miss Vivian says we have to save paper but I*
> *culd write on the bak of hers.*

Gina put the letter down. A sad plea from a sad little girl. She knew it would take Cheryl time to adjust, and it would be a painful process, but knowing it didn't make living it any easier. Sniffing back tears while fingering the locket that lay close to her heart, she flipped the letter over to read Vivian's message.

> *My friend. We got a report saying you made the trip to*
> *Manila safely, and you are now waiting for a residence*
> *pass. My fingers are crossed for you. We've moved since you*
> *left, and Davy is talking about moving again. We just got*
> *settled, but now hear that patrols are in the area. Cheryl*
> *is a real trooper. She's still crying for you, but she is willing*
> *to accept Maggie's and my hugs and cuddles that settle her*
> *down for periods of time. She's going to be just fine, Gina.*

*Go about your business in Manila with a guiltless heart.
I'll keep you informed of her needs. With that said, this
last move I lost my comb and toothbrush. My little one
needs shoes, size three or four. Anything that will protect
her feet. Maggie and I are both craving something to
read. I miss you terribly. I wish you luck. Viv*

Gina folded the letters. How she yearned to help them, but she was
hidden away in the hacienda. Later, she asked Millie to purchase shoes
for Leah and gave her money from what Marcus had given her. She
asked Franca for books and magazines to send to her friends, and Franca
was more than generous, also donating soap, shampoo, toothpaste, and
personal items. Gina packaged the items into a bag and asked Miguel
to deliver them. It was a start—a very small one, but a start.

When Franca announced that Gina had an appointment with Colonel
Ito at eleven o'clock that morning, Gina choked on her coffee and
coughed until her face turned red.

Franca thumped her back. "Señor Estevez will be representing you.
Just stay calm, and you'll do fine."

Calm wasn't Gina's worry; her own rancor was. Could she face a
senior official of the military police without oozing hostility? Was her
loathing of the Japanese apparent? Would it show on her face? In the
mirror she practiced keeping her body relaxed and her expression bland,
but venom bled from every pore.

Señor Estevez had a bushy mustache, was taller than most Filipino
men, and wore his white suits with style. Gina had met him when she'd
first arrived at the hacienda but had seldom seen him since. She waited
for him in the foyer, and when he arrived, he counseled her to let him
do most of the talking. If Colonel Ito asked her anything, she was to

keep her answers brief. Before getting into the car, he signaled her by putting his finger to his lips and nodding toward the driver. During the short trip, he remained preoccupied with a sheaf of papers. Gina stared out the window and rehearsed her history—born in Milan, raised in Canada.

At the city hall, they sat in a stuffy room crowded with others waiting for their appointments with government officials. Gina covered her nose and mouth with her hand and furtively looked around, thankful not to see old friends, former neighbors, or social acquaintances who could point a finger or blow a whistle. She wiped beads of nervous sweat off her forehead, and by the time she and Señor Estevez were summoned to appear before Colonel Ito, her head was pounding.

"Don't forget to bow," Señor Estevez whispered as they entered the inner chamber.

Colonel Ito sat behind a large desk in a cavernous room, a secretary on one side and an aide on the other. Behind them stood two Rising Sun flags. The colonel was scribbling in a notebook, and Gina, her knees feeling wobbly, detected the scratch of the pen on paper and the tick of the wall clock as the hand jerked one second forward.

After pushing the notebook aside, Colonel Ito lit a cigarette, and Gina desired one of her own to calm the nervous energy that was making her fingertips tingle. He addressed Señor Estevez in heavily accented but understandable English. "What brings you here today?"

"A residence application, sir." The Spaniard told the rehearsed story that Signora Angelina Aleo had left Manila to visit friends on Bataan and had lost her house and papers in the bombing. His voice sounded strong, but he stood stiffly with his hat in his hands. Gina relaxed her face, hoping to give the appearance that this meeting was just another day's errand to run; however, sweat ran in rivulets between her breasts.

Colonel Ito turned and spoke to her. "Where were you born, Signora Aleo?"

"I was born in Milan, Italy, Colonel."

"And what brought you to the Philippines?"

"I came with my husband. He was killed in a mining accident several years ago." She felt a flush of anger rise to her cheeks, knowing the Japanese had killed Ray or imprisoned him, and she prayed the colonel wouldn't see it.

Not taking his eyes off her, the colonel leaned back in his huge chair and folded his hands over his stomach. "I spent a summer in Florence years ago. Beautiful country. Beautiful language. Say something in Italian for me."

She forced a smile. It had been a while since she had spoken Italian, but her grandmother's favorite phrase popped into her mind. "È un buon giorno per avere una buona giornata"; "It's a good day to have a good day." She widened her smile, hoping to win his favor, but his gaze was blank, and she suspected he had not understood a word she'd said.

"Very nice. I like poetry. How is it you speak English without a hint of an accent?"

Gina stopped smiling. Though the tone of his voice was pleasant, the question carried a dark undertone. "I grew up in Vancouver, Canada. I went there to live with my aunt after my parents died. They speak pretty good English in Canada, sir."

Beside her, Señor Estevez's body jerked. The room went quiet, and Gina heard the tick of the clock again. She swallowed hard, wishing she could take back her last words.

Colonel Ito laughed. "They speak pretty good English in Canada."

Others in the room laughed, and Gina let out a breath she hadn't realized she'd been holding.

Colonel Ito became serious again. "Signora Angelina Aleo. You need a means of support. What is it you do?"

Gina stammered, "I—ah . . ."

Señor Estevez intervened. "If I may, sir. I am responsible for Signora Aleo's support until she obtains the proper papers that give her freedom to move around Manila. She has extensive experience in music and dance education. I expect she will very soon become a welcome contributing educator in our new great society."

Gina's jaw dropped in surprise. Señor Estevez had never shown interest in her future plans. She quickly closed her mouth.

Colonel Ito glanced at his watch. "Very well. Signora Aleo, step up here, please, and raise your right hand." He read a short mandate for her to swear to, promising that she would be loyal to Japan and not collaborate with the enemy.

"I promise," Gina said without hesitation, for in her mind she had her own definition of the word *enemy*.

Colonel Ito gave her a residence pass to sign, on which her signature looked oddly wiggly. He countersigned the document, and after final bows, Señor Estevez ushered Gina out of the office.

The ordeal had taken less than fifteen minutes, but Gina felt wilted. Not until she was outside the building did she allow elation to sweep over her. She was rid of the restrictions that had kept her in hiding, and her real work could begin. She couldn't stop grinning, but Señor Estevez's warning pricked her happy bubble.

"You're past a hard step, but you must be vigilant. Wherever you choose to live, you will be spied on by neighborhood sentinels. Any missteps will be reported to the authorities, and you would be picked up for questioning."

Approaching the car, Señor Estevez again motioned for her to be silent. He settled in the back seat, opened his briefcase, and buried his face in a folder of papers. However, at the hacienda, Franca opened a bottle of champagne, and they cheerfully celebrated Gina's freedom and her flexibility to work in the underground.

Chapter 14

ARMIN GABLE

I observe the anguish of others with such a detached lethargy
I fear I've lost my moral compass.

—Ray Thorpe, Cabanatuan prison camp, October 1942–
January 1944

With her residence pass in hand, Gina searched for a place of her own to live, a laborious task, with Japanese soldiers billeted everywhere. Being persistent and not wanting to spend a centavo more than she had to, she found a room. It included a single bed, a couch, a table and chair, a hot plate, and a coffeepot. A window overlooked a small fenced yard. She shared a kitchen, a bathroom, and a hall telephone with two other renters. It wasn't fancy, and it wasn't even clean when she moved in, but the rent was cheap, and it would do.

She found a job working twenty hours a week at a diner. The pay was a pittance, but it helped to not deplete the money Davy and Marcus had given her. She missed Vivian and the way they had shared expenses, responsibilities, and their secrets and longings—and Cheryl, who had always lovingly been underfoot.

⌐⌐

Not long after getting settled and anxious to get on with the task to
which she was assigned, Gina searched through the bureau drawer for
a specific bra and her small scissors. She checked that the blinds were
closed and her door locked, a behavior bordering on obsessive. Keeping
the light only as bright as she needed to see, she picked stitches out of
the bra, separating the outer fabric from the lining, and plucked out the
list of resistance contacts from where she'd hidden them. She selected
three names that sounded familiar—Riker, Almacher, and Gable—and
she memorized the addresses.

The front gate squeaked. Her heart quickening a beat, she listened
closely. She had seen Japanese soldiers come into the yard to pee by the
palm tree. Afraid of a bang on her door and a barked order to open it,
as had happened to a housemate, she quickly refolded the damning list
and tucked it back into the secret pocket and put the bra back in her
drawer. After turning out the light, she sat in the dark, hearing noises
from outside: shuffles, hoots, shouts of halt, dogs barking, a scream of
pain, a siren's wail, a gunshot—nothing out of the ordinary, she was
learning.

⌐⌐

Over morning coffee and a biscuit, Gina practiced her pitch to a Señor
Riker, one of Theo's trusted acquaintances. "Good morning, Señor
Riker. I'm here on behalf of Dr. Theo Parker, a mutual friend. May
I have a moment of your time?" She checked her image in the mirror
before she left her room and hoped she looked credible in her second-
hand clothes.

After summoning a taxi, she gave the driver an address in a neighborhood populated by the city's wealthy businessmen. As he steered
his horse through the neighborhood, she noticed the once-beautiful

yards had lost their gardenlike aspect. Tangles of unkempt yellow bells lined the driveway and walkway of the house belonging to the Rikers. Children's toys littered the front porch, and Gina tripped over a metal truck. Nudging it aside with her foot, she squared her shoulders and rang the bell. After what seemed a long time, a Filipino maid opened the door.

Gina flashed her practiced smile. "Good morning. I'm Signora Aleo. I'm here on behalf of Dr. Theo Parker to see Señor or Señora Riker."

"The Rikers not live here anymore."

"Then I'm sorry to bother you. Do you know where I may reach them?" Gina glimpsed a flash of a kimono and heard a command barked in Japanese. The maid slammed the door shut, and Gina jumped back at the impact. A bit wild eyed, she returned to the waiting taxi. "Did you know Japanese are living here?"

"No, ma'am, but they all over the city."

Her own house was close by, and nostalgia tugged at her. Was her once-pristine neighborhood as shabby as this one? She wondered if Japanese women were wearing the jewelry Ray had given to her for anniversaries and birthdays or just to say he loved her. And if the original paintings she'd coveted and Ray's coin collection had been sent to Japan. On reflection, she decided the risk of being recognized by a neighbor turned sympathizer, however low, outweighed her curiosity. She gave the driver the address to Mr. and Mrs. Almachers'. The name was familiar, and she searched her memory for a connection . . . a charity function? There had been so many.

She rang the bell, and a Filipino maid answered.

"Good morning. I'm Signora Aleo. I'd like to speak to Mr. or Mrs. Almacher on behalf of Major Davy McGowan."

"Yes, ma'am. Wait here, please." The maid closed the door.

Returning, the maid said, "Mrs. Almacher does not know a Davy McGowan. She asks that you leave."

"But maybe her husband . . . ," Gina managed to say before the door closed. Her ire rose, and she mumbled an obscenity before returning to the taxi to contemplate the value of continuing this task. People living in Manila were skittish for good reasons. Raising funds for Davy and Theo, even among their own friends, was going to be harder than she'd anticipated. Well, three was a charm, she thought, and having decided to give it one more try, she gave the driver the third address.

The ride was just long enough for Gina to compose herself and to think about how to readjust her approach. The house was grander than the previous two and unkempt like the others. She looked around for signs of Japanese occupation. Not seeing any, she rang the doorbell. An elderly gentleman with thinning white hair and intense brown eyes answered it. His white linen suit and starched shirt were impeccably tailored but threadbare and too big for his shrunken body.

"Good morning." She affected what she hoped was a warm smile. "I'm Signora Angelina Aleo. I'm here to see Mr. Armin Gable on behalf of Major Davy McGowan, a mutual friend of ours."

The man scanned her up and down and then glanced at the taxi waiting at the curb. "I'm Armin Gable. What do you want?"

"Major McGowan gave me your name, sir. I understand he's a friend. May I please have a moment of your time?"

Mr. Gable led her into his study and motioned for her to sit in an expensively upholstered but well-worn chair. He sat behind a mahogany desk piled with books and papers. Artfully arranged on the wall behind him were a dozen photographs of Mr. Gable shaking hands with various legislators and military commanders, some from the previous war. Prominently displayed was a shadow box holding a 1924 Olympic gold medal. She was feeling hopeful for a successful encounter.

"How do you know Davy?" he asked in a raspy voice.

Gina brought her focus back to him. "Our children were in the same class at school. I worked on school committees with his wife."

Mr. Gable half closed his eyes. "Aleo, Italian, but not raised in Italy. Your husband's name perhaps. Do I detect an American inflection in your speech?"

Gina's eyes blinked rapidly, and she took note that the frail man had a discerning ear. "No, sir. My parents were from Italy. They died when I was seven, and I went to live with my aunt in Canada. I've never been in the United States. I came to the Philippines with my husband, Ricardo Aleo. He was from Italy, and we met when he was traveling through Canada. He swept me off my feet, so to speak. He died in a mining accident soon after our daughter was born." The lies rolled off her tongue.

Mr. Gable continued to gaze at her. "I've seen you before . . . at the Alcazar Club, November 1930. You sang 'Pirate Jenny' from *The Threepenny Opera*. Not bad, if I remember correctly." He displayed a wide grin of yellowed teeth.

Rattled by this turn of conversation and his steel-trap memory, Gina struggled not to squirm under his gaze. "Yes, sir. I'm impressed. How did you remember?"

"Voice. Body movement. A person gives away a lot without realizing it. You're quite transparent."

That wasn't what Gina wanted to hear, and she tilted her chin up to mask a sinking feeling. "I worked at the Alcazar for a while after my husband died, but it's neither here nor there. Today I'm here on Davy McGowan's behalf."

"Yes, Davy. When my wife died, I lost track of him and . . . what is his wife's name?"

"Sissy," Gina said, suspecting that he already knew.

"A nice woman. What happened to them?"

"She's interned at Santo Tomas with their son, Harry. Davy was captured by the Japanese and left for dead by the side of the road. He's hiding in the mountains." She felt buoyed by Mr. Gable's interest.

"Davy organized a guerrilla unit to harass the Japanese, and he needs support. He gave me your name as someone who would help."

"I see. So that's why you're here, asking for money. How do I know what you're saying is true? Do you have a letter of introduction from Davy? One written in his own hand?"

She didn't. She hadn't even thought of it, and that was a mistake. "No, but what I do have are the names of good friends, like yourself, who might be willing to help him."

"Names the Kempeitai would like to see for sure. Just how many doors have you knocked on this morning identifying yourself and those you're supposedly helping?" He tapped his fingers on the desk. "Young lady. You aren't ready for this kind of work. Do you have any idea what you're getting into? Imprisonment, torture, death . . . a quick one if you're lucky."

Not ready! Gina's rising frustration overflowed. She jumped up, and the chair toppled and banged on the floor. "I realize exactly what I'm getting into. I'm intimately familiar with what the Japanese do. I was in the town of Pilar when they marched our half-dead troops through there, and I saw what the Japs did to them. Now thousands of Americans—men, women, and children—are hiding in those mountains living in the direst conditions. They need food, clothing, blankets, and weapons to fight the Japanese. If you're not interested in helping, I'll find someone who is. Now, if you'll excuse me." She tried to leave but ran into a uniformed maid who was blocking the doorway.

"Stop," Mr. Gable ordered. "Sit down."

Gina stayed, but she defiantly remained standing while the maid put down a bamboo tray with glasses of iced tea and then righted the chair.

Mr. Gable remained unruffled by Gina's outburst. "A bit of a spitfire, aren't you? You'll have to curb that, or you'll find yourself in trouble. Sit down."

This time she obeyed and sat with her arms crossed, questioning whose side of the war this man was on. The thought made the back of her neck prickle.

"You come into my house and ask me for money without offering proof of what you claim. You may be a Japanese sympathizer."

"I'm—" she started to protest, but he held up his hand.

"I know who you are. You played your hand several times in the last few minutes. At least one of your parents was Italian. Your speech idioms are from the United States—West Coast, Seattle, or Portland. You came to Manila a single woman, most likely with an entertainment troupe, and met your husband here. He never worked in the mines, and I suspect you're not a widow, at least not yet."

Gina tilted her head up and stared down her nose at him. "Everything you said is a guess. How could you possibly know anything about me?"

"You told me yourself. If your husband died after your daughter was born, and if she is in the same class in school as Davy's son, that would have been 1936, not 1930. Furthermore, if you were married to a miner in 1930, you would have been holed up in some mining town in the mountains, not singing at the Alcazar. Shall I go on?"

Her face paled as she listened to him unraveling her lies. With a dread rising inside her but needing to hear it, she nodded.

"The calluses on your hands tell me you have recently been living a hard life, so I believe you were in the mountains, and you may have run into Davy McGowan."

She folded her hands to hide the few calluses that hadn't yet softened.

His glare held contempt. "Haven't you been warned about revealing too much information? It will trip you up every time."

"Yes, I have. Señor Estevez—"

His voice rose again. "Never reveal a name! Until you learn to hold your temper and control your penchant for blurting out whatever is in your head, you are a danger to Davy and anyone else who needs covert support." He flipped his hand in dismissal. "You can go now."

She stood with her arms down and fists clenched like a child being chastised. "But Davy—"

He flipped his hand again and turned his back.

Gina slunk out of his house and into the taxi, thinking he was right. She didn't understand the ways of the new Manila, and she was not ready, but worse, not suited for the work she had been tasked to do. Her fund-raising skills, which had once brought her accolades, now were a detriment, and she could put others in danger with her naivete. Rocking with the rhythm of the clip-clopping horse, she ruminated—she had made all the wrong decisions. How could she have been so stupid? Embarrassed and tearful, she wanted to curl up and hide.

Chapter 15
GETTING STARTED

*My hand goes to today's meal, a chunk of bread in my pocket.
It brings me great consternation . . . shall I eat the ration
immediately to quell my worst hunger pangs or divide it into
discrete fare and risk its theft?*

—Ray Thorpe, Cabanatuan prison camp, October 1942–
January 1944

In the morning Gina woke up in a dark mood, and her hand went to the half-heart locket. She missed her daughter and wanted her back. Worse, she was surrounded by Japanese soldiers of whom she was terrified. Vivian had tried to warn her. Why hadn't she listened?

She picked up the morning newspaper and read the headline: Supply Ship Arrives with Aid for the Philippine People. "Rubbish," she muttered. The Philippines were being pillaged; every day loads of stolen wares and hundreds of pounds of rice and beans were trucked to the docks to be sent to Tokyo. No wonder prices were so high.

If she couldn't raise funds for Davy, at least she could work for him. She needed another job. In this morning's paper there were two ads for cooks, and she circled them, but being a cook would be her last resort. A promising ad caught her eye. Rosa's Cabaret was auditioning singers from eleven to one o'clock today. It was a job she could do, but 'it would be risky, increasing her exposure in the city. She jotted down the address. No harm in checking it out. She looked at the clock. She had two hours.

It had been a while since she had sung for anyone other than family and friends. She spent some time vocalizing scales and sang "I've Got a Feeling I'm Falling," a catchy tune with a good dance beat, pretending she was facing an audience.

She arranged her hair, pulling one side back and clipping it with a barrette. The only makeup she had was a lipstick, which she applied, and then she rubbed some on her cheeks and softened it with a dusting of talcum powder. After evaluating her image in the mirror, she darkened the rouge on her cheeks slightly, hoping it masked the toll of thirty-four years.

Dressing for an audition from the selection in her closet was tricky. All she had was her waitress uniform, which she'd had to purchase; an aide's uniform she wore when she volunteered at Remedios Hospital; and the dresses, slacks, and blouses she had been given from the charity shop. She selected a pale linen dress that complemented her dark coloring and left the top buttons open to show a bit of cleavage. The only heeled shoes she owned were from the charity closet, too, and a size too small. She peered in a mirror. *Not too bad*, she decided. Her face was not as dewy as it had once been, but her body was taut from the long treks in the mountains.

While riding in the calesa, she practiced breathing exercises to steady her nerves. The calesa stopped at Rosa's Cabaret, which sat between Yee's Chinese Restaurant and Irma's Bakery. Gina felt sweat trickle down the back of her neck as she stepped into Rosa's, the lobby full of, she guessed, nineteen-year-olds. She filled out the application and sat down in the first empty chair to get off her feet, feeling very much like someone's great-aunt.

Once started, the auditions went quickly—a girl called into an inner room, the sound of a piano, and a short vocal that Gina would evaluate: off key, thin, squeaky, not bad, very nice. Most girls slumped out with mascara leaving black streaks on their faces, and Gina assessed them as they walked by: too heavy, bad complexion, not too bad. Her name was called. Feeling every eye was on her, she pretended to be the queen of the swanky Alcazar Club as she entered the inner room.

It was drab and stank of beer and cheap perfume. Cigarette-scarred tables were scattered haphazardly around. A trim woman with hair the color of straw and wearing slacks and a loose-fitting blouse sat alone at a table facing a small stage. In her hand was Gina's application. She spoke with a German accent. "I'm Rosa Engelhard. Let's see what you can do." She pointed toward the stage, where a pencil-thin man sat at an old upright piano.

"Your music?" He extended his hand.

"I didn't bring any. Can you play 'I've Got a Feeling I'm Falling' in G major?"

He nodded and played a few bars. Gina snapped her fingers in time to the music. As she calmed down, the voice she had always relied on materialized: full, on pitch, and as smooth as silk. Moving around the stage, she sang to the audience of one as if it were a roomful.

Rosa motioned for her to stop and jotted down a note on Gina's application. "I'll be contacting my choice in a few days. Thank you for coming in." She dismissed Gina with a wave of her hand.

On the way out, Gina perceived the others watching. *Too old*, she knew the young girls were thinking. *Probably so*, she thought, let down by the quick dismissal.

⌒

At home, the shoes came off first; then she plucked off the barrette and shook out her hair. The linen dress got replaced by the aide's uniform.

She was due to volunteer at Remedios Hospital, an obligation she had made to Father Morgan. Establishing a rapport with him and Dr. Lopez worked to her advantage, both being on Davy's list of those who worked with them in the underground.

Volunteers were picking up lunch trays; cutlery and dishes clinked and clanked as they were transferred, and the smell of banana pudding lingered. She was scheduled to work with Dr. Lopez in Emergency, which meant filling out forms and cleaning and restocking the room after its use.

She found Dr. Lopez alone in the treatment room, covering the body of a young Filipino who had been left on the hospital doorstep more dead than alive. While jotting on the chart, the doctor said, "This city's a brutal place. Have you ever thought about going back to the mountains?"

She sensed his weariness. "No. You can't get away from brutal these days. I have a doctor friend who's working with the guerrillas. You know him; he was on staff at Philippine General. Dr. Theo Parker."

Dr. Lopez's head snapped up. "Theo?"

"Yes. He lived next door to me. His wife, Vivian, is my best friend. Theo's why I'm here. He runs a clinic of sorts . . . if you can call a hut in a guerrilla camp a clinic." She detected an understanding in Dr. Lopez's expression.

An orderly arrived and wheeled the body away, and Gina began to gather up bloody sheets and instruments. Dr. Lopez stopped her. "No one is in the waiting room. Tell me more about Theo."

She told him Theo had been with the Ninety-First Field Hospital on Bataan when the Japanese had captured the peninsula and how he had rescued her, Vivian, and the girls on the day of the death march. "He left us at the Ramos Ranch and came back to Manila for supplies. He had to stay in hiding while he was in the city. My maid helped him out."

"I remember. I didn't see him, but I knew he was here. I gave him as much as I could without raising suspicion. Where is he now?"

"Higher up in the mountains. He met up with Major Davy McGowan. I think you know Davy. What started out as a small group of refugees turned into a guerrilla camp. Davy and Theo sent me here to raise money to support them."

"Why didn't I know? And how's it going?"

She shrugged. "Slow. I'm just starting. Maybe you'd like to help him out again?"

Dr. Lopez appraised her for a long moment as if he were thinking an idea through. "How do you send money to him?"

"I have a runner."

"You trust him?"

"Yes. Without a doubt."

He took a wad of cash from his pocket and peeled off a few notes. "Tell you what. Send this cash to Theo and have him send a letter back stating he got it and information about what he's doing. I'll show the letter to my colleagues. They'll be glad to support him. Theo has many friends."

That evening Gina put together a package of various necessities for Vivian and Edna, a deck of old maid for Cheryl and Leah, and the money for Theo from Dr. Lopez with instructions to return a letter of receipt. After contacting Miguel, she added a note to Vivian.

Hope the enclosed helps out. Should be able to get more to you soon. Especially lonesome for Cheryl tonight. I miss her hugs and chatter. Making important contacts. Auditioned for a new job. Sending my love to all. Kiss Cheryl for me. G.

Chapter 16

ROSA'S CABARET

Thoughts of escape never leave me. I plot. I plan. I try to dupe myself into believing I wouldn't care that nine innocents would die horribly in my stead. I stay.

—Ray Thorpe, Cabanatuan prison camp, October 1942–
January 1944

Gina awoke to a knock on her door. She had a call on the shared telephone in the hall. She looked at the clock, which read 11:15 p.m. Groggy, she stumbled to answer it. The caller was Rosa Engelhard. Her voice sounded husky.

"Angelina, this is Rosa. I'd like to offer you a job at the cabaret. You'd be working four nights a week from six to eleven. You'd need a slinky dress, and be prepared to sing two sets, six songs. Could you start tomorrow night?"

The pay she offered was good, plus tips, and the hours wouldn't conflict with her job at the diner. Gina didn't have a dress or appropriate shoes or sheet music for one song, much less six, and the time to prepare was short. Afraid if she said no, the job would disappear, she accepted it.

When she hung up, her thoughts whirled. After all the years away from the stage, could she pull this off, or had the entertainment world, where once she was so successful, changed too? She barely slept that night, song fragments dominating her fractured dreams.

～

She needed a dress and shoes that she neither could afford nor wanted to spend a single peso on. Chan's and Heacock's would be expensive. Instead she'd try Malate Church's charity closet. The skirt she was wearing was from there, and though slightly worn, it was finely made.

Two women were sorting clothing by sex, size, and condition. Gina nodded hello, then went about her business looking for something slinky, as Rosa had suggested. There wasn't anything like that, but she did find a black silk sarong patterned with red, pink, and white flowers and green vines. It was really quite beautiful, and the only flaw she found was a frayed seam at the hemline, an easy fix with a needle and thread. She paired it with red strappy heels, and she wondered whether the sarong and shoes had been donated together. By a shelf of books she found a box of sheet music and selected six songs she already knew. Keeping her focus, she avoided the children's department. That would be for another day. On her way out she left a peso in the donation box.

Makeup for her cheeks and eyes, which she'd not worn since returning to Manila, was an expense she couldn't avoid, but at the *sari-sari* store she kept the purchase to a minimum, her only splurge a bottle of red nail polish for her fingers and toes.

～

Gina arrived at the cabaret early, carrying a long linen bag containing the sarong. Her grocery tote held her makeup, music, shoes, and a gardenia for her hair, clipped off the tree in her yard. She found Rosa

Engelhard seated at a desk in a small, smoke-filled office, brushing dandruff off the shoulders of her exquisitely tailored gray suit. On her finger she wore a huge diamond-and-ruby ring that reminded Gina of her own expensive jewelry now lost to her. She motioned Gina to a chair. "Thank you for coming in on short notice."

"It was no problem," Gina answered in a voice she hoped sounded controlled.

All business, Rosa continued. "You'll work four nights a week and do two sets each night. Between sets I expect you to mingle with the customers . . . chat them up, push the drinks. I'll pay you in cash at the end of each night, plus you keep any tips you get. We open at six o'clock and close at eleven, so you'll have time to get home before curfew. I'm going to promote you as Angelina D'Licious."

"What?" Gina choked on the moniker. "No! I'm not a . . . a . . . D'Licious anything."

"It brings the customers in. Take it or leave it."

Gina contemplated her weak position. It was a paycheck, and if it panned out, she could send Davy money every week. "All right," she agreed, but she tasted bile.

Rosa reached for a ring full of keys. "Come with me; I'll take you to the dressing room." Rosa minced toward the door in too-high-heeled shoes. Gina, still stinging from the name change, grabbed her purse and dress and followed.

Feathery boas in pinks, greens, and blues; outrageous oversize hats; sequined masks; and even a leather whip hung on hooks along one wall of the dressing room. Tables held jars, pots, pencils, and tubes labeled Max Factor and Elizabeth Arden. The lights, vivid colors, and familiar odors took Gina back in time to her whirlwind years with the Follies.

Rosa hollered over the chatter of a half dozen women. "Listen up, everyone. This is Angelina D'Licious, our new singer. Be nice and give her some room at the dressing tables."

Gina heard a few snickers and felt the critical stares of the women passing judgment on her hair, skin, figure, and pale-blue blouse from the charity closet. She smiled and tried to appear nonplussed by their evaluations. "Pleasure to meet you," she muttered.

There was a chorus of welcomes and hellos in different languages and accents, and then the women returned to their own preparations, several struggling to squeeze their curvaceous bodies into identical glittery red-and-gold chemises cut low to expose pushed-up cleavages. Garters that dangled from under black ruffled panties held up thigh-high stockings. Stacked nearby were red-and-gold-sequined top hats. As the women dressed, some chattered about dates gone sour, tight shoes, and sore feet.

Rosa pointed to a metal locker and handed Gina a key she took off the ring. "You can keep your things in here. A bell will ding three times five minutes before you're to be onstage. Keep track of where you are on the schedule. Don't be late, ever. You stay until the last act is finished, in case I need a fill-in. If you don't show up for work, you're fired."

A skinny young man wearing a black-and-yellow-striped sports coat, a white shirt, and a green bow tie entered the dressing room, and Gina recognized him as the pianist who'd played at her audition.

"Rosa," he yelled, "the Chinaman's here to see you."

Rosa turned to Gina. "You remember Julio, don't you? He'll finish showing you around." She tottered out on her too-tall shoes.

Gina hung her sarong in the locker, thinking it might be too sophisticated for this tacky venue, with its bevy of beaded and bangled cabaret entertainers.

"So you're the new girl." Julio looked her up and down. "I'm surprised. I remember you from the audition. I thought you a little highbrow for this joint."

"Highbrow?" She chortled, thinking back to the months she had lived in a nipa hut. She thought that experience had humbled her.

"Yeah. There's a certain air about you. Never mind. You'll do fine." He swung his arm toward the door. "Come with me, madame." He talked fast and walked faster, and she trotted along beside him. "You'll enter here, stage right." He led her past the moth-eaten stage curtain.

She noted the scarred floors. Everything looked worn, and the whole place smelled musty. Peering into the theater, she saw the same disarray of tables and chairs as when she'd auditioned and was surprised the room hadn't been cleaned up for the show. Maybe Julio was right. She was a bit of a snob, an attitude left over from years of working in classier places. She saw Chan, her Chinese tailor, standing at the back of the theater talking animatedly to Rosa, a strange place for him to be, she thought. "Do you know him?"

"Yes. Yee Chan. He owns this building. Did you bring your music?" Julio slid onto the piano bench.

"Yes, it's in my bag."

"That's okay. What's your first number?"

"'Put Your Arms around Me, Honey.'"

"Good choice." Julio played a few chords. "I can follow you. The mic's over there." He bobbed his head toward the microphone on its stand. "Go ahead. Give it a whirl."

It took Gina a moment to figure out the microphone. Once she had, Julio played a few bars of the chorus, and she began to sing. Heads poked into the theater to check out the new girl, and they clapped when she finished. She smiled and bowed and then turned to Julio. "Thank you. That breaks the ice. How many other musicians are there?" She didn't see any evidence of a band.

"No others. Just me. Were you expecting more?"

"Well, maybe one or two."

"Hey. I can make this old upright sound like an orchestra." He showed Gina a mouth organ that hung around his neck and a unique drum he kept under one foot. "Chinwag with the audience during your set, and I'll respond with the piano now and then. You've been around. You know the shtick."

Gina nodded hesitatingly. She knew the shtick from a long time ago, a skill she could only hope would come back quickly.

Backstage, Julio pointed out the lavatories, the stage door, and the night's schedule, which was tacked to the wall. "You'll be going on after Inez and Arielle, our hula dancers. Just so you're not surprised, the crowd—"

Julio was almost mowed down by a woman wearing a rose satin bra and floral sarong wrap skirt. Her shiny black hair hung in waves to her waist, and the scent of jasmine lingered behind her. Julio jumped out of her path. "Speak of the devil, that's Arielle. She's always in a hurry. I'll introduce you later. Hey, Sammy," he called to a man wearing a top hat and tails, "come over here and meet Angelina, our new singer; she's fantastic, a cut above the rest of you freaks."

Gina gasped, but the magician laughed and produced a red flower out of the air and handed it to her.

"Thank you. You're very quick." She tucked the flower behind her ear.

Recorded music, a lively dance tune, began to play over the PA system. Julio, seemingly unable to stand still, soft-shoed to the beat, and Gina admired his abundant energy.

"That tune signals that the doors are opening and the party's about to start. You'd better get yourself ready."

Back at the dressing room, the women in red-and-gold chemises and sequined top hats were scurrying out of the door. Gina stepped back to let them pass by before entering the now less crowded room. She saw Arielle with a needle and thread repairing a broken bra strap, and sitting beside her, dressed in a similar costume, was Inez, Gina guessed. Both were beautiful Filipino girls with dewy skin and burnt-almond eyes.

"Welcome," Inez said. "Great job out there, Angelina. You'll knock 'em dead."

"Thank you. Please call me Gina."

Arielle and Inez went back to their last-minute preparations, brightening their lips and cheeks and slipping leis of pink-and-yellow plumeria around their heads, necks, and ankles.

The flurry of preperformance preparation helped calm Gina's first-night apprehensions. Upon retrieving her makeup from her tote and settling at a dressing table, she peered into a mirror, seeing that her eyes sparkled and her cheeks were pink. *A good start.* She darkened her lids and lashes and applied rouge to her cheeks. Siren-red lipstick added more color. *Still a little pale.* She patted glitter along her cheekbones. *Better.* Pushing one side of her hair back, she clipped it in place with a barrette and then pinned in the gardenia. *Good enough.* She then slipped into her beautiful sarong and strappy red shoes.

Inez was watching her. "Are you new to Manila? I haven't seen you around."

Wary of personal questions, Gina remained vague, a stretch for her usually friendly manner. "No, but I just started working again. It's been a few years."

The call bell dinged for Arielle and Inez, and they hurried out, their tawny skin glistening, black hair swinging, and dark eyes shining huge under layers of purple shadow and dazzling pink highlighter.

Gina overheard: "Did Julio warn her about the crowd?"

"I'm sure she knows."

Gina wondered what she needed to know. Was it a rowdy bunch? She'd faced unruly audiences before, but not without beefy security men standing by. Jitters were threatening to dry out her throat, not a good thing before going onstage, and she sipped water from the jug on the side table.

A pixie-faced woman came into the dressing room, took off her sequined hat, and flung it on the chair. "You're on next, hon. Knock 'em dead."

"Thanks. I'll try. Um . . . is there something I should know about the audience?"

Pixie-Face fluffed her flattened hair. "Just the usual SOBs. Don't let them get under your skin. If they sense you're nervous, they'll heckle the hell outa ya."

"Thanks. I won't." Gina left the dressing room feeling more confident. She knew all about hecklers.

At the stage entrance she peeked from behind the dusty blue curtain and watched Inez and Arielle dance a slow, sensual hula to the hollow beat of tribal drums and the wailing vibrato of steel guitars. She let her body sway in unison with theirs, remembering the motions from her years with the Follies.

The music stopped, and as the dancers exited the stage, Julio came to Gina's side. "Here we go. First I need to push the piano into place; then I'll play a few measures of your song and introduce you. Hey, don't look so worried. You'll do fine." He straightened his green bow tie and stepped onto the stage.

Gina listened for her cue, soon hearing the first bars of "Put Your Arms around Me, Honey," and Julio bellowing over a background of jabber: "Give a rousing welcome to Rosa Cabaret's newest songster, the most delightful and delectable Miss Angelina D'Licious."

To the clamor and whistles of a rowdy crowd, Gina swirled out from behind the curtain ready to woo them as she had done on stages around the world, absorbing their energy and feeding it back. There was no other feeling like it, and in this minute she realized how much she had missed it.

Julio winked, and with her smile open and wide, she spun to face them and saw a room packed with Japanese soldiers, their arms reaching toward her, their eyes leering, their mouths grinning and yammering. One tried to jump on the stage, and fear descended so fast it swept her breath away.

She placed her hand on the piano to steady herself and gaped at Julio, who nodded encouragingly and played the introductory bars of music again. But Gina's mind stayed blank, and her jaw locked.

In his raspy baritone, Julio sang the first lines of the song: "Nighttime is falling; everything is still. Cupid is calling every Jack and Jill . . ."

Hearing the lyrics brought Gina out of her shocked state, but her usually graceful movements were bizarrely jerky and her smile oddly skewed. She continued the song, her voice thin, warbling from her constricted throat. When done, she couldn't think of a single thing to say to the mass of leering faces an arm's length away. Her gaze darted to Julio, who played grand flourishes on the piano and segued into the second song. Gina stood dumbstruck. The audience turned ugly, booing and heckling. Her insides churning, she stumbled off the stage and out the back door. Gulping in the fog heavy air, she folded her arms tightly over her stomach to control convulsing tremors. Weak kneed, she leaned against a fence post.

Inez appeared with a glass of water in one hand and a bottle of whiskey in the other. She handed the water to Gina. "Heaven help you. Are you okay?"

Gina sipped the water, not feeling okay, her heart still pounding so hard she felt the pulse in her ears. "Yes," she said through gasps. "I'm just a little sick. It must have been the chicken I ate. I'm more embarrassed than anything." She accepted the cigarette that Inez offered and the whiskey that she poured into Gina's water glass.

Inez talked in a voice just above a whisper. "It's the Nips, isn't it?"

Gina focused her gaze on Inez, who was stunningly exotic and with an imperial guise, the descendant of an ancient ruler, perhaps. Afraid to compromise her newly adopted cover, an expat of Italian descent, Gina drew deeply on her cigarette. "I have no problems with the Japanese. Why should I?"

"Have it your way, then." Inez stepped toward the door.

"Wait! If the Japanese trouble you, why do you work here?"

"You're kidding."

"No. Tell me. I want to know." Gina's voice broke.

"The lack of options. My teaching degree isn't worth a pittance since the Japanese took over the schools. I was a dance minor, so luckily I have my talent to fall back on. I feel fortunate to even have a job. You auditioned. You saw the line of wannabes."

Inez started to leave, but Gina stopped her. "How can you mingle with them?"

Inez turned toward her. "I've steeled myself not to care who's in the audience. You can't get away from the Japs, Gina. The buggers have infested Manila, and this dump is no worse than other places I've worked. Stay around long enough and you develop a shell. You learn they're just men away from their women. They're horny and depressed. If you're smart, you learn to play on their emotions, smile a lot, befriend them, and then use them for your own benefit. It takes the sting out."

Gina stood openmouthed, contemplating this woman with a beautiful face and tough inner core. Did she not know the cruelties and perversions of the beasts she was entertaining?

Inez smirked and handed her the whiskey bottle. "You're full of hate like the rest of us. It's written all over your face and in the tightness of your body. To survive in Manila, you'd better learn to hide that real quick." Inez disappeared inside.

A documentary of atrocities rolled through Gina's thoughts, and she cried to the closed door, "I will never, ever, in a thousand years befriend those butchers!" She heard the words in her head: *You'll be surprised at what you will do.* She glanced around, but she was alone in the alley.

Through a boozy haze, Gina finished her second set, and afterward she shadowed Inez and noted how she worked the tables. "You're too smart for your britches," Inez cooed to a grinning Japanese officer. She plied the bleary-eyed man with more beer and silly talk, stroking his fingers and murmuring, "I like men with strong hands." They both snickered, he relishing the attention and flattery from a beautiful woman and she tucking money into her satin bra.

On the ride home, with her thoughts reeling, head pounding, and stomach sour, Gina considered her options. No matter the path, she'd have to manage her fear of the Japanese in order to work in occupied Manila. As the horse clip-clopped along in a hypnotizing rhythm, her direction became clearer. She would follow Inez's lead, disguise her hate behind a bodacious smile, and use the Japanese, their power, their knowledge, and their pockets full of money to support Davy's guerrillas.

Chapter 17
TROUBLE FOUND

*Never arouse me from the throes of a nightmare, for nothing
is ghastlier than waking to this reality.*

—*Ray Thorpe, Cabanatuan prison camp, October 1942–*
January 1944

Gina didn't realize how difficult it would be to mask her true feelings,
how much energy it would take, or how easy it was to brood and forget
to flash her bodacious smile. The first weeks after accepting the job at
Rosa's Cabaret, she didn't sleep; despite the numerous baths taken, the
tedious number of sheep counted, and the anesthetizing effects of the
alcohol imbibed, she remained anxious, fearful, and wide eyed, tossing
and turning in her bed. Dark circles appeared beneath her eyes that
makeup didn't camouflage, and not having an appetite, she noticed her
dresses fit looser.

The second time her mind went blank and she forgot the words
to the song she was performing, Julio took her aside. "I didn't expect
this of you."

"And just what did you expect?" she snapped and turned away to hide her humiliation.

"More savoir faire." He grabbed her arm. "You're worldlier than most of these yahoos. What's going on? Are you ill?"

His face, long and handsome, attested to his Spanish ancestry. He was always ready to help, and he played the hell out of the old beat-up piano. "No, I'm not ill." But then she confessed, "I've lost some friends, and I can't . . ." She checked herself before saying more. What did she really know about Julio, except that he seemed like a nice guy? "Never mind; I'm just overtired."

"Ah. Tired. It's an easy fix." He showed her a bottle of pills he took from his pocket.

She peered at the Japanese label. "What is it?"

"Philopon. Methamphetamine. The Japs gobble them like candy." He opened the bottle. "Here, take one. It'll perk you up."

Gina stepped back. She should have recognized the source of his mood swings and erratic, high-energy behavior. "No. I never take anything stronger than aspirin."

"Your call. But there's no reason to suffer."

She saw Rosa standing at the back of the room. After Gina's disastrous first night, Rosa had called Gina into her office for *a talk* and told her to shape up or move on. Needing money for rent, food, and clothing and to support her friends in the mountains, Gina couldn't afford to be on Rosa's bad side.

She tried to take a deep breath, but it felt like a band of steel kept her chest from expanding. Gazing at the bottle of potent energy pills Julio was holding, Gina wavered. What was one little pill? She held out her hand, and Julio shook half the bottle into it. She swallowed one with a sip of water. The restriction of her breathing soon disappeared, and she sang her second set robustly, and then she joined Inez at the tables and dazzled the patrons with her sharp wit and wisdom.

Later, at home, she completed the household tasks she had not gotten around to and then baked a batch of cookies for her housemates using the last of the rationed sugar . . . but that was a worry for later. She crashed on the couch around noon and woke up just in time to go to bed for the night, waking in the morning to a wave of paranoia. Terrified, she retrieved the pills to flush them down the toilet, but remembering the Japanese audience she'd be facing that night, she put them back in her purse.

⌒

While Inez was tutoring Gina in the craft of manipulating the Japanese, the two became friends. Inez had a son the same age as Cheryl named Rizal.

"He's named after José Rizal," Inez said, "a poet, a doctor, a hero, and my great-grandfather. He was executed in 1896 for leading a revolution against Spain's rule." She contemplated for a minute. "He was only thirty-five . . . same age as my husband is now."

"Where is your husband, Inez?"

"He's with the army on Mindanao, the island south of Luzon. I haven't heard from him in a while."

"I'm sorry," Gina said. "It must be very hard on you." She knew she was speaking for herself too. Not a day went by when thoughts of Ray didn't cross her mind.

Arielle, Inez's younger cousin, was as vivacious as Inez was circumspect. Gina learned that underneath her vibrant exterior, she was mourning her brother, who had been killed on the forced march, and pining for her American husband, who was imprisoned in Cabanatuan.

"I have a friend who might be there." Gina kept her inquiry vague, having professed to be a widow. "Is there a way I can find out for sure?"

Arielle shook her head. "The place is locked down. Nothing gets in. Nothing comes out. I want to send my husband money. I haven't found how to do it." She sniffed. "But I will."

The two women were able teachers, and between them and Julio's ready supply of Philopon, Gina was able to hide her feelings and work the tables with a degree of aplomb. She soon had the customers pigeonholed into categories: the uncomfortable Filipino nationals who mistakenly wandered in; the rude and rough Japanese soldiers, sailors, and civilians, the mainstay of the clientele; and the Japanese naval officers just off their ships and wanting to be entertained. Gina gravitated toward the naval officers, who were older, more refined, and more generous with their money, which she funneled to the guerrillas.

She found the entertainment at Rosa's Cabaret lackluster and vaudeville-like, with a variety of acts. The most popular performers were the dancers, Inez and Arielle, and also a husband-and-wife team whose routine was more acrobatic. Second in the popularity contest that Gina held in her own mind were the musicians, like herself and the Harmonies, a trio of singing sisters. With his high energy, Julio was in demand, engaging the audience, starting his set with something flourishing like "Rhapsody in Blue" and then taking requests. He seemed to know every song that had ever been recorded, and the crowd, if boozed up enough, sang along. She learned he had studied music at Silliman University on Negros, an island south of Luzon. The audience ignored the string of ventriloquists and their grinning dummies, magicians in top hats, and comedians who told off-color jokes that the Japanese never got.

Though not very creative, Rosa proved to be a tireless business-woman, greeting every customer at the door and lavishing personal attention on them throughout the night while overseeing the bar, the cash flow, and her staff. She was always stylishly dressed in beautifully tailored clothes and had a penchant for gaudy jewelry. She was married to a German businessman, but she had a paramour, Arielle told Gina, a member of the Kempeitai, an on-again and off-again relationship that dictated her moods. Tonight Rosa directed Gina to attend to a Japanese naval commander sitting alone at a table and nursing a beer.

He was young for an officer, his face smooth and skin tight. Gina stopped at the bar for her usual drink, a bubbling ginger ale served in a martini glass, and another beer for the officer. A Philopon boosting her daring, her insides didn't quake when she approached him. She forced a smile, placed the drinks on the table, slid into a chair, and started her well-practiced teasing. "What's a handsome man like you doing sitting alone? You don't have any friends?"

He grinned, showing a chipped tooth. "Not as pretty as you." Already a bit tipsy, he slurred his words and reached out and touched her arm.

She fought against showing revulsion for this man, who represented evil and death, his touch as lurid as a gash. "I don't believe that. There are many pretty women in Manila. I bet a strong young man like you plays sports. Do you like jai alai? I could reserve a court time." She slid her arm away.

He frowned at the rebuff and reached for a cigarette. "I have no time for games. I'm shipping out the day after tomorrow."

"But you could come back to visit." She provided him a light, the flame reflecting in the dark of his eye. "Maybe we could get to know each other better then."

He sat back, smiled, and blew out a stream of smoke. "I like that, but it's not for me. I'm taking my men to Lingayen Gulf. It's too far away to visit."

She faked disappointment. "What's an important man like you doing stationed way out there?"

"Lingayen Gulf is heavily fortified." He sat up, making himself look taller. "I have several hundred men under my command."

"I don't believe you," Gina teased. "You're too young to be so important. You must be very smart."

Inez brought a dish of peanuts to the table and sat with them.

As usual Inez's presence was well timed. "Inez, would you believe that this handsome officer is old enough to have several hundred men under his command?"

"Four hundred," the officer interjected.

Gina addressed Inez. "Don't you think it's a shame . . . he's going to be stationed in Lingayen Gulf. He should be here, where the action is."

"It's heavily fortified," the soldier repeated. "Thirty thousand men are there."

Gina and Inez continued the flattery and cajoling of the talkative young officer, who needed to boost his importance in the presence of the inconsequential bar girls. However, it was not lost on Gina that thirty thousand Japanese soldiers fortifying Lingayen Gulf might be information General MacArthur would like to know.

In the morning she put together a package including a few things requested by Vivian; a miniscule amount of money for Davy, all she could give; and the information about Lingayen Gulf.

Many customers were young and exuberant, in port for a few days, and seeking a fun time. Others were in port for a longer term, waiting for orders or for their battle-scarred ships to be repaired in dry dock. Inez pointed to a table of three newly arrived Japanese officers. "The good-looking one has been here a few times. Seems he's a fan of yours. I asked around. His name is Tanaka, Admiral Akia Tanaka. Go over and say hello."

Gina hadn't known she had a fan, and she was impressed that he was an admiral. She sauntered over to the table. The Harmonies were singing a boogie-woogie, and she had to shout. "What can I get for you gentlemen?"

All three ordered a beer.

When she returned with their order, the Harmonies had finished their set. The other two officers nodded and clapped, but Admiral Tanaka remained unresponsive.

"You're not a fan of boogie?" She noticed he was a handsome man, his hair thick and stylishly cut, his face fine boned, and his features even.

He replied in English without a hint of an accent. "I'm not a fan of noise. If you must shout for us to hear you, soon you'll damage your voice, and that would be a dishonor. I come to this unpleasant place to hear you sing."

Gina took a chance and glanced at this man's face to see if he was teasing her. She saw no threat in his gaze or demeanor. "Thank you. It's kind of you to say that."

"I say it in all sincerity. You should be working in a better place where your talent is appreciated. You see, the pearl of a good life is beautiful music." He flashed a crooked smile.

She should be singing at a better place . . . his place, Gina surmised. She'd heard the flattery, come-on lines, and innuendoes dozens of times, to which she would feign misunderstanding, respond with humor, or, if sensing aggression, quickly retreat. She chose to repeat his poetry. "The pearl of a good life is beautiful music. You seem a cut above, sir. It's been my impression that the Japanese crowd is a rowdy one. To you, I'll dedicate my next number. What would you like me to sing?"

"Do you sing Gershwin?"

"Backward and forward."

At first he frowned at her answer but then chuckled. "Then I'd like to hear you sing 'Summertime' . . . forward, please."

Gina smiled. Julio played a piano rendition of the popular tune, and now she wished she'd taken time to practice it with him. "'Summertime' it is, Admiral Tanaka. I hope you're not disappointed."

His face creased into a delighted grin, but her smile wavered. "Summertime" was Ray's favorite song from the opera *Porgy and Bess*, which they had seen a few years ago. He had purchased the original cast recording and often played it in the evening while he wound down from his day. She broke eye contact and made up an excuse to leave the table. Later, with Ray on her mind, she poured her heart and soul into Gershwin's hypnotic lullaby.

The night dragged on later than usual, a group of sailors out for a party refusing to leave until Rosa told her bouncers to throw them out. A scuffle ensued, and Gina cowered in a corner away from flying debris. However, a mirror nearby shattered, and shards of it covered her shoulders and slipped down the front of her dress. Gina froze. Over shouts, whacks, and the crack of breaking furniture, a woman screamed, and the lights went out. When the lights came on, the sailors were ejected with kicks to their backsides.

"Idiots," Inez said while in the dressing room helping Gina pick the glass off her skin. "I think we got it all. We ought to get hazard pay working in this joint. It's getting late. You want to share a taxi?"

Gina looked at the clock. "I can walk. I still have time. Thanks, though. I'll see you tomorrow." She didn't mind walking home after work, a pleasant interlude between a busy night and her lonely room. She closed her locker and dug into her purse to find her keys. They weren't there. She dug deeper but still couldn't find them. Irritated, she dumped the contents of her purse onto the table, but still no keys. Where could they be? She searched her locker and her pockets. In the bathroom—why would she take them in there?—but she looked anyway. She finally found the keys in the toe of a shoe in her locker. Grabbing them, she slammed its door shut, locked it, repacked her purse, and left fifteen minutes before curfew. She'd have to hurry tonight.

Toward the end of her walk, the normally busy streets had emptied of people, and streetlights cast long shadows on the sidewalk. She passed a closed sari-sari store and an empty bar. Feeling uncomfortable alone on the street, she looked over her shoulder and hurried toward the safety of her rooming house, two doors down.

"Halt," rang through still air. "Halt!"

She silently gasped, "Shit," before turning and bowing to the sentry, who wore a white helmet and carried a baton. "I'm sorry. I'm late," she babbled, and she dug in her purse for her identification.

He tilted her chin up and compared her face to her picture and shouted something she didn't understand.

"I worked late. I live there." She pointed to the nearby house. "I live there." She pantomimed with her fingers. As she saw no understanding, her jaw clenched.

"You late!" he shouted and whacked her across her shins with his baton.

Gina jumped back and screamed. *Son of a bitch.*

He handed her papers back. "You not come out late again. You go."

All night long she ruminated over the uncalled-for abuse, knowing she wasn't alone, as Julio had been arrested and held in jail overnight, and Arielle was sporting a black eye after tangling with a sentry who patrolled the night streets snagging prey.

Gina was awoken early the next morning when Miguel knocked on her door. "I sorry to wake you, Miss Gina. I in a hurry."

She told him of the encounter with the sentry.

"You want me to tell Major Davy?"

"No, please. Don't bother him with it. I was caught outside after curfew. I'll be more careful." She handed him an envelope of money, and he gave her two letters, the usual exchange of money and information. After Miguel left, Gina brewed a cup of coffee and opened the letter from Vivian, always wanting the latest information about Cheryl. Vivian wrote that Cheryl was turning into quite a whiz at math—her dad's daughter, perhaps? She said Edna had ripped her last pair of pants, and the material was so thin it wouldn't hold a mend. Maybe Gina could find something Edna could wear.

The note from Davy was not as easy a fix. He needed more money to purchase guns and ammunition, and prices on the black market were skyrocketing. Gina felt at her wit's end. She was living on what she made at the diner and sending every cent earned at Rosa's to the growing band of guerrillas. She had found two more donors from Davy's list, and Dr. Lopez had recruited other doctors to contribute medical supplies. Still, she couldn't keep up with the demand. She needed a third job. She'd been volunteering a few hours a week at Remedios Hospital for a while now. Perhaps she could qualify to work as a nurse's aide at Philippine General. She'd apply today.

━━

Upon entering the dressing room at Rosa's, Gina heard shouting coming from Rosa's office. "What's going on?" she asked Inez, who was applying a rainbow of makeup to enhance her already beautiful eyes.

"Rosa's on the rampage again. This time she's after Julio. This dump would sink without him; you'd think she'd cut him some slack."

"What'd he do?"

"He didn't show up last night. Said he overslept." Inez turned toward Gina, one eye made up and the other one not, a Picasso-like effect that confused Gina's vision. "It's her, anyway, not him," Inez alleged. "She's been a real bitch lately. Probably got ditched by that policeman guy she's been dating." Inez turned toward the mirror. "Come to think of it"—she closed one eye to apply liner—"she's been ignoring the customers, and that's a high crime to those egomaniacs."

Julio burst through the door of the women's dressing room, carrying the contents of his locker in a paper bag. His face was black with rage. "The little bitch fired me. Just like that." He snapped his fingers.

"Nooo," a frizzy-haired woman cried. Half a dozen other women gathered around Julio, all talking at once.

"She can't fire you."

"That's the thanks you get for working your butt off."

A blue-eyed woman said, "I'm sorry, babe. What are you going to do now?"

"I won't go hungry." He laughed half-heartedly. "Cheers, freaks." He ripped off his green bow tie and put on his striped jacket before slamming the door behind him.

The room went quiet.

Rosa appeared, her eyes snapping and her face flushed. "Let that be a lesson," she barked. "All you people are replaceable." She tossed down the revised schedule for the night. "Gina, you'll work the tables until I find another piano player."

It was a long night for Gina, disheartened without Julio's energy to keep her upbeat and no musical sets to perform to break the monotony of the ghoulish grins, fumbling hands, and innuendos from table after table of patrons.

Rosa hired another piano player, who never showed up, and then she hired a third one, who was competent but missing Julio's vigor. Without his energy and direction, the flow of the entertainment flagged, with long, irregular intervals of time between acts that left the stage dark and the audience cold. However, busy with her own complicated love life, Rosa didn't seem to notice or to care.

Julio kept in touch with Gina and Inez. He always said he was doing great, picking up enough bar jobs to pay the rent. What more could anyone ask for in these times? Had either heard of anyplace hiring musicians? Something permanent would be nice. But then, what was permanent anymore besides death? Gina knew his unrest, but there was nothing she could do to help. She was barely tolerating her job at Rosa's Cabaret, the spirit of the place having left with him.

Inez and Arielle came into the dressing room sweaty from having just finished their set. They both gulped water kept in a jug on a side table. Inez said, "Be warned. There's a table of Jap civilians. One is drunk as a skunk and mouthy as hell. We got off the stage as fast as we could."

Gina looked up from the mirror, beginning to feel the rush of the Philopon she'd taken. "Is Rosa on top of it?"

"She ordered the bartender to water his beer. Just be careful."

When her turn onstage came, Gina scanned the audience. In the far corner were the three Japanese men Inez had warned about—all dressed in black suits, white shirts, and black ties, all smashed, all chain-smoking, and one giggling—the heckler, she guessed.

Gina delivered her practiced banter and songs while being interrupted by the garbled comments from the corner table—"You pretty lady. I love you"—which she ignored, but the heckler was being egged on by his equally drunk companions and becoming louder and more aggressive.

"We meet later? I suck your tits."

The audience reacted to this intrusion, laughing and craning their necks to see from where it came.

"You like me. I show you first-class time."

Anger boiled up, and Gina blurted, "Sir, are you always this stupid, or is this a special occasion?" She laughed, a bit manic, and addressed the audience. "Give the little man a hand, folks. He wins the prize tonight for being the biggest pain in the ass."

The piano player punctuated her comeback with a rumble of a minor chord. The audience clapped and roared with laughter. Every head turned toward the heckler, whose face was black with rage.

Hoping the incident was over but knowing that Japanese men could be cruel, she murmured into the microphone, "I mean, I'm just here to entertain you, and I thank you, Mr. Heckler, for helping me do my job." However, she knew there was more to it than that. She had wanted to see that man squirm, and it felt good. She instructed the pianist to play the introduction to "Little White Lies," an entertaining ditty. Soon the audience was tapping their feet, and all seemed fine.

Afterward, Rosa hissed, "Are you out of your mind? The men at the corner table were just having fun. It happens all the time. You never respond—ever. They are demanding that you apologize. Get over there and humble yourself."

Men requesting her presence was part of her job, but approaching a hostile table was always dangerous. Gina's glance at the heckler met a scowling face. "I don't think I should."

Rosa's mouth became an angry slit. "Do as I say, or you're out of here."

Gina swallowed hard and acquiesced, knowing she needed this job. Winding her way through the room, she felt the gaze of the three surly men following her. Rosa was wrong. These men weren't just having fun. She pasted on her practiced smile. "Good eve—"

The heckler slammed his glass on the table. "This beer tastes like pee. Get me another." He shoved his glass toward her, and she caught it just before it toppled.

"Yes, sir." She turned to flag a waiter, but then, to her shock, the heckler whacked her hard on her rear. She jumped and turned back, seeing only the maw of a mouth on a scowling face.

"*You* get me a beer," spewed from the maw. "In Japan woman wait on a man. You obey our rules now!" He jammed the lit end of his cigarette against her bare leg.

Gina yelped so loudly at the searing pain that every head in the room turned toward the corner. Reflexively, she slapped her abuser hard on his face and hollered, "You son of a bitch!"

He lunged toward her, spilling beer down his pants, but his companions held him at bay while Gina ran in panic to the safety of the bar, where the bartender gripped a baseball bat he'd retrieved from under the counter. The three drunkards upended their table, splattering beer and shards of glass on nearby patrons, and then they left the cabaret.

While Rosa and her staff cleaned up the mess and mollified the affected patrons with sweet talk and more beer, Gina, faint with pain and fear, inspected the blistering burn on her leg.

"Bastards," the bartender muttered and gave her a wet towel and glass of water.

Rosa, her eyes snapping, came to Gina. "My office. Right now."

Gina, not knowing what lay ahead, limped behind Rosa, who slammed the office door closed. "Are you a total idiot? Do you realize what you've done? A face slap is the highest form of insult."

Gina, expecting sympathy, tried to show Rosa the burn on her leg, but the woman turned her head away.

"You're fired. Clean your things out of your locker, and be gone in ten minutes. Your night's wages will pay for the damage you caused."

"I didn't . . . ," Gina tried to protest. "I need—"

"Just get out of here," Rosa screamed with a wild wave of her hand.

Seeing no recourse, Gina limped from Rosa's office to the dressing room, where long-faced women had gathered.

Arielle covered the burn with a salve. "My mom makes this. It's cooling. Here, take the jar . . ."

Inez offered, "I'll go home with you."

"No. I'll be okay."

"Then I'll clean out your locker."

A redheaded woman said, "I'm sorry, honey. I would have done the same thing." Two other women nodded in agreement.

The bartender handed her another cold towel. "I called a calesa. It should be here in a minute." He offered her a peso from his pocket to pay for the ride.

Gina forced a smile. "Thanks, but I can pay."

He pushed the money into her hand. "Take it. You may need it."

The piano player was thumping a rousing tune, and the mood in the cabaret was merry again.

Gina limped through the stage door, and it slammed behind her. The air was heavy and smelled of grease, and with no moon, the alley was dark. She could see the outline of the calesa at the end of the alley, and she was halfway there when she heard a giggle. Shivers creeped up the back of her neck, and she turned to run back to Rosa's just as three inebriated Japanese stepped out of the shadows. Two wrenched Gina's arms behind her. She struggled and screamed, feeling pain in her shoulders, her hair being pulled, and her head being yanked back. The heckler repeatedly slapped her face with the front and back of his hand, then punched her in the stomach.

"Hey!" the calesa driver shouted, and Gina heard a whip crack. The abusers dropped their hold on her and fled. Gina buckled forward and fell to the ground.

"Is she all right?" she heard someone say through a fog of pain and felt hands on her face and body.

"I think she fainted. Let's get her inside."

The fog began to lift. "I'm all right," she insisted, not knowing if she was. Sitting up, she took several gulping breaths and assessed her body, feeling the sting of the slaps, the ache of the punch, and the burn on her leg. She stood, a bit wobbly. "I'll go home now."

"I'll come with you," Inez said.

"No. You need this job. I'll be all right."

"You can't go alone," Inez argued.

The calesa driver said, "I see she gets home safe." He took Gina's arm and led her to the buggy.

"I'll come by in the morning," Inez said.

———

Inez cleaned out Gina's locker and delivered her belongings along with a fifth of booze and a pineapple upside-down cake. Gina's face was pink from the slaps and her lip swollen. "Are you in any pain?"

"Nothing a couple aspirin didn't help, except this cigarette burn on my leg. Arielle's salve numbs it some."

The bitch session that followed condemned Rosa Engelhard of crimes just short of murder. Inez confided, "Rosa said you needed to be brought down a peg, Gina. The creepy old hag. She knew the Nips were out there and ordered the piano player to keep the music loud to cover your cries."

Gina mumbled through her swollen lip, "What? Tell me you're kidding. Who told you that?"

"Edwardo. Eddie. He's the new bartender. He's the one who found you."

"He paid for the calesa. Is he in trouble with Rosa?"

"I don't know. They've both been quiet. Do you know what you're going to do now?"

That thought, even more than her discomfort, had kept Gina awake most of the night. "Maybe a nurse's aide job at Philippine General. I know a doctor who will put in a good word for me. I live pretty cheaply." Discouraged beyond reason, she blinked back tears.

Inez came to her and held her hand. "You should open your own place. If you do, I'll come with you. Arielle will too. Have you thought about it?"

Gina started to laugh but quickly stopped and put her hand to her sore lip. She had, but only in the context of what she'd do differently than Rosa: clean the bathrooms, nix the ventriloquist and his dummy, replace the worn stage curtain. Most importantly, support Davy's growing guerrilla unit with the money Rosa spent on her gaudy jewelry. "It's something to dream about, but practically, I can't even support myself."

"Things will work out. They always do. Are you hungry? Have you eaten?"

"No. It hurts my lip. I wish I had some ice."

"I'll go down to the corner store and get ice cream. We can eat it with the cake."

"You don't have to."

"I want to. I'll be back in a few minutes."

⌒

Gina stretched out on the couch and closed her eyes. She hadn't slept well last night and soon was dozing, dreaming she had burned down the cabaret with Rosa trapped inside, but the dream got twisted with the burning of her cottage, and she woke up in a sweat screaming, "Cheryl! Leah! Maggie!"

Someone knocked on her door. Still breathless, she shuffled to answer it.

A delivery boy looked at her swollen lip and then over her shoulder into the room. "I heard someone scream. Are you all right?"

"Yes, thank you. It was just a bad dream."

He handed her an envelope of fine ivory paper, her name and address written in calligraphy. "Looks like you have an admirer. One with a steady hand."

Tipping him, she closed the door. She inspected the envelope front and back and then carefully slid her finger under the flap to open it. Inside was a card ornamented with a tiny bird perched on the limb of a cherry tree. Gina read the haiku message:

My pretty songbird,
Your pain is causing sorrow.
My wish is your peace.

—Akia Tanaka

It was a sweet gesture and a calming message from a Japanese naval officer, a gentle man, she thought . . . a good customer. She wondered if he'd been in the audience last night. Not knowing what else to do with it, she put the puzzling card in the drawer.

Downhearted, she went back to the couch and her pillow. She'd have to tell Davy there would be no more deliveries of money, however little, or supplies for the women and children in the camp. Thinking of Cheryl, she started to cry. She could go back to the mountains; that was an option. She'd be with her daughter and could at least cook for the camp, a service of some value.

Inez returned, her eyes bugged open and her hand over her mouth. She put a pint of ice cream on the table and sat down hard on a chair. Fanning her face with her hand, she said, "You won't believe this, Gina. Rosa was found this morning floating in the Pasig River."

Gina gasped. "What? Who? Why?"

"It's all I know."

With Rosa's sudden demise, the cabaret was closed. The police investigated the death, but with so many bodies being found in the river, in fields, or even in the streets, not much came of it. Gina felt no sorrow, except for losing her source of income. Today, she was stopping by Rosa's to pick up a few things she had left in a storage closet.

Ling, a young man from the Chinese restaurant next door, guarded the entrance, and the magician, carrying a bag of his belongings, was leaving as Gina entered.

"Horrible thing to happen. Horrible, horrible," the magician said in passing.

A door in the dreary vestibule led into the large main room, with a bar along the back wall, its generously sized stage, and evidence there had once been a dance floor. Gina had no good memories of this place, except the friends she had made. She went directly to the storage closet and, after rummaging through the mess, found the bag she had come for. Retracing her steps, she found Chan in the main room jotting notes on a clipboard.

"Chan," she said, seeing his face in a scowl. "Terrible what happened to Rosa. Have you heard anything more?"

"No, but Rosa Engelhard had many enemies. Look what she did to you. There still bruise on your face."

Gina's hand went to her lip. How did he know what had happened?

Chan said, "She cheat many people, including me, out of money she owe. Look how she left this place. She fill it up every night with Japanese hooligans. Everything broken. No tenant will rent it from me like this."

Gina's eyes blinked rapidly. She gazed around the room to hide her interest, but she couldn't conceal the lilt in her voice. "Oh, I don't know. A little paint, new curtains. Are you looking for any kind of business specifically?"

"It's set up for a nightclub. Everything is here. Missy Gina, I hear you sing. You good. You bring new customers. Men with money. If I find someone to take over, you come back. I give you a job. Please excuse, now."

Over the next few days an idea percolated—would Chan back her if she offered to take over Rosa's space? She had no money and no prospect of getting any, but she did have a game plan he might be interested in hearing given his hatred for anything Japanese, his village in China having been pillaged by them in 1937 and many in his family killed. Would he even consider it? She decided to find out and worked on her approach.

Chapter 18

CHAN

I acquire a pair of shorts stitched from a gunnysack. I have learned to be grateful for the smallest mercies.

—Ray Thorpe, Cabanatuan prison camp, October 1942–
January 1944

When Gina arrived at Chan's, Mei came from the back room. "Good morning, Missy Gina. Long time I not see you."

"Yes, I was away for a while."

"And Mr. Ray?"

Gina slumped a little. How much she'd like to say that Ray was home with Cheryl, and she could hardly wait to show him the new dress she had purchased. "Yes, Mr. Ray too."

Mei leaned over the counter and whispered, "I thought because you American . . ."

Gina bent closer and whispered back, "I'm Italian, Mei. I know I never mentioned it. I was born in Milan, but I left when I was a child. I'm using my maiden name, Angelina Aleo—it's Italian, not American." She stood up, smiled, and said in her regular voice, "Would Chan have time to see me?"

Mei nodded and held back the curtain so Gina could pass through. The smell of fish frying and the wail of a baby filtered down from the upstairs living quarters. The workroom, once bustling with activity, was empty today, the bolts of silks and satins neatly stacked on shelves, women no longer needing formal dresses for their social lives of pre-war Manila. Mei led her to a small office, where Chan, surrounded by invoices and ledgers, was adding a column of figures on an abacus, his fingers flying over the clicking beads.

"Excuse me, Chan." She stepped into his office.

"Missy Gina." He put the abacus aside, removed a ledger from a chair, and motioned for her to sit down. "It always good to see you. What brings you here today?"

She tried to look nonchalant, as if the reason for her visit were an everyday occurrence. "A business proposal, sir." She saw no change in his expression. "I'd like to rent what was Rosa's place, and open my own nightclub. You know I can entertain an audience, and you said yourself that I attracted new business, the ones you preferred, the men with money. I could continue to do that."

Chan rocked slightly forward. "I sure you could. Do you run business before?"

She had hoped Chan wouldn't ask that. She hadn't even finished high school, having dropped out in her senior year after winning a talent contest and a contract with Follies Musical Revue Inc. Nor had she held a job since marrying Ray until her few months at Rosa's, and that had ended in disaster. "No, sir. Not a business, but I was chairman of the Junior League's fund-raising committee for three record-breaking years and was awarded a plaque of commendation. I had to keep meticulous records."

Chan nodded. "It good, but different, but still . . ."

He seemed to be contemplating, and Gina anxiously waited.

He said, "It might be working. You smart lady. I need two months' rent in advance and a twelve-month contract. I renew yearly."

Gina had known this was coming too. Her house was in the hands of the Japanese, and her wealth had disappeared. Who in their right mind would lend her a cent? "Chan, I have no money. You're going to have to trust I'll make good on my promises. I have a plan—"

He put up his hand to stop her.

She quickly interjected. "Please listen. There's something important I must tell you. I found that when a little tipsy, the Japanese officers are easily manipulated. I learned to use that to my advantage. I can sweet-talk them out of a lot of money and sometimes information. It's like a treasure trove waiting to be mined." She paused, letting that sink in, and then said, "I want to open my own club. Others who think like I do want to work for me too. We'll cater to the wealthiest of Rosa's Japanese customers."

Chan sat as still as a rock, his hands in his lap and his face stony, but she could see a pulse beating fast in his neck. "You bring me shame. I thought you entertain our friends working to keep our country free. But no, you entertain the enemy for your benefit. You no different than Rosa. You leave now." He waved his hand dismissively and reached for his abacus.

Gina blinked. His shame stung like a slap, but he had it all wrong. She persisted, "Please let me finish. There's more you need to know."

His glower conveyed his aversion. "It folly. Even your own people call you a traitor."

"So what's new in these times? Everyone is living a lie. Please let me explain, Chan." She told him her plan of a club to cater to the wealthy Japanese officers and her intent to support a guerrilla unit at the officers' expense. She hoped he saw the irony and the value of it.

His eyes betrayed a flicker of interest, but he still resisted. "Impossible," he grunted. "You have much to hide. You stay safe only if you stay noiseless."

She knew that was true. Drawing attention to herself was a peril she'd lived with since she'd returned to Manila, and now she would be increasing her exposure to a dangerous level. Adamant, though, she leaned close to him and peered into his worried face. "We're trapped on this island and living under cruel Nipponese rules. I hate what they are doing to us, Chan. I need to do something with my rage."

She perceived his countenance softening.

Encouraged, she hurried on. "I'm only asking that you help me get started. I need a backer. I saw the money Rosa pulled in. I want that money and any information I learn to support the resistance . . . the guerrillas in the mountains. I've done the math. Even paying you back with interest, I could do that. My guerrilla friends are living and fighting in squalid conditions. They need help, Chan. Many are your friends too. My daughter, Cheryl, is there."

"And Mr. Ray?"

As always when she explained Ray's situation, Gina's voice sounded strangled. "I don't know, He was on Corregidor. He's been missing for months." She placed her diamond-and-sapphire ring on the table. "It's my wedding ring. It means a lot to me. It's the only collateral I have."

After a moment, he picked up her ring and inspected it, but then he pushed it back toward her. "I find out more. Come back. Two days."

Gina left Chan's curious how he was going to "find out more" and encouraged that he had not rejected her outright. With no desire to go to her lonely room, she walked along Escolta Street and observed her reflection flickering by in the shop windows. Who was that aged and worn woman staring back at her? She turned her face away and beat herself up again with her thoughts . . . her child was unhappy . . . but she was, too, and scared and vulnerable. Two sad peas in a pod, waiting for the Japanese to leave, waiting for Ray to come home to them, waiting for their lives to stop drifting without direction.

In Heacock's toy department, for two centavos she purchased a Carmen Miranda paper doll book that included two paper dolls, nine long gowns, and many headdresses, hats, and turbans with feathers and fruit. Cheryl would love it, and so would Leah. She rode the elevator to the mezzanine, where there was a café, once a hangout for her and her Junior League friends.

Cutlery clinked on ivory plates and conversations buzzed as the hostess seated her at a small table next to the railing, where she could view the sales floor below. The menu had changed, and so had the clientele. Missing from the crowd were the blonds and redheads, the blue eyed and green eyed, the tall and the hefty, the pantsuited and skirted, anyone who looked even vaguely American. Gina wished for a slice of pineapple-and-banana bread with cream cheese but spent her last centavo on a cup of tea, feeling guilty even at this meager indulgence, knowing her friends were sometimes going hungry.

On the intercom, Ella Fitzgerald's "Cry Me a River" played, and the bluesy, pure tones of the chanteuse brought on a more profound bout of melancholy. Gina's gaze flitted around the room, and she witnessed compassionate pats and expressions of condolence between long-faced people sharing their sorrows. Gina knew the power of music to manipulate moods, and it was one she could use to her advantage in her new endeavor, should it come to fruition.

Chapter 19

PEARL BLUE

*I labor to heed the sage advice from a seasoned inmate—
stand tall and appear robust to save your body, and search for
moments of solitude to save your sanity.*

—*Ray Thorpe, Cabanatuan prison camp, October 1942*
January 1944

Visions of her own nightclub dominated Gina's thoughts, and sitting on
the couch in her room, she jotted down notes, listing things she would
have to consider. She'd name it Pearl Blue, a reminder of Ray's pearl-
blue eyes. She contemplated bringing Inez and Arielle into her confidence. She could use their help, and she trusted them, both having lost
family members to the Japanese invasion. There would be the mundane,
like applying for an operating permit and a license to serve alcohol.
She didn't have a clue where to start. More exciting was dreaming up
the ambience—posh and dimly lit—and the entertainment, from wild
to seductive to melancholy, calculated to lure in the Japanese patrons,
charm them, and then woo them to unguarded moments when they
would loosen their lips and empty their pockets for Davy's guerrillas.
She heard a knock on her door. It was Inez.

"I was just at Rosa's picking up my stuff. Here, this is yours." She handed Gina a box of eyeshadow, glitter, rouge, and lipstick. "I ran into Julio. He's still looking for a job. I hope you don't mind, but I told him what we're thinking about doing—"

"You what? Nobody's thinking about doing anything."

"Well, if you do, he got really giddy. You never know if he's up or down, but we have a piano player if you could work with him."

"I could," Gina replied. During her years in show business, she had worked with perfectionists and prima donnas, the quirky and the suicidal. She'd learned to tolerate their unpredictability and admire their zeal. "I'd want Julio to lead my club's band. I'm thinking three or four musicians. A percussionist who could keep up with you and Arielle. A jazzy sax behind me at the end of the night. My club would be different from Rosa's. No clowns, ventriloquists, or comedians. I'm picturing us doing standards, jazz and blues, and spectacular ethnic floor shows. You and Julio have the education and the talent. I think we could pull it off."

"And you've got the worldview," Inez replied. "I think we could too."

"It's all hypothetical, of course."

"Of course."

Gina's head was full of ideas she hadn't thought about in over a decade. She was in her element again, and the plan set her thoughts spinning. Now, if she could only convince Chan to back her.

⌒

On her ride to Chan's, Gina felt tied in a knot. She raised her shoulders high and tight, squeezing them into the muscles of her neck to loosen the tension. It didn't work; the butterflies of anxiety still fluttered in her stomach.

Flora J. Solomon

She entered Chan's office with a brisk step and a phony smile and sat tautly in the chair he offered. Feigning confidence, she tried to read his inclination, but there was nothing in his manner to give him away.

As he took a breath, his nostrils flared slightly. "I check. I ask around. I learn you smart lady. You work from your head"—he touched his temple—"and your heart." He touched his chest. "I proposition you."

She stifled a smile.

He sat back and laced his hands over his stomach. "You have important mission. You fool Japanese and help American soldiers. I help you with it. We must move fast. Every day business closed, we lose money."

Chan took a paper from his desk drawer and handed it to her to read. The hand-printed document stated the terms of their agreement. The rent for the building was less than she had expected but still a lot. As she wrestled with the amount, the silence stretched between them until Chan said, "I help you run business until you learn. And I give you special deal for rent and protection."

Gina frowned quizzically.

"My number-three son, Ling, come with rent. He stand at the door and watch out for you."

"That's very kind," she said, touched by his concern for her safety, and not hiring security was one less expense. She could finally quit the diner job and forget about working as a nurse's aide. She could give Pearl Blue her full attention, and Chan believed in her. It was a good plan, so why did she feel so jittery? She gathered her courage and took the plunge that she hoped would change the lives of those depending on her in a positive way. "All right. Let's do it."

He handed her a pen and the documents to sign. At the top was his name, Yee Chan.

"Chan! You own the restaurant next door to Rosa's too."

"Yes, Missy Gina. We do business with you. Make dim sum for your customers."

"I wasn't planning on serving food."

"Not food . . . dim sum. It come on little platters. Easy. My number-one son, Mak, bring in steam cart. No mess for you. Make customers thirsty. Drink more beer."

"We'll see." She dipped the nib of the pen in the inkwell, dabbed off the excess ink, but didn't sign the document. "There's one thing. The place is run down. You'll need to clean it up before I can use it."

"How clean?" Chan asked, which Gina thought would be funny if she weren't about to make one of the most important decisions of her life.

"At a minimum, paint, curtains, renovating the bathrooms. I'll give you a list. I'd like to put it in the contract."

Chan took the contract back, and Gina nervously waited for him to decide. He said, "I add dollar figure and time of two weeks to make it pretty for you." He added the information.

When Gina signed her name and the date, relief that the deal was done turned to euphoria, and a multitude of plans started to whirl in her head. She took a minute to compose herself before she could say, "Thank you. I won't let you down."

"Not me, missy. Our guerrillas. You not let them down."

Gina sat back with her hand over her mouth and tears in her eyes. Chan had totally bought into her plan. "Our guerrillas," she repeated.

Later at home, a nagging worry stalked her—the path she was choosing was risky. Was she up to the task? She called Inez and told her the news.

There was a moment of silence before Inez replied. "You're not fooling me, are you? You got a fairy godmother or something?"

"Sort of. It's scary, isn't it? Meet me at Rosa's—umm, Pearl Blue—at nine o'clock in the morning. Bring Arielle. There's something I need to pass by you. I'll call Julio and Eddie. Oh . . . how do you feel about us serving dim sum?"

As Gina approached Pearl Blue the next morning, she was greeted by the mouthwatering smell of honey and cinnamon coming from the bakery next door. She followed the scrumptious odor into the bakery.

A blonde, angular woman was filling shelves with round loaves of warm bread and long jelly-filled strudels. The woman's smile was welcoming. "What can I get for you?"

Gina held out her hand in greeting. "Hi. I'm Gina. I've been here a few times—you may remember me. I just want to tell you that I'll be opening a new nightclub next door soon."

The woman's welcoming smile faded. "I'll tell you right now, right to your face. I will hold you responsible for any damage your customers do to my property."

Taken aback, Gina said, "I don't expect there to be any trouble."

"We'll see about that. You keep that riffraff in line, or I'll give you and that Chinaman plenty of trouble." She turned her back.

Old bat, were the first words that came to Gina's mind. What had brought that on? Not wanting to make an enemy, she said, "I'm sorry you had problems in the past. I expect my customers to be, umm, better behaved." She clamped her mouth shut and left.

The front of Pearl Blue faced Manila Bay, which was filled with Japanese troopships, battleships, tankers, barges, and destroyers—a distressing sight but all the better for her business. The cabaret signage that hung overhead would be the first thing to go, she decided as she unlocked the door. The inside was dingier in the morning light, and it smelled bad too.

Not long afterward, Inez and Arielle walked in, Inez carrying a box of pastries.

Despite her lousy encounter with the baker, Gina's mouth began to water. She selected an apricot-filled pastry. "I take it you didn't mention to the bakery lady you were bringing these here."

"Her name is Irma. Should I have?"

Gina relayed the story of her unhappy introduction, the sting of it still pestering her.

"Oh." Inez wiped raspberry filling off her chin. "I applied here a while back when it was still the Opus Club. It attracted mostly dockworkers, and it got rowdy sometimes."

Gina was feeling antsy, not sure how to tell Inez and Arielle her real mission. Maybe she should have been up front earlier, but then there had been no reason to. "Before you agree to work at Pearl Blue, there's something you need to know. There will be more going on here than what meets the eye. I'm aiming to make this place classy to attract the wealthy Japanese in port or working in the city. If you agree, the three of us will work together to woo money and information from them that we pass on to the resistance. That's the whole of it. You don't have to stay with me."

Arielle said, "It's not much different than what we're doing now. I work my butt off every night for enough money to live on."

"The difference, Arielle," Gina said, "is I'm putting you at a greater risk. I know how good you are at charming the Japs, but this clientele will be higher class, wealthier, more knowledgeable, and more savvy. We're going to have to measure every word we say."

Inez said, "You've been doing this all along, haven't you? I knew there was something different about you the minute I met you. So what is this resistance group you're supporting?"

"A small band of guerrillas. They sent me here to raise money so they could fight the Japs."

"And how's it going?"

"It's been spotty. You see how I live. This is my chance to make a real difference, and I'm willing to take the risk."

"Anybody else involved?"

"No, just the three of us, if you stick with me. Oh, Chan too. He's all in. You know many of his family were killed by the Japs in '37."

"I'm in," Arielle said. "My brother and three cousins are guerrillas, and my husband's in a prison camp. I've been itching to do something . . . anything."

"Me too," Inez said. "This is going to make coming to work really interesting."

"Thanks, you two. Hearing your comments over the past months, I was sure you'd want to fight back, but I had to ask."

⌁

Eddie arrived carrying a bag of donuts, and a minute later Julio came in with a loaf of freshly baked bread and something fuzzy and yellow. He handed Inez the bread and put a tiny wiggling kitten into Gina's hands. "Here . . . happy business warming."

Gina glowered at him. "You devil. How am I supposed to care for a cat."

He removed a bottle of milk and a tin of flea powder from his pocket. "Not much to it, boss. It'll live on mice. There's a mess of them in here, no doubt." He poured the milk into a saucer Eddie retrieved from the bar, and they all watched the kitten lap it up. The milk gone, Julio sprinkled the fur ball generously with flea powder.

"The mother cat was dead, and this one was trying to nurse on her." Julio couldn't have tugged any harder at Gina's heartstrings.

"Let's see what we got here." Julio picked up the kitten to check the gender. "Definitely a Leo."

Arielle giggled. "A Leo. It's kismet, Gina. You've got yourself a kitten." And so Aleo the Cat joined the family.

⌁

After finishing the pastries and rinsing their fingers in the rusty water that spurted from the faucet, they gathered around a table. Gina said,

"Okay, folks, here's the skinny. Chan is happy to have us as new tenants. He is willing to do some renovations, but he wants it reopened as soon as possible. Inez and I have talked about opening a place of our own, without ever thinking it would happen. We have some ideas."

It felt surreal to Gina to sit here with her friends, now employees, planning an endeavor that finally could be the answer to Davy's needs. Her thoughts spun. Where to start?

"First thing," she said, "the talent in this group isn't being utilized. I'm thinking high-end floor shows on the weekends to draw in the patrons who want more than a cabaret. A band, beautiful costumes, ethnic dances. There'll be a hefty door charge to limit the rowdies. On weekdays, more laid back but still high end. With the harbor right outside our door, we can target the Japanese naval officers."

Inez interjected, "That will take a while to pull together. We'll have to hire dancers and musicians, and there is the choreography and costumes."

Gina nodded. "I think a two-stage opening would work. We can get this place cleaned up quickly and open it for music, social dancing, drinks, dim sum, and such."

"Dim sum?" Julio said, petting the kitten, who was purring loud as a lawn mower.

"Ah yes," Gina said. "Not my idea. It will be brought from Yee's. Later we have a grand opening with the floor show. Maybe around Christmas. Eddie, I'm assuming you want to be in charge of the bar and waitstaff. Keep whoever from Rosa's staff wants to stay, but check them out first. Julio, hire the band; Inez and Arielle, find and coordinate the dancers. I'll run the place."

Julio mumbled under his breath, "Heaven help us."

"What did you say?"

"The kitten cometh," he said, holding up the cat.

They all had worked at Rosa's and had become inured to its shabbiness, but today they were viewing it with an eye to renovation.

"Your overall impression?"

"Squalid."

"It's not that bad."

"Then seedy."

Arielle pointed to the Mars and Venus symbols identifying the lavatories. "These have to go. There's a hole in the wall. Eddie, stand on the toilet. What can you see?"

Eddie peeked through the hole. "You don't want to know."

"That's sick."

"Is there a name for this paint color?"

"Laundry Gray."

"Bad Mood."

A mouse skittered across the floor of the small, greasy kitchen. "Get it! We'll mount it and make a collection."

Everyone groaned.

"I've got dibs on this furniture."

"I'll arm wrestle you for it."

Gina started up the stairs. "You guys aren't much help."

She had never been upstairs, where Rosa had had an apartment in which she'd stayed on nights she couldn't or didn't want to return to her home. Gina unlocked the door and stepped into a room beautifully furnished with plush sofas and chairs and high-end tables and accessories. To the left was a small kitchen and to the right, a bedroom. A large window overlooked the bay. Everything about this apartment was impeccable. Gina opened a closet door and saw Rosa's suits, blouses, and shoes neatly arranged according to color. She blanched and stepped back, finally feeling the shock of Rosa's death. Who had killed her and thrown her body into the river? Imagining it gave Gina a chill.

Inez and Arielle came into the room and found Gina peering into the full closet.

"Jeepers," Inez said, "this gives me the creeps. Who do you think did it?"

Gina pointed to the back corner of the closet. "The safe's open and empty. A burglar?"

"Or her husband. She was running around."

"Or her boyfriend. I heard he was a psycho."

Gina closed the closet door. "Or an enemy. She had several, so I heard. I'll ask Chan to have someone clean the place out."

⁓

While the others talked, haggled, and encouraged, Arielle sketched a floor plan using colored pencils and a large pad she had brought with her. She showed Gina her rendering. "I did most of this last night. What do you think?"

Arielle had designed a room softly lit with ivory-shaded lamps mounted on cream-colored walls. Shimmery gold fabric draped from the ceiling to the floor, covering the windows and curtaining off the stage. Round tables of various sizes were positioned about a dance floor, and settees and small coffee tables were placed at intervals along walls decorated with framed tropical prints. Two smaller side rooms that had always been closed up were available for a quieter setting or games of cards or dice. A hostess would greet the patrons in a newly screened-off vestibule.

"This is so exciting. What do you think about this for tablecloths?" Arielle showed Gina a swatch of fabric printed with a riot of tropical flowers and birds in shades of corals, emerald green, and midnight blue. "I know the woman who paints it. She'll be glad for the work."

"Your design is . . . it's beyond words, Arielle. The room looks like an elegant salon. You could do this professionally. Have you thought about it?"

"Once I did, I finished a year of design school. I met my husband there . . . he was an American studying architecture. We were married for only two weeks before he was called away. He's a prisoner at Cabanatuan."

Even the word *Cabanatuan* struck an uneasy chord in Gina and a longing for Ray, thoughts of him always just under the surface. She quickly turned her attention to Arielle's design. "We're on a tight budget. We can't afford this."

"There's not much expense here. The floors and the bar can be sanded and stained. We'll use lots of paint. Lots of fabric . . ."

"I love them, but the settees . . ."

"Two or three. We get them cheap, and I'll fix them up. The table covers too. The unpainted fabric is inexpensive, and I can help my friend paint it. I'll ask the girls at the orphanage to do the sewing. They work for a few pesos. It helps keep them fed."

"I heard the orphanage closed."

"No. When the Japs raided it, they only took the girls over twelve years old. Most of them are sewing parachutes in a Nip factory west of town, but the prettier ones, well . . ."

Arielle didn't need to complete her sentence. Gina knew that young girls were being kidnapped from orphanages and girls' schools all over the islands and put to work in one lurid capacity or another. Her thoughts went to Cheryl, Leah, and Maggie, all potential targets for a barbarous enemy. It heightened her resolve to help the guerrillas fight back fast and furious, an outlet she needed as much as she needed to breathe.

~

Inside, the old Rosa's Cabaret morphed from dark and dreary to elegant rooms with soft lighting and sophisticated appointments. The large dining room with the stage and bar became the Orchid Room, and the smaller rooms were labeled Hibiscus and Jasmine. With a light twist of his arm, Chan had agreed to furnish one of the empty rooms upstairs at Pearl Blue as an employee lounge and, at Davy's request, to construct a hidden closet. Outside, the pièce de résistance hung over the front doors: **PEARL BLUE** in glowing white neon, donated by Inez's uncle, who was a master glassblower.

Julio assembled a five-piece band from a motley collection of friends who could all play multiple instruments and were delighted to have a permanent job. Inez reached out to her college classmates and found two women and three men eager to dance at Gina's new establishment. They resurrected routines they had choreographed in their college dance classes and dug through backs of closets and in old trunks for costumes. Eddie retrained most of Rosa's waitstaff and ordered them crisp white uniforms.

Ten days after signing the contract with Chan, Gina took out an ad in the *Tribune* and the *Philippine Free Press*, "Under New Management," and hung a sign over Pearl Blue's door, **OPEN FOR BUSINESS.**

Chapter 20
MOVING FORWARD

*I sleep cuddled with three others in a bunk built for two. My
close nighttime companions bring me warmth, comfort, and
a sense of safety.*

—*Ray Thorpe, Cabanatuan prison camp, October 1942–*
January 1944

The first weeks Pearl Blue was open, business boomed as the population
checked out the new place in town. Always circulating and listening to
her customers, Gina overheard comments: "Nice in here"; "Quite an
upgrade"; "No food except dim sum?"; "Pricey for what they're offering." Gina paid Chan his rent and sent money to Davy and a few
niceties to Vivian, thinking she was finally on the right road. The staff
prepared for Pearl Blue's grand opening. Gina, needing help with mar-
keting, sought out Franca, who today was volunteering at Remedios
Hospital.

Seeing Gina, Franca put down her pen, folded her arms, and
ordered, "Shut the door."

Warmth rose from Gina's chest to the roots of her hair. "You have
a right to be angry. I can explain—"

"Angry!" Franca exploded. "Señor Estevez almost had a stroke. He told you that you might be watched, and for pity's sake, Gina, what the hell were you doing . . . working at that whorehouse? I never would have guessed it of you."

Gina dropped into a chair. "Wha . . . what are you talking about?"

"That . . . that place. That name. Angelina D'Licious."

"I didn't choose it, and Rosa's Cabaret wasn't a whorehouse . . . well." Gina thought back at the comings and goings. "I was a singer. That's all. I swear."

"It doesn't matter. What if you're recognized as an American? You're putting us all in danger. Don't you realize that, or don't you care?"

Gina knew Franca's anger was justified. "Of course I care, but I have a daughter to support, not to mention Davy's guerrillas, and I don't have a rich husband to take care of me." Franca's face hardened, and Gina hoped she wouldn't be thrown out of the office. She added, "Rosa's is closed now, anyway. She was found floating in the Pasig. You must have read about it in the *Tribune*. Do you have a few minutes? I have something important to tell you."

Franca uncrossed her arms and motioned for Gina to continue.

Gina admitted, "Rosa's wasn't the best place to be; most of her customers were Japanese. But while I was there, I found I could manipulate them—wheedle them out of their money and information. It seems I've found a new talent, and I've opened a nightclub of my own—"

Franca put up her hand. "Stop right there. That's the silliest thing I ever heard. You can't fool around with the Japanese—"

"Why not? Your husband does it every day, cooperating with President Laurel's puppet government while smuggling Americans like me into Manila."

Franca bristled. "Keep him out of it. We're living in a do-or-die society. He pledges his allegiance to the Japanese and works with Laurel, or he becomes a prisoner in Fort Santiago or a body floating in the Pasig River. You took the same pledge, if I remember."

"I did . . . and I took it as insincerely as Señor Estevez did, and you did, too, I suspect."

"You're in dangerous territory, Gina. I think you'd better leave."

"No, please. Just hear me out. I'm trying to do what I was sent here to do in the only way I know how, Franca. I tried soliciting money from the list of names Davy gave me, and except for Dr. Lopez and a few others, I got almost squat. I can barely support myself working in a diner or as a nurse's aide, much less a guerrilla unit." She swallowed to regain control of her shaky voice. "My new place is different from most nightclubs. It's posh and expensive and designed to attract the wealthy Japanese, and there are thousands of them in Manila and on those ships anchored in the harbor. I have driven people working with me . . . beautiful, bilingual, talented people who are motivated to lend a sympathetic ear to a lonely Jap in the name of helping the United States win this horrible war. Whatever money the Japs spend on a hefty door charge and overpriced drinks, and any information they spill, is being used against them."

Franca's voice softened. "That's all well and good if it works. What makes you think the little turkeys will come to your posh place?"

"Because I know what they like. They want to be served. They want to be pampered and flattered. I'll give them that plus classy music and beautiful, exotic dancers."

A wry smile crossed Franca's lips. "For that, every male on this planet will be there." She opened the desk drawer and retrieved a pack of cigarettes. "Where do I fit into your plan?"

"I need help with promotion. We opened a month ago, serving drinks, social dancing, and such. We have a band, and I schmooze with the crowd and sing a few show tunes. We're planning a grand opening soon with a full floor show. I'm hoping you'll come and bring your friends." Gina saw a crease form on Franca's forehead, and she leaned forward and said, "The place needs an air of . . . ah . . . swank."

Franca struck a match and lit a cigarette. "Swank?" she said through a smoky laugh.

She nudged the pack toward Gina, who tapped out a cigarette and lit it and then put out the match with a shake of her hand. "Yes, swank . . . and the publicity your society friends generate just from showing up. In return, I offer them a stocked bar and entertainment that will knock their socks off."

"A onetime shot. That's it?"

"No. I want them to come back, but initially, I'm interested in splash."

"Gina, I'm sensing there's more behind this endeavor than money."

"I have friends being hunted like animals in the mountains. They need support. What other reason would I need?" Franca leveled her stare, and Gina's eyes rapidly blinked an involuntary response. She whispered, "You don't want to know what I've seen."

"You're probably right. There're plenty of horrors to go around. What time frame are you thinking about?"

"December first."

Franca didn't reply right away. "How long did you work at Rosa's?"

"Three months. Long enough to see what was going on."

"Your background, Gina. You sang at the Alcazar Club?"

"Briefly. I traveled for several years in America and Europe with the Follies before coming to the Philippines. I can *do* entertainment. I've found a backer, and I moved into Rosa's place."

Franca snubbed out her half-smoked cigarette. "I'd like to help, but I must run this past Señor Estevez. I can't guarantee he will allow me to involve our friends."

"But you'll try."

"I will. I'll tell him everything you've told me. And I wish you luck."

"Thanks." Gina stood up and started for the door and then turned back toward Franca. "Thank you for all you've done for me. I hope someday I can return the favor."

On the trip home, the horse plodded along in heavy traffic. Gina fussed with her notes and chewed on her thumbnail, wondering if she had oversold her skills and Pearl Blue's swank.

Later, in her office, Gina kicked off her shoes and went over the invoices on her desk, her least favorite job of her new undertaking. Liquor prices had gone up and were now more than she'd budgeted, and laundry costs were higher than expected. She'd have to cut back, somewhere, until she built a clientele, if she ever did. Maybe her vision of an upscale nightclub near the rough-and-tumble dock area was ill conceived. What would Ray do? He was the numbers guy in the family. She put the invoices aside and pushed back her chair. What she really wanted right now was to be with Cheryl. She'd seen this cute gingham dress at Heacock's with a white lace collar. It came with matching hair ribbons. If only—

In her last letter, Cheryl had written that she loved, loved, loved the Carmen Miranda paper dolls, each *love* decorated with hearts and stars. A bit of her spunk returning? Gina closed her eyes, thinking this office a lonely place. Filled with family and friends, the nipa hut, despite its bugs and resident birds, in some ways had been a better place. She hadn't realized it then. She dozed for a minute.

Waking up with a start, she shook her head to regain focus and then picked up the phone and ordered daily ads to be placed in the *Tribune*, *Gazette*, and *Philippine Free Press* newspapers:

Grand Opening
December 1, 1943
Manila's Newest and Hottest Nightspot
Pearl Blue
Spectacular Floor Show! Dance Floor! Live Band!
Drinks and Dim Sum
Make Your Reservations Now!

Chapter 21

GRAND OPENING

As I decorate a sad little Christmas tree with string and origami animals made from gum wrappers, I suffer endless longing for Angelina and my precious daughter, Cheryl.

—Ray Thorpe, Cabanatuan prison camp, October 1942

January 1944

Julio's personal collection of recordings included everything from Wagner to Joplin, most of which he could play renditions of on the piano. When Gina went from her apartment down the stairs to Pearl Blue, he had Ella Fitzgerald playing on the sound system. "Sit with me for a minute," she said. "What time is the band coming?"

"They'll be here by five. We're still set up from last night's practice."

"If I don't get a chance, tell the guys they clean up real nice."

"Yeah, well. Gil doesn't like the black tux, and Layden says he feels like a pussy in the peach-colored ruffled shirt. Christ, Gina—"

"Tell them to grow up. It's only for the weekends, and it adds a touch of class."

"Personally, I think my striped coat and lucky green bow tie are classy enough."

She opened a bag of macadamia nuts and beckoned to Ling, her security man. He was a younger version of Chan and trained in the martial arts with both fists and weapons, as were all of his brothers and sisters. Approaching, he moved with the graceful ease of a fighter comfortable in his toned body.

She pointed to a chair, and he sat down. "I had my window open last night and thought I heard someone outside. It might be nothing, but I'd like you to check it out."

"Yes, ma'am. I rake near the foundation yesterday. If anyone there last night, I seeing footprints."

"You raked . . . ?" For as young as he was, Ling knew his job. He'd insisted she have bushes and debris removed from around the foundation of the building and lights mounted by the kitchen and stage doors. Inside, he'd secured the windows, triple-locked every door, and had a one-way mirror installed in her office so she could view the vestibule and the Orchid Room. "If there's trouble, I expect it will be tonight. Did you find extra help?"

"Yes, my sister, Biyu. She put man's face to the floor in two seconds." He grinned. "I time her. I check outside right now."

Julio watched Ling leave. "Are you expecting Rosa's monkeys?"

"Possibly. Or Irma, the bakery lady. She's not happy we're here."

━━━

Backstage was in a state of opening night chaos, with dancers in various stages of dress warming up their back and leg muscles. At the barre, Margo and her dance partner, Manny, bickered their way through a warm-up routine—he a perfectionist and she a master of the quick retort. Gina whiffed the fruity odor of pot, and she barged into the men's dressing room. "Who's got one burning?" she demanded. "You know the rule. No drugs before the show."

Hores, a tall dancer as thin as a pencil, answered. "We're doing good. Leave the door open on your way out, will ya? It's hotter than the devil in here."

"Just put it out," Gina snapped, aware she ruled from a weak position, with every musician and dancer hired essential to the show.

In the women's dressing room, Gina sniffed the scent of orchids and tuberoses from the island dancers' coronas and leis. With a sprained ankle tightly wrapped, Arielle sat in a corner, gluing pheasant feathers onto an elaborately plumed and beaded headdress that Hores would be wearing. She held up the headdress. The beads and shells jangled, and the feathers wobbled. "I'm not sure this glue will dry in time." She chuckled. "Hores might molt on the stage."

"Don't tell him that," Inez warned while applying a second coat of mascara. "He'll have a breakdown worrying about it." She stopped her makeup routine to light a cigarette "My friends are out partying right now, and I'm missing all the fun. They'll probably show up drunk as skunks tonight." She chortled. "Just a warning."

The list of the night's plagues was growing longer—injured and bickering dancers, pot-smoking musicians, a faulty headdress, and the high probability of sloshed patrons. Nothing unusual, Gina knew. Still, she couldn't shake the jitters. She reached for a cigarette, then put it back in the pack, afraid it would irritate her throat.

Ling stepped into the dressing room, carrying a foul-smelling bag at arm's length. "Animal horns . . . goat, ram, bull. I find bury in the yard." He held up a black, moldy one.

The women recoiled. "Ugh. Really? What for?"

"Seems you cursing. Each horn buried in the yard bring six years bad luck." Ling rattled the bag. "Four in here. Maybe more outside."

Gina didn't believe in curses. "Just get them out of here."

As she turned and walked away, she heard someone ask, "Can you reverse it?"

Standing in front of the full-length mirror, Gina slipped on her dress, an understated low-cut black number with a fitted bodice, spaghetti straps, and a long slim skirt that skimmed over her trim figure. Her hair was parted to cover one eye when she tipped her head just so. Large diamond-and-antique-gold earrings dangled around her face, and a matching bracelet sparkled on her wrist.

Bing Crosby crooning "O Tannenbaum" drifted in from the Orchid Room, bringing on memories of Ray making origami kittens, birds, and dragons for Cheryl to hang on her own small tree. The child had saved those ornaments in her treasure box, which was gone now, like everything else.

Julio came up behind her and fastened the clip on the back of her dress and gazed appreciatively at her reflection in the mirror. "You're a vision of success, boss."

That was the impression Gina wanted to portray. In reality, the jewelry was borrowed from Chan. "Money begets money," she had said when she'd approached Chan about wearing the jewelry stashed in his safe, most pawned by the once-wealthy American women interned in Santo Tomas. Gina turned the bracelet around on her wrist, wondering who'd worn it last. With a sigh, she turned her back to the mirror and to her memories and questions.

The music changed to "Carol of the Bells" to lighten the mood, so Gina knew Pearl Blue's doors had opened. From behind the one-way mirror in her office, she and Inez watched as Petra, the full-lipped, green-eyed, socially elegant hostess greeted and seated guests.

The dining room filled with Manila's art and political personalities, Japanese military officers, physicians and staff from the Remedios and Philippine General hospitals, and professors from the University of the Philippines. Inez's sloshed friends gathered together on the settees. Gina felt slightly heady when she saw Hajime Ichikawa, who conducted the symphony at the Manila Metropolitan Theater, arrive on Petra's arm. A pear-shaped photographer from the *Philippine Free Press* circulated the room, snapping pictures.

"I think you've hit the jackpot," Inez said.

"Thank God, we've got one hell of a show for them." Her mind flew through everything that could go wrong, from injured dancers to equipment breakdowns. "If we can pull it off."

"Don't tighten up, Gina. We're ready. Keep positive."

Gina heard her cue and flung a red feather boa over one shoulder. On her way to the stage, she called, "Break a leg," to the women dancers. Passing the men's dressing room, she waved and repeated the sentiment in Italian: *"In bocca al lupo."*

The band was playing a popular melody, and when Julio saw Gina standing in the wings, he winked at her and then continued solo on the piano while purring melodically into the microphone, "Ladies and gentlemen. We'd like to welcome you to the grand opening of Manila's newest nightspot, Pearl Blue. Our goal is to entertain, enthrall, beguile, and captivate you this evening. We hope you love the show and will come back to visit us . . . and next time bring your friends along. Now, it is my great pleasure to introduce Pearl Blue's most perfect pearl, our own wonderful songbird, direct from the stages of Venice, Rome, and Florence, Italy: Signora Angelina Aleo."

Breathe, Gina coached herself. *Let it flow.*

Piano and drums segued into a subtle *123-12* syncopation, the stage lights darkened, and Gina strolled into the spotlight and assumed the eighteenth-century persona of Pirate Jenny, who lived in a crummy German town and toiled as a maid in a cheap hotel while suffering gawks and taunts from her cruel oppressors . . . and planning her revenge.

Gina slunk around the stage, watching her audience's reaction, flipping the red boa, slipping between German and English, whistling to punctuate a point while melodically spinning the tale of Jenny's imaginings: a thick fog in the harbor, a black freighter appearing, a town under siege, and Jenny's soul-satisfying retaliation before sailing away with the pirate invaders. The performance ended abruptly with a flourish on the piano and the bang of the drum. Gina felt elation and relief that she'd completed her number without a memory lapse or a trip. She bowed deeply to the applauding audience and acknowledged Julio on piano and Giorgio on drums.

Covered with a fine sheen of perspiration and with her dress sticking to her in inconvenient places, she addressed the audience. "Welcome to Pearl Blue. You may have recognized Pirate Jenny from *The Threepenny Opera*, written in 1927 by Kurt Weill and Bertolt Brecht. The opera was wildly popular when it opened. Within a year it had been performed in cities all over Europe. Everybody knew the songs." She whistled a few bars of "Mack the Knife." Smiling, she made eye contact with Franca, who gave her a wink. "I'm going to let you in on a fantasy of mine." She paused, taking the time to observe the effect of this teasing admission on their upturned faces. "I've been singing and dancing since I was a young girl—"

Giorgio tapped the snare and clanged the cymbal.

Gina turned toward him and put her hands on her hips. "It wasn't *that* long ago—"

The audience laughed.

Gina laughed, too, and continued. "Ever since then, I've dreamed of opening my own nightclub. In my fantasies, my desire was to entertain the best people—the generous of heart and the knowledgeable of mind—people like yourselves who are the backbones of society." She gestured outward. "And here you are. Right in front of me. I'm honored to be in your presence. Thank you for coming tonight. I hope you enjoy the show."

For the next thirty minutes Gina held the audience in the palm of her hand as she alternately bubbled with vitality and gently caressed them with a medley of songs from Cole Porter and selections from the bluesy Billie Holiday's songbook. The spotlight followed her when she left the stage to circulate among the tables to tease and cajole or to straighten a crooked tie or wrap the boa around a bald head while she sang the playful tune "I Get a Kick out of You."

When she returned to the stage, she stood beside the piano. "Please give a hand to our talented band: Julio on piano, Sedrick on strings, Giorgio as percussionist, Layden on the horns, and Gil on everything else." She gestured toward them, and the band stood and bowed to enthusiastic applause.

Before the crowd had time to catch their collective breath, the curtain opened to a full moon peeking through a densely jungled setting and the figures of three women stomping their bare feet and shimmying their grass-skirted hips to the wild beat of percussion instruments and the wail of a wooden flute. The audience remained standing as the beaded and tasseled island dancers fanned out over the stage, followed by the two drummers, their mostly naked bodies brightly painted and their oiled hair pulled into tight knots on top of their heads.

Gina watched Arielle from the wings, worried that the young girl's injured ankle wouldn't hold her, but Arielle proved that she had grit, giving the dance all she had. Eddie came to Gina's side and whispered into her ear, "Thought you should know. Ling saw one of the waitstaff going into the utility room. He caught him trying to break into the fuse box."

Gina turned abruptly. "To interrupt the show? Where's the man now?"

"Ling tripped him when he ran, and Biyu chased him out the stage door." Eddie smirked. "Sissy."

Gina didn't see any humor in the intrusion; there was more at stake than Eddie realized. She scowled back at his silly grin.

He shrugged and uttered, "Ling recognized him as one of Rosa's monkeys. Don't read too much into it."

That one of Rosa's monkeys had infiltrated her staff was a significant concern to Gina. "We can't let that happen," she barked and saw a puzzled look cross Eddie's face. "Sorry, nerves," she mumbled. The dance pulled her attention back to the stage.

The flute stopped its wail. In its place the hollow, rolling beat of a kettledrum preceded the appearance of a figure emerging from behind the curtain, dressed head to toe in black, moving on all fours, slinking smoothly as a panther around the edges of the stage, stalking the dancing women. A warrior appeared next, as slim as a pencil. A loincloth covered his essentials, and a tall headdress of hackle feathers, seeded beads, and coconut flowers elongated his figure. A belt of dried grasses circled each ankle, and he carried a spear. He whistled to the women, who turned, saw the roaming panther, screamed, and scrambled away.

"Super," Gina whispered to the island dancers as they came backstage. "Arielle, how's the ankle? You going to be all right for your next number?"

"It's okay. I'll wrap it later and take another aspirin."

Onstage, two flutes moaned a counterpoint duet as the warrior and panther circled, their eyes intent on each other's every step and twitch, one advancing, the other retreating, the warrior prodding, the panther clawing and hissing.

From behind the curtain, Gina assessed the audience, which sat motionless in a tense rapture, and when the panther crouched and sprang, she heard their collective gasp.

The warrior whirled away in a series of grand jetés, and again man and beast faced each other, one hissing, the other growling. The warrior attacked, and a battle ensued in a cloud of arms and legs, feathers and fur, untamed, ferocious, and feral. The warrior raised his spear overhead, and to the clang of a cymbal, he thrust the tip deep into the heart of the snarling foe. He circled the animal, watching it writhe and die, and then sank to his knees, his back bowed and head bent low, his hand to his face in the posture of prayer and profound remorse.

Gina sank into a chair as exhausted as if she had herself fought that battle.

The program continued with Julio's piano rendition of Gershwin's "Rhapsody in Blue" and concluded with a jerky marionette number performed by Inez and Arielle.

Gina sighed with relief that the hastily put-together opening night had gone without a hitch, and it had been magnificent. When she returned to the stage to close the show, she struggled to hide her giddiness. "Thank you for coming. I hope you enjoyed the show and will tell your friends about us. We're open Tuesday through Saturday for music and dancing, with a full floor show at eight p.m. on Friday and Saturday nights. Have another drink; enjoy the dance music. As soon as my lovely and talented dancers catch their breath, they will be out to chat with you."

The crowd dispersed to the bar and dance floor or to the smaller Hibiscus and Jasmine Rooms to converse in intimate clusters. Gina moved among the guests and graciously accepted their praises and wishes of good luck in her new venture. Upon seeing Franca, she whispered into her ear, "Thank you for bringing your many well-heeled friends. I owe you one."

Franca returned the whisper. "A big one, and soon I may be calling it due."

Gina stepped back, curious as to what was in store for her, but Franca changed the subject. "My dear, you do me proud. How did you put this together in such a short time and on a shoestring budget? You and your staff are most certainly talented."

The dancers reappeared, the men in black jumpsuits and the women in hand-painted sarongs with white orchids pinned in their hair. They joined Gina to schmooze with the crowd, Inez and Arielle seeking out the Japanese officers on whom to lavish their special attention.

Later Gina, Inez, and Arielle toasted each other with the last drops of champagne. Inez removed the orchids from her hair and shook her head, letting her dark tresses fall to her shoulders. "I feel like magic happened. Look, my hands are shaking."

Already a little tipsy, Gina said, "Don't sell yourselves short, either one of you. What happened here tonight was the result of hard work."

"Here's to hard work and magic." Arielle held up her glass in a toast.

"To success," Inez uttered.

"To those Japs—the officers we were mesmerizing."

They clinked glasses.

"Do you think they'll come back?" Arielle asked.

Inez let out a hoot. "You kidding? Most assuredly, and they'll bring their friends. Isn't that what we are all about? Here's to the Japanese, our rich and unwitting partners. May many flood our doors."

"To the guerrillas in the mountains and the men in the prison camps," Gina added. "God bless them." She silently added, *To Ray and Cheryl. May this crazy endeavor help bring them home to me.*

The mood became wistful but triumphant, and the three exhausted women left Pearl Blue arm in arm, giggling like schoolgirls giddy from too much champagne.

Chapter 22

DIGGING DEEPER

Mother Nature favored us with a meteor shower of fiery brilliance, a sparkling and welcome interlude in an otherwise joyless day.

—Ray Thorpe, Cabanatuan prison camp, October 1942–
January 1944

Chan had a stake in Pearl Blue being successful, and he mentored Gina to get her started by supplying names of safe vendors from whom to order materials and services and from where she could purchase liquor for almost nothing. He introduced her to creative bookkeeping techniques to hide profits and cautioned her to burn all communications.

Under his guidance and Gina's creativity, Pearl Blue became the new hot spot in town, and business quickly increased. Tonight, a weeknight, toe-tapping tunes played over the PA, and already couples were dancing, a sign of a spirited crowd. Julio would keep the music loud and the energy high, a recipe for a healthy cash flow.

Eddie's waitstaff scurried from table to table taking orders and serving beers and cocktails. He had added several pretty young women to his staff who refilled bowls with snacks, emptied the ever-full ashtrays, and schmoozed with the customers. Gina had hired Biyu, Ling's sister, who floated around the room, lending a hand where needed, but her real job was security backup.

Gina circulated through the crowd, dodging the waiters, bowing to the Japanese men, putting on a show, chatting, and playfully tapping the shoulders of those customers she knew. Ling prowled between the front door and the bar, and when Gina caught his eye, she gestured toward table 10, with its group of already inebriated young officers. She strolled to the table and spoke loudly over the jazzy music and clink of glassware. "Welcome to Pearl Blue. What ship are you fellas from?"

"*Kongō Maru*, my pretty." The young officer pawed her backside.

Gina stepped away. Her eyes narrowed. *You scum* went through her head. She saw Ling step forward, but she signaled him with a slight movement of her left hand that she could handle it. "You misunderstand my establishment, sir. What you're looking for is down the street." She saw a flicker of rage and prepared herself for a slap, but the others at the table whooped and guffawed, deescalating the danger. Hiding her edge of anger, she smiled and said, "Have you tried the dim sum? It's excellent with the beer."

A lieutenant gobbled peanuts like he was hungry. "What kind of a joint you have here? Is that all you have to eat?"

"Yes, sir, but there are three choices tonight." Gina waved the dim sum waiter over, the smell of hot sauce and shrimp making her stomach growl. "Are you men going to be in port long? You must come back on Friday or Saturday for our floor show. Lots of pretty girls—no touching allowed." She grinned at the man with the roving hands, but his gaze had turned to Inez, who was laughing with him and refreshing his beer. Biyu and a tawny-haired waitress came to the table to bestow friendly attention and to help serve the chicken-and-shrimp dumplings, curry puffs, and vegetable buns from the dim sum cart.

The booze, the spicy food, a bevy of attentive women, and the cover of music loosened tongues, and Inez later told Gina that the men were from a fleet leaving port in a few days for Shanghai, where they were delivering airplane parts to a factory. Over the first months of operation, Gina and her staff had charmed information from army brass and navy elite about troop movements, road and bridge conditions, and ship repairs.

Inez sidled up next to Gina and whispered, "The man at table 16 asked to speak with you privately. I think that's his wife with him."

Gina looked over and saw a Filipino man, fortyish she guessed, unremarkable in appearance, wearing a stylish white suit and dark-rimmed glasses. His wife was dressed in a flowered suit, expensively tailored, and ruby-and-diamond jewelry. "Any hint what he wants?"

"No. What do you want me to tell him?"

"That I'll meet him in my office. When I leave, give me five minutes, and then bring them to me." She circled the room again before slipping away. After entering her office, she checked for anything inadvertently left out, though she was meticulous about destroying sensitive documents.

Inez knocked on Gina's door. "This is Mr. and Mrs. Emilo Sak."

Up close, the woman looked vaguely familiar, and Gina felt a prickle of fear. "I'm pleased to meet you. What can I do for you?"

The woman spoke first. Her voice was soft. "You may not remember me, Mrs. Thorpe. My name is Imelda. We worked on a community project together to collect school supplies for the less fortunate children in Manila. Our little girl, Ella, and your Cheryl are the same age."

Gina's heart thumped, and she struggled to remain composed. "Yes, I remember you. I'm Angelina Aleo now. And how is Ella?"

"That's why we're here." Imelda turned to her husband.

"Please," he said. "I know this is startling to you, but we come as friends. Two years ago, Dr. Theo saved Ella's life—her appendix burst, and she almost, well . . . it was a hard time for us. We've recently learned he is working with the guerrillas. We want to help but don't know how to contact him. Imelda remembered that you were friends with his wife, Vivian."

Gina wondered how Emilo had learned about Theo working with the guerrillas, and she certainly wasn't going to confess to knowing it. "I have no idea where Vivian and Theo are. I'm sorry, but I cannot help you."

"Of course. I understand. I give you my card. If you learn more, you pass it on, please."

Gina waited until Emilo and Imelda Sak left before she picked up the card he'd placed on her desk. It read,

E. J. Sak Industries
6543

She showed the card to Ling. "Do you have any idea who this is?"

His eyebrows rose. "E. J. Sak. Emilo Sak. He owns munitions factory in northern Luzon. You give card to Major Davy. He knows what to do with it."

"So this guy's for real then?"

"Very real."

—

It took only a short time for Gina to pay Chan back the money he had loaned to her to get Pearl Blue started. Her good luck weighing on her mind, she purchased apples, mangoes, bags of rice and beans, three small red fire trucks, and a coloring book and crayons and divided the goods into three boxes: one for Sissy and Harry; another for Stella, Ruthie, and the two little boys; and the third for Edith and her frail mother. She put them behind the bar and said to Eddie, "When you leave today, please drop these off at the package line at the University of Santo Tomas."

"Sure enough, Miss Gina. I've heard it's nasty in there. You got a minute? I need you to go over these latest orders—something isn't adding up."

While Gina was helping Eddie reconcile the deliveries with the invoices, the front doorbell rang. "Want me to get it?" Eddie offered.

"That's all right. I'll take care of it."

Admiral Tanaka, who had been away for weeks, was standing at Pearl Blue's front door. Gina had read in the *Candor*, an underground newssheet secretly passed among certain employees, that the United States and Japan were fighting battles in the Marshall Islands. She wondered if he'd been involved. "Admiral Tanaka. Come in out of the heat. What can I do for you?"

He stepped inside. "Thank you. I came to ask a favor."

"Have a beer while you're here. You look like you could use it." Fact was he looked haggard, with sallow skin and bags under his eyes. At the bar, she filled a glass with his favorite beer and skimmed the foam off the way he liked it. She wondered what favor he had on his mind—a celebration of some kind, maybe. That would be fun.

He accepted the beer and took a long drink, then rested his arms on the bar like he was tired. "My colleagues are waiting; I only have a minute. I'll be in Manila for several months. I'm looking for a place where my friends and I can play cards. It's pleasant in your Hibiscus and Jasmine Rooms . . . would one be available for us to use one or two afternoons a week?"

Instinctively, Gina didn't like the idea of having Japanese officers in Pearl Blue during the day. Guerrillas sometimes stopped by disguised as workmen, and her rehearsing dancers and musicians felt free to mock their Japanese customers, sometimes getting raunchy as they laughed and let off steam. She dispensed another beer to give herself time to think. "How many would there be?"

"Just four for poker or mah-jongg. We won't be any trouble."

"I wouldn't expect you would be, Admiral." At least not in the way he meant. But it was a dangerous request, and she scrambled for a face-saving way to refuse it. Nothing quickly came to mind. She felt his questioning gaze and forced a smile. "Certainly. It would be my pleasure." Even before the words were out, her mouth went dry. She'd have to warn her staff.

"You are most gracious, Signora Aleo." He finished his beer. "We will compensate you, of course."

"There's no need, sir."

When the admiral left, Eddie puckered his lips and blew a silent whistle. "Words of a master manipulator. He asks a favor he knows you can't refuse."

"I didn't have time to think," Gina mumbled. She dumped the beer she had drawn down the sink . . . maybe she could pick up information for Davy. She said aloud, "Having the officers here might keep Irma off our back. She doesn't bring those doughnuts to us out of the goodness of her heart, you know. I suspect she's the neighborhood sentinel. It's best we go about our business—keep our eyes open and our mouths shut."

Days passed quickly. Admiral Tanaka had brought three officers to Pearl Blue twice now to play mah-jongg, and there had not been a problem. Gina had closed the curtain on the door to the Hibiscus Room and played classical piano music over the sound system just loud enough to block carefully held conversations.

Today Pearl Blue was quiet, and Gina had errands to run. A calesa was waiting. On her way out the door, she ran into Miguel. He handed her a letter and said, "I just came from Major Davy's."

Gina recognized Vivian's handwriting. "Did you have a chance to talk to her?"

"No, ma'am. She cold and hot with malaria. Miss Maggie angry, because Miss Vivian gave her medicine to the guerrilla soldiers. Dr. Theo give Miss Vivian shots that take her headaches away, but he angry, too, because he only has one needle, and the shots hurt. It is very sad in the mountains. Everybody angry and hurt."

Dr. Lopez had told Gina he couldn't keep up with the medical needs of Davy's growing guerrilla camp. "I'll tell Dr. Lopez what you've said. Maybe there's more we can do. Did you see Cheryl?"

"Yes, ma'am. She and Leah found some baby bunnies they feeding. She taken care of good. No need to worry about her."

"Thank you, Miguel. You look exhausted. Go home to get some sleep. Spend some time with your wife and kids."

⌁

After finishing her errands, Gina walked to Luneta Park, a large urban park that skirted the shores of Manila Bay. She often spent time there when she wanted to be alone or to find peace by lingering in the gardens or walking along the water's edge. She sat on a bench in the shadow of the monument dedicated to José Rizal, Inez's great-grandfather and her son's namesake. Before taking Vivian's letter from her purse, Gina checked for Japanese guards who monitored the park. Seeing none close by, she opened the letter.

> *My friend. I miss so much having you to talk to. We share so many memories. Cheryl and Leah are in their school class with Edna right now. Edna's a good teacher, even with her meager supplies. She thanks you for the notebooks and pencils you sent in your last package.*
>
> *Cheryl is excited about her birthday. She has grown two inches since the last time she was measured, and she has two new front teeth and two are missing. Red is her*

favorite color this year, and she asked for barrettes for her birthday. She could use shorts and shirts. She might like a coloring book and crayons. She's doing fine, Gina. She and Leah play well together, and she's helpful around the camp. She's quite a little imp and keeps us entertained.

In your letter, you asked me to be truthful and tell you what it's really like living in a guerrilla camp. I gave your question a lot of thought before I settled the answer in my own mind. I can say with all my heart that life is good because we're free, though the manner in which we're living is a perversion of the concept.

Since your return to Manila, the guerrilla band has grown, and we are always on the move in order to evade capture. We are now a company of men, a squad of women, and a handful of children who can quickly and quietly evacuate our makeshift hovels in the middle of the night, taking only necessities, which means guns, ammunition, food, medicines, and as many clothes as we can wear on our bodies. We trudge always uphill, climb over fallen trees, scale cliffs, slip in the mud, and hope the ever-present rains will obliterate our telltale tracks.

We've been at this camp for a few weeks. It's high on a densely forested ridge and miles from the Japs' nearest military stronghold. I feel safer here than I have in a while. The main trail leading to the camp goes straight up a cliff, and machine guns salvaged from downed American planes guard the mud-slicked and thorny side and back trails. A low rocky area in the center of the ridge forms a natural amphitheater and hides our campfire light, which is heavenly—we went many weeks without the warmth of a campfire. Our moves to new camps are practiced and efficient. A few days after our arrival here, the men had built a score of huts, Theo had set up his clinic, Edna had a working kitchen, and Marcus had arranged for ongoing transport of food and supplies to us. Both are tireless workhorses.

I'm sitting in a nipa hut, on a rough-hewn bench at a makeshift desk squeezed beside a bunk where Maggie and I sleep. Leah and Cheryl have the upper bunk, and Theo sleeps on a cot in the clinic. My job is to keep track of the camp's duty roster and finances. Your last contribution bought us a desperately needed supply of rice, beans, blankets, and mosquito nets. Some things we can get from the local people; others Davy brings back when he raids the Japanese storehouses, but more and more we are forced to turn to the black market, where prices are skyrocketing.

Davy said to tell you a million times thank you for everything you are doing. We could not survive without the money you send and the backers you find for us, some who are very generous. Davy is checking out the tip you sent about a Japanese warehouse in the area. We could use those supplies if it pans out. He has developed into a strong but cautious leader. In the early days when there was no creed, nor rules, nor long-range plans, his philosophy had been to hit and run, often with disastrous outcomes. Many men were lost then and hard lessons learned. Most attrition now is from disease.

Theo's staff in the clinic includes Maggie, a chaplain, and two Filipino women trained in first aid. They treat everything from gunshot wounds to foot fungus with no more than scraps of provisions and the vile-smelling herbal remedies Maggie cooks up on a primitive stove. The medical supplies and medicines Dr. Lopez is sending

*are lifesavers in a literal sense. I, myself, have periodic
episodes of malarial fevers.*

*You may not know this, but some of our contacts
have visited your club, and they have nothing but good
things to say about it. I'm so proud of you. Thank you for
everything you are doing. I miss you terribly but don't
wish you here. I'll give Cheryl an extra hug for you.*

Love in war and peace,
Vivian

Gina examined a smear on the letter . . . Vivian's tears or raindrops?
She sat for a while with her eyes closed, listening to the lapping water
on the shore and contemplating how primal life in the guerrilla camp
was, staying one step ahead of Japanese patrols while scrounging for
life's basic necessities, not knowing what the next hour or minute would
bring. Gina's eyes filled with tears of sorrow for her friends' dangers and
hardships, and her soul filled with guilt for abandoning Cheryl to it.
She folded the letter and tucked it into her brassiere.

A Japanese soldier riding a bicycle appeared, and a prickle of fear
went up the back of her neck. The brakes squeaked when he stopped.
He barked in garbled English, "What is your business here?"

Vivian's letter burned like a hot poker on her breast, but Gina
calmly rose from the bench and bowed, avoiding the guard's eyes,
instead noticing his belt buckle, the crease in his pants, and his polished shoes. "I'm out for a walk," she said, wondering if he had been
watching her.

He parked the bike and strode toward her, coming so close she
could smell the pomade he used on his hair. "Who are you waiting for?"

She stood straight but kept her eyes lowered, noticing a scar on his
chin. "Nobody. I'm just enjoying the beauty of this park."

"Why should I believe you? You wait for someone." He grabbed
her purse, and her instinct was to grab it back and run, as she might

have done to a thief a year ago, but she squelched the impulse. As she watched him paw through her purse, her mind ticked through what was in it: her pass, a comb, a lipstick, a sanitary napkin, and a few pesos.

He found her pass and tilted her chin up with his fingers, and she fought not to pull away and prayed he wouldn't notice the locket that connected her to Cheryl and yank it off her neck. At first chance, she would tuck it into the pocket she had made in her bra, it safer hidden away—as was her child. For a moment his eyes lingered on her generous breasts, and Gina held her breath. He put the pass back and shoved the purse into her chest. "You sit here, and I watch for who comes to meet you." He got on his bike and pedaled away.

Tethered by his watchful eye, Gina sat on the bench, seething and praying no one would come to sit beside her. Vivian's written words came to her: *Life is good because we're free, though the manner in which we're living is a perversion of the concept—*

After a while she left with no ramifications but aware of the perverse nature of her freedom. She and every blessed person on this Japanese-held island were prisoners in one sense or another, and the realization made her breath catch.

<hr />

The first thing Gina heard when she opened the door at Pearl Blue was Julio bellowing, "Holy shit! Are you crazy?" She hurried to the back and saw him standing beside a delivery of clean laundry. Nested inside were rifle parts and boxes of ammunition sent from E. J. Sak Industries.

"Rifles?" he hissed when he saw her. "I suspected there was more to this little venture of yours than getting rich. You're working with the guerrillas, aren't you?"

"Shhh!" Gina said, afraid a deliveryman could be close enough to hear Julio. "These are for our protection."

"So you say. Just what else do you have stashed in that hidden closet upstairs? Whatever it is, I could help, but noooo, you don't trust me, do you?" He thumped his chest with his fist. "Me!" He started to pace.

Gina had seen Julio flying high and deep in depression, but she'd never seen him angry . . . or was it hurt at her distrust? "You're not exactly the Rock of Gibraltar, you know. Half the time you're strung out on drugs. Where do you get all those pills? From the Japs?"

"What difference does it make? I hate them as much as you do. I deal with it in my way." He stopped pacing and faced her. "Do you want me to leave?"

"No. Don't leave. You're too important here." She lit a cigarette to buy time to think of what to say. She decided to tell the truth. "It's why I came to Manila. To raise money for a small band of guerrillas . . . my friends. If you tell anyone that, we'll all go down . . . including you. You're more involved than you realize."

"So a little blackmail's not beneath you?"

She shrugged. "Whatever it takes. Now that you know, I could use your help. Admiral Tanaka will be here this afternoon, and this stuff needs to be put out of sight. It will be gone in a couple of days."

Julio's anger dissipated as quickly as it had flared. "Just tell me what you want done, boss." He helped her carry the contraband to the hidden closet.

Trusting Julio was risky, but what choice did she have? She had been caught red handed. Best to draw him close. She hoped she wasn't wrong.

Chapter 23
THE UNDERGROUND

In this subhuman existence, illusions of my favorite foods force their ways into my thoughts, an unwanted and cruel torment.

—*Ray Thorpe, Cabanatuan ⊔⊔⊔⊔ ⊔⊔⊔⊔ Camp, October 1942–*
January 1944

Gina woke up with a headache and in a foul mood. She had dreamed that she was reunited with Cheryl, but the child had rejected her and run away screaming that she wanted her real mom. Gina took an aspirin and drank a cup of strong coffee, but it didn't help her achy head. The telephone rang. It was Franca.

"I didn't wake you up, did I? I tried your office phone, but you didn't answer."

"Sorry, I'm slow getting started this morning. Today's Cheryl's birthday."

"Oh, Gina. I'm sorry. You want to be with her. When my boys grew up and left home, those first few birthdays were hard for me to get through. It must be even harder with a small child. I called to invite you to lunch. Why don't you come. It will do you good to get away from Pearl Blue for a couple hours."

Gina didn't even feel like getting dressed, much less going out to lunch. "I don't know . . ."

"Please come. I have something I want to talk to you about."

"Can you tell me over the phone?"

"No. What I have to say is for your ears only. Please . . . come at noon."

Gina rubbed the spot that hurt between her eyebrows with her fingertips. "All right, at noon." Franca had a way of making an invitation sound like a summons.

By the time Gina arrived at Franca's, her headache was gone, but she still felt blue. Franca handed her a gift wrapped in birthday paper and with a big red bow. "It's one of my favorite books, *Heidi*, by Johanna Spyri. I've read it at least a half dozen times over the years."

"Cheryl will love this. Thank you. There are few books in the mountain camp, and she loves to be read to. Vivian says she's starting to read by herself."

Franca took Gina's arm. "Let's walk in the garden. I had Millie make up her special chicken soup for you, and it should be ready in a bit. There's nothing like it to soothe a soul." She led Gina outside, where beautifully tended lilies, beds of fragrant jasmine, and bunches of white plumeria edged the crushed-stone path. They walked past the waterfall and stopped at the grotto that held a statue of the Blessed Virgin. Franca said, "What I have to tell you has to do with the well-being of our prisoners."

Gina came to attention. "Have you heard something about Ray?"

"No, I'm sorry, I haven't. But this could have an impact on him. The doctors are running a smuggling operation out of Remedios Hospital. It started several months ago. One of our drivers noticed that ambulances leaving the Camp O'Donnell prison were searched, while strangely enough, ambulances going into the prison camp were not. We've sent in meds, money, and food that way. I keep waiting for the operation to blow apart. It's too easy."

Gina was surprised all that was going on right under her nose but wondered what it had to do with Ray.

"The issue is," Franca said, "O'Donnell is closing, and the prisoners are being transferred to Cabanatuan prison camp. Isn't that where Ray is?"

"I haven't heard anything officially, but the men captured on Corregidor were taken there, so probably."

Franca gestured for Gina to sit on a bench under a magnificent bani tree, its canopy spreading a wide twenty-five meters. It was cooler in the shade. Franca said, "The doctors and I, and some others involved, want to continue supporting the prisoners, but it's going to be trickier smuggling supplies and medicines into Cabanatuan. I've contacted a resistance worker in Cabanatuan City. She says she knows you. Her name is Clara Jacob."

"Clara! She's the nurse who found Davy by the side of the road in the mountains. She brought him to our camp and nursed him back to health. Last I knew is she had applied for a job with the Red Cross in Cabanatuan City. I like Clara. I've wondered what happened to her."

"She's going to be in Manila next week, and she asked to see you. I've arranged a meeting with her and a few other people in the resistance. I'd like you to come too."

Franca had caught Gina's attention. She wanted to know more about the plan to smuggle supplies into Cabanatuan and maybe to Ray, but she cautiously hung back. "Who are these people? Can you give me names?"

"Not until you commit. You'll have to trust me. I can tell you it's a handpicked group."

Gina wasn't surprised. Names were obscured and jealously held. "I need some time to think about this. Other people will be impacted."

"Of course. I know it's not an easy decision. Come—I see Millie is signaling that lunch is ready."

The more Gina thought about Franca's invitation to meet with a small group of resistance workers hoping to penetrate Cabanatuan prison camp, the more she was inclined to say yes. Ray might be there or held in some other loathsome camp, and also it was her chance to meet like-minded people willing to work for a cause. When back at Pearl Blue, she called Inez and Arielle into her office and told them about O'Donnell prison camp closing and the Manila resistance moving into Cabanatuan. "Right now, only a handful of people know Pearl Blue's true mission. If I get involved with this larger group, it puts us at higher risk of being detected."

Arielle's foot tapped in the air. "I don't care about risk. My husband's in Cabanatuan. It's what I've been hoping and praying for. I'll do anything I can to help."

Inez paced in front of Gina's desk. "Cabanatuan. That's big time. Do you know what you'll be doing?"

"Not yet. I'll find out at the meeting."

"Do you trust these people you'll be working with?"

"I'd trust my life to the organizers, and I was told it's a handpicked group. As soon as I commit, I'll find out more."

"I had friends who were in O'Donnell. Their stories are brutal. I trust your instincts, Gina. Find out more, and if you feel comfortable with it, I'm in too."

Gina felt the relief of having decided, and when Inez and Arielle left her office, she called Franca on the phone. "I've covered some bases here. I'll come to the meeting. Tell Clara I'm looking forward to seeing her."

"I thought so. Come prepared to introduce yourself. You'll need a code name."

Gina sensed she was about to enter a world where nothing was what it seemed to be. She bent down to pet Aleo the Cat, who was slinking around her ankles. "Kitty," she said to Franca. "My code name is Kitty." There was a knock on her door. It was Arielle.

"Gina, there's a man here to see you."

Gina put her hand over the receiver. "Do you know who it is?"

"I've never seen him before. He looks sort of scruffy."

"All right. I'll meet him in the Jasmine Room. Tell Ling to stay close by." She returned her attention to Franca. "Gotta go. Someone's here to see me."

Gina met the scruffy man in the Jasmine Room. "I'm Signora Aleo, and you are?"

"Lieutenant Francis Willard, United States Army, ma'am." He spoke with a tinge of a drawl and kept his voice barely above a whisper. "Father Morgan sent me. I got separated from my unit. I want to go to the mountains and join the guerrillas but I need help getting out of Manila.

Gina scanned the man's face, thinking he looked too young to be a lieutenant, but maybe he was exaggerating his rank to impress her. His wide-set eyes, light coloring, and lanky build reminded her of a younger Ray. She felt a pang of longing. "Why do you think I could help you?"

"Father Morgan said you could put me in touch with someone who could get me past Major McGowan's security." His gaze shifted to the window and quickly back. "It would help a lot if you wrote me a letter of introduction."

Gina doubted Father Morgan's involvement. She scrutinized his face and his manner. He looked and sounded like an American soldier, and there were hundreds living in hiding in Manila. Still, she remained cautious. "I don't have any idea who Major McGowan is. I don't know where Father Morgan got that idea."

Willard's face fell. "I understand . . . me walking in off the street and everything. One has to be extra careful these days. But if you could spare a few pesos so I could get a haircut, and maybe your husband has an extra suit of clothes I could have. I'm too visible on the street like this." He pointed to his army pants. "It's all I have to wear."

Gina wavered. The request was meager, and his story might be true. She thought of Ray in need of kindness and being rejected, and her hand went to her pocket where she kept a few pesos. But then a jerk of his glance out the window again stopped her action. Scowling, she took a step back. "Who do you take me for, and what makes you think I'll give you anything? Get out of here!" She shooed him away with a flail of her arm.

Surprise crossed his face and then anger. He stepped toward her, his jaw clenched.

Gina backed away quickly, her steps jerky. She put a chair between herself and him. "Get out," she hissed.

"Bitch. You'll get yours." Sneering, he opened the door and left.

Gina heard Ling's voice coming from the dining room, and she hurried to where he was talking with Inez. "Ling. Follow that guy. Don't let him see you."

Ling wasn't gone long, and his report gave Gina the jitters. Willard had gone straight to a Kempei waiting on the corner. Realizing how easily she had nearly been duped by a man with a handsome face made Gina weak kneed. She slumped in the closest chair, ruminating on what she had done to attract the Kempeitai's unwanted attention. And now Franca was asking her to increase her exposure.

~

With more than a little trepidation, Gina arrived at Franca's the following week to meet with a faction of Manila's giant underground. She saw only Father Morgan's vehicle parked in the driveway and wondered if she was one of the first to arrive. She lifted her chin and rang the doorbell.

Millie led her to the dining room, where drinks and canapés were on the buffet. About a dozen people—Filipinos, Spanish, Chinese, and Europeans—were dressed in business attire and sipping cocktails. Gina did a double take and inwardly groaned. Standing in profile by the fireplace was Armin Gable, who not only had turned down her request to sponsor Davy McGowan but had chased her, shamefaced, from his house. By the looks on their faces and adversarial stances, he was arguing with Franca. When he saw Gina, he frowned and turned his back.

Gina slunk to the buffet and selected a drink before approaching Father Morgan. "Do you know everyone here?" she whispered.

"Yes, we've become a close-knit group. Many are native to the Philippines; some are socially prominent, others politically connected. All have a unique skill. We work toward one goal—to aid the prisoners in the camps. We seldom meet as a group; it's too dangerous. But we're taking a new direction, and we need a new strategy."

Gina discreetly nodded toward the fireplace. "Can you tell me about him?"

"That's Armin Gable. He's a retired banker from Zurich. He's an interesting fellow. During the last war, he interrogated deserters who'd crossed the border into Switzerland. He can spot an imposter a mile away, a valuable talent to us."

Gina almost spilled her drink. An interrogator. She should have guessed. Given his low opinion of her, she wondered whether he had vetoed her inclusion in the group.

Father Morgan glanced at Gina's scowl. "Everyone is here by invitation. We welcome you as a worthy resource to our mission, Gina."

Gina shrank inside. He'd guessed what she was thinking; there must have been a discussion of her shortcomings. Across the room she saw Clara Jacob. "Excuse me, Father. I know her. I'd like to say hello."

Just then Franca clapped her hands. "I know you're all busy people, so please take a seat at the table, and we'll get started."

Once all were settled, Franca addressed the group and reiterated the purpose for coming together—to set up a collaborative effort with the resistance in Cabanatuan City to aid imprisoned soldiers. She gestured to her right. "Clara Jacob is here representing the network. She'll tell us about the tight security at the Cabanatuan prison camp and what her group is doing to work around it. Not to state the obvious, but who is in attendance and what is said today does not leave this room.

"Before we start, we have some new members, so let's go around the table and introduce ourselves. I'll start: I'm Señora Franca Estevez; call me Franca. I'm the go-to person. If you have a problem or a question, come to me. If I can't help you myself, I'll direct you to someone who can. My code name is Butterfly. Please use it whenever you contact me." She nodded to Gina.

With every eye on her, warmth rose to Gina's face. "Angelina Aleo; I go by Gina. I'm honored to be invited to join this group. I'm the owner of Pearl Blue, a nightclub. I'm not sure why I am here yet. My code name is Kitty."

"I might add," Franca said, "if you haven't been to Pearl Blue on Friday or Saturday nights, you must go. The floor show is spectacular." She gestured to Father Morgan.

"Father Brady Morgan, priest and chief scrounger. The garage at Malate Church is available to store supplies you gather until they can be delivered to Cabanatuan. There are many problems to be worked out, but we're up to the challenge. Written and phone messages should come to True Heart."

"Dr. Hernandez Lopez. I'm on call for all medical issues. I procure medical supplies and some drugs through the Remedios Hospital accounts. Call me Loopy." He nodded to the woman sitting next to him.

"Hi, and welcome to our new members. My name is Jean Caffey. I've been providing interest-free loans to prisoners at Camp O'Donnell. I hope to continue to do so at Cabanatuan. I accept IOUs written on any scrap of paper the prisoner has at his disposal. Levi is my code name."

Gina pondered the code name: Jean . . . Levi, easy to remember. She glanced askance at Armin Gable, the next one to speak.

He cleared his throat. "Armin Gable. I beg my wealthy Italian, Swiss, and Chinese contacts for money. No more needs to be said. You can call me Bashful."

Gina swallowed a guffaw. She could think of a dozen other code names more fitting, like Bully or Tyrant, though she had to admit he had been right at the time: she hadn't been ready to take on the task assigned to her . . . and maybe, according to his standards, she still wasn't.

Franca said, "Armin's contacts have been very generous. We hope that continues." She nodded to a younger man next to Mr. Gable.

"Lulian Jonesy. Reporter and photographer for the *Philippine Free Press* by day, and author of the underground newsletter the *Candor* by night. We got the *Candor* into Camp O'Donnell. I hope we can get copies into Cabanatuan. As always, if any of you have information suitable or unsuitable for print, contact me. My code name is Clark, as in Clark Kent."

Gina recognized Jonesy. He'd taken pictures at Pearl Blue's grand opening night. So he was the author of the *Candor*, a one-page rag sometimes left behind the bar at Pearl Blue reporting Japanese and Allied movements, skirmishes, arrests and releases, rumors, and atrocities meted out by the Kempeitai. She wondered if Eddie, her bartender, was involved with Jonesy and if the *Candor* was sent to the guerrillas. Davy could use the information the sheet reported. She made a mental note to contact Jonesy.

"I'm Mrs. Hahn. I offer shelter to anyone who needs to be hidden for a few days. I'm an artist, and my husband is a chemist and a genius with dyes. Between the two of us, we forge credible documents. My code name is Belle."

"Freddie Sulet, accountant. Like Bashful, I have access to foreign funds. Slapstick."

"Rinaldo Torio, enforcer. I'm new to the group. Call me if you're in a jam. Bull."

Enforcer! And the guy was built like a bull. Gina crossed her arms over her body, hoping she never had to use his services. The aura of the group suddenly took on a darker quality.

"Bai Guang, pharmacist, Teddy Bear. I find drugs for you to send to prisoners. Price is higher, but most I still can find."

So that was how Dr. Lopez was able to send quinine to Davy, even though the Japanese had blocked its shipment. This meeting was bringing some things into focus for Gina. She hadn't been working alone but had been navigating the periphery of this larger group.

"Clara Jacob, Red Cross nurse stationed in Cabanatuan City. Barton, as in Clara Barton. I'm also new to this group. Thank you for inviting me."

Franca stood. "As you see, our talents are diverse, and our reach is wide. Not only do we work to support our men in the prison camps, but we back a number of saboteurs and disrupters to keep the Japanese off balance. Now, if there are no questions, please welcome Clara."

Gina clapped louder than anyone for the woman whom she knew to be a good nurse, a rebel, and an adventurer.

Clara stood, straightened her navy pinstriped dress, and cleared her throat. "Thank you for inviting me here today." Her voice shook slightly. "I work for the Red Cross. Like everything else, the Red Cross is administered by the Japanese. My current assignment is to provide health care to the Filipino civilians in Cabanatuan City and its outskirts. By Japanese rule I'm forbidden to provide aid to Allied soldiers." She fumbled with her watch. "I've never been very good at following rules."

Her audience chuckled.

After the laughter, Clara seemed to relax, and her voice strengthened. "Thousands of Japanese soldiers are living in Cabanatuan City, and hundreds are billeted inside the prison camp itself. Franca has told me what you are doing at Camp O'Donnell. It's commendable, but the Cabanatuan camp is a much larger and far more dangerous place. You cannot take the same risks. Those of us wanting to help realize the desperate needs of the men inside, but until recently we've found it impenetrable." She hesitated, looking over the group. "But there's still hope."

"Amen," someone in the audience said.

"Thank you. Yes, there's still hope. The Geneva Convention requires POWs be paid for their work. Pay averages about twenty centavos a day, about ten cents, depending on the prisoner's rank. They use the money to purchase cigarettes or food, but it's not enough; they're dying of starvation and disease."

Gina hugged her arms tight around her, trying to block the thoughts she couldn't deny. *Please not Ray. He's smart. He's frugal.*

"We have found we can pass small amounts of money to the prisoners who are outside the camp on work details. On any given day, about four thousand men work on the farms, cut wood in the forests, rake the airfields, or dig graves in the ever-growing cemetery. My young niece, Trixie, has organized a cadre of women who have food-vendor licenses and are allowed to approach the prisoners outside the gates. The women sell a prisoner fruit or a bag of peanuts for two centavos; then they give him the purchase and five centavos in return. That's our basic model, and we'd like to expand it, but we don't have the resources. These women also wear men's shoes and extra shirts to work and leave them behind for the prisoners to find. It's dangerous. If either the women or men are caught, they are beaten or worse."

Mrs. Hahn asked, "Just selling peanuts and fruit outside the gates seems narrow in scope. Are there other avenues we could use too? Where else are the men spending their money?"

"There is a camp canteen, where they can purchase cigarettes and limited food. Provisions such as clothing and blankets are sent in from the Swiss Red Cross, which the prisoners are allowed to buy . . . that's after the Nips have pilfered the best for themselves. Additionally, civilians set up huts along the roads where the men travel to work. They sell food, drinks, cigarettes, hats, shoes, and whatever. This is one avenue for us. On a larger scale, select prisoners are assigned to purchase rice, beans, and other supplies in bulk for the camp at the marketplace in Cabanatuan City. I see this is where our best opportunity lies. Currently, no stalls are available, but we've found a man named Dion who owns three. One of his sons died from typhus at O'Donnell—Dion's no sympathizer. We haven't approached him yet, but he's our best bet. I've been inside his stall, and I think he's already smuggling goods to the prisoners. He uses clothing racks on wheels to create blind spots in his stalls. There are diversions, like porn magazines he keeps in his office, and he opens the curtain to make them visible when he sees the guards coming. Women with babies and children with pets magically appear to divert the guards' attention."

Franca raised her hand. "The guards aren't suspicious?"

"Not that I've noticed. They ogle the women and play with the children. I saw a guard leave with a girly magazine shoved down his pants. I suspect that while the guards are distracted, Dion is loading the prisoner's cart with bags of rice and beans containing contraband."

"If we get involved, won't the guards notice if the prisoners are suddenly spending more money?"

"Not if we're careful. There are nine thousand men in Cabanatuan. They can absorb a lot of money and contraband without it causing a ripple."

Franca raised her hand again. "Have you learned anything more about Dion . . . as a man?"

"Just that he has a big family and they all work at the stalls. The oldest son owns two other stalls on a side street. He was on the death march and spent time in O'Donnell. He made it home, but his younger brother didn't."

Father Morgan stood. "Just as important as resources is the exchange of information. Would Trixie or Dion be willing to send a note to someone inside?"

"We haven't approached Dion yet, but I'm sure Trixie would, if she knew whom to contact."

The room came alive:

"I know an American doctor—"

"I have a friend—"

Gina raised her hand. "I think my husband—"

The meeting lasted through the afternoon, and it was decided that Trixie and her cohorts would continue to smuggle small amounts of money to the prisoners in their peanut and fruit purchases with more money provided by the Manila resistance. As soon as an internal contact was found, Trixie would send in a note written by Father Morgan. Additionally, Clara was to explore opening supply huts along the prisoners' work-detail routes and to contact Dion to see if he would be interested in working with the Manila resistance. A committee was formed to explore ways of transporting larger volumes of goods from Manila to Cabanatuan City without being detected.

Franca clapped her hands to quiet the group. "We've made a lot of progress today, and I want to keep the momentum going, but let's step back for a moment. We know the risks, not just to ourselves but to our families and friends. Remember to keep a tight lip, to use code names in telephone communications, and to destroy anything written. We've established a phone chain, and I'll add the new members to it. We each have two people to call if one of us is picked up by the Kempeitai. The list is redundant, purposely, so no one gets overlooked. Use the code 'So-and-so is on his or her way to school.'"

Kitty is on her way to school. A chill went up Gina's spine as the danger felt real and significant.

Franca stood. "We can adjourn. Gina, please stay. Clara would like to speak with you."

The others left a few at a time so as not to be conspicuous to anyone watching. Clara and Gina huddled together at one end of the table. Clara squeezed Gina's hand. "It's good to see you again. How did you end up here?"

"Davy thought I'd be useful in Manila. Pearl Blue supports his guerrillas."

"A nightclub. How intriguing. I always knew there was something special about you. You have a certain flair. Is Cheryl with you?"

"No, she's at Davy's camp with Vivian. She just had a birthday; she's seven." As hard as she tried to hold back, Gina teared up.

"You're missing her."

Gina lowered her voice. "With all my heart, but it's more than that. What I'm hearing is scaring me. When I left Davy's camp, it was a small group, and life was hard, but it was bearable. It about tore me apart to leave her there. It's far from a picnic here in Manila, but I want my child with me."

"Do you think Cheryl is in danger?"

"I don't know. Maybe. The guerrilla unit has grown, and the Jap patrols are always two steps behind them. They move around a lot. Half the stuff I send them gets left behind. Vivian's malaria has kicked up again, and there's no quinine. Food's always scarce."

Franca joined them, and the conversation changed. "Clara asked specifically that you be here, Gina. I'm glad you could join us."

"It's been eye opening, but I don't know what you expect from me."

"I can answer that," Clara said. "To support the men in Cabanatuan prison camp, we need to establish a supply route from Manila to Cabanatuan City . . . trains, trucks, drivers, storage garages, trusted workers, and so forth. I'd like to get guerrilla support to guard the truck route and storage garages. Also, we need men on the docks at the train station to police our shipments. It's important that I meet with Davy McGowan, and I haven't been able to contact him. Franca thought you could help."

It was a simple request for Gina to handle. "I can send him a message with one of my runners and tell him what you're doing. It's up to Davy to respond. Remind him he owes you his life!"

Clara sniffed. "Good thought. I'd like to set up a meeting with him to explain what we're doing. I've been told I can be persuasive."

Gina had no doubt that Clara was persuasive. "Anything's possible. I'll help where I can." Gina was hesitant to ask her a favor, not wanting Clara to think her request was a tit for tat. "I suspect my husband's a prisoner at Cabanatuan. Could you help me find out for sure?"

"I can try. We need to find a contact inside the camp first. I have Trixie and Father Morgan working on it. Once that's established, if all goes well, information will flow in and out. You'll need an identifier . . . some code he would recognize, like his mother's name or a favorite song. There are nine thousand men in Cabanatuan and probably a couple dozen Rays."

Nine thousand men and a couple of dozen named Ray. Gina wondered the odds at finding her Ray.

Chapter 24
JONESY

I follow the teachings of my church, but watching a guard bludgeon a man to death with the butt of his rifle mocks my piety and leaves me questioning.

—Ray Thorpe, Cabanatuan prison camp, October 1942–
January 1944

It was show night at Pearl Blue, a more formal night of entertainment. The musicians had arrived, and the dancers were warming up. All day Gina had been moody, it being her fourteenth wedding anniversary, and Ray was still at the mercy of the Japanese.

Upon entering her office, she found what looked like scrap paper slipped under the door, but a tiny dot in the upper left corner identified it as a coded message from Davy. She turned on a lamp, and when the bulb was hot, she held the paper near it and watched Davy's directive, written in lemon juice, emerge in the heat. *Guerrillas reorg. Desperately need radio. Send in pieces with multiple runners. Parts okay.*

Gina knew some background relevant to Davy's requests. The guerrilla bands, scattered throughout the Philippines, were now organized along military districts. Davy, promoted from major to colonel, now had thousands of men under his command, and his need for a radio was greater than ever. Thinking Jonesy might be helpful, she placed a call to him. He didn't answer his phone. Tearing Davy's note into small pieces, she burned it in a large ashtray she kept for that purpose.

She checked the one-way mirror to watch arriving customers, mostly Japanese military brass, government officials, and business leaders with their wives or dates for the evening. She was heartened to see a mix of regulars and new faces. Scanning the crowd, she searched for those customers known to be volatile, calculating, or information givers or seekers—anyone who with a point of a finger had the power to pitch her into peril. Satisfied that she knew her audience, she slipped into her simple red silk dress and elegant jewelry and joined Margo and Manny backstage, both clad head to toe in black leotards. "I'm not feeling ready," Margo confessed.

"You'll do fine," Gina whispered. "Think positive."

The house lights dimmed, the audience quieted, and Julio murmured the welcome and introduction while playing soft arpeggios on the piano. On her cue, Gina entered stage right to the beat of a drum and eager applause. She stood in the spotlight beside the piano, faking a smile and an upbeat attitude, hoping it would raise her spirits.

"Good evening. Welcome to Pearl Blue, my friends. It's good to see all of you here, new faces and old faces . . ." She stopped and put her hand to her lips. "Um, maybe I should say familiar faces."

The audience laughed.

Gina laughed and hoped it didn't sound as fake as it felt. "I have a special program for you this evening. My dancers Margo and Manny have been working very hard on a new routine. You're the first to see it performed, and we hope you love it. They'll be dancing to one of my favorite French love songs, 'Ouvrez Votre Coeur . . . Open Your Heart,' written by Jean Leroy."

Julio played the slow introduction in a lilting waltz tempo, and Gina joined in, first humming and then presenting a moving rendition of the song's haunting lyrics of love and yearning.

"Open your heart to me, and share the passion that lies within . . ."

At the end of the first stanza, she paused while Julio played an interlude. Thoughts of Ray were intruding. A lump had risen in her throat, and she worried she couldn't get through the rest of the number. She glanced at the stage, hoping that Margo and Manny were poised and ready.

On a cue from Julio, the curtain opened to reveal the shadows of a man and a woman behind a backlit screen with their arms and legs extended in the precise posture of a waltzing couple.

Gina continued the song—"Ouvrez votre cœur et partagez la passion qui se trouve dans . . ."—casting sly glances at Margo and Manny, who were performing a delicate dance of longing, their supple bodies gracefully coming together and breaking apart in sultry configurations, creating sensual shadow images on the screen. Gina detected the rising excitement of the audience, who murmured oohs and aahs at the unexpected eroticism of the dancers' choreographed movements. She caressed the final phrase—"Je vous aime," I adore you—in a lover's hoarse whisper. The backlights dimmed, and the dancers' silhouettes vanished.

A hushed aura permeated the room, and Gina stood with tears rolling down her face. From the audience, she heard sniffles from women and snuffs and coughs from men who took pride in being stoic. When Margo and Manny came from behind the screen to take their bows, the patrons rose to their feet in a loud standing ovation. A relieved sigh escaped Gina's lips as the dancers bowed to the fervent applause, but then she quickly left the stage and told Inez to take over.

In her office Gina broke down and sobbed out the wretchedness she had been fighting all day. How much longer would she be able to hide behind a gay facade and entertain an audience she both loathed and feared?

By the time Inez came into her office, Julio had the audience gaily singing Japanese pop music from the 1920s and 1930s. "Are you all right?" she asked.

"I am now. Thanks for taking over."

"It's okay. You need to talk?"

"No. It's over. Today is my fourteenth wedding anniversary. You'd think I was the only one missing my husband."

"You're not. Both Arielle and I have had our turn with the boo-hoos, just not on stage while singing love songs. Why didn't you say something?"

"I thought I could handle it. I guess I was wrong."

~~~

The show over, the dance floor was opened, drinks refreshed, and dim sum served. Gina, having recovered her composure, mingled with the crowd, greeting those she recognized and welcoming those new to Pearl Blue. She stopped at the bar, where Arielle, wearing a flowered sarong and a lei of orchids, was playing rock, paper, scissors with an officer. "Paper covers rock," she said and laughed as the officer downed his beer and ordered another. Eddie put the beer in front of him and refreshed Arielle's ginger ale. He signaled for Gina to come behind the bar, where his baseball bat was placed for easy access. He kept a loaded gun in a locked drawer.

"We're almost out of beer. The shipment's late again. I've told the waiters to push the liquor."

Pushing the liquor was cost effective; Gina got it almost for free, the owner of Manila's largest distillery working with the underground, but beer was a popular drink at Pearl Blue. She said, "Call Yee's and see if you can borrow a keg."

Just then, Gina heard a flurry of excitement and saw Petra leading an entourage to a favored table. "It's Baal-hamon, the actor," Eddie said.

The young man was truly a delight to the eye, loose limbed and with every feature perfectly placed in his sullen, baby-soft face. With him was an older man, impeccably dressed in a well-tailored black suit. Each man escorted two women, one on each arm, beautiful and skimpily dressed showgirls. It wasn't unusual for Manila's luminaries to arrive at Pearl Blue in their own flurry of pomp and circumstance. Gina treated them royally, providing every amenity and the particular attentions they craved.

She strolled over. "Welcome to Pearl Blue. What brings you to my little place down here by the docks?"

The older man stood, his chair scraping on the wooden floor, and he weaved on his feet. "Come sit with us, Signora Angelina Aleo. A beautiful name for a beautiful woman." His voice was as smooth as good chocolate, and he pulled back a chair for her to sit. "I came last Saturday to see your show. Spectacular. Your voice has the fullness of a choir, and the timing of your program is of professional quality. What else can I say?"

Drinks came, and it gave Gina time to evaluate this blast of flattery. She demurred. "You're much too kind, sir."

He leaned into her. "Not kind at all. I'm a damn good businessman. When Japan wins the war, I will move my company to Hollywood. You come with me, and I'll make you a movie star. Your name will be in lights. You'll be the toast of the town." He reached into his pocket and handed her a business card that read, *Eiji Fugio Productions, Agent to the Stars. Hollywood, California, USA.*

Gina smiled at the silliness and slipped the card into the pocket of her dress.

Mr. Fugio continued in his boastful way. "You dance like Ginger Rogers. Would you like to meet her? When we get to Hollywood, I can arrange that."

"You flatter me, sir. Of course I'd like to meet Ginger Rogers, but I'm happy enough here in little ole Manila."

"Don't be coy. Fame can be yours. Look at Baal-hamon, here."

She smiled at Baal-hamon and received a scowl in return. He peered at her breasts with half-closed eyes. "I'd like to see you do a fan dance, like that woman Sally Rand."

Gina's hand flew to her chest as she half chortled and half gasped in surprise at the insinuation that she was a stripper. "Ah-ah . . ."

Mr. Fugio laughed loudly. "What do you expect from a kid?"

As if on cue, Julio began playing the theme song from Baal-hamon's recent movie, and Gina silently thanked him for rescuing her from a sticky situation. She stood and announced Baal-hamon's presence and led the audience in applause, knowing he and his entourage would return to Pearl Blue along with his many loyal followers.

She said goodbye and good luck to Baal-hamon and his hangers-on and joined Jonesy at the bar, where he was hunched over a plate of dim sum. She asked, "What you got there?"

He poked at one of the gelatinous dumplings with a small fork. "Chiu Chow, fun guo . . . shrimp, pork, and peanuts." He picked up a talon-shaped body dripping with sauce and held it out to her. "Fung zao . . . steamed chicken feet. Want it? Dim sum's meant to be shared."

Gina ate the spongy-textured tidbit and licked the sweet soy sauce off her fingers. "What will we be reading in the morning paper?"

"Bad news or good?"

"It's all bad, isn't it?"

Jonesy's chin jerked up in agreement, and he huddled close to her. "Lieutenant Stevenson and his guerrilla unit were captured yesterday. You familiar with them?"

Gina remembered the odd duck of a kid named Stevenson, who had shown up at Davy's camp asking to see their leader. She'd laughed at him that day. "Lieutenant Robert Louis Stevenson. He recruited his ROTC schoolmates."

"That's him. They never set up a base camp, just kept moving from place to place giving the Japs shit. They were captured in a barrio near Angeles. The Kempeitai rounded up the local men, women, and children, hooded half, then shot one at a time until someone broke." Jonesy talked while he devoured a dumpling. "It's just one of their dirty little games."

Gina knew the Kempeitai's cruelty. Hearing it always sickened her.

A Japanese officer pushed his way to the bar and stood next to Gina. Her insides tensed, but she greeted him with a smile.

Jonesy stopped talking.

After the officer got his beer and left, Gina leaned closer to Jonesy and whispered, "I have a friend who needs something. I think you may be able to help. It's hard to talk now. Can you stay until closing?"

"Yup. Got nothing to do but keep my eyes and ears open. Great hole-in-the-wall for intrigue, this place."

Gina bristled. *Hole-in-the-wall?*

⌒

After closing, Gina turned off the neon sign and locked the door. She poured whiskey for Jonesy and mixed gin and vermouth for herself. Jonesy spun around on the barstool and surveyed the lit room. "I came here when it was Rosa's. You've done a nice job cleaning this place up."

Gina smirked. "You just called it a hole-in-the-wall."

"Just an expression. I hang out in a lot of dives."

"What do you think of our floor shows?"

"Too highbrow for me, but you've got an audience. I've heard you pack the place with the best and the brightest of Hirohito's Imperial Navy. You must pull in a bundle."

"It's enough to buy groceries." She took a cigarette from a pack on the bar. Jonesy lit it for her and one for himself. She said through a cloud of smoke, "Tell me your story."

"Not much to tell. I'm native. Graduated from the University of Santo Tomas and joined the army. My unit was stationed in northern Luzon when MacArthur ordered the army to retreat to Bataan. I vacationed on Bataan when I was a kid, and I saw it for the trap it was. I slipped into the mountains. I guess technically I'm a deserter." He took a long drag on his cigarette and blew it out his nose, squinting. "I came back to Manila just before the Japs' big entry. I swore allegiance to their imperial asshole, and they kept me on at the newspaper. What they didn't know is before they showed up, I smuggled out a new radio and replaced it with a junker from the storeroom." He snickered, glanced at his drink, and pushed it away. "Too much of this. Got any water?"

At the mention of a radio, her heartbeat picked up a few thumps per minute. Out of habit, she played dumb as she poured a glass of water with ice and lemon. "You have a radio? You have a death wish?"

Jonesy shrugged. "The Nips have to find it first, and they won't. It's right under their noses."

"How far does it reach?"

"Why are you asking?"

"Just am."

"Australia. Sometimes San Francisco. It gives me a different perspective of what's going on. Contrary to what you read in the rag I work for, the United States took the Mariana Islands. One by one they're neutralizing Japanese bases in the Pacific. Did you read about it? I reported it in the *Candor*."

"No. I didn't see it."

Jonesy thumped his knuckles on the counter. "Damn. And that's my problem. There's no circulation. The *Candor* should be all over Manila and in every prison camp and read by every guerrilla. I desperately need help with distribution."

Gina was quick to pick up on his frustration. "And I know someone who desperately needs a radio."

Jonesy's stare was blank at first, and then he laughed. "Son of a bitch. You're working with the guerrillas. I knew it. You are sharp, baby girl."

Gina's stare bored back into his. "As you might take notice, asshole, I'm not a baby girl."

He laughed again. "Touché. I need to piss." He left for the men's room.

Gina debated how much she wanted to reveal to Jonesy. He was Filipino and knew the desires, customs, and habits of the people, plus he had contacts she didn't and vice versa. Since he'd been vetted by those in the network, she felt he could be trusted. He liked his liquor, but he knew when to stop. When Jonesy returned, they both started talking at once.

"I can distribute—"

"Sorry, but I can't give you a radio—"

"I didn't figure you could. Do you have any components? My guys will take anything they can get."

"That I can help you with."

Gina bit on her lip. "There's something else."

"Your price comes high, baby . . . uhh, lovely lady. What is it?"

"I'd like you to listen around and tell me what rumors are in the air about us, you know, being friendly with the officers or whatever. There's an admiral, Akia Tanaka. He's become a fixture at Pearl Blue. He likes our programs, and I've let him use our side rooms for mah-jongg."

Jonesy scratched the back of his head and grinned. "You getting involved?"

"I'm married."

"Does that matter?"

"Of course it does. Keep it quiet. This world thinks I'm a widow. It's important that I know what Admiral Tanaka is hearing. . . that's all."

Jonesy grabbed the whiskey he'd rejected earlier. "Deal. I'll keep my ears open for rumors about Pearl Blue and gather up some radio parts. You help me increase the distribution of the *Candor*."

They toasted to their new alliance.

He glanced at the clock. "Shit, it's after midnight."

Gina knew his concern. Booze and questioning at Fort Santiago were a dangerous combination. "You can stay here tonight." She saw his grin. "Don't get your hopes up. There's a couch in the employee lounge. You'll share it with Aleo the Cat."

Chapter 25

ADMIRAL AKIA TANAKA

Visions of Gina enter my mind hourly and bring me moments of bliss. But as I look at my shrunken body and swollen feet, I feel uneasiness. How could she love . . . this?

—Ray Thorpe, Cabanatuan prison camp, October 1942–
January 1944

Sometimes Gina needed to get away from the ringing phone, the clank of glassware as Eddie restocked and cleaned the bar, Julio and the band practicing a new arrangement, or the dancers working up a new routine. Outside Pearl Blue it was no better, with the shouts, whistles, honks, and sirens of crowds and traffic. At one time she had embraced the bustle of the city, but more often now she desired quiet and solitude. It was those times that Gina walked to Luneta Park and entered a different world, one of stretches of green grass, benches under massive bani trees, and the gentle lap of water on the shoreline of Manila Bay. Here, she could decompress, dream, and think.

Today Gina was deep in thought as she strolled along a path in the quieter area of the park away from the neoclassical government buildings and monuments that drew crowds. The shimmer of light through the trees and the crunch of gravel under her feet fostered relaxation. She filled her lungs with air, her chest expanding, and then blew the air out slowly and with it the tension her body greedily held. In a state of well-being she sat on a park bench next to a man reading a newspaper, it hiding his head and most of his body.

"Good morning," she murmured.

The man lowered the paper and turned to look her way.

"Admiral Tanaka?"

"Signora?"

Without another word, he handed her the fashion section of the *Washington Post* and resumed his reading.

The *Washington Post*? She read of the latest fashion trends, which were all about creating an hourglass silhouette with padded shoulders, nipped-in waistlines, and skirts that covered the knee. More women were buying pants, this season also high waisted with a wide leg shape. Gina assessed the dress she was wearing, a shapeless number she'd purchased on sale at Heacock's, thinking that maybe a belt would give her the nipped-in look coming in style.

She put the newspaper down and watched a doe and her spotted fawn foraging for berries under a bush and squirrels playing tag in the trees. She noticed the admiral watching too. "Admiral Tanaka, did you order the entertainment?"

"Yes, special for you. Do you come here often?"

"As often as I can get away. It's close to Pearl Blue. I need to see the sky and the trees. It refreshes me. How about you?"

"It reminds me of home." He folded the newspaper into a precise package and put it on the bench. "Would you like to walk with me?"

What would it hurt? It was just a walk in a public park, though she'd have to measure her words. "Certainly," she said and stood and straightened the skirt of her dress. "And where is home?"

"Sometimes I wonder that myself. Tokyo. It's where my family lives."

They walked through a field of wild cosmos to a nearby pond and watched the ducks swimming among the lily pads and the turtles sunning on the pond's edge. The admiral retrieved a handful of animal crackers from his pocket and threw one into the water. Three ducks paddled toward the floating cracker, and he threw another. Soon, six ducks were paddling within his throwing distance and then a dozen. He laughed and threw out the remainder in his hand.

"Do you have children?" Gina asked and saw a smile light up his face again. It was a handsome smile.

"Yes. Two boys. Riku is twelve years old. He's quiet and studious. He's away at school most of the year and just beginning to pull away from his mother. Soru just turned six, still a small child, but he's a bit of a . . . what do you say . . . piston."

Gina laughed. "Pistol."

"Yes, a handful for his mother, but he's bright. He'll go far with a steady hand guiding him."

"You must miss them, being so far away for so long."

"I do, but we're at war, and I owe a debt to my country. And you, Signora, what brought you to this beautiful island?"

She laughed. "A husband. What else? I was born in Milan but grew up in Canada. I met my husband there. He was an engineer and was offered a position at a diamond mine in the Sierra Madre. We thought it would be a great adventure. Unfortunately, it ended in tragedy. There was an accident, and he was killed." She knitted her eyebrows appropriately, but her voice caught whenever she mentioned her fictional husband.

"I'm sorry. I can only imagine your sorrow. Do you have children?"

"No." The denial stuck in her throat. "I'd like to have some someday, a girl for her daddy to spoil and a boy to carry on the family name." How was it she lied so easily?

A Japanese family—father, mother, and two children—approached, and the admiral's gaze followed them so longingly as they walked through the field of flowers that Gina wondered if he were visualizing his own family. He handed the children the remainder of the animal crackers in his pocket and then stood back to joyfully watch them feed the ducks.

They searched and found the path that meandered through a lush forested area, where Gina could hear nothing but birdcalls, winged flutters, and the rustle of leaves. The admiral stopped periodically to point out a rare plant or a beautifully flowering bush. The trees thinned, and they passed a playground where children were playing on the swings, seesaws, and a merry-go-round while parents and grandparents sat on benches sipping sodas.

Ahead, Gina saw the majestic shores of Manila Bay, the sunshine on the water sparkling like diamonds. At a kiosk nearby, the admiral purchased two sodas, and they sat on a bench that overlooked the water, the breeze off the bay refreshingly cool after their walk.

Feeling emboldened by the admiral's friendly manner, Gina said, "Besides the banter at Pearl Blue, I've never talked to an admiral in the Japanese Imperial Navy. You're very impressive, sir. You do know that?"

The admiral blushed and grinned. She could see he was pleased, and she, encouraged by his acceptance of her flattery, pushed a little further. "Tell me something about yourself."

She learned that he was the third son of seven children, his father an intermediate-rank samurai. He'd had a happy, though strict, upbringing. As a young man, he had been adopted by the childless Tanaka family to carry on their rank and name.

"You were adopted as a young man?" Gina reiterated, not sure she'd heard right.

"It's a common practice. I was given opportunities I never would have had, and my adoptive parents' legacy stayed intact. Through their contacts, I was able to study at Harvard University and work as a naval attaché in Washington, DC."

A Harvard graduate and a naval attaché; it accounted for the *Washington Post* and his Americanized ways. "How long were you in the US?"

"Five years. Three at Harvard studying business and mechanical engineering and two in Washington, DC. It's a beautiful country, the United States. I traveled a lot while I was there. Unfortunately, my country doesn't realize the vastness of our adversary's resources. We should have dealt more terrific blows early in the war to deplete them. Maybe they would have then negotiated to end it."

Gina felt her jaw clench and her breathing quicken at the thought of her beloved homeland being annihilated for what end besides greed, an ugly human condition never to be overcome even by love and shared values?

He looked off into the distance. "Unfortunately, we awoke a great sleeping giant. The sneak attack on Pearl Harbor spurred the US to revenge. I doubt Japan can hold on another year." The sadness in his voice revealed his yearning for home and his great love for his country.

A sheen rose on Gina's cheeks. She left the bench and walked to the water's edge. She wondered if he realized the importance of what he had just told her and if he would remember later and regret it. Or was he naive enough to think her a safe confidante? She doubted that. Maybe the information was already widely known. Or maybe this was a test . . . too heartfelt, though; it didn't feel like a test.

He joined her at the water's edge.

She turned toward him. "It's not what I read in the newspapers, sir. Japan is stripping the islands they capture of their natural resources, and she is stronger for it. I think your assessment is overly negative."

Seemingly pulling out of his funk, he grinned. "My wife says that about me all the time. Come—let's take the path along the bay back to the city."

The long view of the bay had always been a stunning sight to behold, with sunsets so magnificent they took on an aura of the surreal.

She and Ray had spent many an evening on their lanai, basking in the beauty while sharing the day's events. Gina squelched the urge to try to glimpse the red roof of her house just behind her and up a hill. Instead she looked outward to the water. "Which one of those many ships is yours, Admiral? Impress me."

He didn't immediately answer, like he was trying to formulate what to say. "None, unfortunately. My ship is in repair at Cavite. It will be there awhile."

Gina clamped her jaws shut, remembering what she'd read in the *Candor* about gruesome fighting and heavy casualties in the Marshall Islands. It was hard to cheer on the good old USA when the admiral walking beside her might be mourning his lost men. She squelched her impulses and said instead, "I'm sorry to hear that."

Japanese planes roared overhead so low that Gina clapped her hands over her ears and ducked her head, "I'll never get used to that!" she shouted.

"What?" the admiral said just as a volleyball flew at his face. On reflex, he slapped at the ball, sending it into the water.

Two teens were right behind it. "Sorry, Mister," one yelled as he passed by; the other yelled, "Shit." On returning, the ball and the teens were black with oil. A rope of seaweed trailed from one's ankle.

If she squinted, Gina could just see the top of a submerged tanker and the Rorschach-like image its bleeding crude left on the water's surface drifting toward the shore. The admiral bent to pick up a dead bird blackened with slick, and he flung it as hard as he could into the brine.

"It wasn't always like this," Gina said, looking around and seeing wreckage from strafed and sunken boats floating in the water and their detritus lining the shore. "Watch where you put your feet."

Even though for the most part she was enjoying Admiral Tanaka's company, Gina was anxious to leave it. She declined his suggestion to stop for ice cream, saying she had things that needed to be done before tonight's show. They parted ways at the Rizal Monument with a handshake.

She mused all the way home.

It should have been Ray walking with her today, but he was languishing in some prison camp, a best-case scenario. She put her hand over her heart, where long ago on Bataan a seed of hate for anything Japanese had been planted. She felt it still there, hankering to germinate, threatening her tightly held order of all things life preserving.

Be very careful, Gina.

She looked around, thinking she'd heard Father Morgan's voice. *Don't let hate for the Japanese strip your life of vitality. Use that energy for the greater good.* She had followed his teachings . . . but at what expense? Her husband's? Had her noble intentions turned on her in a twisted way? Had one man blurred the beliefs she had so tightly crafted and held? Was she losing her direction?

After the night's show and closing up Pearl Blue, Gina lingered in the shower, then slipped on her favorite nightgown, the material washed to gossamer softness. In bed, she lay in the dark, and when sleep didn't come, she reached for the pillow that should have been Ray's. Pressing it to her face, she prayed for the scent of him, but the pillow smelled only of Ivory soap. She hugged it against her breast as if it were his beloved body, and in time her aspect softened, her breathing slowed, her guard weakened, and rational thoughts faded away, allowing her to dream without filters of a pleasant day with a pleasant man who loved his family and country as greatly as she did hers.

Chapter 26

TRIXIE

*I mull over my latest predicament. What is it I crave more—
my last cigarette or the bowl of watery soup it will purchase?*

—*Ray Thorpe, Cabanatuan prison camp, October 1942–
January 1944*

When Gina opened Pearl Blue's cashbox, it was so stuffed with Japanese-issued pesos that newly released hundred-peso bills fell to the floor. She scooped them up. *Worthless junk.* The Mickey Mouse money was choking the economy. She counted the income, then divvied out sums she needed to pay rent, utilities, and salaries for her staff; noted the amounts in a ledger; and placed the money in envelopes that she would hand deliver. Not recorded were generous donations sent to Davy that she backed out of her income, making Pearl Blue's bottom line look close to breakeven.

So intent on her work, she was startled when a young woman appeared at her office door. Gina hastily closed her ledger and cashbox. "How did you get in here?"

"I sorry. I not mean to scare you. A man named Julio let me in."

Julio, of course. Pearl Blue was like a second home to him, and he often came in early, using the quiet time to compose his music.

In a glance, Gina evaluated the small-statured person, who was wearing white shorts, a flowered blouse, a floppy hat, and boots. When she removed the hat, her beautifully textured skin attested to a Chinese ancestor, and notably, one eye was brown and the other green. She didn't look dangerous, but who knew these days? "What can I do for you?"

"My auntie Clara said it safe to come to you. My name is Trixie. Maybe you know me as Elf."

"Trixie, yes, of course. It's safe to come to me." It wasn't unusual for runners for the underground dressed as deliverymen or workmen to arrive at Pearl Blue to give or receive information. Gina knew many by sight and others by code names. She motioned to a chair. "Please sit."

Trixie clutched a bag that she kept on her lap. "I come to Manila to visit my cousin and bring a gift for her new baby. I have good news for you. Her husband's father—his name is Angelo—owns a house outside Cabanatuan City. The prisoners from the camp pass by on their way to work in the forest. My cousin say Angelo gives the prisoners bananas and peanuts when he can get them. I will talk to him when I return to Cabanatuan. Yes? Maybe we can help him."

"That's definitely a yes. We'll provide him with whatever he needs. How does he get around the guards?"

"I ask my cousin that too. She say some of the guards away from the prison camp are better. They want to keep the prisoners healthy so they can work, so they allow them to take extra food when it there. I figure when we get set up, we pass notes and money like on the farm." Her smile revealed beautiful teeth.

Gina had known that Trixie was young, but not this young. Sixteen maybe. And pretty. She should be in school learning reading, math, and history, not selling peanuts on a prison farm where the guards were known to be cruel. "Could you work with Angelo? It might be a safer job for you."

"No, I stay at the farm. We doing good work there, and I avoid the guards. My dad worked for Mitsubishi, and I went to school in Tokyo. When I hear the guards say they go in one direction, I go in the other. I dress in rags like a beggar lady and work slow. They think my mind slow, but I fool them." She flashed her brilliant smile again and opened her bag. "I have something important to give you."

She unwove a strand of hemp with a hairpin, revealing a hidden pocket that held a letter that had been folded up small. She held it out to Gina and giggled. "We did it." Her eyes could not have shone brighter if she had been holding the Holy Grail. "It from Pastor Nelson. He goes by Lightfoot. He a prisoner at Cabanatuan."

A note from inside the Cabanatuan camp. It was what she'd been hoping for, and Gina's face flushed with excitement. "How did you get this."

"Like we planned. Father Morgan wrote a letter and addressed it to Pastor Nelson. He wrote that he could smuggle money and letters into the camp, but he needed a contact, someone who came outside on a work detail. He wrote that the peanut vendor with one brown eye and one green eye could be trusted. That is me. I put the letter and fifty pesos in a bag of peanuts and passed it to one of my regular customers. Then I waited, very nervous. I opened my eyes wide to everyone." She grinned and bugged out her eyes.

Gina chuckled at the antics, but she felt concern. "My dear. Do you know the danger you're in? Has your aunt Clara explained the risks you're taking and what the consequences could be?"

"Yes, ma'am. Auntie Clara try to stop me, but I do this for my uncle, Auntie Clara's husband, who was killed by Jap soldiers for no reason at all, and for my best friend, Rosamie, who was raped and killed in a most brutal way. I do this for all the girls in the Japanese workhouses. No one will stop me as long as I'm free."

Gina felt her face skew, and she swallowed hard.

Trixie continued. "Two days ago, a prisoner called Eugene gave me this letter wrapped in a peso bill. It is for Father Morgan. He is out of town and will not be back until tomorrow. I have to leave Manila this morning. You give it to him, please?" She gave Gina the letter.

Gina could hardly believe what she held in her hand, the first wedge into the prison camp. "Yes, the minute he returns." Gina opened the cashbox and handed Trixie a handful of pesos in small denominations. "To put in your bags of peanuts."

"Or to buy cigarettes. We hide them in the fields under the green bean plants. They as good as money inside the camp." Trixie placed the pesos in the secret pocket of her hemp bag and took a minute to weave it closed. She chuckled. "It is a game, you know, and I not as stupid as those Jap guards think. I must go now to catch my train."

When Trixie left, Gina dialed Franca's number. "A little elf just left my office. She's barely out of her childhood. What the hell are we doing? Anyway, game's on."

─═

After the initial contact had been made with a prisoner inside Cabanatuan, a pipeline developed that carried small amounts of information and money in and out of the camp. Father Morgan suggested that the prisoners write notes to trusted coworkers and friends asking for their support. One day, when she was at Malate Church, he handed a letter to Gina.

To Willie. I'm pleading for your help. Nothing could have prepared me for the horrors of this camp. There is no escape except death, and each minute I'm here, I feel closer to it. There are angels working on my behalf, soliciting money so I can buy food. Please be generous when they come calling, my friend. Every peso buys me one extra day. I live only for liberation. Red

When she handed the letter back, Father Morgan said, "Unfortunately, I couldn't find Willie."

"What are you going to do with this letter?"

"Burn it with the others that can't be delivered."

"Father, let me reply to them."

"I can't let you do that." Father Morgan folded the missive and put it in his pocket. "There's sadness and ugliness in these letters."

"Yes, but there is also hope for a reconnection. It makes me sad to think of these men waiting for an answer to a letter that will never come. I'll write and say hello and that we know they are there—and that we love them."

Father Morgan removed the letter from his pocket. "Are you sure, my dear girl?"

"Yes, I'm very sure."

⌖

It was more important than ever now to keep Pearl Blue a viable establishment, and a challenge was keeping the entertainment fresh. Gina and her staff had created a repertoire of songs and dances from which to select each week's floor show. Thursday became a popular and profitable "Men Only" night when exotic dancers, who worked for a pittance and tips, were hired to tease those customers with a salacious nature. The extra income was marked to be funneled to the prisoners in Cabanatuan prison camp.

⌖

On Friday night, the crowd was slow to leave. Eddie closed the bar, and Gina turned on the room lights. A wolf-faced Japanese lieutenant, telling a story to his audience of hangers-on, caught Gina's attention.

She gathered napkins and tablecloths from nearby tables to be close enough to listen.

"At the old Chinese cemetery. Six. Naked and crying. Digging their own graves. Haw, haw, haw." The lieutenant's audience laughed along with him, but a dark affect came over Gina, and her fingers involuntarily wadded up a napkin.

"Got the big-nosed pigeon in my sight." The lieutenant held up his arms as if aiming a rifle. "Took careful aim. Squeezed the trigger. Got him with one shot." He moved his arms so Gina was in his fictitious aim. "Bang!"

Gina's eyes practically popped out of her head. She winced and felt the blood drain from her face. But everyone's gaze was focused on her, so she laughed along with the others. "Congratulations, Lieutenant. And who was the recipient of your well-aimed bullet?"

The lieutenant sat back in the chair, puffed up and basking in the limelight. "Some ROTC kid. His band of guerrillas was caught cutting our communication lines. We hunted them down like the dirty little rats they were."

A toast with empty beer glasses completed the lieutenant's moment of fame, and Gina wobbled away, trying not to be conspicuous. She passed by Arielle. "Finish closing up for me, please," she murmured and then hurried to the backstage bathroom, where she retched up the day's meals. How could she even pretend to be friendly with anyone of this cruel race?

Woozy, she retreated to her office. Hidden under a false bottom of a desk drawer were several copies of the *Candor* to give to Miguel to distribute to the guerrillas and also an envelope from Father Morgan that had been delivered just before showtime. She picked up a copy of the *Candor* to read and put it aside, then opened Father Morgan's envelope. Inside were undeliverable letters from the men in Cabanatuan. She shuffled through the top few, noting their distinctively American handwriting. Upon hearing her office door opening, she turned, surprised she had neglected to lock it, always a habit before opening her secret drawer. She saw the wolf-faced lieutenant and quickly pushed the letters beneath a manila folder. She said in a voice as steady as she could muster, "Can I help you?"

"I need to piss. Where's the *benjo*?"

"Up front," she directed.

The lieutenant stepped inside her office and closed the door.

Gina felt her heart thump and her mouth go dry, and she surreptitiously pushed a button under the front lip of her desktop.

"Nice place you have. I hear you especially like Japanese officers." He giggled and lunged for her, and Gina swiftly moved, causing the letters to scatter to the floor.

"Get out," she hissed and wished she had a club in her hands.

The lieutenant chased her around the desk, his feet slipping on the strewn papers, and Gina prayed he didn't recognize them for what they were. The door burst open, and Eddie barged into the office, swinging a baseball bat, with Arielle right behind wielding a fire extinguisher. Seeing the two of them, the lieutenant stopped his chase and put his hands up. "Sorry. I looking for benjo, and pretty lady invite me in."

"Get out," Gina gasped, and she reached out for Arielle, relieved the two had responded quickly to her call.

Eddie pushed the lieutenant out the door.

Arielle stayed with Gina. "A fire extinguisher?" Gina asked. They both snickered.

"It seemed like a good idea," Arielle said. "I was going to aim at the creep's face." She looked the extinguisher over. "I'm not sure how it works, though."

Gina picked up the papers off the floor, seeing the headline in the *Candor*: ROTC Kids Murdered. She handed the *Candor* to Arielle. "I laughed at a good kid for being brave, and now he's dead. As if the world isn't cruel enough, I added to his pain. He was just a kid!"

Arielle read the news. "You knew these guys?"

"Not well. Our paths crossed." Gina rubbed both temples with her fingertips.

"You're all worked up, Gina. Let me help." She pointed to Gina's office chair.

Gina leaned her head back, and Arielle massaged her temples in a slow rotating motion. "We all make mistakes. I slapped my baby sister once because she was crying. Does that make any sense?" She moved her fingers in tiny steps along Gina's hairline to the center of her forehead and back again, her touch as light as a butterfly.

Arielle continued the downward movement to the front of Gina's ears. She spoke softly. "Inhale through your nose. Fill your lungs. Now exhale slowly through your mouth. Repeat it if you want to. Take your time. Feel yourself sinking. Deeper." She stayed quiet while Gina felt herself relaxing into a comfortable state.

"When you're ready, picture your guilt as hundreds of bees, pesky bees around your face and in your hair, but with a movement of your finger, poof, they disappear." Arielle gently pinched Gina's ears between her thumbs and forefingers, moving from the lobes to the top. Gina saw the troublesome bees, hundreds of bees buzzing around her, and felt her index finger move ever so slightly. Poof. The bees were gone. Tightness around her mouth loosened, and her lips parted.

Arielle continued down Gina's jawline while whispering, "Live in these few moments of blessed peace." She pressed her thumbs into the base of Gina's neck on either side of the spine and then moved with gentle pressure in tiny circles upward. Gina felt as if she were floating.

"Better?" Arielle lightly ruffled Gina's hair to bring her back.

Gina took a long breath and let it out as a sigh, realizing how much she missed being touched. "Much better. You're God's gift to the demoralized. Where did you learn that?"

"From my mother. Before she married, she worked for a Chinese doctor. She learned about herbal medicines, massage, and acupuncture. And the importance of thinking positive. You need to sleep, Gina."

"I'll go upstairs in a couple minutes. I want to look through these letters first."

Arielle left with a hug and a wave.

Gina yawned and then selected a letter addressed to her, it not unusual, some of the men corresponding with her regularly now. This one was written on the back of a food-can label and folded into quarters. It was hard to read, as many letters were, pencils available to the men no more than nubs.

> *Miss Kitty. I heard you are looking for your husband Ray. I knew a Ray who mentioned a wife and little girl. He was tall, blue eyed, and blond. Nice guy. Engineering type. He might be your Ray. He left Cabanatuan about two months ago on a convoy that never returned. Rumor is the men are being shipped to Japan to work in the mines. I hope this news gives you some peace of mind. Whisper*

Gina jumped up from her desk and trotted to the main dining room. "Arielle! Arielle!" she called, waving the note that carried the good news that Ray was alive and had been in Cabanatuan all along. However, Pearl Blue was empty. She went back to her office to reread the precious missive and savor the good news alone. Finding a pen and paper, she wrote,

> *Dear Whisper, I thank you from the bottom of my heart for letting me know that my husband is alive. I cannot express my joy. He is a good man, as I know you are too. There are signs that the war is winding down—the Japs cannot replace the ships and planes that are being destroyed in great numbers. Our PT boats are harassing Japanese convoys south of the Solomon Islands, and our marines now occupy New Georgia and New Guinea. It's*

been reported that Emperor Hirohito has stated his coun-try's situation is now truly grave. Try to keep your spirits up. I'm looking forward to meeting you in person outside those prison gates. Forever grateful. Kitty.

Gina answered a few other letters. After putting them in a water-proof case, she placed it under a floorboard on the back porch to be picked up by an unknown runner and delivered to Clara and then smuggled into the prison camp.

Chapter 27

HARD DECISIONS

I'm sailing in rough waters. With each pitch and roll, I enter-
tain thoughts of death's comforts, but I am too much a coward
to take my own life, so I endure.

—*Ray Thorpe, Enoura Maru, China Sea, January 1944*

February 1944

Gina stepped outside to get the morning newspaper. Christmas music drifted from Irma's Bakery. The year 1943 was almost behind them, and the war between Japan and the United States still raged, two whole years, so much longer than she had thought the war would last and an eternity to be away from her husband and child. Would they ever make up the missed time together?

December's morning air was already hot and sticky, and in her office, Gina turned on an electric fan to get a breeze blowing. She answered the ringing phone. "Good morning. You've reached Pearl Blue. How may I help you?"

It was Ling. He had a friend who worked at Cavite Navy Yard who kept him informed of unusual activity. Ling passed it along to Gina. He said, "The cooks busy last night. They making two new dumplings: har gow, filled with shrimp, scallions, and bamboo shoots, and Chiu Chow, filled with pork and peanuts and flavored with hot mustard. They pack our largest refrigerator full. I add a dozen each to your order?"

"Please do, and thank you." She substituted *containers* for *dumplings*, *guns* for *bamboo shoots*, *ammunition* for *hot mustard*, and *largest ship's hold* for *refrigerator.* She deduced the Japanese had loaded containers filled with munitions into their largest ship's hold. It was time to update Davy. Her hand was on the phone to call for a runner when Clara arrived at her office.

Gina scooted her chair back and noted the nurse's baggy eyes and hollow cheeks, but then who didn't look drawn during these days of endless work, incredible stress, and increasing uncertainty? "When's the last time you got any sleep?"

Clara slumped into a chair. "Let me think . . . I don't remember." She rubbed the back of her neck, squeezed her shoulders up, and then took a deep breath. "I just want to tell you that Davy's a gem. He's cute too. I'd consider marrying him if he wasn't already married to what's-her-name."

Gina grinned. "Sissy. And there's a child, Harry. You may want to shop someplace else."

"I'm not shopping. I have this need to escape sometimes. Anyway, he's working with us. He already had his guerrillas on the docks and at the train stations in Manila and Cabanatuan City, so getting their protection for our shipments wasn't a problem. Dion scrounged up a couple supply trucks, and Davy assigned men to be drivers."

Davy could be stubborn, and Gina appreciated hearing the good news. "Thanks. It's a boost." She opened the safe and retrieved an envelope of money she had collected from Pearl Blue's popular Men's Night. "Split this between Trixie and Dion." From her desk drawer, she retrieved two repaired eyeglasses that belonged to the prisoners and handed them to Clara.

Clara untucked her blouse and put the money in a pouch she wore under her clothes. She placed the eyeglasses in her purse and in turn handed Gina a broken denture wrapped in a handkerchief. "Here's another job for the dentist."

Gina inspected the denture before putting it away. "It's the third one this month. What's going on?"

"My guess is given their diet, the guys' mouths are shrinking, and the dentures are loose. Or a heartless guard has taken to socking them in the face. Could be either."

"Yeah. Nice place up there. Have you heard any rumors about the Japs getting suspicious of our activity?"

Clara straightened to attention. "No. Why?"

"Trixie said she overheard two Jap guards talking about how skillfully Americans stretched their money. One guard gestured like he was pulling a rubber band. Do you think Dion is being too generous?"

Clara frowned and shook her head. "No. He's too shrewd, but I'll warn him. Trixie probably has already. He's sly, too, Gina. I've watched him work. He moves our merchandise within and between his stalls. He brings in extra family members to work on the days Americans shop, so there are always a lot of people around. His daughters flirt with the guards and bring their babies for a distraction, and his sons work as stock boys or pose as customers. He moves them around like he does the merchandise. Luck was on our side, finding him."

"What about the workers. Could one be a sympathizer?"

"I don't think so. If there was, the Kempeitai would be all over us. I think the guards were just gossiping. It's a popular pastime."

Where there's smoke, Gina thought. "Maybe we need to scale back . . . for our workers' safety."

Clara practically jumped out of the chair. "No!" Then she said in a softer but urgent voice, "We can't scale back. We're supporting several hundred Americans, but there are thousands more we're not reaching. Disease is the killer. The men are dying by the dozens from lack of basic medical care, and without sulfa drugs, dysentery is epidemic. And they need soap. They don't even have enough soap to go around, for Christ's sake."

Gina listened. Clara's argument to scale up to benefit more prisoners was as valid as her reasons to lie low and decrease risk for the workers. She took a minute to light a cigarette, and then she nudged the pack toward Clara. "There's a lot at stake here. I'll pass your concern by Franca and Father Morgan."

"You'll emphasize how important it is?"

"I will. In the meantime, talk to Dion about ways to get more drugs into the camp. He may have some ideas. I'll scope out a supplier. Some of the Chinese and Swiss drug houses are still open."

Clara added her own suggestion. "The Red Cross has a plentiful supply." She sat back and folded her arms. "We could hijack their truck."

Gina looked hard at her friend and coworker. "You're not kidding, are you?"

Clara gathered her things to leave. "No. I can get a schedule and a route for you to send to Davy. Just tell me when."

⌒

Whenever Clara came to Manila, she left Gina with sticky questions to ponder. She went to the bar and poured a whiskey, the balm that sometimes brought a measure of comfort. Perched on a stool, she couldn't sit still, so she paced between the bar and the window, obsessing about the opposing choices—increasing the workers' risk or denying the prisoners life-saving drugs. At the piano, Julio played a few scales before teasing Gina with the familiar three-note motif of Beethoven's "Appassionata." She stopped her pacing to listen.

Julio's nimble fingers charged up the keyboard, where they got hung up on a trill that partnered with the quiver Gina felt in her chest, and then the music plunged to the lowest registers of the old baby grand, where he pounded ominous discordant chords that mirrored her doubt. For the next twenty minutes, Gina fixated on the frenzied jumble of instability and constant expectation, effected through incessantly hammering triplets; eruptions of sharp, nervous counternotes; and unrelenting drive, until her body involuntarily twitched in search of blessed resolution.

So deep was her engagement that she didn't hear the man coming up behind her, and when he appeared in her line of vision, she gasped and leaped up in fright.

"Sorry to frighten you, ma'am. I rang the bell, but nobody answered. My name is Lucas. You have a delivery from Graydon."

Since the guerrillas had consolidated, they sometimes used Pearl Blue as a meeting place for representatives of the various factions. They'd arrive disguised as businessmen, deliverymen, merchwmen, or even beggars, but they all had one thing in common . . . Graydon, a fictitious colonel, friend, or family member. Wearing a suit coat, this man didn't look like a deliveryman, and Gina's hackles went up.

Lucas's gaze shifted around the room, and he inspected the side rooms. "Anyone here besides the piano player?"

She stammered, "No." The minute the word left her mouth, she wished she hadn't uttered it. She hoped Julio was watching her back as she followed Lucas to the delivery entrance at the rear of the building.

Lucas scanned the parking lot before opening the door of a beatup Chevrolet sedan. A man struggled to emerge from the back seat. A fedora covered his hair, and a mustache disguised part of his face. "Davy McGowan," Gina uttered when recognition hit. She held out her hand. "You're a sight for sore eyes. It's been a long time."

Chapter 28
BEGINNING OF THE END

Sleet blankets my shoulders, and frozen mud forms on my shoes. I walk to the mine shaft, musing how lucky I am to be working underground, where there is no wind.

—*Ray Thorpe, Fukuoka #17, Japan, February 1944–*
September 1945

Gina cocked her head to one side to study Davy. His white pants and jacket and blue shirt with large patch pockets were pressed and as stylish as they came these days, but they hung loosely on his too-thin frame. She noticed him assessing her also and speculated about his evaluation . . . tired, worn.

"It's good to see you, Davy, but what the hell are you doing in Manila? There's a bounty on your head."

"Business. You. My wife and kid. I'll fill you in later." He glanced around. "Nice place. Aren't you going to ask me to sit down?"

"No, sir. You're in Jap territory. We'll go upstairs to my apartment, where it's safer. Lucas, you can wait at the bar. Have Julio get you a soft drink."

Gina led Davy up to her apartment, noticing he still limped, an attribute she'd seen listed on the wanted poster hanging in the post office. Davy chose a straight-backed chair by the window. She poured them both a whiskey. "How did you get here?"

"Me and my men rode for two days in a boxcar, buried under palm leaves." Davy gulped his whiskey, and scorn spewed from tight lips. "The Nips fumbled the ball. North of Capas they couldn't get the boxcar door open. Fucking idiots. We were inside with our guns drawn, just waiting. Think I lost a couple pounds sweating."

"Where are you staying?"

"With Mr. and Mrs. Hahn. They have a hidden room in their house." He crossed his legs and uncrossed them and then settled, sitting on one hip like the other hurt him.

Gina poured him another whiskey, which he slugged down, so she left the bottle next to him. "Catch me up, Davy. What's the latest news?"

"The good news is MacArthur has virtually destroyed the Imperial fleet at Leyte Gulf, and with our superior sea and airpower, Iwo Jima will soon be in our pocket too. I expect MacArthur's troops to be in the Philippines in three to six months. The bad news is the Japanese are frantic, and the closer our troops get to the Philippines, the more unglued the Nips are becoming. They won't give up these islands until their last man dies. Pearl Blue has served its purpose. The guerrilla army has government backing now. MacArthur is providing us with consultants, money, weapons, and radios. It's time you gave up this place and came back with me to the mountains."

Gina couldn't believe what he was saying, and she replied with a grin, "So that's why you're here? To rescue me from the big, bad Japanese and take me back to your mountain cave?" When he didn't show a hint of a smile, she added, "You're the most hunted man on Luzon; why should I go anywhere with you?"

"Because I know you need to be reunited with Cheryl, and I'm giving you that chance. I feel the same about Sissy and Harry. The war-prisoners department of the Jap army took over the administration of Santo Tomas. They've ousted the Filipino vendors who sold the internees extra food, and they shut down the package line. Sissy and Harry are living on watery rice and not a lot of it." He hefted himself out of the chair and started pacing. "Holy Mother of God, I've got to get them out of there."

Gina dropped the grin. She knew the package line had been closed, her donations having been rejected. "I'm sorry, Davy. If anyone can get them out, you can. I suspect you have a plan."

"And a backup. My men have been working on the inside for weeks. We're breaking out two women and three children. We'll have them out in four minutes from start to finish and then disappear into thin air. We've had a lot of practice playing cat and mouse with those bastards."

Gina's foot was tapping of its own accord. "Successful or not, there will be retaliation. Are you willing to let others pay a heavy price for your obsession?"

"I've learned to wall things off." He returned to his chair. "I want to get Sissy, Vivian, you, and the kids off this island before MacArthur lands his troops. A window has opened up, and it will be a short one. Our supplies are being smuggled in by submarine. Women and children are being smuggled out. I want all of you on one of those subs."

How many times had she dreamed of getting herself and Cheryl off this island? She pondered the consequences. She couldn't go anywhere, not yet. She had responsibilities beyond why Davy had sent her here. Hundreds of prisoners in Cabanatuan would die if the resistance abandoned them. She asked, "What's the window for the submarines?"

"Two months. Three, tops."

"I need to finish up some things here. I can't leave just yet. Too many people are counting on me. I'll get to your camp just as soon as I can. A couple weeks. A month at most. If a sub comes before I arrive, send Cheryl with Vivian, and I'll follow on the next one. Please promise me you'll keep them together. I want Cheryl off this island with or without me."

She saw Davy's jaw clench and release. "You're taking a huge chance."

"I'll be okay. I have friends. We look out for each other."

"Friends? You have no friends here. What you have is an underground network, and it's every man for himself. When it goes down, it will go down fast, and you may not have time to escape. Have you thought of that?"

Before she could answer, there was a knock on the door. Gina jumped up, and Davy reached for the gun under his jacket. He hissed, "Don't answer it."

"Boss." It was Julio's voice coming from behind the door, and Gina exhaled a sigh of relief. She opened the door a crack, and Julio whispered, "Admiral Tanaka's here with Captains Katsura and Hatayama to play mah-jongg. He wants you to be the fourth."

"Criminy," Gina whispered and felt a rush of warmth to her face. "It's Tuesday. They're not supposed to be here." She patted her chest with the palm of her hand. "Get some music on. Something distracting. Tell them I'll be down in a few minutes. Did they see Lucas?"

"No. They went straight to the Jasmine Room."

"Tell Lucas what's going on and to stay scarce."

She turned to Davy and put her finger to her lips. "Three Japanese naval officers are downstairs, and they want me to be the fourth for mah-jongg. It's not unusual; I fill in sometimes." She paced in a circle. "They'll be here all afternoon. I'll keep them distracted. You have to leave."

"What naval officers? Who are they?"

"Regular customers of mine: Admiral Akia Tanaka and Captains Katsura and Hatayama."

"Holy Mother of God," Davy whispered as he vaulted out of the chair. "Admiral Akia Tanaka? Here? Downstairs? Gina! Are you kidding me? Do you know who he is?"

Davy's tone told a lot, and the hair stood up on Gina's arms. She rubbed them as if they were cold. "I know a little about him. He likes good music and mah-jongg. He supports Pearl Blue by bringing his friends here. They're generous with their money, and it's all gone to you, Davy McGowan, along with information they inadvertently let slip."

Davy paced in a circle while running his hand through his hair.

"What?" Gina said. "What's so wrong?"

"I'll tell you what's so wrong." He paced to the window and back. "Tanaka is a vice admiral and a protégé of Admiral Isoroku Yamamoto. The two were central in planning the attack on Pearl Harbor."

"No," Gina choked, holding her arms tight against her body. "That's ridiculous. I don't believe you."

"You'd better. Tanaka's ship's the *Musashi*, one of the largest battleships in the Japanese navy. It carries the most powerful antiaircraft guns developed, the devil of our airmen. He's responsible for the fall of Bataan, and his fleet's attacks almost blew Corregidor off the map. Wasn't Ray on Corregidor?"

"You know he was." She quickly sat down, her mind processing what she'd just heard. "You can't possibly be right. He told me he was against the attack on Pearl Harbor. I sent that information to you when I heard it. He didn't think the Japanese had enough resources to win a war against the US."

"And those views almost cost him his life. He has many enemies among his own people."

Gina could barely speak. "How could you possibly know?"

"It's my job to know my enemy. One of our subs torpedoed the *Musashi*, and it's been in dry dock at Cavite Navy Yard. My men have been monitoring it. Right now, it's being loaded with thousands of tons of munitions."

Ling had reported the same. She recoiled in a whirl of confusion. "I've got to go downstairs." The menacing look on Davy's face scared her. "Promise me you won't do anything stupid."

He seemed to be seeing right through her. "Not stupid at all. I'm going to take down Tanaka, and you're going to help me."

Gina blanched. "You're crazy, Davy McGowan."

"I'm perfectly lucid. I've got you, Lucas, and the advantage of surprise."

Gina didn't recognize the man standing not three feet from her, and a zing of a chill went straight up her back. "There's no way in hell I'll help you."

She felt panic rising and pivoted to look out the window. She had to compose herself, slow down her racing heart. She had to think clearly. She took a deep breath and turned toward Davy. In a voice as strong as she could muster, she laid out her case. "If I'm connected to you in any way, my operation blows apart, my staff will be arrested, and thousands—think of it, Davy—thousands of American prisoners in Cabanatuan will suffer greatly for it." She hoped the steel of her stand conveyed her message, but the look on Davy's face was noncommittal. "Admiral Tanaka will not be taken down or hurt in any way while he's at Pearl Blue. You and Lucas must leave. Julio will tell you when it's safe."

Davy's face turned black with menace.

"Did you hear me?" Gina said. Her voice rose from a whisper to a hiss. "There will be no violence at Pearl Blue! You have to leave!"

She went to the bathroom and ran cold water over her wrists. In the mirror she saw a woman with wild eyes and a hive on her upper lip. Her stomach churned, and she thought she might be sick. How could Admiral Tanaka have fooled her so thoroughly into thinking he was a regular guy with the simple hopes and dreams of every man? Or was Davy wrong? Tanaka, after all, was a common Japanese name . . . Davy could be wrong. She disguised the hive as best she could with lipstick. It itched like the devil. When she left the bathroom, Davy was gone. *Thank God.*

Gina's relief was short lived; on her way to the Jasmine Room, she peeked out the window and saw Davy's car still there.

Julio whispered, "He and Lucas are in your office."

That damn son of a bitch. "Julio, get them out of here as soon as you can." She wiped her sweaty palms on her skirt, composed her face, and turned on the charm before entering the room to greet the Japanese officers. Mah-jongg tiles were laid facedown on a table, and Julio had brought in drinks and bowls of peanuts. She recognized the compilation of Chopin's Études playing.

"Good afternoon, gentlemen. I'm sorry to keep you waiting. You caught me by surprise." She bowed to each one and slid into the empty chair. She cautioned herself to keep calm and not talk too much, like she tended to do when under stress.

Admiral Tanaka started the game by drawing and discarding a tile, and the play proceeded around the table as players sought to collect specific combinations, following a myriad of complex rules and Asian conventions. Not knowing Davy's intentions, Gina played poorly, her glance often going to the curtain and her fear of what he might be doing overpowering her ability to think. She furtively watched the admiral, looking for clues to his real character that she had missed. He gave nothing away.

Even though the conversation was limited by the click of tiles and incoherent mumbles, today, Gina sensed a change in these men. There was a lightness about them not apparent in these weeks they'd been waiting in port for their ships' repairs to be completed. Between games, she smiled broadly, hoping the sunny beam didn't look as fake as it felt. She teased, "You dour gentlemen are almost cheerful today. It must be the Chopin. Should I play his works for you more often?"

Admiral Tanaka looked directly at her, and she struggled to hold her poise. "You are most gracious as always, Signora Aleo, but this is my last visit to Pearl Blue. I'll be leaving Manila soon."

She lowered her gaze. So Davy wasn't wrong. With her world turned upside down, she didn't know how to feel about this man, whom she'd believed had a kind soul—but now she knew of the cruel heart under his gracious exterior. She swallowed down bile before leaning forward. "Oh, that makes me sad. When will you be sailing away from me?" She noticed a slight downturn of his mouth. She placed her hand on his arm, hoping it wasn't her demeanor cautioning him to trouble. She hurriedly added, "I'm sorry. It's not my place to ask your business. I wish you a safe trip, Admiral, sailing or flying, business or pleasure." Turning, she smiled. "And you gentlemen. Are you leaving me too?"

Both captains nodded.

"Then that calls for a toast." She left the room to get a bottle of whiskey. She whispered to Julio. "Please tell me that Davy's gone."

"Wish I could, boss. He and Lucas are in your office. Davy's been on the phone the whole time."

"Damn it! What's he up to?" She selected a bottle of Old Crow and placed it on a tray with the whiskey glasses, filling her glass with ginger ale. She pressed her hand on her chest and closed her eyes. "I think I'm having a heart attack."

"It's stress, boss. I have a pill . . ."

"No. I need a clear head. The officers are shipping out. I'll keep them busy with a little goodbye party. Try to get Davy out of here. If he won't go, tell him to stay hidden."

"It's not like he'd listen to me," Julio mumbled and lifted the heavy tray for her. "What's with your lip?"

"It's a hive. It itches like hell." She added more lipstick. "Does it show?"

"Not much. Be careful in there." He cocked his head toward the Jasmine Room.

Chopin's Polonaise no. 6, a raucous, toe-tapping military composition, played over the PA. She paused and pasted on a smile before entering the Jasmine Room. Pouring generous measures of whiskey, she passed the glasses around, offering a toast to clear skies and safe trips. Mahjongg tiles were stirred and stacked, and the game began again, the players drawing and discarding tiles to form melds in their quest to complete a legal hand. However, the game of skill and strategy soon deteriorated and was abandoned altogether as toasts "to our ships at sea and to our planes in the air" went around, then around the table again. The men began trading war stories. Gina steeled herself to sit and seethe.

"Excuse me, please." Admiral Tanaka rose and left the room.

Holy shit, where is he going? She pretended to listen to the stories flying around the table, but her questions were stepping on one another: Would the admiral see Davy? Would Davy try to take him hostage? What the hell was Davy doing on her telephone? When the music stopped, she cocked her ear to pick up sounds: glass breaking, a telephone ringing, her office door banging, or was that the bathroom door? Her eyelids batted with each ring, thud, and thump, and she lowered her head to hide the tic. *Damn it all, where are those two men?*

Not able to sit still a minute longer, she jumped out of her chair just as the admiral returned. She quickly sat down and assessed his demeanor—calmly balanced or a raging bull? He remained standing, his hands on the table and his fingers splayed as if his body were seeking stability.

Gina felt sick in the pit of her stomach.

Admiral Tanaka said in his usual well-modulated voice, "I dislike interrupting this party, but I have many things I must do to prepare for my departure."

The others agreed, and they gulped down the last of their drinks and boxed up the mah-jongg tiles.

Gina stood, took a deep breath through her nose, and composed her face into what she hoped was a pleasant expression.

Admiral Akia Tanaka turned to Gina. "You're a formidable woman, Signora Angelina Aleo. I'll never forget you. Had we met in happier times . . ."

"That would have been lovely," she said and knew at some level she meant it. She bowed slightly.

As soon as the Japanese were out the door, she hurried to Julio, finding him sweeping up the remains of a water glass he'd dropped. The look on his face warned her of trouble. "Tell me the worst."

"Colonel McGowan and Lucas left a few minutes ago. He's been on the phone the whole time. He told me to tell you to keep the Japs here as long as you could, that he was setting up an ambush. He promised it would be away from Pearl Blue."

Gina sank into a chair, and Julio handed her a glass of water. "Don't faint on me yet," he said. "There's more. I think Admiral Tanaka saw Colonel McGowan leaving Pearl Blue. He watched out the window as the colonel and Lucas got into the car. I don't know if the admiral knew what he'd stumbled on."

"What are the odds?"

Julio shrugged. "My guess, fifty-fifty. He may not have recognized Colonel McGowan's face, but there's that limp. You need to let Colonel McGowan know he may have been spotted."

Gina called the Hahns' and left a cryptic message. After hanging up the phone, she patted the itchy hive on her lip, which had grown to the size of a US dime. *Damn Davy McGowan and his arrogance. Damn that son of a bitch!* Her anger turned to fear. "What now, Julio?"

"We wait and see."

After days of nothing happening, Gina let down her guard. She picked up the phone to call Jonesy. She heard a click, and she quickly hung up. *Tapped.* Again a feeling of doom fell over her like a shroud.

As if on cue, Jonesy showed up with copies of the *Candor* for her to distribute. She pointed to the phone. "It's tapped. What can I do?"

"Be careful what you say. You know the codes, right?"

"Pretty much. It's the first I've heard the click."

"Be sure to tell your staff." He held out a copy of the *Candor*. "Did you hear about the breakout at Santo Tomas? Gruesome stuff."

"No!" She snatched the newsletter from his hand.

Santo Tomas Internees Escape

Two women and three children escaped the confines of Santo Tomas Internment Camp late Wednesday night under the cover of darkness and in the confusion of a fire in the shantytown area of the campus. A hole was found in a brick wall at the back of the compound along with three dead Japanese guards.

The Japanese retaliated by torturing and executing four internees suspected as being complicit and five others selected at random while the population in the camp were gathered in the courtyard to witness the punishment.

Two escapees were identified as the wife and son of Colonel Davy McGowan, one of the most powerful guerrilla leaders on Luzon.

Gina handed the newsletter back to Jonesy, unable to feel joy at Davy's success. "How much horror can one take before one becomes immune to it? If we don't get away from this, we'll all be raving idiots soon. Do you have any good news?"

"Not good, but interesting. A couple of dockhands attacked your Admiral Tanaka as he was boarding his ship. Sailors killed the dockhands and threw them into the river. Can you fill me in? What's the story here?"

Gina sat with her hand covering her mouth. She had no desire to share her complicated feelings about Admiral Akia Tanaka with Jonesy or anyone else. "I knew he was leaving. That's all. How is he?"

"No worse for wear, I've heard."

The Philippines was a perilous place to be living in 1944. Every day people were picked up on the street, marched out of offices, or plucked out of beds to be taken to Fort Santiago and grilled by the Kempeitai. Increasingly, bodies were found floating in the Pasig River. Clara told Gina that the number of Japanese sentries in the market in Cabanatuan City had doubled, putting Dion's stalls and their smuggling operation in greater danger.

On an unusually gray day, she received the phone call from Franca that she had been dreading—"True Heart is on his way to school"— Father Morgan becoming the first of their network to be arrested by the Kempeitai. Gina could barely dial the telephone to pass the grim message on to Jonesy and Mrs. Hahn as prearranged and then to warn Julio, Inez, and Arielle to be on guard. That night, the four huddled around the bar, drinking beer and eating peanuts, their nerves jumpy, nobody wanting to be alone. The next day Armin Gable, known as Bashful, and Freddie Sulet, the accountant known as Slapstick, were detained by the Kempeitai.

Inez said to Gina, "I'm taking Rizal to my mother's. I'm scared. If I disappeared off the street, he'd be alone. Have you thought about closing Pearl Blue?"

Gina had, weighing the increased danger to herself and her staff against the diminishing needs of the guerrillas and the increased needs of the prisoners in Cabanatuan. "I'm going to let it ride for a while, but I'll warn the staff we could close overnight. Everyone should have a plan to disappear into the city or the mountains, should one of our staff be picked up by the Kempeitai." Just saying that out loud gave Gina the shivers.

Inez said, "Most of us are local. We know where to hide. How about you, Gina?"

"At the first sign of trouble, I'm going back to the mountains and will leave the island by submarine. I'm setting it up."

"Don't wait too long, will you?"

"No, I'll be watchful. You too."

～

Irma's Bakery always drew early-morning crowds, and people were passing by with their bags of breakfast sweets. When Gina picked up the morning newspaper by her front door, she stood for a moment and watched the children walking to school.

Cheryl had been safe in the mountains with Vivian for almost two years now, a long time in a short childhood. Did she remember anything of her life before the war . . . the parties and pretty dresses, the cuddles at bedtime, playing hide-and-seek in the house on rainy days, dancing as a threesome in the moonlight with Ray?

Julio's band was practicing, and music floated into Gina's office, where she had settled at her desk to attend to her mail. She opened and read a letter from a prisoner to his girlfriend:

Dear Elena,

You're probably surprised to hear from me after so long a time. I'm a guest at the Son of Heaven's royal mansion here in Cabanatuan prison camp. A bout of tuberculosis laid me low, followed by dysentery, followed by . . . enough of that. I'm on my feet, metaphorically. I'm really just lying on a hard, stinking floor feeling lonely and thinking of our time together enjoying the best the Pearl of the Orient had to offer.

Rumor has it our navy is trouncing the Imperial forces, and it's my dream to take up where we left off before all hell broke loose. If that's not in the stars for you, please write to me anyway. I need to know someone is out there beyond His Highness's golden gate.

Love in yearning,

Georgie

Gina chewed on the end of her pen. Undeliverable letters were hard to answer. She wrote,

Dear Georgie,

I'm sorry we could not locate your girlfriend, so your letter was not delivered. On the bright side, you must know there are many people outside the golden gate who are working on your behalf. The Nips are losing ground, so please take heart in that. In the meantime, when you're lonely, write to me, and I promise to answer. Please use a code name.

Yours in war,

Kitty

From the pile Gina selected a letter addressed to Kitty from Sparrow, a sassy kid from a small town in Iowa. They had been trading jokes for a while. She wrote,

> Hey, Sparrow,
> Did you hear about the magic tractor? It went up the road and turned into a field.
> Ha-ha!
> Last count in the Philippine Sea: Nips, 3,000 dead, to Allies, 100 dead.
> Hold on to your hat. Victory bells are in your future.
> Kitty

There was a rap on her open door, and Gina looked up and recognized Ricco, one of Davy's most trusted guerrillas. He stepped in and handed her a note. "It's from Davy."

"Thank you. Get yourself a beer at the bar. I'll be out in a minute."

She closed her door and took cash from her safe. She scribbled a note to Vivian and another to Cheryl and then put the cash and letters in an envelope.

She found Ricco at the bar, guzzling beer and looking pleased. She handed him the envelope. "Give this to Dr. Theo. I heard that a supply of quinine was smuggled in by submarine. Tell him to check the black market."

"Thanks. That's good news. Not much is around."

Gina drew herself a beer and sat with Ricco. "Do you know anything about Davy sending the women and children home on a sub?"

"I know he wants to, but Vivian's been too sick to travel."

"Malaria?"

"Yeah. It puts her down periodically. So far she's always pulled through."

It wasn't good news. Vivian had to be getting weaker with each bout. "There's a letter in the envelope for her. Be sure she gets it."

"I'll do that." He drained his beer and got up to leave. "Thanks for the beer. It's hotter than the devil out there." He left with a wave.

Gina took her half glass of beer to her office and opened the note from Davy. It was short. Three sentences only:

> *Code breakers decrypted Admiral Akia Tanaka's radio messages and pinpointed his location. US forces blew the* Musashi *out of the water. A victory to celebrate.*

Gina knew Davy wrote in the spirit of good news, but tears clouded her vision. Gone from this world was a beautiful soul—a gentleman, a poet, a lover of music and mind-bending games. Her admirer.

Her enemy?

Her Judas?

Gina slumped back in her chair, remorseful for her part in his undoing and weary of the hostility that had determined it.

Chapter 29
BUSTED

I'm herded here and driven there like one in a flock of sheep.
How much I yearn for solitude.

—*Ray Thorpe, Fukuoka #17, Japan, February 1944–*
September 1945

Valentine's Day had always been a favorite holiday, but now the day was difficult for Gina to get through, her reflections on Ray more poignant and her thoughts of Cheryl more urgent and heartrending.

Planning a special Valentine's Day program at Pearl Blue helped numb her reflections of what had been. She wooed Manila's lovers with hard-to-find miniature chocolates, abundant fresh flowers, glowing mood lights, and Margo and Manny's sensuous shadow dance. A couple arrived whom Gina watched with desirous interest, he a gorgeous hunk of male imperative and she a beautiful deep well of yearning.

New lovers? Those weeks of exploration, sparks of novel discoveries, and unbounded sensations. Newlyweds? A time of abundant physical and psychological intimacy.

Inez eyed them keenly too. "Look at them. Antony and Cleopatra."

The customers lingered until Eddie closed the bar and the band packed up their instruments. Ling turned off the neon sign and locked the front door. As chores were completed, the staff filed out. Inez and Arielle stayed behind and were sipping red wine and eating chocolates with Gina. Ling approached the table. "Miss Gina, I must talk to you."

"What's on your mind, Ling?"

"On Friday I must accompany my father to present a document to my third cousin. I needing the night off. Biyu taking my place."

Arielle whooped. "A document? Would that third cousin be a girl?"

A flush crept up Ling's neck and across his cheeks.

Arielle continued her tease. "Gina, I think our young stud is about to enter marital bliss. Fess up, Ling. We'll keep your secret."

"Yes, ma'am." He grinned. "If she have me."

"Well, if she won't, I know two others who will," Inez said as she pushed out a chair. "Here, sit down. Tell us about her. Do we know her? What's her name? Is she pretty?"

Ling remained standing, his eyes shifting as if he were looking for an exit. "No, you don't know her. Her name is Jade. She as pretty as a budding rose. Miss Gina, Friday night?"

"It's no problem, Ling. Congratulations."

"Thank you. I lock up everything, and security lights are on. I come back in the morning and let the cleaning staff in." He left with a bounce to his step.

Gina slapped at Arielle's arm. "You're terrible. No more teasing. Everyone deserves some time in the sun."

"Don't be a sourpuss, Gina. He can take it. Didn't you see the twinkle in his eye?"

⌐

Gina had a love-hate relationship with her apartment over Pearl Blue. After a tiring night's work, she embraced the solitude, but often she found it a lonesome place with only Aleo the Cat to keep her company. Holidays always brought on a special sadness, remembering the used-to-be days of secrets and surprises with her husband and child.

Tonight, she especially missed Ray. She had no connection to him—not a letter, not a picture, not Cheryl's wide-set eyes and square-chinned face to remind her that he had ever existed. With nothing tangible, her memories were becoming fragile, like whiffs of delicate scents that dissipated in the slightest breeze, and the thought of losing him frightened her.

Miguel had delivered a letter from Cheryl, thanking her for sending the Valentine candy with its printed messages: *Love Me*, *Be Mine*, and *Forever Yours*. She picked up the note and read it again, noticing how much Cheryl's handwriting had improved, no more squiggles or backward-facing letters. Her child was growing up without her. Others were shaping her memories and values. Would Gina ever survive the guilt? Would Ray ever forgive her for abandoning their daughter? It wasn't supposed to be. MacArthur had promised a quick resolution, not a multiyear war.

One day at a time, she reiterated in her thoughts, knowing it was a ploy to drag her feet. She could close Pearl Blue tonight if she chose to and be reunited with her daughter. The decision had never felt as viable as it did on this Valentine's Day.

The apartment too warm, she opened a window that gave her a view of the bay. A Japanese fleet, newly arrived, was a commanding sight, and she turned off the lamp to take in the imposing patterns of bridges, turrets, towers, and massive guns shadowed against a full moon. A shiver went up her back. Would the war never end? With her indecision to stay or leave Manila still unresolved, she climbed into bed, promising herself she would make up her mind one way or another in the morning.

Hours later she stirred and turned over in her half sleep, dreaming she heard a scuffle of shuffling feet and the squeaks and pings of bicycles. "Speedo!" she heard called in her dream. She awoke with a start, sat up, and listened. The noise wasn't a dream but was drifting in through her open window. She peeked out and saw hundreds of shuffling prisoners of war marching to the docks. "Speedo," rang again, this time punctuated with a crack of a whip. She jumped back from the window so fast she stepped on Aleo the Cat, who let out a yowl and scurried under the bed. Gina stayed on the floor in the dark listening, certain that nothing good was happening.

After the last soldier passed by, she quickly dressed and slipped out the stage door. The air was warm and wet and every light a halo. Keeping low, she crept through the alley behind the restaurants and shops, hearing rats scurrying in the garbage. The docks lay just ahead. She crouched behind pilings and witnessed the prisoners being loaded onto barges, motored into the harbor, and herded into the hold of the *Nissyo Maru*, a rusty merchant ship, the old vessels often targets for American bombers. Gina clenched her teeth to keep from yelping her anguish. Seeing all that she needed to, she retraced her steps, being careful to stay in the shadows. But as she approached Pearl Blue, she heard, "Halt! You there! Halt!"

Oh, my lord! No! Please no!

She sprinted to Pearl Blue's stage door, bounded through it, and locked it. Panting, she scurried to her office and fumbled in her desk drawer for a pencil, her hand shaking so hard she could barely hold it. She scribbled a note describing what she'd observed, the date, time, and—what was the name of the ship? The name of the ship? She scrawled *Nissyo Maru*.

A bright light shone through the window, illuminating her desk, her chair, and the trash can before swooping around the walls. Gina stood with her body flattened behind the door, where the beam couldn't reach. The light disappeared, but thumps came from the front of the building, a command to halt, and then a gunshot.

Gina's ears rang from the blast, and she stifled a scream, certain she was in mortal danger. Gulping air, she rushed to the stage, opened the top of the piano, and slid the note between the piano's middle C string and its hammer. Another gunshot and the front door crashed open. *Lordy!* She ducked behind the folds of the stage curtain and stood still as a stone statue. Her heart thumped a tattoo, and sweat beaded her forehead.

Her hearing acute, Gina detected every footfall coming from the front door, through the vestibule, and into the Orchid Room. The sentry stopped on the dance floor, and she prayed the stage curtain wasn't rippling. Through a gap in the fold, she watched the beam of his flashlight reflect in the mirrors and sconces on the walls, and sweep over the bar. Gina shifted her weight, and a board creaked. The beam swiftly came to the stage. She held her breath and wished herself invisible.

In a violent sweep, the curtain was ripped away, leaving her prey to the grip of a beefy hand. She yelped and cringed back, but the sentry grabbed her hair and yanked her forward, where she tripped and landed at his feet. He jerked her up, his fingers digging deep into her arm, and propelled her, kicking and fighting, to where Ling lay facedown in a pool of blood. The scream Gina had been holding inside swept through the air, skipped across the water, and echoed off the mountains beyond.

She dropped to her knees in the puddle of Ling's blood and placed her hand along his neck. *Please, let there be a pulse. Oh God, please.* The kick of a hobnail boot to her ribs tumbled her to the ground. She rose to her hands and knees and shrieked, "You dirty coward. You shot him in the back!"

The outburst earned her a kick to her left jaw, and she sprawled on the ground again, tasting blood and detecting a back-tooth wobble. The guard yanked her up, slapped her face, and tied her hands behind her with a leather thong. He half marched, half pushed her to the dock, where he shoved her into the back seat of a car and slammed the door, missing her legs by a minute degree.

Left alone, she saw Ling's blood on her dress—too, too much blood, beginning to dry and turn crusty. She gulped back her sobs, and tears coursed down her cheeks. *Oh! Ling? Not Ling!* She shook with rage at the uncalled-for death. "Butchers!" she screamed, then shrank down, now fearing her own death and those of Cheryl and Ray.

Her tears depleted, she numbly watched another group of shuffling American soldiers being loaded onto the *Nissyo Maru*, disappearing into the ship's hold, from where many would never return. *All* might not ever return, she amended. She prayed Julio would discover the muted key on the piano and find the hidden note in time to stop the carnage.

As the sun rose in the sky, inside the car heated to sweltering, and sweat ran in rivulets down Gina's forehead and from under her arms. Every bone in her body ached from the guard's kicks and slaps. An officer and his driver entered. Wilted beyond reason, Gina mumbled, "Water, please." A canteen landed in her lap, but with her hands tied behind her, she had no way to drink from it. She leaned back with her swollen eyes closed and parched mouth open. *Breathe in. Breathe out. Survive.*

When the car slowed, Gina forced her eyes open in time to see the massive pillars and arched entry into Fort Santiago, the principal defense fortress of Old Manila, built in the 1590s. She had often played golf on the grounds for charity events, never once giving thought to the many prisoners who'd been tortured and executed over the centuries in the fort's dungeons and dropped into the Pasig River through a hole in the floor.

Those images came to mind, blurring her thoughts as she was hustled inside, where a clerk removed her bindings. Her hands tingled as blood flowed back into them. "The benjo?" she asked in a squeaky voice that sounded terrified. The clerk pointed to a door a few steps away.

She scrubbed her hands clean and then cupped them to guzzle water. The abrasions on her legs and arms stung when she washed the dirt away. A vision of Ling lying dead brought on a wave of agony, and she struggled against more sobs of despair. Her thoughts flew in rampant circles: *Cheryl, Inez, Arielle . . . breathe in. Breathe out.*

The clerk locked her in an empty, windowless room. She paced the perimeter, the magnitude of her situation beginning to sink in. She'd witnessed what she shouldn't have, and there would be a penalty to pay unless she could talk her way out of it. At worst, the impact could be far reaching, from Pearl Blue to Davy's guerrillas to the resistance at Cabanatuan and ultimately to Cheryl. She sat in a corner, her legs drawn up, hugging her knees. Denying her discomfort, she struggled to stifle her fear and began preparing her story.

Time slowed. It seemed like hours she sat in the room, hearing Japanese voices from outside the door but not knowing what was happening. She listened for a familiar tongue—had others of her network been rounded up to squat in rooms nearby, also bruised from the guards' rough treatment? Ling came to her thoughts, and a sob erupted from deep inside her. *I'm so sorry, so sorry.* What Chan and Biyu must be going through today. Upon hearing a key in the lock, she gasped and pressed her body against the wall.

A guard approached her carrying a stick and a hood.

"No, please," she begged, "you don't need—"

She stumbled out of the room and into another, her vision shrouded, a guard gripping her already bruised arm. Shoved into a chair, she clutched the armrests like they might be her only salvation. She heard the rustle of paper. A voice said, "State your name."

She stiffened. She knew that voice. It belonged to an officer in the Kempeitai, skinny as a rail and fox faced, a regular customer at Pearl Blue. She garbled her name, it painful to speak. "Signora Angelina Aleo."

"Do you know why you're here?"

"Yes, sir. I was out after curfew. I can explain."

"Go ahead."

She swallowed and took a painful breath, her rib cracked from the guard's cruel kick. "I was asleep in my apartment on the second floor of Pearl Blue, the nightclub I own. My bedroom window was open. I woke up and thought I heard a child crying. I went outside and looked around. I didn't find a crying child. I must have dreamed it. I'd just turned to go back inside when the guard saw me."

There was a rustle and a lengthy discussion in Japanese.

The officer said, "Signora Aleo. Do you swear everything you said is the truth?"

"Yes, sir."

"For your own good, you must tell us the truth. The Japanese are smart people. If you lie, we will know it, and being a woman won't protect you. We treat man and woman the same. Do you understand?"

His message chilled Gina to her core, and she gripped the chair arm tighter. "I understand. I have nothing to hide. I have no reason to lie." Picturing Ling lying in a pool of blood, she struggled to hold her voice steady.

The officer grunted. "I have here the arresting guard's report. He says he saw you on the dock after curfew. You ran when he approached and didn't stop when he called for you to halt. He followed you to Pearl Blue, a place of business, where he found you inside hiding behind a curtain." The officer's voice was thick with insinuation. "What were you doing on the dock after curfew?"

"The guard didn't see me on the dock. I was outside my own establishment, sir."

There was another unintelligible discussion, and her mind wandered to Chan and Biyu. Had they been awoken by the gunshot and witness to the scene? She sniffed back tears and choked, it hard to breath under the hood.

The interrogator broke into her thoughts. "The guard ordered you to halt. Why didn't you stop?"

Gina feared an uphill battle. "Because I didn't hear him. I must have been inside already. That's when I heard a gunshot. Did the guard tell you he killed my security man? He shot him in the back!" She hiccuped a sob. *Don't let them see you cry.* She felt someone standing close to her. She curled her body tighter, fearful of what he might do.

"Signora Aleo. What did you see when you were on the dock?"

The central question, Gina knew. "Nothing. I was never on the dock."

The blow came as a surprise, hitting her over the loose tooth, the pain so intense it radiated to her shoulder.

"I'll ask you again. What did you see?"

"Nothing," she cried. "Please don't hit me. I didn't see anything until the guard put me in the car. Then I saw the ship's crew being loaded. That's all."

The officer paced. "The ship's crew?"

"Yes. I guessed it was the crew. My eyes had swollen almost shut and were full of tears. I didn't consider it unusual. Ships come and go, and so do the crews." The menacing presence who'd hit her was beside her again. She drew away.

The interrogator asked variations of the same questions until Gina's voice gave out, and she couldn't speak above a whisper. After the interrogator left the room, a guard removed the hood.

Gina closed her eyes to the brightness. Her jaw was so sore she could barely move it. She felt she had answered the interrogator's questions to his satisfaction. She would return to Pearl Blue, close its doors, and flee to the mountains.

She opened her eyes and tried to stand, but an acute pain in her side doubled her over. She folded her arms tight to her body and struggled to breathe. The guard ordered her to remove her shoelaces, a ring she was wearing, and the bobby pins from her hair.

She protested. "What for? I answered your questions. I have nothing more to tell you."

The sergeant cuffed her hands behind her, grasped her arm, and propelled her bent and squirming along thick-walled hallways, down a flight of stairs, and through several archways and locked doors to a long corridor of cells.

"Stop," she cried. "I shouldn't be down here. This can't be happening. I'm innocent of any wrongdoing." She smelled mold and filth and heard the rustle of bodies moving, stifled coughs, whispers, and troubling moans. A guard unlocked a cell door, released Gina from her cuffs, and pushed her inside a five-by-eight-foot cell.

She perceived a premonition. *I'm going to die here.*

Chapter 30

INTERROGATION

How thin the veneer—that which we call civilization! Is there meaning in all the suffering?

—Ray Thorpe, Fukuoka #17, Japan, February 1944–
September 1945

Gina felt the gaze of five curious women. She stumbled over another dressed in fatigues and sleeping on the floor. "Sorry," she mumbled, recoiling from the dirty-looking woman at her feet.

"No talking," the guard bellowed and threatened her with his baton, but she stepped out of his reach and stood with her back to the stone-block wall. She swayed, her knees buckled, and she slid to the floor, praying that somehow the message had been sent to the others in her network: "Kitty is on her way to school."

A woman wearing a badly stained business suit turned her back to Gina, and a Spanish mestiza holding a black shawl tightly over her shoulders eyed her suspiciously. When the guard left, three nuns dressed in stained white habits clustered around and handed Gina a cup of water and a chunk of dried bread. In a whispered babble, they all quizzed her at once about what was happening outside.

Her jaw swollen and not able to talk above a whisper, Gina related what she'd last heard from Jonesy. "There's fighting in the Philippine Sea. They've disrupted the Jap supply lines."

A round-eyed nun introduced as Sister Agnes peered into Gina's face. "We hear airplanes. Are they Japanese or American?"

"It could be either, but the Japs are getting weaker. They don't have the resources to replace the planes and ships they're losing."

"We can tell when the Nips lose a battle," a nun named Sister Bruna quietly hissed. Underneath the grime, she had a sassy young face. The back of her tattered habit attested to her menstruating without protection. "The guards forget the Lord says, 'To give us this day our daily bread,' the yellow-bellied bastards."

Gina blinked, surprised at Sister Bruna's choice of words.

Sister Margaretta, who carried herself with an air of authority, sucked in a sharp breath, but she didn't admonish the young sister

"How long have you been here?" Gina asked Sister Bruna.

"Twenty-nine days. If I had my watch, I could tell you the hours, minutes, and seconds, but the guards stole it."

Gina's sore jaw clenched, sending pain to her ear. She could never survive a month inside this moldy gray cell crammed to suffocating with unwashed, lice-ridden bodies.

A guard approached, and the women stood and remained silent, as required.

Gina detected the guard taking special notice of her. She endured his unwelcome stare. A pervert? A customer of Pearl Blue? If so, an ally?

For days Gina sat nearly mute, mourning Ling's death and crazy with worry about what was happening to her friends and coworkers outside the walls of Fort Santiago. As her body healed, she craved exercise, but in the tight confines, she could barely move without stepping on someone. Her ears desired quiet, but every impassioned shout, every clang of an iron door, every footfall of the guards echoed off the rock walls. She wished to plead her innocence, but time passed, and she feared she had been forgotten.

The Spanish mestiza offered no succor. "You'll be summoned by interrogators in five minutes, five days, five months, or maybe never." She drew her shawl tighter over her shoulders.

Infested with fleas, Gina continually scratched.

"Don't do that," Sister Bruna warned. "If a bite gets infected, it won't heal. We're not getting enough essential foods. I taught hygiene in the convent school. I know all about nutrition and health."

Gina stopped scratching the bite that now stung. The sister didn't look old enough to be a schoolteacher. "What did you do to end up in here?"

"I lived by a higher law than one being imposed on me." She sniffed and jutted her chin up. "My sisters and I ran a canteen for the prisoners on a work detail from Bilibid Prison. They marched by twice every day. We sold the usual candy and cigarettes, but we added what we called"—she glanced around—"manna from heaven."

This young sister's exuberance and positive outlook on life reminded Gina of Arielle, and she suppressed an urge to wrap her in a protective hug. "Prayers?" she asked.

"No, well. Sort of." She whispered from behind a cupped hand. "Radio messages. Agnes had a radio hidden in the convent." She lowered her hand and grinned. "We slipped a few words of interest into the prayers we said for the prisoners as they walked by. A guard caught on, and the jig was up. The Kempeitai came for us before sunup and dragged us away from our morning service."

Gina lowered her head, not wanting Sister Bruna to see the look of horror on her face. Punishment for possessing a radio was death. *Lord, please help this child.*

Sister Bruna's chin trembled ever so slightly. "All of us in this cell are doomed, I'm afraid. The woman in the business suit . . . she had a buy-and-sell business that allowed her to travel. She tracked down

Japanese hideouts and reported back to the guerrillas. I don't know any-thing about the Spanish mestiza except her name is Lolita. She keeps to herself. The one in fatigues—she's a guerrilla with the Hukbalahap, the Communist Party. They hate everybody, Americans and Japanese alike."

Gina remembered hearing Davy rant against the Huks, their guer-rilla bands plentiful in the mountains and as brutal as the Japanese patrols.

Sister Bruna reached out for Gina's hand. "I'll pray for your soul."

Gina was touched by this young woman, whose future looked hopeless but who, somehow, retained a generous attitude. "Thank you, Sister. I'd rather you pray for our survival."

"Yes, of course. I'll do that too."

A guard led Gina up a flight of stairs and through a windowed hallway that, after days in the gloomy cell, seemed overly bright. The screened windows let in a refreshing breeze, the river below presented as a blue ribbon, and the flowers in the nearby garden appeared as splotches of glittering pink, purple, and yellow. Gina soaked in the view and gulped in deep breaths of fresh air.

She was led to an interrogation room, a small windowless space. A round-faced captain and a sergeant who had the pointy nose of a Chihuahua were sitting at the table, shuffling through a folder of papers. In place of a chair for Gina was a knee-high bench, the top lined with split bamboo. She wondered how she was expected to sit on the cutting surface.

"Kneel," the captain ordered, indicating the bench.

"What?" Gina asked, not sure she had heard correctly.

"Take off your shoes. Dress above knees. Kneel on the bench."

She balked at the command, but she had no choice. She took off her shoes, pulled the skirt of her dress above her knees, and gingerly knelt on the surface, the sharp edges of the bamboo digging into her legs from her knees to her toes. Her body tightened, and she held her breath, trying to make the weight lighter.

"Sit back," he ordered.

Bastard. It was a word that was coming into her mind more often now. She slowly lowered her body onto her heels, a sensation of entering a tub of scalding water, and she couldn't help a gasp from escaping. She groaned inwardly. *Breathe. Get through it.* Panting, she forced her focus outward and saw the folder of papers on the table was thicker than before. Not a good thing—the Japanese were doing their homework. She wondered whether the note hidden in the piano was in the folder, a certain death sentence for her.

She was quizzed on numerous matters she had answered before, and she stuck to her story that she had been outside Pearl Blue because she'd thought she'd heard a child crying and that she had never been on the dock. However, her attention to detail was being sabotaged by the numbness in her feet due to lack of circulation. Afraid she'd lose her toes, she wiggled them.

The sharp-nosed sergeant consulted with his superior, and when he returned to Gina, he asked, "Signora, you claim you were raised in Canada. Have you ever been to the United States?"

Gina felt a flush she hoped her inquisitors didn't see. "Just once when I was a child. It was a family vacation. My aunt wanted to see the Grand Canyon."

"You never returned?"

"No, sir."

"You never went to Hollywood, California?"

Hollywood, California? Where had that question come from, or more importantly, where was it going? "No, sir," she answered—but then she remembered the business card she'd slipped into the pocket of her dress: *Eiji Fugio. Agent to the Stars. Hollywood, California.* So the Kempeitai had searched her apartment. What else had they found?

She was meticulous to obsession with letters and lists, burning them as soon as they came into Pearl Blue, but still, the searchers had found that obscure business card—*in the pocket of her dress!* The image of them pawing through her private things gave her the creeps.

The sergeant paced. "We have it from a reliable source that you are friends with Ginger Rogers, the Hollywood dancer, and that you were often a guest at her home in Hollywood, California."

A reliable source? Eiji Fujio? Why in the hell was he lying about her, or was it his sullen protégée, Baal-hamon? She could only guess—they were Japanese operatives or just greedy sons of bitches. Or had she been set up? A target of an extortion scheme gone bad, perhaps? Gina's mind was muddled and screaming *danger.* "I know who your source is. He's lying to you. Let me be clear—I've never been to Hollywood, and I've never met Ginger Rogers." She tensed, waiting for retribution.

The sergeant screamed into her face. "You lie. You go to Hollywood. You friends with Ginger Rogers. You an American citizen. Who you spying for?"

She cringed back from the spray of spittle. "Nobody. I'm not a spy."

"We'll see." The sergeant nodded to the captain, who picked up the phone and spoke into it. Two beefy men wearing white pajama-like uniforms came through the door. As they approached Gina, she sensed greater danger with each closer step. "I swear to you on my mother's grave," she cried, "I'm not a spy. I've never been to Hollywood." Her protests unheeded, the men in white dragged her off the bench and into another room, where they strapped her to a table. "No! No! I'm telling the truth. I'm not an American. I'm not spying for anyone," Gina yowled, just before one brute forced a water hose into her mouth.

Later, the two men in white helped Gina stumble back to the interrogation room. She noticed the torturous bench had been replaced by a chair, the smallest of mercies. Her wet dress clung to her, and her throat felt raw from paroxysms of coughing up inhaled water. She shivered with anger and the aftereffects of the vicious treatment. There was no truth in this room, only insanity, and she had no defense against it.

"Are you ready to talk now?" the officer asked.

"Yes. I'm not a spy. I've never been to Hollywood, and I don't know Ginger Rogers."

The officer kicked her off the chair, and she landed hard on her left shoulder, the pain shooting to her wrist. She lay with her eyes closed, thinking a nightmare couldn't possibly be as bad as this dire situation. Her thoughts went to an orphaned Cheryl, and her heart squeezed so tight she felt faint.

The guard half carried and half dragged her back to her cell, her left shoulder painfully clicking. When feeling came back to her legs, the razorlike cuts burned worse than she had ever imagined. The nuns clucked around her with their prayers and cold rags. "Thank you, Sisters," Gina said, taking comfort in their ministrations.

And so began days of endless questions and alternate tortures: the razor-sharp bench, the water forced down her throat, and always the beatings to coerce her to admit she was an American spy working with the guerrillas. There were nights she was thrown back into her cell with cuts and cigarette burns she didn't remember getting. The women in her cell did what little they could to ease her suffering. "Brutes," Sister Margaretta muttered when applying wet compresses to Gina's bloodied legs.

"Scoundrels," Sister Agnes mumbled and offered a prayer.

Gina gave the Japanese nothing for their brutal efforts, never confessing that she was an American spy, their focus of inquiry. Each night, as she lay on the stone floor writhing in pain, she felt she had won a small victory.

The guards changed hourly and strode the corridor from one end to the other and back, and the women were required to stand when they passed by. Gina had learned to recognize certain gaits and gave her oppressors names: Cracker Jack, who was all business; Drippy, who sniffed and snuffed; Fruitcake, who was greasy and uttered lewd comments; and Sicko, who magically appeared whenever one was using the benjo.

Gina craved any food other than the starchy rice *lugao* served twice a day, often dreaming about bowls of steaming vegetable soup or fragrant, mouthwatering pineapples and mangoes just out of her reach. She desired privacy for her personal ablutions, soap with which to clean her wounds, and a blanket for the comfort of wrapping her body in warmth. On the nights she couldn't sleep, when the stone floor cut into her hips and ankle bones, she practiced her story in her mind—born in Italy, raised in Canada—going over the smallest details. However, as deprivations increased, so did her memory lapses, and she agonized over her deteriorating mental acuity, which increased the probability she would give away her true mission.

She jerked awake from a recurring nightmare where she was running through a fog, being chased by a big dog, the cur gaining ground in each successive dream. Tonight, it had nipped at her heels. She sat up, her heart thumping as if she'd run a sprint.

"A nightmare?" she heard whispered from a corner.

Gina turned to see the speaker was Lolita. "Yes. It keeps coming back." She climbed over two sleeping bodies to sit next to her.

Lolita reached under her black lace shawl and produced a cigarette and a match. She lit the cigarette, took a drag, and handed it to Gina, who sucked on it hungrily. "Where did you get this?"

"From a guard who wanted to be friendly."

Sex for cigarettes . . . how far would one have to fall?

Gina learned Lolita had been arrested almost a year ago for possessing a letter from John Boone, a known guerrilla leader. Her trial was coming up soon, and she expected to be executed. She said, "The letter was planted in my bag. I told the Japs a hundred times I had no knowledge of it." She took the cigarette from Gina and inhaled the smoke as if it were life giving. "When the Nips get something in their heads, they never let it go . . . ever."

Ever! Gina heard, and it gave her the willies.

Under the once-beautiful shawl, Gina caught a glimpse of healed scars and oozing sores. Was she seeing her future? The thought precipitated days of hopelessness.

A guard again came for Gina. Barefoot, flea bitten, and wearing the same bloody dress in which she'd arrived, she followed him to the interrogation room, trembling inside but with her back straight and her head held high. "Appear robust. Don't show fear," Lolita had counseled.

The interrogators arrived, smelling of bacon and beer.

One officer looked over her file and then ordered her to take her position on the split-bamboo bench. The agony of it radiated from her toes to her teeth.

"Signora Aleo, we believe you are an American spy working with the guerrillas. You know what we can do. You will save yourself much pain if you work with us. Are you ready to tell the truth?"

Fighting back pain, she stated, "I've been telling the truth. I have nothing to hide. I'm not American. I'm Italian by birth. I grew up in Canada. I own a nightclub in Manila. I know nothing about the guerrillas."

The sergeant twirled his club, and she tensed her body.

He flipped a letter close to her face. "Is this your handwriting?"

Her first fearful thought was that they had found the note she had left in the piano for Julio and the death sentence it would be for the hundreds of men trapped in the hulls of the merchant ship *Nissyo Maru*.

She focused on the squiggles. In the best of times her handwriting was illegible, and tearing from a swollen eye further obscured the cursive. She blinked several times, and the message came into view. It was a note she'd sent to Dion about a shipment of demijohns and calamansi, or cal, as she had abbreviated it, and he'd returned the note with the word *received* and a *T* written on the bottom. It would have been burned with other notes, and she wondered if the Japanese had been sifting through the burn barrel in the alley behind Pearl Blue. She'd have to think fast, and that wasn't good. "I'm not sure. I can't see very well." She took the letter from his hand and held it close to her face. "It could be."

The officer snatched the letter back. "It's signed on the bottom, T. Who is T?"

T was for *Tarzan*, Dion's code name, but she wasn't going to confess that. "He's a farmer named Tadeo who supplied my club with demijohns of calamansi lemonade."

"This Tadeo. His last name?"

She quickly said, "Sanchez."

The two interrogators exchanged a glance. "Signora. We picked up Tadeo Sanchez yesterday. He's a runner for John Boone's guerrillas. He gave us your name as a supporter of the camp."

Liar, she wanted to say. There was no Tadeo Sanchez who knew her name in any context. She was tired of this charade, the accusations and innuendos. Without thinking, she blurted, "I've never supported John Boone's guerrillas. Somebody is lying, and I know it's not me, so it must be either Tadeo Sanchez or you."

Her impudence cost her a slap across her face. Her head flew back, and tears came to her eyes.

"Maybe two weeks in the dungeon will teach you respect."

"No, please. I didn't mean it. I'm not disrespectful. Please, no!"

The door burst open, and two guards grabbed Gina and propelled her down a flight of stone stairs to where green moss blanketed grand stone archways and tunnel-like walls. She detected the smell of river water, the Pasig below, and anxiety creeped from her toes to her ears. *The dungeons.*

One guard left while the other opened a small door to a dark, fetid cell and cautioned her, "Careful. The jamb's low. Don't bump your head; the stone's mighty hard." After locking the door, he handed her a lit cigarette through the bars. "Why are you here?"

Gina, surprised at his act of kindness, sucked on the cigarette and held the smoke in her lungs for as long as she could before blowing it out. Her voice croaked. "They think I'm an American. I'm not. I'm Canadian of Italian ancestry. Canadian, not American."

He lingered. "I went to school in the United States. San Francisco. Good education system. My sister's still there. She's a nurse."

Bile rose in Gina's throat. How dared he. How dared this little piece of slime take advantage of the best America had to offer and then so viciously turn on its people—like Admiral Tanaka had, too, she sadly and finally admitted. "Good luck to you." She hoped she sounded civil; she sure didn't feel it. "You got another cigarette?"

The cell was barely long enough for her to stretch out full length. The only natural light came from a little rectangular hole high up on the stone wall. Beyond the bars, a guard sat at a table drinking from a bottle of what she guessed was sake. She sat on the floor with her back to the wall, her hand on her breast, checking to see that the locket, her only connection to Cheryl, was still there. She waited, anticipating the unknown, dreading the day, and frightened by every footfall.

＿＿

Days passed slowly by. In her solitude she mulled over the last weeks— the physical pain and fear; the innuendoes, intimidations, and accusations of the guards and interrogators; her story, which had become convoluted; and her self-flagellation when she became confused and gave grist to the enemy to mill. She had endured it all. Her body had been broken, but it would heal, and her mind remained sane, she self-assessed. She drifted in and out of sleep, sensing her mother's presence in the cell with her, a comforting affect. Hearing her own snoring, she cased her surroundings through half-closed eyes.

A flurry of activity stirred her, and she stood to watch as two guards dragged in a stumbling prisoner. Jonesy! His head lolling, he looked half-alive, like her. She bit down on her tongue to keep from crying out his name. She heard his barred door clang shut, and her emotions bounced like a rubber ball between a frenzied high and profound horror, and she questioned her self-assessed sane mind.

～

That night a soldier, an all-American, blond-haired, blue-eyed kid looking worse for wear, was lashed to the bars of her cell and beaten in her full view with a leather strap wound in barbed wire. She recoiled with each blow, her eyes squeezed shut and her hands over her ears, trying not to register the boy's screams of agony or feel the splash of his blood on her legs or the oozy bits of pulp from his disappearing face that landed on her arms. The beating stopped, but the kid's suffering didn't, and he was left lashed to her cell's bars, moaning in anguish. Gina crawled to him. "I'm sorry," she whispered. "I'm so sorry." As she laid her face on the coolness of the slippery floor, her resolve weakened. The Japanese hadn't been able to break her silence, but now she feared they could break her spirit. She wept until there were no tears left in her to cry.

The beatings of the sacrificial soldier continued the next day until he no longer responded and was dragged out by his feet. Never had Gina felt so guilty. Never had her soul been so dark and her will to survive in this cruel world so frail. But she couldn't break. So many others would suffer. Someone needed to know she was alive. Mustering what mental and physical strength she had left, she crawled to the bars of her cell and screamed as loudly as her raspy voice allowed, "You asshole. I'm not your baby girl!"

The effect was immediate. The guard, so drunk he couldn't stand, roared something in Japanese and hurled his bottle of sake at Gina's cell, where it shattered on the bars and covered her face and shoulders with shards of glass.

⌒

An answer came a few days later when she heard a tap, tap, tap as a priest, stripped down to a G-string and working from the outside, emptied the benjo. As deftly as a magician, he plucked a note from under his skimpy garment and dropped it into the bucket. Gina whispered, "Thank you, Father," to the ghost of a priest, and when sure no guards were watching, she plucked out the note and wiped the slime on her dress.

Sitting with her knees up to block the guard's view, she read Jonesy's cryptic note: *Butterfly is in mountains. Your staff scattered. PB closed. US planes spotted, warships approaching. Keep your spirits up, lovely lady.*

Gina perceived hope in his message: her friends were alive, though in hiding, and the American army and navy were coming to the rescue. She blocked out the negative thoughts her mind tried to dwell on and allowed her spirits an uptick.

There were no other notes from Jonesy, and not long after she witnessed his broken body being dragged out, and he didn't return. She guessed his fate and mourned the gutsy reporter who'd given his life in service to spreading truth and hope. She wondered if he had a family and wished she'd gotten to know him better.

She discussed her wretchedness with Ray, the two-way conversations so realistic it was as if he were sitting beside her.

"I've seen too much cruelty. I'm losing my will to fight. I'm afraid my body is dying anyway, and my mother is watching over me. Would not a sweet death be my ultimate comfort?"

You're treading dangerous waters, Gina.

"I'm drained dry. I have nothing left to give to you but your freedom from me to live your life and raise our daughter."

My dearest, don't lose hope. Find refuge from your emptiness in my unending love. Let it fill you. Let it maintain you during these lowest of low times.

Gina saw Ray's shimmery image, vital and tender. While holding Cheryl in one arm, he was beckoning to her with the other. Cheryl was laughing and wildly waving—in anticipation, Gina wondered, of the family's reunion? Gina's hand went to the locket, her lips lifted into a smile, and she allowed herself to retreat into her inner self, the only place where life's riches were still within her grasp.

The day Gina was taken back to the women's cell, Lolita was taken away and didn't return. Soon after, the Huk guerrilla and the businesswoman disappeared. The rumor was that they had been executed, and it was not lost on Gina that all three had been accused of working with the guerrillas. In constant pain and hunger, she feared her days were numbered, and in weak moments she mourned for her motherless child and sent all of her love to Ray.

Other women replaced those lost, and each one brought information, one revealing that MacArthur had the guerrillas united and well supplied, and they were ready to move beyond their hit-and-run strategy and fight the Japanese directly . . . old news, Gina knew, and she feared the woman a plant.

Deep in her own thoughts, Gina hardly noticed a new woman was being shoved into the cell. When they glanced at each other, their eyes locked, and both quickly looked away.

The nuns handed the woman a cool cloth to hold on her injuries and then pumped her for the latest news, but she said she had nothing to tell them. She sat alone in a corner with her eyes closed.

After dark, Gina lay down beside her. "Hello, Belle," she whispered to the woman, Mrs. Hahn, who had forged so many of her documents.

"Kitty, thank goodness it's you. No one knew if you were alive."

"How long have you been here?"

"I don't know. They've been keeping me awake day and night. No meals to speak of. Today a guard rammed my head into a wall. Now my eyes won't focus."

Gina had seen it before, some guards partial to hitting prisoners' heads.

It took Belle a moment to swallow. "There are things you must know. I'm weak, and I don't know how long I can last, so just listen. The Japs are onto our network. They captured a supply truck going to Cabanatuan. They brought the driver here."

Gina had to listen closely to catch Belle's words.

"Slapstick and Levi were killed. Franca, Jonesy, and Armin Gable have disappeared. I don't know if they were arrested or are in hiding. Father Morgan was arrested again. My husband, Mr. Hahn, was shot." Her voice broke. "He was a good man, a good man. I'm . . ." She sniffed. "I'm likely to face more questioning. Oh, Kitty, I'm so scared."

Gina held her, and they quietly cried together. It was all she could do; there were no words to comfort life's worst horrors and deepest sorrows.

Belle curled fetal and mumbled, "Something doesn't feel right in my head."

Gina felt Belle's body relax as she drifted into sleep, glad she was getting a short respite from the anguish of a cruel day; however, Belle, the artist, the forger, the provider of a hidden room when one needed a safe harbor, didn't wake up in the morning.

Gina watched the guards cart Belle's body away, just one more to be burned in a pile, the acrid smell of it permeating all of Manila. Who was left in the resistance to support the men living like rats in Cabanatuan? Where was Davy McGowan? Was Cheryl still with Vivian? Were they in the mountains or on a submarine headed to a place unknown? What was holding up MacArthur's return? And always, where was Ray?

Chapter 31
RELEASE

To find refuge from my empty existence, I escape into my past.
My mind plays with the trifling things from my childhood,
and I find solace there.

—Ray Thorpe, Fukuoka #17, Japan, February 1944–
September 1945

Gina had been a prisoner in Fort Santiago for four months when the nuns, whom she thought of as friends more than cellmates, were executed for possessing an illegal radio. She missed their fluttery ways and their whispered conversations. In another world . . . how many times had the thought come to her lately? Another world. A sane world. A loving world.

Her grilling resumed. She sat in a straight-backed chair in a small, dreary room with her knees together and hands folded, trying to look unconcerned, but the setting itself caused disquiet, now that she knew the evil power of her inquisitors. The officer today was new to her, and she wondered of his disposition. He introduced himself as Captain Sato and took his time shuffling through the ever-growing folder of papers before handing her a letter.

Hey, Sparrow,
Did you hear about the magic tractor? It went up the
road and turned into a field.
Ha-ha!
Last count in the Philippine Sea: Nips, 3,000 dead,
to Allies, 100 dead.
Hold on to your hat. Victory bells are in your
future.
Kitty

Gina's heart hammered, and she felt a blush rising from her neck to her hair roots. So what Belle had told her about the network being compromised was true, but how deeply?

Captain Sato sat on the edge of the desk, wearing slacks and an open-collared shirt, looking more like a schoolteacher than an interrogator. His voice was modulated, and he came right to the point. "Signora, we have reason to believe you're Kitty."

She handed the letter back, her palms feeling moist. "It's not mine. I don't know anyone named Sparrow or Kitty."

"So you deny you wrote it?"

"What if I do?"

He shrugged a shoulder. "It's of no consequence to me . . . or you. We'll bring Sparrow back. We have many ways to get to the truth."

Gina envisioned the blond kid in the dungeon beaten to a pulp at her witness. Was Sparrow to be another kid sacrificed? This one in her stead? Captain Sato let silence linger between them, as if giving her time to think on it.

"I'd hate to see that happen," he finally said. "He seemed like a nice young man. He talked about his wife and two-year-old son."

Gina folded her arms to conceal a shiver. What if she did confess to being Kitty? The issue was only a letter to a lonely kid, hardly a violation of significance, and it might shift the questioning away from her involvement with the guerrillas, a weightier crime. "Don't bring him back. I won't deny it. I'm sometimes known as Kitty."

The captain stood. "Good. Now that we've got that established, we can move on. Tell me, who is Sparrow?"

Gina's hand flew to her lips when she realized how thoroughly she had been manipulated. "I don't know." *You scum*, she added in her mind.

Captain Sato let the silence stretch between them again as he shuffled through her folder. "Miss Kitty, you've got some explaining to do. Shall we get started? Who is Sparrow?"

Gina felt she had no choice but to play along, but she'd parse her words. "I don't know. I wrote letters to 'Dear Prisoner.' He answered. Several prisoners did. They're all lonesome and hungry. I can't give you their names. They all used a code."

"I see. You, and maybe a few of your friends, wrote to the prisoners out of compassion."

"No, I worked alone."

"Okay. If it were me, I'd have recruited a few friends, but let's let that go for now. How did the letters get delivered?"

"I don't know."

"Of course you do. You wrote a letter. What did you do with it?"

Gina felt as if on a slippery slope, and she didn't know how to stop sliding. "I put them in a pouch on my back porch, and a kid picked them up and left others."

"Who?"

"I don't know. I never saw him."

"Do you know how the letters got inside the prison camp?"

"No."

Captain Sato lit a cigarette and offered her one, which she hungrily accepted. "Miss Kitty, what you've described is a sophisticated operation. Getting mail inside a prison camp takes cunning and cooperation. Who are you working with?"

Gina knew a net was closing around her, and she had to buy time to think. "Sir. I know you've got me in a compromised position. I will cooperate with you to the extent that I can." She felt her toes wiggling inside her shoes.

A sergeant came into the room and whispered to the captain, who frowned and then returned his attention to Gina. "I'll give you one chance to prove yourself." He searched through a folder and handed her a piece of paper. "Fill in the blanks." He left the room.

The sergeant stayed behind, looking like he wanted a nap. Gina moved to a chair in the corner, not having a clue how she was going to "cooperate," and hoped she hadn't gotten herself into a worse situation. As she studied the paper, she saw it was a list of code names. Next to her name, Kitty, someone had written *Signora Aleo*. So the captain had known all along. She scanned the list for Stargazer, Davy, and Flash, Miguel, two names that would link her to the guerrillas, her certain demise. Neither was there, and she exhaled a sigh of relief.

This list in her hand seemed to be an advantage, but how to use it was a puzzle. She studied it closer and saw, from what she had learned from Belle and Jonesy, she could sort the people into groups by circumstance: those unknown to her and those who were free, in hiding, missing, captured, or gone from this physical world. She began to plan her deception.

When Captain Sato returned, Gina restated that her knowledge was limited, but she'd help where she could. She handed the captain the list. "I know this person; her code name is Levi. Her real name is Jean Caffey. She's independently wealthy. A widow or divorcee, maybe. She asked me to include money in specific letters. I didn't see any reason not to. I was already sending a little bit myself. She had me address them to someone called Twilight."

"Do you have an address?"

"No, I never saw her. We never shared personal information. She sent the money with a Filipino maid named Maria." Gina pointed to another name, Clark. "This is Luhan Jonesy. He's a reporter with the *Tribune*, I think. He likes to hang out with the Japanese officers at Pearl Blue. He is always looking for a story."

"Can you describe him?"

"A little taller than me. Filipino. He always carries a notebook and camera."

For the next weeks, new names were added to the list, and Gina pretended to cooperate with Captain Sato and the other interrogators, giving information in bits and pieces about those she knew were dead or in hiding and making up stories she knew couldn't be traced and fake code names like Twilight. She wondered how much they believed. But they let her talk and talk.

"Robert Sulet was my accountant. Once when I was in his office on Canal Street, someone came in asking for Slapstick. It might have been him. Maybe not. His office was destroyed in the bombing."

One interrogator grinned a lot. "A pleasure to meet you, Signora Angelina Aleo. I spent many delightful Saturday nights at Pearl Blue. It was always crowded. You must have made a lot of money." He left the implication hanging.

Gina recognized him by the star-shaped mole on his face. "Yes, sir, I did. But over the rent and utilities, I spent a lot on salaries, costumes, interior repairs, and alcohol. You Japanese are a rowdy and thirsty bunch. Pearl Blue was barely breaking even." Knowing the cost of many entries in her account books, like the alcohol she got nearly for free, were greatly inflated, she offered the proof. "The books were in my office. I expect you have them."

Other code names never appeared, and Gina believed the Japanese had not yet broken the supply chain from Manila to Cabanatuan. It was possible Clara, Dr. Lopez, and Dion were somehow still smuggling money and drugs into the prison camp. It was excruciating not knowing. Gina sent a prayer their way.

Captain Sato conducted today's interrogation. Of all the officers, he was the most reasonable, not given to fits of temper and angry slaps. He handed her a new list of code names, and she saw Bashful—Armin Gable—was on it, but there were no others she recognized.

She waggled the paper. "The list is changing. The underground is changing. I can't help you sitting in a cell." She watched his face for a change of expression . . . a downturned mouth or a squint of his eyes. "I'm an entertainer. I can get a job at a club and keep my eyes and ears open. I'd report back anything I heard." She knew the request was a long shot, dangerous even, if he considered her to be conniving.

"Why would you want to do that, Signora?"

"Because I see the future, and I want to be a part of it." She wondered if that sounded as false to him as she knew it to be. Japan's future in the Philippines would be short lived when General MacArthur returned.

"It's not my decision, but I'll pass your proposal along and put in a good word for you."

However, weeks dragged on with more of the same dither and dance. She spent days in her cell without a break from the boredom and then hours with the interrogators, some subtle but formidable like Captain Sato and others physically brutal. She gave up only enough information to keep herself alive. She had seen other prisoners after they were no longer useful disappear from their cells and never return, and she was beginning to have bad feelings about it.

⌒

Captain Sato broke the news. "A date has been set for your trial, Miss Kitty. I put in your record that you'd been cooperating. We broke up a resistance ring due to your help."

Gina held back a gasp. She didn't think she had given the investigators anything useful. Quite the opposite. She'd led them into many blind alleys. "Do you know the charge?" There were only two: a spy or an abettor—death or life.

"No." His forehead wrinkled. "We'll both have to wait and see."

Back in her cell, Gina's thoughts went to the nuns, Lolita, and the two women guerrillas, all executed by hanging or firing squad. Her hand went to her throat, which was so tight it hurt to swallow, though she didn't fear death. She'd already been to the edge from the beatings she'd taken and starvation she'd suffered. Wouldn't a quick death be easier than one calculated to draw out the agony?

More disconcerting . . . she'd be forced to leave life before her mission was done. She had a child. Her chin dropped to her chest, and she mourned the time she'd never have to watch Cheryl grow into the beautiful woman she was destined to be.

Gina wrapped herself in a blanket, lay down, and turned her face to the wall. She whispered, "Ray . . ."

The courtroom pulsed with fear as downtrodden prisoners shuffled in to stand one by one in front of the stern-looking judge who sealed their fate: freedom, imprisonment, or execution by hanging or firing squad. With each minute that passed, Gina's breathing became more restricted. When the prisoner before her was sentenced to death by firing squad, Gina's knees buckled. The man behind her caught her before she hit the floor. No one else stirred.

Her name called, she stood before the judge, feeling dizzy and her insides turning to water. She focused her wavering vision on the flag-draped photograph of Emperor Hirohito over the judge's head. She wanted to scream, *Stop! I have a child who needs me. I beg for the court's mercy.* The petition went unsaid.

In both Japanese and English, she was charged with aiding and abetting the enemy. The judge looked over the top of his glasses. "What is your plea?"

"Guilty," she croaked, relieved she wasn't to be charged as a spy. She stole a glance at Captain Sato, whose head slightly nodded.

The judge returned his gaze to the paper in front of him and pronounced, "The punishment for aiding and abetting the enemy is life in prison."

Gina's knees gave again, and the guard held her up, her full weight leaning on his arm around her waist. *No, no, no,* formed in her head. *I have a child.*

The judge, oblivious to Gina's rag doll composure, continued speaking. "Because of the mercy of His Imperial Highness, the emperor of Japan, and a recommendation of leniency, your sentence has been commuted to twelve years' confinement at hard labor. You will be incarcerated at the Correctional Institute for Women in Mandaluyong. If you try to escape, your time will be doubled, and you'll be taken to Japan to finish your sentence."

Tears of relief came unbidden . . . her life to live, however hard. Twelve years . . . an interlude, not a lifetime. An interlude . . . her mind whirled in a confusion of emotions. Cheryl would be twenty years old before she could hold her in her arms again. Not a lenient sentence at all, but a heavy punishment.

After the sentencing, she was taken to a room and ordered to sign several documents that she scanned but failed to grasp their meaning. In this topsy-turvy world, what did it matter anyway? Her immediate thought was to get outside the cold gray walls to breathe fresh air and to see the sun again. *The sun!* Stoic, she scribbled her name, Signora Angelina Aleo, on whatever the guards placed on the table in front of her. It wasn't her real name anyway, and that fact gave her a bit of pleasure.

Chapter 32
GINA AND THE GUERRILLAS

I sense a void within myself and fear a complete mental breakdown. My captors execute their insane. I worry this will be my fate.

—Ray Thorpe, Fukuoka #17, Japan, February 1944–
September 1945

Wearing the same tattered clothes she'd arrived in and her hair in a wild tangle, Gina walked into sunlight so painful to her eyes that she covered them with her hand and peeked between her fingers. She took a long breath of fresh air scented with gardenia. A guard placed her in the back seat of a car and slid in beside her. *Praise be*, she thought as they passed through the massive pillars and arched exit of Fort Santiago, *it's really happening.*

The car passed the Manila Hotel, pristine in the sunlight, and crossed over the Jones Bridge, the Pasig River running underneath, its shore lined with bancas and cascos, the gypsies' flat-bottomed dinghies. Nothing appeared to have changed in the months she'd been jailed. The car turned north toward the women's correctional institute. Gina tilted her head back and closed her eyes, woozy from the motion. Her lip throbbed from a recent slap by a guard.

She didn't know how long she dozed. She was in a half dream of what might lie ahead, twelve years incarcerated in a women's prison. Meager meals, Captain Sato had told her, working during the day, and her own bed at night, no physical abuse. It didn't sound so bad if she didn't let Cheryl and Ray cross her mind, that pain too raw to touch. She slapped at a louse that was crawling into her ear, a souvenir from Hirohito's hell house.

She heard the guard beside her snoring and felt the car slow, then stop. She opened her eyes and saw the muzzle of a gun pointed toward the back seat. She screamed and dove for the floor just as the gun fired and the world around her exploded in a spray of red. Huddled in a ball and shivering, she heard another bang and felt strong hands dragging her body from the car. A disembodied voice yelled, "Run!"

"No! No! No!" She fought and screeched like a terrified animal, but her abductor was male and strong, and he shoved her into the back seat of another car and slammed the door. The driver revved the motor, and the car fishtailed down the road. She banged on the window with both of her fists.

A man sitting beside her said, "It's all right, Gina. You're with friends now."

She recognized the voice. Marcus? In disbelief, she turned and reached out to touch him. It really was her friend from the mountains. Her mind reeling, she stuttered, "Wha, what—?"

"You were just rescued."

She didn't understand, and she didn't feel rescued. Her heart was about to bounce out of her chest, and she was heaving for breath.

He handed her a wet towel and tumbler of whiskey. She wiped off her face and hands and gulped the whiskey, feeling the burn all the way down. In a minute she took a full breath and started to cry.

Marcus said, "I'll tell you more later. For now, just know that you're safe. Can you hear me? You're safe. By the time the Japs realize you're gone, we'll be in the hills."

Marcus wrapped her in a blanket. She saw tears in his eyes. She rode a long while with her head on his shoulder and his arm holding her snug against him. Was this an oxygen-deprived dream?

⌐

"Where are we?" she asked sometime later. All she could see were trees, so many trees—was this really happening? The wheels of the car crunched on a rocky road. Two men sat in front, and she was with Marcus in the back.

"We're in the foothills of the Zambales Mountains. We have another three hours to drive; then we'll stop for the night. Drink some water. Try eating some of this mango."

She did as she was told. The water went down easily, and the mango tasted sweet on her tongue. "Did I sleep?"

"If you could call it that. You're pretty jumpy. Do you need to stop?"

She had no liquid in her. "No. Thank you. Can you tell me what happened?"

"We bribed a guard. We knew when you were released and where they were taking you. My men held up traffic on both ends of the road while we got you out. We knew by the time the Japs realized you and their car were missing, we'd be in the hills."

"You killed the guard sitting next to me." Remembering the sound of the gunshot sent cold shivers through her. She held her arms tight to her chest.

"Yes, and the driver. The Japs' car was taken to a shop, where it will be chopped into parts and repurposed by guerrillas. We work fast, and we don't leave a trail. We'll be stopping for the night at a coffee plantation owned by Cecelia Torres and continue the trip in the morning. We'll get to Davy's camp tomorrow evening."

"Is Cheryl there?"

"Yes. She's fine, Gina. You'll be surprised when you see her."

Strangely numb, she didn't feel the joy she expected to feel when told she'd be reunited with her daughter. "Did you tell her I'm coming?"

"No. There're too many unknowns. She has adjusted well. Best to keep it that way."

Marcus's message carried a dark undertone. This trip could still go awry.

Though it was warm, she stayed wrapped in the blanket for the security of it. She watched the scenery go by, the trees . . . short and tall, scrubby or reaching up to the blue sky, pale-yellow foliage to the darkest green blue, lacy or thick leaved. Why had she never noticed the variety? A farm with its hills and furrows, bushy plants all in a row, a nipa hut, a pond, a child riding a carabao. The ordinariness of it soothed Gina's soul.

She took a cleansing breath and let the sweetness of the air fill her with hope of a finer life. Her thoughts went to her daughter, and a smile came to her lips. What would she say to her besides *I love you*? How would they ever make up the lost years?

"Tell me about Cheryl," she said to Marcus.

He crossed his arms. "Well, she's about half a head taller than you remember, and she's skinny as a rail, but she's healthy. Edna holds school classes for all the kids in the camp—the number varies, five or six. Cheryl is reading well and is exceptional in math."

"Like Ray," Gina said. "She doesn't get that from me."

"What she does get from you is talent. She's always organizing skits and plays for the kids to do. She's lively and has a fun sense of humor." He was quiet for a moment, as if contemplating. "If you've ever wondered, you made the right choice, leaving Cheryl with Vivian.

Life hasn't been easy, but she's been part of a family. When Viv was sick, Maggie and Edna stepped in, so there was continuity."

Gina had wondered a thousand times if she'd made the right choice. "I thought about her every day. Viv was good about writing, and she had Cheryl write to me. I watched her grow up through her letters." Gina chuckled at her memories. "She was always expressive—even as a tiny baby she'd wiggle and coo, so bright eyed. As a toddler she was a scamp . . . she kept me running, let me tell you. I may have my hands full with her." She was so ready, she told herself, but then why did she feel so detached?

The roads became narrower and steeper. Soon they arrived at a cabin surrounded by terraced fields of coffee plants. The door of the cabin opened, and a gray-haired woman wearing men's pants and a work shirt appeared.

"Please come in." Cecelia waved them forward.

When Gina stepped out of the car, her knees buckled, and she landed in the dirt.

Amid a flurry, Marcus picked her up and carried her into the cabin and laid her on a couch. "I'm sorry," he said. "I wish I could make this trip easier for you."

Cecelia handed Gina a glass of water to drink and a wet cloth to wipe off her face and hands.

Feeling foolish, Gina drank the water. "Please don't fuss. I'm a little weak, but I'm okay . . . really," she said, though she ached and itched from head to toe.

Cecelia turned to Marcus. "How is Theo doing?"

"Okay," he said, and Gina noticed the slight nod of his head toward her, making her question what was going on with Theo.

After Cecelia adjusted the heat under the pot of beef stew cooking on the charcoal stove, she returned with a glass of milk and a biscuit for Gina. "My dear, you need . . ." She sighed. "You need so much. Would you like to rest, or would you like to shower or eat?"

Gina was hungry, but she felt an urgency to wash away the grime and stench of four months in prison. She felt a louse on the back of her neck, and she slapped at it. "I'll shower first. I'm afraid I don't have any clothes."

"That's not a problem. I have clothes for you. The shower's outside. I put a stool in there so you can sit." She handed Gina a towel, a bottle of shampoo, and a bar of medicinal-smelling soap. "I make this myself. It will rid your body of lice and fleas. Don't get it in your eyes. Take this too." She added a toothbrush and cup of warm water. "It's salt water. If you can't brush, just swish. It will help your gums heal."

Inside the bamboo stall, Gina kicked off her shoes, peeled off her dress stiff with grime and dried blood, stepped out of her underpants, and unhooked her brassiere. Before tossing the bra on the pile of throwaways, she opened the seam and extracted the half-heart locket dangling on a gold chain. She and her daughter would be reunited tomorrow, and the thought both thrilled and terrified her.

The water, warmed by the sun, gushed from the rain barrel over Gina's head and shoulders and dripped off her nose, chin, and elbows. She washed her hair first with the medicinal soap and then the shampoo, it bubbling into a wonderful froth. Starting with her face, she lathered every inch of her body, getting inside and behind her ears, under her chin, under her arms, between her fingers and toes, and to her privates, where the soap stung inflamed tissue. After rinsing, she lathered from top to toe again, then towel dried. It was the first time she'd seen her body in a while. Her skin hung loosely on bone and was lizardlike in texture and awfully scarred, scabby, and bug bitten. A few open sores oozed a yellow fluid. She'd have to stay covered not to scare Cheryl. She wrapped herself in the towel and went inside.

"You're safe. I chased the men away," Cecelia said. "There are clean clothes for you on the bed." Cecelia glanced at her and groaned. "Ooh, my dear child. What did they do to you?" She wiped tears from her eyes and then rummaged through a cupboard for ointments and lotions.

In the bedroom, she said, "Drop the towel. I want to see every inch of you." She dabbed the ointment on the open sores that dotted Gina's body. "Animals," she mumbled. "Anything hurt on your privates, honey? Don't be shy."

Gina felt a blush rise to her face. "It hurts when I pee."

"You can use this ointment there too." She handed Gina the pot. "Drink lots of cranberry juice. As much as you can. They're in season. I'll make the juice and send it with you." She rubbed lotion on Gina's mottled skin from her forehead to the tips of her toes, then pointed to a towel for her to wrap in. Putting a drop of oil on the palms of her hands, she ran them through Gina's hair from the roots to the tips, massaging her scalp. "I'll cut your hair later, if you like." Gina thought she'd found heaven. "One last thing; then I'll get you fed." She clipped Gina's toenails and fingernails.

Tears of gratitude came to Gina's eyes. She dressed in cotton underwear and scrubs; fastened on the locket, liking that it sat over her heart; and left the room feeling less the animal that had arrived and more the woman she was.

⌇

Five sat around Cecelia's table: Gina, Marcus, Cecelia, and the two guerrillas who had accompanied them. At the charcoal stove Cecelia ladled out bowls of beef stew from a simmering pot. She sliced homemade bread, scooped butter from a tub, and put them both on a plate. Marcus filled glasses with fresh mountain water.

The wonderful sights and smells made Gina's stomach growl in anticipation of a real meal. The guerrillas finished first and excused themselves to finish preparing for tomorrow's trip up the mountain.

Gina ate slowly, her teeth loose and some painfully infected. When sated, she had an overpowering desire to sleep, but leaning on her elbows, she stayed at the table. "Can you tell me what happened the night I was arrested?"

"I know some," Marcus said. "I talked to Chan. He's been watching for you too. He told me his daughter, Biyu, heard the shot that killed Ling and saw you being dragged away by the Jap guard. She contacted Inez, who started a . . . a . . . ?"

"A phone chain. Each of us had two people to call."

"That's it. Both Biyu and Chan were arrested but released. None of your employees showed up for work. I can't tell you if they were found and questioned. I just don't know."

Gina winced and prayed not.

Marcus continued. "The Kempeitai searched Pearl Blue and kept it under surveillance for a while. It's still empty as far as I know."

"I left a note for Julio, my bandleader. Do you know if he found it?"

"I don't."

Gina had expended her last ounce of energy, but she inquired, "Inez and Arielle?"

"They disappeared into the city, Gina. It's the best I can tell you."

Marcus had prepared a cot for her with quilts and a pillow. As tired as she felt, she couldn't settle down. She peered out the window. "Are you sure no Nips followed us?"

"I'm sure. A squad of Davy's men have been with us every step of the way. We have another long day tomorrow. Get some sleep."

"First tell me what's going on with Theo."

Marcus and Cecelia exchanged a glance.

Gina frowned. "You've got to tell me."

Marcus glanced at Cecelia and back. "Vivian died three weeks ago. It was malaria. She suffered from it off and on for a long time. The whole camp is taking it hard. You're needed up there. It's good you're coming."

Gina's eyes rapidly blinked. Not Vivian . . . her best friend, her confidante, her link to an older, kinder world. She waited for emotions to sweep over her, but she felt no sorrow; she shed no tears.

Marcus looked on. "I'm sorry, Gina. Are you all right?"

She didn't answer him. She lay down on the cot and turned her face to the wall. Had the Japanese beaten all normal emotions out of her? Or had she built a wall so thick nothing could penetrate it, even the death of her dearest friend? Had she lost a most basic human emotion, her capacity to grieve?

In the morning Cecelia's son arrived with an oxcart lined with a kapok mattress and filled with munitions and food for the camp. Marcus helped Gina climb aboard, where she could either sit or lie down. "This chariot can't handle steep cliffs. I hired Negritos to carry the munitions and you up the cliffs when we get that far. We should be at the camp before nightfall."

She had no intention of being carried into the camp, and she made good her aim that evening, asking the Negrito ferrying her piggyback to please put her down. She squared her shoulders. "Thank you. I'll walk from here." She took a step and wobbled. "Marcus, I may need your arm."

Gina walked to the guerrilla camp with Marcus's support. Upon turning a bend, she said, "Stop here." She thought she knew what to expect from Vivian's letters, but what she was seeing and smelling was rawer. The camp was situated under a thick canopy of trees, and the area was damp and dark, and foul odors emanated from the latrine and graveyard. Small huts and lean-tos, put together from bamboo, scrap metal, canvas, or even packing boxes, gave the camp the look of the dirtiest slum. Her shoulders dropped in a slump, and she weaved on her feet. She would never have left her daughter to live in this horrible place, far meaner than the nipa-hut camp of two years ago.

She watched Cheryl from afar, playing hopscotch with Leah. Her black hair was pulled into a ponytail, and she moved as gracefully as a colt . . . or a dancer. Gina observed the scene with incredible pride at how her baby had grown into a beautiful child.

"Your foot touched the line, Leah. You're out."

"No, it didn't. You need glasses, Cheryl."

Gina couldn't help but chuckle. Some things never changed . . . except the voices, older, more assured. She couldn't contain herself any longer, and she nudged Marcus forward.

Cheryl turned and looked her way, then turned back and resumed her game.

Gina's bubble burst. Her daughter didn't know her as this woman years older in mind and body. Gripping Marcus's arm for stability, she felt an ache in her throat.

Marcus patted her arm. "She didn't see you. You're in the shadows."

Gina shook her head. "It's been too long. I'm too changed. She doesn't remember me."

"That's not true. She has a box full of every letter and card you sent to her. She won't let anyone touch them. Come on." He led her to where the girls were playing. They stopped a few steps away.

Gina hesitated, afraid Cheryl might not recognize her voice. "Cheryl? Sweetheart?"

Cheryl whirled around, and her eyes widened. "Mama!" she cried and ran into Gina's arms, a wisp of a girl as light as a feather, and Gina squeezed her as tight as she dared against herself.

Cheryl pulled back, and her eyes searched Gina's face. "Is it really you? You're not a dream this time?"

Gina knelt down and smiled through her tears. "It's really me. I'm not a dream, and I'm not going away again."

Cheryl looked around. "Is Daddy here too?"

With her hand, Gina brushed Cheryl's dark hair off her forehead, feeling its little-girl softness, and then caressed her cheek. How much she wanted to say yes, her daddy was here, and they'd all be together forever and ever. "No, not yet. As soon as this war's over, we're going to find him. I have no doubt."

Cheryl wrapped her arms around Gina, hugging her like she'd never let go.

Gina heard Theo say, "Welcome back."

Marcus helped Gina stand up, and when Theo hugged her, she bristled. "You're in pain," he whispered.

She nodded. "I've learned to live with it. I'm sorry I couldn't have done more for Vivian."

"She felt the same for you, Gina."

Leah, blonde like Vivian, clung to Maggie's side. "I'm glad you're back," Maggie said. "Cheryl asks for you every day." Gina reached out for Vivian's girls, and they stood in a close circle for a moment, each blinking back tears. "We'll talk later," Gina whispered.

A woman with a young boy joined the group of well-wishers, and she realized it was Davy's wife, Sissy. "Welcome back, Gina," she said. "Thank you for the packages you left at Santo Tomas's gate. They saved many a day."

Eight-year-old Harry, a young version of Davy, offered his hand. "Thank you, ma'am. I liked the fire truck a lot."

Gina was overwhelmed seeing her friends and family gathered again, but each now with their own story of sadness and deprivation. When she stumbled, Marcus grabbed one elbow and Edna the other. "You're bunking in with me," Edna said.

A good assignment, Gina thought, always comfortable in Edna's presence.

～

In the subsequent days, Cheryl stayed close to Gina, who followed her daughter's every movement and held on to every word. She was the picture of Ray with his wide-set eyes and smile, though adorably snaggletoothed. She was self-sufficient, taking care of her own physical needs, and responsible, helping Edna in the camp kitchen.

In a private ceremony, they clipped their half hearts together as one, and Gina hung the completed locket around Cheryl's neck. Cheryl inspected the pretty locket, which hung almost to her tummy, and grinned. "I'll never take it off."

Today they were playing rummy with a deck of worn cards, and Gina was impressed how quick her daughter was to order patterns and combinations. However, the child was quieter than her usual exuberant self. Gina said, "Miss Vivian told me you're really good at math."

Cheryl shrugged. "It's easy."

"Maybe you can be an engineer like your dad."

"What's an engineer?"

"A person who uses math to solve problems. Your dad's good at that too."

Tears pooled in Cheryl's eyes.

Gina put the cards down. "What's the matter, honey?"

Cheryl's tears turned to a blurted sentence. "Leah says Daddy's in heaven like her mother."

Gina couldn't get her arms around Cheryl fast enough. She drew her close, saddened she couldn't disprove, without a doubt, Leah's comment. "Nobody knows that. There are many soldiers who are missing. Some are hiding in the mountains like Mr. Marcus and Colonel Davy. Others are in prison camps like Miss Sissy and Harry were. Some of our soldiers have been sent to Japan to work in their mines and factories. We won't know until the war is over where Daddy is. All we can do, honey, is keep our love strong."

Cheryl cuddled into Gina. "I hate the war. If I was president of the United States, I'd outlaw all wars." She was quiet for a while and then patted Gina's chest. "You're not really sick, are you, Mama, like Miss Vivian?"

Gina hugged Cheryl closer and kissed the top of her head. "No, I'm not really sick. Mostly I'm tired and weak from not having enough food. I'm better already, and I'll be even better after I eat that stew you and Miss Edna are cooking."

Cheryl sat up. "That's what Miss Edna said. We put in extra carrots for you. You want to play Miss Mary Mack?"

"I guess. I don't know what it is."

"It's a hand-clapping game. I'll teach it to you. Put your hands up and clap like I do. Ready? One, two, three . . ."

> Miss Mary Mack, Mack, Mack,
> All dressed in black, black, black,
> With silver buttons, buttons, buttons
> All down her back, back, back . . .

Under Theo's care, Edna's pampering, and Cheryl's endless menu of hand-clapping games, which always brought laughter when Gina bungled them, Gina slowly regained her strength. When able, she visited Vivian's grave, finding solace sitting quietly reminiscing about their carefree days living a good life in a colonial society and then on a more sober note how they had changed. How they had dug in and done what had to be done in the nipa-hut camp, however distasteful and hard, working as a team, always supporting, encouraging, and protecting each other under the harsh bridle of their Japanese invaders. She promised Vivian that she would love and nurture Leah and Maggie like they were her own and keep their courageous mother's memory alive. *I'm so sorry I couldn't do more to help you, my dear, dear friend. It wasn't supposed to end this way.*

Per Theo's instructions, Gina was encouraged to walk, and Edna accompanied her, imparting information and introducing her to other residents. "How many people live here?" Gina asked.

"Permanently, around a hundred and fifty American soldiers. Some have wives and children with them. Most of the Filipino guerrillas live on farms or are laborers in the towns. Since the units consolidated, it's a huge network. If needed, Davy and the other district leaders can muster thirty thousand guerrillas here on Luzon alone."

"How do you feed everyone living here?"

"It's hard. We plant gardens and hope they come to fruition before we have to move out. We're always scrounging. We depend on people like you. We miss the money you sent from Pearl Blue. The farmers provide what food they can, but Japs take their crops in taxes, and they barely have enough to feed their families."

They stopped to say hello to an American soldier and his Filipino wife, who were playing cribbage on a homemade board. Both wore Japanese army jackets with visible bullet holes, Thompson submachine guns were within their reach, and pistols were strapped to their hips.

Edna tapped the young man on his shoulder. "Jerry here is one of our radio men. This is his wife, Maria. She's going to have a baby soon."

"Congratulations," Gina said, but out of earshot, she said to Edna, "This is the last place I'd want to have a baby."

"There are worse, Gina. There are some families hiding in the swamps. You have no idea what the Japs do to these people when they're captured."

Edna was wrong, but Gina had no desire to go down that road of thought.

They began walking again, and Edna pointed to a hut larger than the others. "That's Davy's. He led a patrol on a mission. He should be back soon." They passed by one of the many makeshift kitchens, where a woman was tending to a pot of mungo beans simmering over a wood fire.

"Wouldn't the fire tip off Jap patrols?"

"It's always a chance, but we have multiple rounds of security. If the Nips penetrate our perimeter, you'll hear a warning shot. You'll need a weapon." She pointed. "There's a path behind that tangle of bamboo. It leads to a cave about a mile up, where we store supplies off-site so we can vacate this camp at a moment's notice. We've learned a lot since you were last with us. Still, it's a cat-and-mouse hunt, Gina. It's a crummy way to live." She paused before adding, "But I guess you know all about crummy."

"Yes, but it was a different kind of crummy. In Manila I was comfortable enough, but I was face to face with the Nips. I had to constantly censor everything I did, every move I made, everything I said. There was no time to relax. No letting down my guard. The danger and stress take a toll."

They were walking toward Theo's clinic when Cheryl and Leah caught up with them and displayed the ivory-and-ocher clay beads they'd just finished making.

"My mom showed us how," Leah said.

The child was so thin she hardly cast a shadow. Gina admired the beads. "They're very pretty. Your mom had many talents, Leah, and you are so much like her. I'm sure she's smiling down on you right now."

Leah beamed. "She showed me how to poke holes in them before they dry. That way we can string them together. We're going to make bracelets and sell them when the war is over."

Gina complimented the girls' entrepreneurial drive, thinking it was good as anything to keep their minds off the ugliness around them. They left to hunt for an elusive vine used to string beads.

"I'm a little dizzy. I need to lie down, Edna. I'll check out Theo's clinic later."

Resting on her cot in Edna's nipa hut, Gina was startled by a young Filipino soldier who came through the door holding up his pants.

"Sir," the kid said to Edna in a mixture of his dialect and English. "I need thread. I no can hold up my pants and do drills. The tear is big."

Edna rummaged in a box and found a needle and thread. "You mend them here." She pointed to a bench where he could sit and sew.

His eyes got large. "No, sir. I go alone to my hut."

"You're not leaving here with my only needle and thread. No one's going to look at you, and for Pete's sake, call me Miss Edna, not sir."

"Yes, sir." He retreated to the bench, turning his back before slipping off his torn pants.

Edna glanced at Gina. "New kid from the village. They stay here a few weeks for training. Davy's lieutenants drill them to exhaustion. It toughens them up quick enough."

Enough to die? Gina wondered.

She returned to her reading. Soon, another young man stepped through the door, looking so much like the first one they could be brothers. "Excuse me, sir. Colonel Mu? ... ... my he want to see you pronto."

Edna dropped what she was doing and shooed the kids out of the hut. She turned to Gina. "Davy's orders always come pronto. Want to come?"

~

On the way to Davy's hut, Edna warned, "Word came that this mission didn't go well. Sergeant Errol was killed, and Cimbo, a guide, is missing. Steel yourself for a tirade." Edna stopped for a minute and squared her shoulders before entering the hut. Gina followed her.

Marcus was already there, and Davy, scruffy and haggard, was pacing in front of him, flailing his arms. "What do you mean, we're out of rice? My men haven't eaten anything but swamp spinach for days. They'll be shittin' green for a week." He turned to Edna and barked, "What the hell is going on?"

Edna answered, her voice as strong as Davy's was loud. "The Japs are marking and mapping trails, and our volunteer home guards can't get their convoys through with supplies. Marcus has begged rice from the local farmers, but they don't have squat left to give us, and we've used up our credit with Mrs. Bueno in Tinian. Where's the money you promised was coming up from Manila?"

Davy's gaze went to Gina. He growled, "Hello, Gina. Welcome to hell."

Gina swallowed her emotions, their parting in Manila not on the best of terms, he having exposed her to undue danger. "You don't know hell like I know hell, Davy."

He stared into her still-haunted eyes. "Just say we've visited different neighborhoods." He waggled his hand at Edna. "Get the men fed. Anything but swamp spinach. If they don't eat, we're going to lose them."

Edna left, mumbling something about a goat, and Marcus followed her, leaving Gina alone with Davy. He sank onto a chair, the muscles in his face twitching. He turned his head away. "The Japs killed Sergeant Errol. They held him in a school turned torture chamber until the last three days, when they hung what was left of him from a tree by his feet and let the birds finish the job. I couldn't get close enough to cut him down without losing more men. You understand that, don't you, Gina?"

She recoiled at his story and understood his need for reassurance, remembering even after successful missions—when he'd return with eyes too bright and carts loaded with food, weapons, and clothing stripped off dead Japanese foes—Davy went through a period of remorse. Missions gone sour took a particular toll. She let him talk out his emotions.

"The Nips retaliate," he muttered. "They'd have killed the townspeople. Lined them up and run them through with bayonets. I've seen it before." He wiped tears from his eyes, and then his gaze focused on Gina. "I couldn't take that chance."

Gina sought to assuage his guilt. "You're a strong, compassionate leader. These men know they are risking their lives. They die nobly fighting to free their country from its cruel oppressor, a cause they believe in."

Davy straightened his spine. Though his face relayed his sorrow, his voice sounded gruff. "A memorial service. Get on it, Gina. Have Edna and Marcus help. Something nice. Have the guys bring their guitars and fiddles." He lit a cigarette and offered her one. "Now, bring me up to date. How are you doing?"

Before she had time to answer, a wild-eyed man burst through the door. "Cimbo's been found. He escaped the Japs. He's in the clinic. He said something about there being an informant in the home guard."

Davy's head jerked up. "Who?"

"He didn't say. He's in and out of consciousness. Dr. Theo's doing what he can to keep him alive."

Davy heaved himself out of his chair. "God damn, I need to talk to him." He motioned to Gina. "Come with me."

"No!" Gina did not want to be witness to any more Japanese atrocities. However, Davy was already out the door, and she trailed him.

Davy limped up the six stairs to the clinic door. Gina dreaded going inside. Sick and injured men lay haphazardly in one large room that swarmed with insects and stank of shit, vomit, old blood, and the dita-bark concoction to treat malaria that Maggie cooked on a charcoal stove.

Theo was leaning over a man, lancing a boil on the patient's groin with a toothpick and Mercurochrome. The soldier lay white faced and gritting his teeth.

The sight made Gina light headed, the feeling made worse because she was holding her breath against the fetid smell. She sat on a stool by the door, covered her nose and mouth with her hand, and swallowed hard.

Maggie grasped the patient's hand. "Take a deep breath, soldier. This will be over in a minute. Count with me. One, two . . ."

The soldier followed the order but let out a roar when Theo's toothpick found the right spot and pus spurted to the surface.

"That's the worst of it." Theo turned the patient over to a Filipino aide to clean up the mess and bandage the wound. He addressed Davy while washing his hands. "If you've come to see Cimbo, he's over there." He nodded toward the back corner of the room, where a body lay under a mosquito net. "He took a bad beating. His right eye may be lost, and the right clavicle's broken. He'll recover unless something internal is going on. I'll know better tomorrow."

"Has he said anything?"

"I don't think so, but ask Maggie. She cleaned him up." Theo waved Maggie over. She was a smaller, feminine version of Theo and second in command at the clinic. She checked the brew she was cooking before joining the men and answering Davy's question.

"No. He moans but hasn't responded since he's been here."

Davy parted the netting, recoiled, then leaned in and shouted into Cimbo's face. "Cimbo! Wake up! Can you hear me?" There was not a flicker of reaction, and Davy said to Maggie, "Get me some water."

Gina, sensing what Davy was about to do, hurried to the bedside. "No. Don't. He's had enough pain. Let him sleep."

Davy ignored her plea. Taking a full jug from Maggie, he flung water on Cimbo's face, and the injured man's body convulsed.

Afraid she was going to lose what little food she had left in her stomach, Gina returned to Edna's hut. Dark, fast-moving clouds hung low, and a gust of cold air hit her like a dire forewarning.

A black-haired kid stood outside her door. "Sir, my brother borrowed my shoes, and he won't give them back—"

"Get out!" she shouted to his astonished face and then to his retreating back.

Despite the ache in her stomach, she gulped a slug of cane alcohol, which burned all the way down, but it soon brought on a sense of calm. She imagined she could become dependent on the mind-numbing effects of this potent brew, but at the moment she didn't give a diddly care.

～

Her hair growing in a messy tangle, Gina took to wearing a floppy canvas hat. To protect her feet, Marcus found her a pair of men's boots that fit if she stuffed them with grass and wore the socks she crocheted from string. Davy gave her a shirt left behind by a guerrilla soldier. When she ventured out of the camp, which she did to forage for food, she wore a Colt .38 in a holster buckled around the waist of her long skirt.

Cheryl and Leah didn't fare much better clothes wise. Both girls had grown and were unusually thin. Both wore simple dresses or shorts and shirts made from mungo bean or rice bags. Maggie preferred cotton pajamas made by nuns from bedsheets found in an abandoned hospital.

It wasn't unusual to see Japanese planes overhead, but in late 1944 they began to drop from the sky. It was a mystery those in the camp speculated about until the radioman came from his hut scratching his head. "The fighting's off Leyte. The Nips are jettisoning small rocket-powered aircraft they call cherry blossoms from the underside of bombers. The pilots steer the crafts straight into American ships. Kamikazes, they're called. Suicide bombers."

"Kamikaze," Edna whispered. "It means 'divine wind.'"

Cherry blossoms, Gina thought. Poetic. And evil. No doubt the pilot was a teen—expendable and indoctrinated by Hirohito's message to the youth presented in poems like the "Song of Young Japan" that aggrandized death and charged the young "to be ready to scatter like cherry blossoms in the spring sky." Inez had said that Rizal mouthed the words of that horrible song without an inkling of the seed that was being planted in his head.

⌐⌐

Cimbo died, and the informant was never identified. Camp guards remained on high alert. Activity increased with confederations of guerrilla leaders arriving to meet with Davy, some building lean-tos and staying several days, putting a strain on Edna's food supply. Wagonloads of tommy guns and carbines were hauled into camp by skinny carabaos and stored in a guarded hut. Davy disappeared for a time and returned with a briefcase full of money.

Japanese planes continued to dominate the skies, though Gina had seen an airplane with a blue star on its underwing she swore was American. Davy called her into his hut. He waved her to sit down and came to the point. "There's been a new development." He lit a cigarette and leaned back in his chair.

By the scowl on his face, Gina knew this wouldn't be good news. She crossed her arms to prepare for the worst.

Davy didn't mince words. "The Japs penetrated your network. Five priests at Malate Church and Dr. Lopez were arrested. Franca's missing. Her husband, Señor Estevez, and Armin Gable were both shot."

Despite her folded arms, Gina shivered inside, hearing this worst of information and envisioning her friends in the most brutal of places. During her months of interrogation, had she given the Japs clues, an unthinkable breach of trust? "What tipped them off, Davy?"

"A prisoner dropped a letter, and a guard picked it up. It was like a match to dry tinder. There was a surprise search of the Cabanatuan camp, and within hours the market stalls you were using to pass money to the prisoners were razed. Somebody warned Dion. His family fled to the hills. He was captured but escaped and went into hiding."

A relief, Dion and his family out. "Clara too? Do you remember her? She was your nurse. And Trixie, her niece? They worked with Dion."

"I don't know the whereabouts of either. Listen, Gina. A submarine is leaving for Australia, and they're taking as many civilians off this island as they can cram in. I want you, Cheryl, and Leah on that sub. Don't fight me on this. MacArthur's going to be here in short order, and it'll get bloody. You know the Japs—they dig in."

Gina knew Japanese cruelty firsthand, and she'd give her life to protect the kids from it. "Who else is going?"

"Sissy and Harry, of course. Edna's leaving, and so are a couple other women and their children. Maggie refuses to go. She says her work is here with Theo."

"When are we leaving?"

"Tomorrow morning. Give Theo your address in the States so he knows where to find Leah. You'll go by horseback to the coast. Pack light. Take your gun."

Chapter 33

THE RESCUE

*I raise my gaze above the mire to the glory of the setting sun.
I feel Gina's presence beside me with uncanny tangibility, her
attendance transcending the physical.*

—Ray Thorpe, Fukuoka #17, Japan, February 1944–
September 1945

Gina prepared to leave the Philippines with mixed emotions. She anticipated a saner life for herself and Cheryl but lamented leaving Ray behind. She promised herself and Ray to return as soon as it was safer to find him or learn his fate, knowing in her heart he would understand her decision.

The thought of leaving Maggie behind was as painful as leaving Ray. "Please, Maggie, this may be your only chance. The Japanese are brutal. Your dad wants you to be safe. Leah needs you."

"I've made up my mind. I'm staying. Dad can't manage this clinic alone, Miss Gina. Leah will be okay with you for a while. She and Cheryl are like sisters."

Gina readied Cheryl for the trip by painting it as an adventure. Cheryl had her few clothes, a bag of clay beads, and decks of old maid and go fish packed and ready to go in a minute.

Leah was not so easily persuaded. Theo gently ordered and Maggie cajoled the unhappy little girl, who sobbed at even the mention of being separated from them.

Cheryl tugged at Gina's arm and whispered into her ear. "I think Leah and Maggie need this." She held up the locket. Gina's heart swelled with pride at her daughter's thoughtfulness.

That evening in a short but enchanting candlelight ceremony, Cheryl handed Maggie and Leah each a gold chain with half a heart locket and demonstrated how they snapped together. Cheryl said, "Wear these all the time. When you're lonesome, just touch the locket, and you won't feel so sad anymore. It worked for me."

"And me too," Gina said and nodded in agreement.

Maggie hugged Cheryl. "Thank you."

And then she hugged Leah. "My sweet little sister. I love you. We'll be together again soon. In the meantime, I promise I'll touch this locket every day."

Leah said, "I saw you touching this locket, Cheryl. You were always crying."

Cheryl sniffed. "Sometimes love feels sad, Leah."

Gina's heart just about broke.

⌒

A caravan of eighteen left the guerrilla camp for the coast to rendezvous with a submarine: Gina, Cheryl, and Leah; Sissy and Harry; Edna; and two other women with three children, along with Marcus as coordinator, two armed guerrillas, and four Negrito guides. Five horses carried supplies, guns, ammunition, and the pilgrims' personal effects. Gina had packed what meager clothing was available for her and the girls, the money Davy had given to her, and her gun.

It was a hard seven-day trek over the mountain, twice the caravan having to scatter and hide from Japanese patrols. Gina was stronger but still healing from the cruel treatment at Fort Santiago, and every bone in her body ached. Her feet started to bleed inside her too-big boots. She kept the girls' spirits up by singing the trail songs they had learned from the cowboys on the way to their nipa-hut camp . . . was that only two and a half years ago? It seemed like a decade.

As they approached the coast, forest cover gave way to conga grass fields and rice paddies, the flatness of the land increasing their danger of being spotted. Gina's gaze often went to the sky, and her ears were tuned to the faintest buzz of Japanese search planes. At long last, seeing the blue of the Philippine Sea, she grabbed Cheryl's and Leah's hands and quickened her step.

A congregation of people came into view: women sitting under palm trees tending to toddlers; men pacing in the sand, their eyes focused out to sea; and boisterous children splashing in the foamy water at the shoreline. Suitcases, boxes, and baskets were scattered in clumps. Armed men, some on the ground and some sitting in trees, watched the perimeter. At the water's edge, several small boats bobbed in lazy waves, and two large squares of white fabric hung high in a tree's branches.

Gina walked straight to the water, pulled off her clumsy boots, and dipped her bloody feet in the brine. Cheryl, Leah, and Harry waded beside her, and soon they and three other children were splashing seawater on one another. Marcus conferred with Major Beryl, the guerrilla officer leading the mission, then waved to Gina, Edna, Sissy, and the others.

"I gave Major Beryl your names. I don't know if you'll get on the sub. The commander's expecting twenty-five people. There are forty-one here."

Gina winced at the news and ran her hands through her hair in frustration.

Edna bristled. "There's no way he would leave us. When's the sub supposed to be here?"

"It might be out there now. It won't surface till the commander's sure the waters are safe. The white flags in the trees signal the beach is secure. We just wait."

Unable to sit and wait, Gina paced the beach and watched the horizon, hoping to get a glimpse of a submarine rising from the depths. Others were doing the same, and she collided with a man wearing a ragged army shirt. "Oh. Sorry."

"No. I'm sorry. I'm not watchin' where I'm goin'." He offered her a cigarette. "What's a pretty girl like you doing in this godforsaken place?"

Gina laughed. It had been a while since a man had called her pretty or a girl, and she doubted she deserved the compliment. "Same as you, soldier. Where are you coming from . . . or better, where are you headed?"

"Coming from Pasay, a prison camp over by Manila. Nips had us diggin' up the entire mountain by hand to build their fuckin' airfield at Nichols." He took a long drag on the cigarette. "There're three of us here. We found a pass the Nips didn' know about. Me, I'm headed to London. Goin' to surprise me mum. It's been two years. She probably thinks me dead."

"Most probably not . . . just don't pop in unannounced and give her a heart attack." A loud whoop came from the crowd sitting under a tree. "Do you know who they are?"

"Plantation owners and missionaries mostly. Said they been hidin' in the mountains. Must've been hard with all those kids."

It was late afternoon before Major Beryl called the refugees together. He had to yell to be heard. "The submarine's a mile offshore. I'm taking all of you out there. It's up to the commander to decide how many he can accommodate. When I call your name, get into a boat. Boat number one, Miller, Dan; Miller, Julia . . ."

Gina sought out Marcus, who had joined the other guerrillas to guard the perimeter. "We won't know until we get out there if we'll be leaving. Just in case, I'll say goodbye now. Thank you for everything." Her eyes misted over.

"Not goodbye. I'm sure our paths will cross again . . . in better times."

"Will you be coming to the United States?"

"No. This is my home. I'll stay here and help rebuild the school."

She regarded him with open fondness. "Good luck, Marcus. And stay off high cliffs."

He gave a raspy chuckle. "That I'll do. Good luck to you, too, Gina. When things get settled, write to me. Edna will have my address."

She handed him her gun. "Take this. I won't be needing it."

With a warm hug, they parted ways.

Major Beryl led the convoy of small vessels into the now-choppy waters.

"I don't see anything." Cheryl shaded her eyes with her hand. "What's a submarine look like?"

"It's just a big boat," Leah replied.

The submarine's nose emerged, followed by the foredeck, the conning tower, the afterdeck, and the stern. It was magnificent to watch, and a cheer went up from the crowd.

Crew members appeared on deck to hoist the American flag, and gunners loaded cannons and pointed them seaward. From his boat, Major Beryl shouted to an officer on the deck, "Permission to come aboard, sir."

Permission was granted. The refugees were left bobbing in the waves. Edna's eyes closed, and her lips moved in silent prayer. She opened her eyes and said, "I can stay here if they can't take all of us."

"So can I," one of the other women volunteered.

Cheryl leaned against Gina. "You won't leave me, will you, Mama?"

Gina heard Cheryl's voice, but her thoughts had gone to Maggie and her unyielding commitment to a noble cause. Gina again felt a tug to work with Davy and Clara, to support the guerrillas, aid the imprisoned, and heal the injured. She looked to the shore for Marcus, thinking he'd take her back to the camp with a little persuasion.

"You won't leave me, Mama, will you?" Cheryl repeated, her voice shriller.

Gina blinked out of her reverie and saw Cheryl's worried face. She sighed. "No, honey. You, me, and Leah stay together, no matter what."

Major Beryl appeared on the deck of the submarine. Gina, Edna, Sissy, and the kids held hands, anticipating his announcement. He spoke through a bullhorn. "The captain welcomes all of you on board."

A cheer went up from the crowd. Gina kissed the girls, and Edna looked skyward and mouthed, "Thank you."

The convoy edged close to the submarine, and a redheaded sailor dressed in white shorts and leather sandals stepped into Gina's boat. He stretched out his callused hand. "Hurry. Leave your bags. We'll bring them on board." The refugees were pulled out of their boats and onto ladders that led to the top of the submarine. They walked a few slippery steps and entered the conning tower, a small room that housed an enormous periscope.

"Hurry—down there." Another crew member pointed to a hatch. "Watch the stairs. They're tricky. Follow the crowd. Don't dawdle."

Carrying her boots, Gina wound down the circular metal stairs, taking hold of the helping hands of the crew. The dark little room she entered smelled of diesel fuel, and every inch of wall and ceiling space held gauges, dials, and switches. "You're in the control room," a sailor said. "We steer the ship from here. Quickly move on, please."

The passengers crowded into the crew's mess, a more substantial space filled with picnic-style metal tables bolted to the deck. Oversize bowls held chocolate candy bars that carried a message in gold bold-faced lettering: *I Shall Return.*

Cheryl flashed a nearby sailor her cutest smile. "How many may I take?"

The bright-eyed crewman answered with a grin, "As many as you can eat without getting sick, young lady. Welcome aboard."

Gina let the girls take two, and she took two for herself. When she tore open the blue wrapper, the aroma caused her mouth to water. She allowed a square to slowly melt on her tongue. In the galley not far away, a coffeepot burbled, and Gina deeply inhaled the delicious aroma. Coffee and chocolate . . . indeed, she'd found a friendly place.

"Crowd in," a steward instructed while reaching to turn on a circulating fan attached high on the wall. The light was blazingly bright, and a scratchy, two-way conversation was broadcast over loudspeakers:

"The guerrillas got the ammo and fags. They're asking for food."

"I'll send them up sandwiches and coffee. It's all I can do. We've got a houseful here."

The steward addressed the nervously excited crowd. "The captain asked me to tell you he is pleased with how orderly you all came on board. We will arrive at the port of Darwin, Australia, in seven days. We travel submerged during the day. Be aware, when we're submerged with this many people onboard, it's going to get stuffy. Take naps, read, play quiet games. We'll surface and open the hatches each day after sunset."

The klaxon blasted, squawking like an old car horn. "Clear the bridge. Prepare to dive," boomed over the loudspeakers.

"We're on our way," the steward said. "Expect some rocking while we're going under the surface. The hissing you'll hear is the ballast drawing water into the tanks to make us descend. You'll also hear the droning of the engines and the churn of the propellers. It's all normal. Relax and enjoy the experience. As soon as the ride smooths out, the cook will put out the food. After you eat, you can pick up your luggage in the forward torpedo room. I'll be there, and I'll have sleep arrangements figured out by then. Welcome aboard."

The mess crew offered plentiful food: ham, turkey, and salami sandwiches with real bread made from wheat flour, not the cassava flour Gina never had become accustomed to; a variety of sliced cheeses; fresh fruit; potato salad; coleslaw; brownies; cow's milk; coffee; and soft drinks.

"The bread tastes funny." Cheryl put her sandwich down. "Can I get some rice?"

"I can't drink this milk." Leah pushed her glass aside.

Gina, Edna, and Sissy rolled their eyes and dug in.

The forward torpedo room was designated to house older children and women with babies. That night Gina made up a bed for Cheryl and Leah to share by padding a torpedo rack with blankets. Cheryl said she had a sick tummy, and Leah cried that she wanted her dad. Gina sat between the overtired girls, an arm around each one, not sure who needed her most.

A white ring formed around Cheryl's mouth, and a trickle of sweat ran down her face.

"Leah, honey. I'm going to take Cheryl to the bathroom. Do you have to go?"

Leah sniffed. "No."

Gina hurried Cheryl to the head, and no sooner were they inside than Cheryl upchucked the chocolate candy and what little food she'd eaten. Gina cleaned her child up in the metal sink and then tackled the toilet's complicated flushing instructions. She missed a step, and the toilet overflowed on her bare feet. Embarrassed, she opened the door and flagged a passing steward. "Um . . . sorry, I need a mop in here."

"Not again," the steward muttered and sprinted away.

Back in the torpedo room, Gina found Leah on the rack reading a story to Harry. Cheryl climbed in beside them to listen.

"Is Cheryl okay?" Sissy asked.

"Yes, thank you. I think the chocolate was too rich, and she's overtired."

"I'll watch her tonight. I'm going to be right here." She patted the makeshift bed. "Harry doesn't want me to leave him."

"That's kind of you. Thank you."

When Leah finished the story and Harry climbed onto his own rack, Gina tucked the girls in for the night. "You are brave girls. I'm proud of you."

Cheryl returned a wan smile and Leah a sigh of resignation.

⸺

Officers had given up their quarters off the wardroom for the women— five bunks in one room, but the room had a door, and Gina appreciated even that little bit of privacy. Walking there, she noticed a new sign posted on the head's entry: *Don't blush. Ask help to flush.* She couldn't help but chuckle.

The steward stopped her. "Ma'am." He shoved a pair of leather sandals into her hands. "The floors are mighty cold on bare feet." He turned and scurried away.

"Thank you," Gina called after him, touched by his thoughtfulness. "What's your name, sailor?"

"Ray," he said as he disappeared through a door.

Gina clutched the sandals to her chest. *From Ray.* No, it was just a coincidence, but she was jolted into a memory of her cheek on her husband's shoulder as they danced in the moonlight that reflected on Manila Bay. She closed her eyes not to lose the scent of him.

In the small bunk-filled room, Sissy, Edna, and three missionary women were already in their nightclothes. One was brushing her long gray hair, and one was reading a *Life* magazine and another her Bible. Gina showed Edna the sandals. "Someone's looking out for me tonight."

The woman reading *Life* magazine hooted. "Get the title of this article, girls—'Is This Trip Really Necessary?'"

She received blank stares.

"It's about rationing. The title tickled me, given the timing of . . . well, everything."

When the lights in the submarine dimmed, Gina snuggled under the blanket and closed her eyes. She heard a click and then Bing Crosby crooning Brahms's "Lullaby" over the sound system. A smile came to her lips. Who would have thought a strapping and seemingly fearless submarine crew would have Brahms's "Lullaby" in their music repertoire?

By the third day, life had fallen into a routine. At dawn, as usual, the klaxon clanged, and an officer shouted, "Dive. Dive."

Going underwater gave Gina the shivers, though once under, the ride was as smooth as skating on ice. With little frame of reference, she lost track of the day and time. "How do you do it?" she asked a crew member who worked four hours on duty with eight hours off in a continuous rotation.

"It's easy, ma'am. If I'm eating pancakes, it's morning."

That afternoon, while she was playing Monopoly with Cheryl and Leah, the carbon dioxide concentration was high, and the girls were listless. "I don't want to play this anymore." Cheryl dropped the top hat token into the Monopoly box.

"Me neither." Leah pushed her race car token aside. "You want to write notes?"

The girls retired to their bunk to write secret notes to each other in the Morse code the radioman had been teaching them.

Gina felt listless, too, and she craved a cigarette. It had been hours since the smoking lamp had been lit, giving the passengers and crew permission to light up. She found Edna on her bunk reading a *National Geographic* magazine she'd borrowed from the crew's library.

"Reading anything interesting?"

"I don't know. I'm just looking at the pictures. I can't concentrate."

That night, when the submarine surfaced and the hatches were opened, fresh air streamed through the sub, and Gina swore she heard a collective sigh. The passengers gulped the salt air and stared through the open hatch at the moon and stars.

Cheryl rubbed her tummy. "It doesn't feel good."

"Mine either, honey," Gina commiserated, wishing she could see the horizon to steady her gaze and quell the queasiness in her stomach caused by the sub's pitching and rolling during surface travel. "Come— there's a sing-along in the mess. It'll be fun."

~

On the morning of the fifth day, just as the passengers were waking up, alarms blared, and a sudden downward movement brought Gina's stomach to her throat. In the corridor, sailors stampeded. Pushing her way through the oncoming runners, she found Cheryl and Leah clinging together. She climbed onto the bunk and wrapped them in her arms, seeing Sissy across the way, hugging pale-faced Harry close to her chest. Wailing children and jabbering parents heightened the chaos.

The steward came into the torpedo room. He seemed at ease and said in a calm voice, "Ladies, gentlemen, children. Everything's all right. We were spotted by a Jap plane, and the captain ordered a crash dive. It's dramatic, but not unusual, given the times. Was anyone in here injured?"

No one answered.

The steward continued. "We're going to stay deep for a while; then we'll go up and look around. We'll keep you informed. In the meantime, breakfast is being served."

The matter-of-fact manner the incident was handled in calmed many passengers, but Gina knew the Japanese never gave up a hunt, and she didn't trust they wouldn't be back. The thought gave her the shivers.

After breakfast, she followed Cheryl and Leah to the crowded wardroom, where they laid claim to a checkers set. The steward appeared, waving his arms and whispering, "Shhh, everyone . . . quiet. Keep the children quiet. The captain spotted a Jap convoy. They don't know our exact position, but any noise will tip them off. All noise-generating systems have been shut down. It's going to get hot in here. Sit tight. Sit still. We'll be out from under the Japs in a jiffy."

The temperature in the wardroom soared to 120 degrees. Sweat poured off bodies, and the steward passed out salt tablets and water. Toddlers were carried, bribed, and cajoled. "Shhh, we must be quiet as little bunnies." Most fell asleep from the heat and lack of oxygen. Gina, terrified at being trapped underwater, listened to the sonar pings of Japanese vessels circling like sharks above them. That night, with the Japanese out of range, the submarine surfaced. Hatches were opened, and fresh air swept through the corridors like a tsunami. The whole of the submarine's population came alive.

⌒

Early on the morning of their arrival at Darwin, the passengers packed their belongings. In single file they ascended the stairs to the conning tower and stepped into the sunlight and the freedom from fear and oppression. Gina held Cheryl's and Leah's hands; only Ray's and Vivian's presence could make this moment a more perfect one.

The officers and sailors, having shaved their scruffy beards and pressed their uniforms, stood at attention on the deck. It was a glorious sight that moved Gina so deeply she couldn't speak, and she hoped the crew sensed her gratitude as she nodded and walked by.

A launch waited to sail them ashore. Two American army nurses, both with shiny hair and perfect makeup and wearing crisp white uniforms, welcomed them aboard. Cheryl stared, and Leah gaped, and Gina, feeling worn, folded her hands in her lap to hide her ragged fingernails. They arrived at the quarantine station at noon and were handed Red Cross bags that contained soap, lotion, a toothbrush, toothpaste, crackers, peanut butter, and apples. They were assigned beds for the night and told where to find the showers.

"I'm going to be a nurse when I grow up," Cheryl announced to the Red Cross workers attending to their needs, the comment earning her and Leah a smile and an extra apple.

Gina, sitting on a clean bed in a large room of beds, read movie reviews in a newspaper someone had left on a table. "Which one shall we see?"

Cheryl clapped her hands. *"Lassie Come Home."*

"National Velvet," Leah countered.

"We'll see both," Gina promised, "and we'll go out for hot dogs and ice cream." Oh, to leave the horrors of war behind and live free of fear again. A new way of life was close, and Gina felt impatient to get on with it.

Sissy sat down beside Gina. "I'm going to say goodbye now. Davy and I have friends in Brisbane, and I'll be staying with them until Davy arrives. Thank you for all you've done for us. Davy said there were weeks when the money you sent to the camp was their only support. I feel guilty that I wasn't able to help. I knew what was going on and felt selfish, always on the taking end."

Gina held Sissy's hand. "What counts now is you're all going to be together soon. Are you going back to the States?"

Sissy shrugged. "We go where Uncle Sam sends us. I'll pray that you find Ray. I know you will. Our men are scattered all over this globe." She stood, and they hugged goodbye with promises of keeping in touch.

Chapter 34

ON FRIENDLY SOIL

Forces beyond my control have taken everything away from me except my freedom to choose how to respond.

—Ray Thorpe, Fukuoka #17, Japan, February 1944–
September 1945

The Red Cross had rented a hotel in Brisbane for civilians being relocated. A woman at the front desk handed Gina a room key and an envelope. "You need to fill out these papers, Mrs. Thorpe."

"How long will we be here?" Gina asked, hoping the stay would be a short one.

"That depends. You're on standby status. It could be two days or two weeks. There are ration coupons in the envelope, and there is a relief clothing center in the building next door."

Before going up to the room, Gina stopped at the Western Union office in the hotel lobby and sent her father a telegram: *RETURNING HOME WITH TWO YOUNG GIRLS. NEED PLACE TO STAY.*

Later, Gina's telegram was returned stamped *UNDELIVERABLE.* Gina folded the message and put it in her pocket. Where was her father if not at home? She rationalized that the nation was at war. It wouldn't be unusual for a telegram to not be delivered.

～

Six weeks passed before Edna, Gina, Cheryl, and Leah stood with a joyful crowd on a military ship's deck as it sailed under the Golden Gate Bridge and into San Francisco Bay. Feelings of warmth and protection washed over Gina, so intense that tears came to her eyes. She hugged each of the girls, Leah subdued and Cheryl excited, knowing that soon she'd be seeing her grandpa Milo.

Wistfully, Edna said, "We'll be parting ways soon. I'll be at my sister's in Akron. You have the address and phone number. If things don't work out in Seattle, you come and stay with us."

"Thank you," Gina said, Edna again offering to lend a hand. "We had some good times in those little huts in the mountains . . . you, Marcus, Vivian, and me. It wasn't all bad . . . was it?"

"No. Not all bad. I won't forget those marathon bridge games."

"The sing-alongs around the campfire."

"Popo."

Gina laughed. "Popo. How could we ever forget Popo?"

An excited buzz came from a group standing nearby, and a woman shouted, "MacArthur's in the Philippines. He landed the US Sixth Army at Lingayen Gulf early this morning. It won't be long now before this war's over, and our men will be coming home."

Cheryl clapped her hands. "Yay! The war's over. Daddy's coming home."

Gina's heart sank, and her voice faltered. "Honey, our troops are fighting real hard, but the war's not over. Daddy won't be coming home yet. We just have to be patient awhile longer."

Cheryl's happy countenance collapsed. "That's what you always say. I'm tired of being patient." She retreated to the cabin and a picture she'd been coloring, letting her hair fall like a veil over her face.

The wet, cold weather in San Francisco chilled Gina, and she purchased coats, hats, and mittens for herself and the girls. She tried calling her dad, but the operator said the telephone had been disconnected. A returned telegram and a disconnected phone: the implication brought on a chill more significant than that from the inclement weather.

After a night in the city and saying goodbye to Edna, they boarded a bus for a multiday trip up the California and Oregon coasts on roads that once were Native American foot trails that wound through numerous river valleys of rugged mountains. Gina had traveled this majestic countryside several times during her early days with the Follies, so very young, a free spirit, honing her professional skills and learning the truths of the world in the gutsiest way.

The bus dropped them off at a substation not far from her dad's house. Carrying their suitcases, they trudged past the fire hall, a Texaco gas station, and a blue trolley car that had been converted to a café, before turning the corner onto Haywood Street. "Just a little farther," Gina said to the girls, who were tired and lagging behind.

The house appeared a block ahead. It was still yellow. She remembered the summer her dad had painted it that bright hue, saying it was the color of sunflowers. At the time, Gina hadn't realized his gift for color and symmetry. As she approached the house, she saw boarded-up windows and a sign on the door that read *No Trespassing*. An ominous cloud obliterated her sun. Where was her dad?

"I'm tired of walking," Leah said. "Where will we sleep?"

Gina had no idea where they would sleep. "We'll figure it out," she said, the concern about her father foremost on her mind. She tried to stay positive. Maybe he had remarried—an interesting thought—or moved into a retirement home, where daily living would be easier. She led the girls onto the porch and peeked through a small window in the front door. Nothing appeared to have changed inside.

"Will the door open?" Cheryl asked.

Gina rattled the doorknob, not ever remembering the door being locked. Her disquiet grew. "It doesn't look like anyone lives here," Leah said, her forehead wrinkled in concern.

Gina noticed the child's lips were blue. With no place to go and beginning to panic, Gina led the girls to the house across the street. A young woman answered the doorbell. Her hair was pulled back in a ponytail, and a baby boy with drool on his chin bounced on her hip.

"Hi. I'm Angelina Capelli Thorpe, and this is my daughter, Cheryl, and her friend Leah. I grew up in the house across the street. My best friend, Lainie . . . um"—in her muddled state, she couldn't remember Lainie's married name—"Lainie Mitchell lived here. Would you happen to know where she lives now?"

The woman knitted her brow. "I don't know anyone named Lainie. Hold on a second." She called over her shoulder. "Hey, Jimmy. There's a lady here looking for Lainie Mitchell. She says she lived here."

A tall, thin young man with his foot in a cast and struggling on crutches came from the kitchen. "You must mean Elaine Schultz." He studied Gina's face. "Do I know you?"

"I don't think so. I used to live there." She pointed to the yellow house. "I'm looking for my father."

The man nodded. "Your father. Um . . . yes." He snapped his fingers. "I *do* know you. You were friends with my older sister. We lived on the next block. It's Elaine Schultz you want. She sells real estate. Her office is about thirty minutes from here. I was just a kid when you left school to travel with a dance troupe. You were the talk of the neighborhood. I can give her a jingle if you like."

His help a vast relief, Gina said, "Would you, please?"

The woman's name was Brenda, and she called the baby Scooter. Jimmy went to the phone and dialed a number. "Elaine? Jimmy. Good. There's someone here to see you." He glanced at Gina and said to Elaine, "No. It's best you come over."

~

Lainie arrived looking professional in a smart tweed suit, a rust-colored silk blouse, and medium-heeled shoes. Her red hair was styled into a chin-length pageboy, and her makeup was subtle and perfect. Surprise flickered in her green eyes when she saw Gina, which she quickly masked with a smile and a hug.

Gina's smile wavered, seeing Lainie robust and groomed, as she had been what seemed eons ago. Gina introduced the girls, who murmured hello and then left to play with Scooter. Jimmy and Brenda retired to the kitchen to make coffee.

Gina was seldom at a loss for words, but she didn't know what to say to Lainie. She sat on the couch with her arms and legs crossed. Lainie sat in a chair and smoothed her skirt over her knees.

"I thought you'd fallen off the end of the earth, Gina. The last letter you sent, you were living in a beautiful house that overlooked Manila Bay, and you had a maid, a cook, and a houseboy. I was up to my elbows in diapers with my third child. You have no idea how much I envied you."

"I admit I was a bit spoiled, but the Japanese changed all that." She tried to mask her chipped teeth by casually stroking her upper lip. "I haven't been able to get ahold of my dad. Do you know where he's living now?"

Lainie spoke softly. "Gina, I'm so sorry. Our letters were returned, and nobody knew how to contact you. Your dad had a stroke a year ago in August. It was a hot day, and he was cutting the grass. It was sudden, and he didn't linger."

Gina had suspected it. How could she not? But hearing the truth felt like a punch. She blinked back the tears she'd been denying.

Lainie moved closer and took Gina's hand. "Is there anything I can do?"

Gina couldn't control the quaver in her voice. "The girls and I need a place to stay. I was hoping my dad . . ."

"You can stay with me tonight. Your dad's house is yours free and clear. I handled the transactions when he died, and I can get the keys. I'll send someone over tomorrow to get those boards off the windows so you can get inside."

⌒

That evening Gina met Lainie's three children and her husband, Chuck, whom she had married a year after graduating from high school. After dinner of macaroni and cheese and green beans, Chuck and the kids did the dishes, and Lainie prepared a pull-out couch in the den for the girls. While Lainie's daughter kept Leah busy with a game of go fish, Gina took Cheryl to the den and told her that Grandpa Milo had died, but they'd be living in his house.

Cheryl's face puckered up. "That's no fair. I want him living there too."

Mother and daughter huddled together, remembering Grandpa Milo, a tall, white-haired, gentle man who had loved Cheryl dearly and grown beautiful flowers. Eventually, drained from the trip and the bad news, Cheryl surrendered to sleep.

Leah came to the door. "May I come in, please? Why was Cheryl crying?"

Gina saw a bedraggled little girl with tired eyes. "Yes, Leah. Come in. Cheryl's sad because she learned her grandpa Milo died."

Leah climbed onto the bed. "I'll help her feel better. I'll hold her tonight."

"Thank you, Leah. You know how much it hurts when someone you love dies."

"I couldn't sleep when Mama died, so Maggie held me. I want Maggie to be here."

"I do, too, sweetheart." Gina lay with the girls until Leah also slept, her arm draped over Cheryl's shoulder.

~

Gina found Lainie in the living room. She handed Gina a boozy hot drink. "You've had a rough time of it."

Gina sipped the drink, feeling the warmth slide all the way down. Chuck had left for his weekly poker game with the guys, and the kids were in their rooms doing homework or asleep. Gina was glad to have Lainie to talk to.

"Rough doesn't cover it." She told Lainie a brief history of her years in the Philippines, stopping just before her involvement with the guerrillas, Pearl Blue, and the horrors of Fort Santiago.

There were tears in Lainie's eyes. "You can't claim your house back?"

"No, everything's gone. I have no desire to return, anyway, unless it's to find Ray. I suspect he was sent to Japan to work as a slave laborer, but I don't know for sure."

"Oh, Gina. I'm so sorry. I can't even imagine. When you're ready, come to church with me. We have a group that helps military families get reestablished. They'll be a good resource for you. In the meantime, we'll get your house opened up and see what needs to be done—probably just a cleaning. Your dad left it in good shape."

Gina nodded. Though homecoming wasn't what she'd expected, she felt like she'd landed in a safe harbor. "Thank you, Lainie. You've always been a good friend."

~

Gina saw that little had changed in her childhood home since she'd last visited. She half expected to see her dad come through the back door with an armful of flowers to arrange in a vase and display on the dining room table.

Lainie followed behind. "My father-in-law was your dad's lawyer. We went through the house together. I cleaned out what would spoil, and we collected and documented your dad's personal papers and anything of value. We figured you'd be coming home as soon as you could."

In the bedroom closet, her father's clothes hung in good order, and his shoeboxes lined the floor. Gina opened the top dresser drawer, feeling like she was invading his privacy. A lump rose in her throat, and she wiped tears from her cheeks with the palm of her hand. "I feel awful that he died alone."

"He wasn't alone, Gina. He had a busy life and many friends. Several of the gardens in the city parks are his design . . . he tended them like they were his children. There's talk of naming the park on Third and Madison after him. There's a plaque there now."

Gina found the news comforting.

The girls skipped into the room, Cheryl wearing a red flapper dress and Leah a middy blouse and navy pleated skirt, both outfits sizes too big. Gina couldn't help but smile. "You scamps have been in my closet."

Cheryl twirled around, and the dress's fringe took to the air. "Did you really wear this, Mom?"

Lainie answered, "She sure did. Your mom was a hot petunia in that dress, with her dark cropped hair and kohl-rimmed eyes."

Gina smirked, her hand over her mouth. "And you, Lainie . . . as skinny as a boy, and a fashion snob. I coveted your pink cloche hat and that long string of pearls you got for your sixteenth birthday."

They both posed like flappers—one knee bent up, toe pointed down, and arms and hands gracefully extended, as they had done what seemed a lifetime ago. The last constraints of their long separation loosened with giggles.

Lainie looked at her watch. "I've got to get to the office." She handed Gina several work orders. "Workmen are coming today to check your furnace, electrical, and stuff. No reason you can't move in if you want. I'll have my son bring your things over and drive you to the grocery store." She handed Gina an envelope. "Your dad left a good amount of money in the bank. Here's a loan to help you get started. You can pay me back later."

Gina established a comfortable home with the cash her dad had left in the bank and a life insurance settlement pending. However, making even small decisions was difficult, like where to place the telephone—in the kitchen or the living room. She wished Ray were there to help. With the scars on her body a constant reminder, her thoughts often dwelled on her months in Fort Santiago, the interrogations playing like a loop in her head, causing her stomach to ache. She wondered if she'd given clues that had put the underground workers in danger as Captain Sato had said. She stressed about her Manila friends . . . were they alive; were they in hiding? Though she was physically safe, anxiety continued to be her constant companion, and some nights she drank too much wine.

She wrote the War Department in Washington, DC, inquiring about Ray and received only a form letter stating his status was "missing in action" and referring her to the Prisoners of War Information Bureau. The bureau had no record of Ray beyond his imprisonment in Cabanatuan. It seemed the US Army had lost track of her husband. *How could they do that!* She wrote the departments and bureaus multiple times as she remembered details she thought might be helpful, but she learned nothing new of his whereabouts.

The girls were enrolled in the same grade school Gina had attended. With them in school, Gina had time on her hands, and she found physical activity blocked her disturbing thoughts.

"That's pretty," Cheryl said of the newly painted peach-colored living room walls.

"It brightens it up a lot, doesn't it?" Gina showed her the pale-green paint she'd purchased for the kitchen and the flowered material from which she'd be making new curtains. "Where's Leah?"

"Upstairs writing in her journal. Can I go out and play?"

"Sure, honey."

Cheryl made friends easily and had a group of girls with whom to play jump rope and jacks on the playground and after school. However, Leah hung back, preferring to spend time alone in her room reading books borrowed from the library or writing in her journal. She helped Gina with household chores without being asked, and when the weather warmed, she planted and tended a spring vegetable garden.

"Leah," Gina said on one sunny day, "the girls are playing hopscotch. Why don't you go out and join them?"

"I'd rather not. They don't play it right."

"You could teach them the rules."

"No. Don't make me." Her chin quivered. She ran to her room and slammed the door.

Gina followed Leah and sat on the bed beside her. "Honey, I'm not going to make you do anything."

Leah turned her face to the wall.

"I know you miss your mother terribly. I do too. She was my best friend, and I loved her so much. I wish you'd talk to me about her. It might help."

Leah shouted, "Stop talking about my mother."

Gina retreated. Leah needed help but rejected any offer of it. Gina was stymied about what to do.

⌐⌐

Heavy fighting continued in Manila, but the Allies had made gains. In February 1945, four thousand internees were liberated from Santo Tomas. At the end of March, General MacArthur declared a victory for the United States. However, the Japanese vowed to fight to the last man's death. All through the summer, both Allied and Japanese troops pounded Manila with heavy artillery, eradicating whole portions of the city and slaughtering tens of thousands of civilians. Obsessed, Gina could not stop reading the news.

To bring closure to the unceasing carnage, on August 6, 1945, the United States dropped an atomic bomb on Japan's port city Hiroshima, and three days later another bomb was dropped on Nagasaki. On September 2, 1945, in the event that was broadcast around the world, Japan signed the formal Instrument of Surrender.

Two weeks later a telegram arrived for Leah:

SAILING. EST. ARRIVAL OCT 15. SEATTLE WA. KISSES. DAD AND MAGGIE

Every day Gina watched for a telegram from Ray that never came, and each day she became more fearful that he hadn't survived.

⌒

At eleven years old, Leah was more a young lady than a child. She had grown during the summer and came up to Gina's chin now. The day of Theo and Maggie's arrival, Leah dressed in a navy skirt, white blouse, pale-blue cardigan sweater, and ballet slipper shoes. Her blonde hair curled onto her shoulders. Outwardly, there was no trace of the rough years she'd lived in the mountains.

When the taxi arrived, Theo emerged first, followed by Maggie. Leah ran from one to the other, and then all three stood in a huddle with Theo's arms encircling both of his daughters. Joy registered on his face, and tears puddled in his eyes.

In the harsh light of the homecoming, Vivian's and Ray's absences were achingly vivid, and Gina struggled against giving in to her rawest emotions. It was not so for Cheryl. Gina found her in the bedroom, her head buried in a pillow. "Dad's not ever coming home, is he, Mama?"

Gina sat beside her and rubbed her back. "I don't know, but we have to believe he will. There are still men in prison camps that haven't been released. We have to be patient." Gina had mulled over the thought of preparing Cheryl for the possibility of Ray's death, but not yet. Not as long as there was a thread of hope. "Come, now. Mr. Theo needs help with the luggage."

≓

While Maggie cut up apples and celery and put them on the table for munching, Gina poked at the roast in the oven and added potatoes, onions, and carrots to the pan. She closed the oven door and waved the heat away from her face with a hot pad.

Theo came into the kitchen. He looked weary, like he'd aged ten, not just four, years. He peeked under a dish towel that covered an apple pie. "Did you bake this yourself, Gina?"

"Sure did. I've discovered I'm a woman of multiple talents." She handed him a cup of coffee. "Where are the girls?"

"Upstairs finishing Leah's packing. How's she doing, Gina?"

Gina pulled out a chair for him. "I have some concerns—"

"She's been trouble to you?"

"No. Just the opposite. She's trying to be too perfect, like she's eleven going on twenty." Saying that gave Gina pause. Had they all aged beyond their years? "I talked to her teacher. She said Leah's a little quiet, but she's a model student. I've tried to get her outside with other kids, but she'd rather stay in her room and read or write in her journal. I feel she's tied in a knot, but she brushes me off when I try to get her to open up."

Theo leaned forward with his elbows on the table. "Does she talk about Vivian?"

"No, but she writes about her in her journal. Don't tell her I peeked."

Every wrinkle in Theo's face deepened. "I'm not surprised. She's our sensitive one. Being around Vivian's mom will help her. They're a lot alike."

Maggie added, "What I remember about Grandma's house is that every room is filled with family pictures going back generations. Photography is a hobby of hers. She has tons of pictures of Mom with me and Leah. I need to see them too. I don't want to forget . . ."

Gina reached over and patted Maggie's hand.

Theo said, "We'll have a proper funeral. It will be good for all of us. We haven't been able to mourn her passing as we should have." His voice trailed off, as if he were entering his own thoughts. He blinked and came back to the present. "Have you heard anything about Ray?"

"Only that he's classified as missing in action. Last week I got a reply from the International Red Cross in Switzerland. It's the main conduit of POW information. They couldn't help either. They said the lists of prisoners provided by the Japanese are incomplete." Feeling a sting behind her eyes, a prelude to tears, she jumped up to check the roast.

Dinner was a success, and there were groans when Gina brought out the apple pie, and a decision was made to serve it later with ice cream. Cheryl and Leah asked to go to the park, and they begged Theo to go with them. Gina and Maggie were left to clean up the kitchen.

Gina surveyed the pile of dishes. "Wash or dry?"

"I'll wash. You dry and put away. That was a good dinner."

"Thanks. I've discovered that I like to cook. I'm turning into my mother." Realizing what she'd said, she turned to Maggie. "I'm sorry. I didn't mean to be flip. It's a good thing. I remember a loving home."

Maggie plunged her hands into the soapy water. "I don't need to be pampered, Miss Gina. I'm not a wilting flower."

"No, you're not. And you're not a child. You can drop the 'Miss.' Just call me Gina."

Maggie grinned at the acknowledgment that she was an adult. "Thank you." She carefully washed and rinsed the glassware and placed it in the drainer. "Do you miss your houseboys and maids?"

"No. I've been content with having my home to myself and the girls. I've enjoyed fixing it up. I grew up here, you know. Funny, I could hardly wait to leave. Now I don't think I ever want to. What are your plans, Maggie?"

"With some studying, I should be able to test out of high school and get into college. I always thought I'd be a surgeon like my dad, but now . . ." She tucked a wisp of blonde hair behind her ear with a soapy finger. "Well . . . things have changed. I've changed. I'm not sure I'm up to the challenge."

Gina flashed the young woman a sidelong glance, thinking Maggie was more than up to any challenge.

Maggie rinsed the soap off the plates and placed them in the drainer for Gina to dry. "I had a few free days in Manila, so I went to Pearl Blue. I thought I'd check it out for you. In the last battles there was damage from strafing, but much of the building is still standing." She hesitated. "The truth is I was curious."

Gina hadn't thought much about Pearl Blue except for the people. She dried the clean plates and began stacking them. "Curious about?"

"You. How you faced the Japanese every day. Just standing on the stage and imagining being surrounded by the enemy audience gave me the creeps. Weren't you scared?"

Maggie was stirring emotions on which Gina had not let herself dwell. "Yes," she admitted. "At first I was terrified. But then I forced myself to focus on what mattered . . . the survival of the families in the mountains and the men in the prison camps. The irony was it was the Japanese themselves who were supporting my cause. It became a game, a dangerous one. For a while, I thought I'd outwit them forever. Inevitably, the end did come."

Gina felt a stir of anxiety. She stopped drying dishes to light a cigarette and inhale deeply, the ritual taking the edge off her discomfort. "My experience in Manila was no more frightful than yours in the mountains. A different focus. A different set of horrors."

"Horrors, yes," Maggie said. "There were plenty of them. I raged at the inhumane cruelty I witnessed every day. I had no outlet like you did, and the rage is still inside of me. Sometimes I relive the worst moments . . . I hear it. I see it. I smell it. I even feel it inside of me. Does that happen to you?"

"It did once." Gina had thought her strange incident an anomaly. "I found this blond kid dead on the road. I even remember his name—Gerald Kent. I sat beside him to keep the crows away until he was buried. Weeks later, I relived every heartbeat of it. I even reached down to close his eyes." She remembered Gerald's wallet and class ring she'd meant to send to his parents. They had gotten lost long ago. How she wished she had sent them. "Is that what you mean?"

"Yes. I'm learning it's not uncommon. Nor are nightmares and panic attacks that turn me into a blubbering idiot."

"Have you told your dad?"

"No. He has his own demons to deal with."

"Maggie, you can't ignore this. You need to talk to him or to somebody."

Maggie stopped washing dishes and dried her hands to light a cigarette. "I know. I'm talking to you. You've always been so strong."

Gina's eyes opened wide. "Is that what you think? You, who at sixteen years old rolled up your sleeves and dug in when I didn't want to get my hands dirty? You, who became the doctor of a budding band of guerrillas? Who was second in command of a clinic under the ugliest and most inhumane conditions? You need to change your definition of *strong*, Maggie."

Maggie contemplated. "It sounds different when you say it that way. I just went day to day, doing what had to be done." She put out her cigarette and tackled the roasting pan with a Brillo pad. "On the ship home, I met a biochemist. He loaned me a couple of his books.

I suspect there are biochemical changes in the brain when the body is under stress for long periods of time. If we can understand what's causing the symptoms, we can learn how to control them. But it's a challenge. It will take years of study before I could even begin to understand it. I don't know if I have the strength or the will to do it."

Gina reached for Maggie's hand. "Please don't think like that. You're exhausted right now and mourning your mother. You'll regain your physical and mental strength. Your mother's passing may always be a burden, but it will soften. Be kind to yourself. Give yourself time to heal."

"But I'll never be the same."

"None of us will. You've seen a dark side of humanity that you never should have. It's part of you now, and you've changed. You started out a determined young woman; now, accept the change and make it work for you. You've already begun to do that . . . seeking to learn what's happened to your body and how to heal it."

Maggie's reply came as a whisper. "Those words are easy to say, but I'm not as determined as you think I am."

"Oh, that's not so. I remember seeing a pretty tough streak of rebellion in you. It drove your mother crazy."

"I know. I feel guilty about that."

"Don't. She knew you'd need that spunk to be successful. She was so proud of you, Maggie, and she loved you so much, even when she was rolling her eyes."

Maggie sniffed and grinned. "Thanks, Gina. I needed to hear that."

The next morning there were goodbye hugs and kisses and promises to visit. All day the family was on Gina's mind—Theo depressed and older than his years, Maggie suffering debilitating anxiety, Leah having pulled into herself—and they all were mourning Vivian's death. How much could the human body and psyche endure without being permanently damaged? That night, she said a prayer for the family in crisis.

With mail going through again, Gina wrote letters to Franca, Chan, and Father Morgan. She wrote that she was doing well in Seattle, but she was still looking for Ray. Her effort was rewarded with a letter from Franca.

October 30, 1945

Dear Gina,

What relief your letter gave me. I'm so glad to hear that you and Cheryl are safe at home in the United States. I worried so. I'm sorry—I do not have information about Ray at this time. I am checking the new-arrival list every few days at the 29th Replacement Depot, where men returning from the prison camps in Japan are being housed before their redistribution. Ray's name has not appeared yet, but keep your hopes up; ships are still arriving.

After spending several months hiding in a convent high in the Sierra Madre, I am now home. My dear husband, Salvador, was arrested not long after you were taken to Fort Santiago. He was killed just days before the Americans returned. I'm extremely proud of the work he did to sabotage the Japanese efforts to conquer the Philippines, our beloved home.

There is more sad news that I feel obligated to pass on to you. Our precious Father Morgan and five other Irish priests at the Malate Church were arrested, executed, and buried in a mass grave. Their bodies are being exhumed and will be given a proper burial. May the wrath of the Lord come down on their executioners.

You'll be interested to know that Inez, Arielle, and Julio are partnering with a chef whose restaurant was destroyed, and they are soliciting funds to reopen Pearl

Blue as a restaurant/nightclub. I wish them luck, but I feel they are going to miss your guidance very much.

Julio asked me to tell you that he found the message about the Nissyo Maru you left inside the piano. Miguel ran it to Davy, who was able to send it to General MacArthur. Hearing that, I did some detective work for you. One of our pilots had spotted the Nissyo Maru and had targeted it for bombing. He got the message that the hold was filled with American prisoners, and he gave up the mission. A submarine followed the Japanese ship and reported that it had docked in Tokyo.

Gina dropped the letter to her lap. So some good had come out of that terrifying night when she'd been captured and Ling had been murdered—perhaps some soldiers on that ship had lived to return home. She resumed reading.

I'm sure you've heard about the devastation of Manila from others. It's going to take a long time to rebuild the city; most buildings in the business district were leveled, with only scattered ones standing, and those suffered extensive damage.

I've lost track of Clara, our tireless Red Cross nurse. Dion was captured, but he managed to escape during the vicious battles after MacArthur returned. He's back in Cabanatuan City working in the marketplace as before. On a cheerful note, Trixie married Dion's oldest son in a life-affirming ceremony that I happily attended.

As for me, Dr. Lopez and I are working with architects to rebuild Remedios Hospital. The army has just bulldozed away the rubble. It's heart wrenching; there are bones in every shovelful, and I cannot stay for more than a minute to watch. Funds are coming in, and when completed, the new hospital will be beautiful and modern. In the meantime, we are working out of makeshift shelters. The American doctors and nurses who are volunteering their time and expertise in this hour of need are a blessing.

I hope our paths cross again after the rubble is cleared, the bad memories have dimmed, and the trees and flowers are in full bloom.

In love and peace,
Franca

Gina sat a long time holding Franca's letter. Would the bad memories dim? Would flowers ever bloom in her heart again? She thought she had become tough and hard and unable to be hurt, but now on safe soil, she felt as vulnerable as ever.

⌒

November came with its cooler days. Cheryl had adjusted to her new life and was doing well in the fourth grade. Knowing she couldn't live on her dad's savings forever, Gina rented space in a building in town, where she planned to open a theater arts studio and teach voice and dance. She was excited to get started on the renovations.

Today she was raking up the last of the fall leaves in the front yard, and the mundane task let her thoughts drift off in any direction. She had enjoyed, she mused, the best Manila high society had to offer, and she had survived the worst the Japanese army had thrown at her. Now here she was, back where she had started: in middle-class America raking leaves. She felt she had changed, but she didn't know how, and in her mind, she began to assess her new attributes.

However, she saw the Western Union boy bicycling on her street. A telegram delivery wasn't unusual, but then why was she holding her breath? She watched him approach, trying to gauge if he was slowing down, or would he whiz by, leaving her still in the abyss of unknowing regarding what had happened to Ray?

The messenger bicycled into her driveway. "Telegram for Mrs. Raymond Thorpe." He handed her an envelope, but Gina's hand shook so hard she dropped it.

He picked it up. "Would you like me to open it for you?"

She noticed red hair curling around his ears under his cap. "Yes, please." She closed her eyes.

She heard paper tearing.

"You may want to open your eyes and read this, ma'am."

She listened to the tone of his voice. Was it upbeat, or were the words delivered in a minor key like a sad song? She opened her eyes and read the message:

IN MANILA. HAD TROUBLE FINDING YOU. NOBODY KNEW A GINA THORPE. CHAN CAME TO THE RESCUE. I'LL BE HOME FOR CHRISTMAS. A MILLION KISSES AND A THOUSAND HUGS TO YOU AND CHERYL. RAY

Gina had no control over the laughter that burst from her followed by tears that coursed down her cheeks. She wiped them away with her sweat-covered hands. "You have no idea the joy," she gushed, hugging the messenger, who stood uncomfortably stiff in her grip.

He flashed a broad grin as he stepped out of her embrace and straddled his bicycle. "My pleasure, ma'am."

"Wait. Don't go." Gina ran into the house and rummaged through her purse, finding only a ten-dollar bill, a lavish tip for the young messenger. She didn't care. She'd just received a million kisses and a thousand hugs, and she wanted everyone to be as rich as she was. Ray was alive. He was in Manila, and he would be home for Christmas.

AUTHOR'S NOTE

During World War II, tens of thousands of American civilians were trapped on Pacific islands and at the mercy of the invading Japanese military. Those surrendered or captured were placed in internment camps, the topic of my first book, *A Pledge of Silence*. Others evaded capture and survived, one way or another, in the occupied country, many of them women alone or with children, which is the topic of this book, *Along the Broken Bay*.

The dispositions of the lone women who escaped capture varied: some colorful, like Claire Phillips, an entertainer who owned a nightclub in Manila; others heroic, like Yay Panlilio, a journalist who became a guerrilla; or gutsy, like Margaret Utinski, a nurse who worked for the Japanese-run Philippine Red Cross; or brave, like Viola Winn, a missionary who fled with her four very young children to live in fear and deprivation in the mountainous rain forests.

My characters are fictional, composites of the personalities of whom I read, and no one person in my research encountered the many travails of my fictional characters. Within that scope, *Along the Broken Bay* paints a reasonable facsimile of life on an occupied Pacific island during World War II.

A word about the epigraphs at the beginning of each chapter. I wanted to keep Ray alive in the reader's mind and settled on following his emotional progression during his three-year imprisonment from anger, disbelief, and curiosity to doubt, questioning his sanity, mentally escaping, and then living in the spiritual. My source for this information was *Man's Search for Meaning*, by Dr. Victor E. Frankl, an Austrian neurologist and psychiatrist and a Holocaust survivor.

For further reading I recommend the following memoirs:

Manila Espionage, by Claire Phillips and Myron B. Goldsmith, 1947. Republished in 2017 as *Agent High Pockets: A Woman's Fight against the Japanese in the Philippines.*

Miss U, Angel of the Underground, by Margaret Utinski, 1948, 2017.

The Crucible: An Autobiography by Colonel Yay Panlilio, Filipina American Guerrilla, by Yay Panlilio, 1950, 2009.

Three Came Home, by Agnes Newton Keith, 1947.

Guerrilla Wife, by Louise Reid Spencer, 1945.

For pictures, videos, and to meet the real people who inspired my fictional story, visit my website at florajsolomon.com.

ACKNOWLEDGMENTS

It's no secret: I had a lot of help putting this book together. Many thanks to the members of the Writers' Roundtable at St. James Plantation who critiqued my raw chapters and were generous with their suggestions. A special thank-you to Evelyn Petros, a novelist, screenwriter, former international opera singer, and friend, who shared with me her experiences in the theater and helped me design Pearl Blue.

Knowledgeable and well-read beta readers are a must-have, and mine were Emily Jane Gillcoat, Beth Arlene Schodin, Barbara White, and John and Pat Whiting. A special thank-you to my husband, Art, who gracefully put up with me living in an alternate world several hours a day and multiple times helped me rescue my protagonist when I had written her into a corner.

Lake Union Publishing, an Amazon imprint, makes publishing a painless process with its cadre of editors and designers. Thank you to Danielle Marshall, Christopher Werner, Tiffany Yates Martin, Nicole Pomeroy, Stephanie Chou, Riam Griswold, and the many others whose names I don't know, for adding their special polish to my manuscript.

ABOUT THE AUTHOR

Photo © 2012 Jerry Dycus

Flora J. Solomon worked as a researcher and analyst in Michigan's university system and health care industry. She started writing after retiring and moving to the North Carolina coast with her husband. Her first novel, *A Pledge of Silence*, won the 2014 Amazon Breakthrough Novel Award for general fiction and was selected as a Historical Novel Society Editors' Choice. When not sitting at her computer creating stories, Solomon can be found on the golf course, on the tennis court, or—most naturally—at the beach.